BLACKLIGHT

DARK YORKSHIRE - BOOK 2

J M DALGLIESH

EXCLUSIVE OFFER

Look out for the link at the end of this book or visit my website at **www.jmdalgliesh.com** to sign up to my no-spam VIP Club and receive a FREE Hidden Norfolk novella plus news and previews of forthcoming works.

Never miss a new release.

No spam, ever, guaranteed. You can unsubscribe at any time.

For Iain & Willie, gone too soon, never forgotten and sorely missed

CHAPTER ONE

THE OVERNIGHT STORM had left the car park treacherous. Pooled water highlighted where not to stop, or walk, once beyond the confines of the interior. There was the distinctive crunch of hiking boots on gravel as he climbed out and made his way to the rear, dropping the tailgate. Pulling the red and black rucksack out and slipping it over his shoulders, he locked the vehicle and cast his eyes skyward. The day was still overcast but held some promise; shafts of light split the grey, changing the landscape beneath from grim to stunning. Far off to the west was an ominous sight. Swathes of rain lashed the distant hillside and he was thankful that the wind direction was favourable.

The rucksack on his back felt nigh on empty, an unnecessary addition to the all-weather gear. Surprisingly there was another car parked up already. This early in the morning, he found that unusual. Granted, he had only been here twice before, once scouting and once to leave his kit but nonetheless, he had never come across another soul. That was the reason he had chosen the location. There were so many better, no, not better, more travelled places that drew in the tourists and locals alike. Leaving the car park from the east side, he set off on the well-worn trail.

Starting out in a valley, the path trekked east before changing direction and tacking north, his destination point would never see him leave the confines of the hills to either side. On a dreary day, such as this, there was always the likelihood that a walker would barely see the sun let alone the views that Yorkshire was famous for. The going was tough as the trail narrowed and the gravel passed into mud. The water drained into the valley, leaving the soil wet and sticky underfoot, slowing his progress. Despite this, his destination was well within a fifteen minute walk. He knew that to be almost exact. The need to make notes was never required. That was his gift. The ability to commit details to memory, even trivial ones, that would slip the mind of lesser people in moments. He knew where to make the turn from the trail; after the boulder, one hundred yards beyond the sprawling gorse ahead.

He heard voices and stopped. The first was young, a girl, and after that an adult male, her father? Their chatter carried to him on the light breeze. Another, a young boy was complaining about his feet getting stuck in the mud. A shriek followed as someone presumably lost their footing. Resuming his course, he clocked them rounding the forthcoming turn in the track, the boy now being led by his mother. The man was at the head of the party, a furrowed brow, born of frustration no doubt. They were equipped for a hike, judging by their gear but none of them looked comfortable.

"Good morning," the father said, glancing up from the Ordnance Survey map, enclosed within a transparent case, hanging by a cord from his neck.

"Having trouble?"

"Is it that obvious? We wanted to visit the bird sanctuary at dawn but we've taken a wrong turn on the way back to the car."

That wasn't surprising. He knew the sanctuary, a well-tended area returned to its natural habitat by a wilderness group over the past eight years. It was easy to get disorientated. The group were good on nature, bad on signage. They planned to not only reintroduce native tree species but also the indigenous animals, wolves and lynx, to national parks in the future. That is, if they managed to overcome the objections of local landowners. It would be easy. *Too easy.* He dismissed the thought. Stepping forward, he located their point on the map before tracing a line with his index finger, walking them through the route back to the car park. Even with the children in tow it would take them under twenty minutes. With many spoken thanks and smiles of gratitude, the family moved on. Once again, he was alone. Picking up the pace the sense of excitement rose within him as it had done at this time in each of the previous three years. He left the trail skirting the heather and jogging up a shallow incline before coming to a stop alongside a solitary silver birch. For some reason this species loved the landscape here and was one of the few managing to thrive.

Looking around, he was struck by the isolation. There was nothing to indicate an urban presence: no roads, artificial light or noise, beyond the breeze passing through the foliage. He was most definitely alone.

Removing the rucksack, he put it on the ground and dropped to his knees. From inside he took out the only item. The collapsible shovel was assembled in moments and with one last look around, he set about digging. Barely five inches beneath the surface, he found the rim and within a minute of that he had unearthed the top. Clearing more space around it, he put the shovel down and used his fingers to pry off the lid to the orange plastic tub, breaking the airtight seal.

Immediately, a smile crossed his face as he examined the contents. There was no evidence of moisture penetration, as he anticipated, and all was as he had left it. Firstly, he took out the length of coiled rope, cable ties and duct tape, placing them all in the open rucksack. Next, he picked up the mobile phone, removing the cover and slotting in the battery from his own handset, deliberately chosen to be interchangeable. Switching it on, he watched as the screen illuminated and went through its start-up process. Putting the phone in his jacket pocket he returned his focus to the container. A resealable bag came out, the three hundred pounds in used tens and twenties were swiftly transferred to his pockets.

A bottle of drain cleaner and a pack of refuse sacks were added to the rucksack. Retrieving a small red and white cardboard box, he opened it to reveal it was full to capacity. Lastly, he took out the semiautomatic pistol and checked it over. The slide was well greased and moved with ease back and forth, as did the hammer. Several years of military service had taught him how to prepare a firearm for these conditions. Releasing the magazine, he loaded it with rounds from the cardboard box and, having replaced it, chambered one. Ensuring first that the safety was on, he put the weapon in the pack alongside everything else.

Quickly reattaching the lid, he buried the container once more, covering the disturbed earth with detritus . Finally, he collapsed the shovel and returned that to the rucksack. Lifting it onto his shoulders he bore the newly acquired weight with ease. With a last glance at the ground, content that almost any sign of his presence was fleeting, he set off back towards the car park. The family came to mind once more, and he wondered whether they had reached their car and set off already. A wave of exhilaration passed over him and he fought to subdue it. *This wasn't the time.* Although, he had been raised to *never look a gift horse in the mouth* and for a brief moment he considered breaking into a run before quelling the urge. That was getting harder and harder as time passed. The recognition of that fact made him stop to draw breath.

There was a process and it was successful. One that had been developed through experience and had never failed him. Why should he change it now? Was this becoming mundane? Perhaps it was time to broaden his horizons a little, mix up the status quo. *Maybe so, but not today.* That would require some thought. Unless an opportunity presented itself again, of course. That would signal something else was at work, a power far greater than him.

Retracing his steps back to the trail, as the sunshine broke through the clouds , he made it to the car park soon after. The family had made worse time than predicted and were still loading the car as he approached. The mother smiled warmly in his direction before leaning in and clipping their daughter's seatbelt in place. The father offered a small wave of acknowledgement. No doubt his pride slightly dented. Their son was hopping around in the rear, apparently searching for something lost amongst their gear.

Whistling a nameless tune his thoughts drifted to the contents of his rucksack, all easily accessible if required. He must have slipped into a daydream of possibilities because he found the father staring at him as he finished stowing their kit, closing the boot to their people carrier. The man stopped and glanced over towards him. At that moment he realised he had stopped walking and was standing in the middle of the car park, watching intently. Still, he didn't move.

The excitement was building once again. This coming weekend was shaping up to be a great one.

CHAPTER TWO

THE DOOR to the taxi slammed shut and the car moved off. Caslin watched as the driver pulled out onto the Fulford Road and accelerated away, in the direction of the city centre, with apparent disregard for the fact he was leaving a police station. Caslin considered sticking him on at a later date. Although, £6.80 was practically daylight robbery, and he felt that he should be able to arrest him for that alone. Telling that to the cabbie however, could've been deemed provocative, so he let the thought pass. Grabbing a ride from someone, hopefully later that day, to collect his car would be far more agreeable than shelling out again.

Crossing the car park, he mounted the steps to the entrance and walked into reception. Linda was on the front desk and he gave her a smile and a wave whilst she returned it, pointing to the clock on the wall, signifying he was late. Caslin's smile broke into a grin. Linda was much like a mother to him, only without the emotional baggage. He was punching in his code to the security door when she drew his attention, indicating a lady seated to his left. Crossing over to the counter, he approached Linda with an enquiring look on his face.

"She's been here since first thing," she said in a hushed tone.

"What does she want?" Caslin asked, equally lowering his voice.

"I think she wants to make a complaint. At least, that would be my guess. She's asking to see a senior officer."

"Who's the unfortunate in the firing line?" Caslin said, smiling as he spoke.

"One of yours, Terry Holt."

His smile faded. That was the last thing he needed. First the car, now this. He considered what on earth his DC had been up to. Glancing over his shoulder, he took the measure of the woman. She was in her early fifties, he guessed, judging by the hair style and clothes that she wore but had the look of someone far older. The skin to her face was heavily lined and despite fake tan, hair dye and a bit of make-up, it was clear that she was losing the battle with time.

"Any idea what her problem is?" he asked without looking away.

"Perhaps you should ask her?" Linda said evenly, with only a hint of condescension.

He glanced back at the civilian desk clerk and smiled.

"Well maybe I will, then. Did she give you a name?"

"Suzanne Brooke."

"Thank you, Linda."

Leaving the counter, he walked across reception and his approach was met with wary eyes. Before he was able to introduce himself, she rose from her seat.

"Are you a senior officer?" she asked, her tone stern and uncompromising. Caslin was slightly taken aback and realised how Linda had formed her conclusion.

"I'm Detective Inspector, Nathaniel Caslin."

"You'll do," she said. "I want to make a complaint."

"You had better come with me," Caslin replied, indicating towards the internal access to the station proper.

"About time."

Caslin glanced at the clock which read 9:48. What a start to his working week.

HAVING FOUND THEM A QUIET ROOM, Caslin got her a cup of tea, himself a coffee and they sat down. Whether he had misinterpreted her attitude or not, he wasn't sure, but there was a definite softening of her stance as they began to talk.

"May I ask what you would like to complain about, Mrs Brooke?" Caslin asked, hopeful that it was something minor.

"Miss Brooke," she corrected him. "But I know I'm a little old for that, so Suzanne will do just fine."

Caslin acknowledged the correction with a nod of his head. She had definitely softened.

"You have an issue with one of our officers?" he asked, as casually as he dared, hoping to cut this off early.

"Yes, Detective Constable Holt," Suzanne glared. "He's not taking my report seriously. I've phoned and visited over the weekend and I'm being fobbed off."

"You'll forgive me. I've been out of the station for a few days. I'm not aware of what he's working on. Could you fill me in?"

Suzanne sat forward in her chair, apparently pleased that a senior rank was prepared to listen. Caslin wondered if she had lost her cat.

"My daughter's missing," she began, emotion edging into her voice. "It's not like Melissa, not at all."

Caslin also sat forward. "When did she go missing?"

"I realised something was up on Saturday morning, when she didn't show up to see Isabel, her daughter."

"She was with you?"

"She lives with me, you see," Suzanne met his eye, tears forming on the rim of hers. Caslin observed the woman across from him, watching her demeanour morph from aggression into nervous vulnerability. "She never misses a day out with her, *never*."

Caslin did a quick mental calculation. Being Monday morning, only a little over forty-eight hours had passed since she had been last heard from.

"How old is Melissa?" Caslin asked. Suzanne frowned. "That was the first question DC Holt asked me as well." Caslin cursed himself silently. "She's twenty-one. And before you say it, I know, she's an adult and can do what she wants."

Caslin held up a hand. "I'm only building a picture, in my mind. Do you have any reason to think that she has come to harm? Have you been to her residence—"

"Of course, I have!" Suzanne interrupted him. "I have a key to hers and she's not been back, I would know."

"Not been back, you said? Do you know where she was on Friday night?"

Suzanne fell silent, leaning back into her chair as a sense of deflation overcame the threat of rising anger. "She was working."

"Where does she work?"

There was a moment of hesitation before her eyes flicked up at Caslin, then dropped back to the table. Caslin knew what that look meant, she didn't have to say it, she didn't want to.

"Not exactly," Suzanne replied.

"What does she do?" Caslin asked again.

"She… she's an escort."

The words appeared to sting as they crossed her lips, her body language signifying resignation. Caslin could immediately see her difficulty in acknowledging what her daughter did for a living but at the same time, it brought her reasoning into focus.

"Why do you think that something untoward has happened to her, other than missing a play date with her daughter?"

"She wouldn't miss it and certainly not without letting me know. She doesn't do this to me, she knows how I worry,"

Suzanne's eyes were imploring him to act, to find a solution. "She's not a street walker, you know—"

"That's of no consequence to me, Suzanne. I promise you," he reassured her. "How then, does she carry out her... business?"

She looked at him then, as if attempting to read his thoughts, assessing whether he really cared or was passing judgement, as so many others had no doubt done before. Her expression was unreadable. "I don't know, Mel keeps that to herself but she always insists she's safe. She's never unaccompanied."

"Her pimp?" Caslin asked. There was no easy way to sugar coat such a question.

She shook her head, "No, it's not like that. She has a driver; all the girls do."

Caslin considered that. This put Melissa in a different bracket to the prostitutes who inhabited the redlight areas of York, or even the call girls who operated independently through wanted ads in magazines or the internet.

"Any history of substance abuse or—"

"I know what you all think but I swear to you, she's clean these days. I would know. I know my daughter."

"Alright, Suzanne. I'll look into it and see what's going on. Would you like to hold on here while I have a word with the investigating officer?"

Suzanne nodded. A brief smile crossed her face before returning to the strained expression that had greeted him in reception. She didn't want to make a complaint. This was a frightened mother who wanted someone to help find her daughter.

MULLING OVER THEIR CONVERSATION, as he made his way upstairs to CID, he wondered what Terry Holt had made of it. He tried hard not to draw any conclusions about his attitude before speaking with him. Holt was a reasonably decent member of the team but he did suffer with preconceived ideas about people from certain backgrounds. That did him few favours with his DI but as Caslin had to admit; Holt wasn't alone. Passing through the double doors into the squad room he gave only cursory responses to the greetings received, making a beeline for the stocky DC, currently hunched over his desk.

"Terry, my office," he said as he walked past, noting the open copy of the Racing Post before him. "When you're finished picking a few losers, naturally."

Several people erupted into laughter as Holt rapidly closed the paper. He stood up and hurried after Caslin.

"What's up, Sir?" Holt asked as he entered the office.

"Close the door behind you," Caslin told him, taking his seat behind the desk. Holt's brow furrowed at that. He had the look of someone who thought he was in trouble. Caslin always kept the door open; usually keen to be a part of the atmosphere of the squad room, a throwback to earlier days. Unless that is, he had something to say. "Melissa Brooke. Talk to me."

Holt hesitated before pulling out one of the two remaining free chairs but Caslin didn't stop him.

"Prostitute, reported missing on Saturday, just gone. I pulled her file," he went on, "multiple arrests for soliciting, shoplifting, possession… the list goes on."

"What have you done to investigate?" Caslin asked. There was no insinuation in his tone, merely a request for cold facts.

Holt thought for a moment. "I went to her address, there was no sign. I made an enquiry at the hospitals under her name, or any anonymous female admitted since Friday night, for that matter."

"No hits?"

"Not one," Holt stated. "Nothing on file with us over the weekend either. Chances are she's sleeping off a rough weekend, or she's on a nice earner."

"Terry, don't make assumptions," Caslin chastised him.

"Sorry, Sir. But what have I got? A mother reports her daughter missing, who happens to be a Tom, less than a day since she last spoke to her. Oh, and she's a junkie. Am I supposed to be surprised? It is the weekend after all."

"Mother says she's clean."

Holt baulked at that. Caslin couldn't tell if the reaction was from disagreeing with the statement or outright surprise that his DI knew so much about the case, having been off for three days.

"They always think they're clean," he countered, Caslin had to agree. "She's got form as well."

"Who? The mother?"

Holt nodded, "Receiving, as well as some benefit fraud, a couple of years back."

"Well, at least you've been busy," Caslin said dryly. "The mother says Melissa had a driver which puts her into the realms of the organised criminals, a cut above your average junkie. Have another look at it. And while you're at it, Suzanne... the mother, is waiting downstairs. So, you can give her a lift home and find out as much as you can."

"Yes, Sir."

Holt didn't argue. He got up and left without another word, his DI having found a direct avenue of investigation that Holt hadn't even considered. Caslin didn't need to say anything further. His expectation was for the DC to put in more effort. About to head downstairs to speak to Suzanne Brooke before she left, Caslin stopped at the doorway, finding DCI Frank Stephens looking for him.

"Just the man."

"Guv?"

"You need to get yourself over to Ripon. Studley Park, to be exact."

"What's going on out there?" Caslin asked.

"We've got a missing girl," Stephens enlightened him. "She didn't show at the Abbey as expected. They've found her car, apparently abandoned, on a lane to the south of the park."

"Okay, Guv but what's this got to do with us?" Caslin said, highlighting that it was a little off their patch.

"I don't always call the plays, Nate. Sometimes I just read them out."

"Fair enough."

The DCI glanced past Caslin, back into his office, taking in the clear desk and barren walls. He shook his head as he turned back to face him, "When are you going to start treating that as *your* office? You could at least put a picture of your kids on your desk, even one of your car, if you prefer?"

Caslin looked over his shoulder and shrugged, "I'll get around to it."

He watched the DCI leave. It had been six months since he'd returned to CID from his enforced absence, on medical grounds. The death of the former incumbent of that office still weighed heavily on him. For sure his surroundings would become more familiar to him but it was low on his priority list. Several sets of eyes fell on him as he stood in the middle of the squad room.

"What's that about, do you reckon?" DS Sarah Hunter asked openly.

Caslin shrugged, "Haven't a clue but…" he pointed to her, "We're going to find out. Get your coat."

"Me, Sir? I was planning to—"

"You're driving."

"Yes, Sir."

CHAPTER THREE

THEIR ROUTE TOOK them north on the A1 before cutting west and eventually picking up the A61, circumventing Harrogate. They were aiming for a remote lane that ran north between the Spa town and Studley Park, a World Heritage site that encompassed the ruins of the Cistercian Fountains Abbey, Georgian Water Garden and the Studley Royal Deer Park. Leaving the A road they picked their way along the narrow lanes, used predominantly by the locals to avoid the traffic on the main arterial routes.

The day was overcast with frequent bursts of heavy rain, bringing down visibility and slowing their progress. Approaching a police cordon, a solitary traffic vehicle positioned across the road, Hunter slowed the car and pulled alongside the lone officer. Following a brief inspection of their warrant cards they were bidden access and directed a quarter of a mile up the lane. Hunter parked the car on the verge, near to several other unmarked and liveried vehicles. Caslin noted the presence of a canine unit and then a CSI van, one usually driven by Iain Robertson, the senior scenes of crime officer in North Yorkshire. The big guns were most definitely out. Clearly this was more than merely a report of a missing girl.

Getting out of the car, Caslin put on his overcoat. This year had been one of the wettest, and therefore coolest, on record. The promise of an Indian summer was becoming hollower as the days passed. Glancing in the direction of the park, he saw the ruins of the abbey, perhaps half a mile away.

His attention was drawn to a red Vauxhall Corsa, parked partly on the road with the front perched atop the verge. Casting an eye over the car as they walked, he couldn't see any signs of damage indicative of an accident or a breakdown. It appeared in good condition and was less than three years old, judging by the plates.

"Glad you could make it," a familiar voice called to him. The tall figure, unmistakably DCS Kyle Broadfoot, broke free of the small group deep in discussion and made his way towards them. Caslin acknowledged the greeting with a smile and took the offered hand. He was unaware that his attendance was optional.

"What do we have, Sir?" he enquired as Broadfoot also acknowledged DS Hunter.

"A twenty-year-old girl who didn't turn up on site, as expected. Her dig leader, and tutor I believe, contacted the parents. They're family friends and he found it strange. The parents became concerned."

"Presumably, they knew that she was due here today."

"Yes, she had spoken of it when they talked on the telephone last night. They felt it out of character. She is very conscientious, apparently, and they knew that she wasn't ill. The father left his office, after his wife called him to see if he knew why she hadn't shown, and drove the route. He found her car here." Broadfoot indicated the Corsa.

"When was all this, Sir?" Caslin asked, looking around the scene.

"A little after 9 a.m."

"They were quick off the mark."

"She was due in from 6 a.m., to make the most of the light."

"Where was she due to work, Sir?" Hunter asked.

"Not work," Broadfoot corrected her. "She's an Archaeology student from the University of York. She's part of a team carrying out some excavations at nearby Fountains Abbey. Using it as the foundation of their dissertation pieces, I understand. They called off the dig last Thursday, due to the torrential rain, and were set to restart again this morning."

"Any sign of a breakdown?" Caslin asked. Broadfoot shook his head.

"What about a struggle?" Hunter said.

"Not that we can see. The car was unlocked, no sign of the keys."

"What about her personal effects: purse, mobile?" Caslin asked.

"Come and see," Broadfoot suggested and led them to the car.

Caslin put on a pair of latex gloves that Hunter passed to him, before opening the passenger door, noting that the vehicle was facing in the direction of the abbey. It would seem that she stopped on her way to the site. A quick glance to the ground saw no evidence of freshly laid down rubber. Caslin figured the damp conditions could well have prevented the tyres from doing so if she had indeed stopped in a hurry. A lack of mud or grass deposits in the wheel arches, positioned on the verge as they were, further indicated to him that this was a controlled stop.

"What's the name?" Caslin asked casually as he stooped low to inspect the interior. Hunter passed around to the driver's side, opening the door, and doing likewise.

"Bermond, Natalie Bermond."

Caslin's ears pricked at the name, "Bermond? The parents?"

"Catherine and Tim—"

"Timothy," Caslin finished.

Hunter stopped her inspection of the vehicle and looked across at him. "You know them, Sir?"

Caslin was snapped back into the present. Standing up, he turned to Broadfoot who answered an unasked question.

"An old friend of yours, I understand?"

Caslin shrugged almost imperceptibly, "I wouldn't go that far... I mean, we were but that was a lifetime ago."

"Well, he requested your presence."

"Really?" Caslin was surprised although that explained the cryptic request for his attendance. Broadfoot pointed a little further down the lane where two plain clothes detectives were speaking with another man, who Caslin barely recognised. Timothy Bermond was no longer the scrawny youth, with a mass of floppy hair that he recalled from his childhood. He was balding and carrying more weight than was probably good for him. Even from this distance, Caslin could see facial lines far more determined than one would expect on someone of his years. No stranger to weight issues himself, he suddenly felt better about his physique as he took in that of his childhood friend.

Returning his gaze to the car, he focussed on the cabin. The gearstick was in neutral and the handbrake was on. The interior was almost immaculate with hardly any signs of wear. The absence of rubbish that often accumulated in vehicles, particularly owned and driven by youngsters, struck him as odd. There was a fair amount of mud on the off-side floor mat, but other than that, it was spotless. Out of habit, he scanned the linings of the roof and sides to see if there was any visible blood residue but found nothing. He saw no mobile phone, coat or backpack, nor any sign of personal items left behind. Hunter met his gaze and he thought that she had come to the same conclusion. Both stepped away from the vehicle. Looking around to the front of the car, Caslin saw Iain Robertson kneeling down a few metres away. Walking over he greeted the gruff Scot with a smile.

"Morning, Iain."

Robertson looked up and returned the smile warmly, "Hello, Nate."

"What have you got there?"

"Tyre impressions," Robertson indicated the depressed earth at his feet, two locations that signalled the front and rear wheels of a vehicle that had left their mark in the grass verge. "Made by a big vehicle, too, taking the width and depth into account... and recently."

"How can you be sure?"

"Lack of water retained in the tread patterns."

"Four-by-four?" Caslin asked.

"Quite likely, I should imagine. As far as it's possible for me to surmise, at this stage anyway. I wouldn't rule out a van of some description just yet though. Spacing between them limits the scope for much else. Short wheelbase van, or an SUV, is my best and most highly educated, guess."

Caslin smiled, Iain was normally modest, despite having the least to be modest about. When it came to the analysis of forensic examination, there was no-one better.

"Did it stop abruptly, do you think?"

"Doubt it very much," Robertson said with confidence. "Look at these tread impressions in the mud. If it had stopped suddenly, there would be more of a scuff and far less detail to the pattern."

"Could you match it?"

"To a brand?"

"Preferably to a vehicle but whatever you can do," Caslin replied, slightly tongue-in-cheek.

"I'll give it a go," Robertson said, smiling.

"Good man," Caslin replied. "Have you taken a look at the car?"

"Of course. I didn't see a lot in it for me though. We'll run the full battery of checks, if the DCS thinks it worthwhile but nothing leapt out as being noteworthy."

"Okay, thanks. I'll catch up with you later," Caslin said, departing. Returning to stand alongside Broadfoot, he found the head of North Yorkshire CID looking perplexed.

"It's a curious one, isn't it?" Broadfoot said. It seemed to Caslin to be a rhetorical question. He answered anyway.

"Not much to suggest anything untoward happened," Caslin said. He looked at the surrounding fields, only the odd building punctuating the landscape to denote that they weren't too far from habitation. This was a lonely place on the fringes of urban life. That was the beauty of Yorkshire once beyond the edge of the towns and cities you were liberated by the landscape. "Any luck with witnesses?"

"Nothing as yet but we have officers knocking on doors."

"To be fair, she could just as easily have met a friend here and left in another vehicle," Caslin said. It was the most plausible of scenarios in the absence of evidence to the contrary.

"The father clearly doesn't think so," Hunter offered.

Caslin glanced over at the man, a worried expression on his face, as he stood deep in conversation with their colleagues. The dog handler was returning, from the northern end of the lane, and it appeared as if he had also turned up nothing of note.

"Perhaps we should speak with him, then," Caslin said. Turning to Broadfoot, he added, "If you don't mind, Sir?"

Broadfoot shook his head, "You'll be reporting to one of the team from Harrogate, DCI John Inglis. You know him?"

Caslin shrugged, "No, never met him."

"That's him over there with Mr Bermond, the one to the right." Broadfoot pointed. He was of slender build and looked as smooth as a film star with the way he carried himself. "I'll introduce you later."

"Thank you, Sir. Am I to be seconded away from Fulford Road?"

"Certainly not. You can carry on with your caseload. Inglis can handle this. Do what you do, Nathaniel, but do it through John."

"I understand, Sir," Caslin confirmed. However, he did feel that he was largely present at the behest of Timothy Bermond and therefore, primarily for window dressing. Broadfoot had, until recently, intimated to Caslin that he had a new role lined up for him but subsequently that had fallen by the wayside. Perhaps Caslin's manner had brought the DCS to his senses.

"Pay attention to this, Nathaniel. We can't afford any slip-ups. Find her and do it quickly, please."

Caslin said that he would endeavour to do just that and set off, Hunter falling into step alongside him. Once out of earshot, although still in a lowered tone, she voiced her thoughts.

"What did he mean by that?"

Caslin smiled as he replied, "You haven't put it together yet. All of this?" he waved his hand in a circular motion, a gesture regarding the police presence.

"It is a little over the top, seems a bit of a fuss—"

"About nothing?" Caslin said.

Hunter nodded.

"Exactly, I mean we don't know that anything has happened but half the force has turned out, including the Prince of Darkness."

Caslin laughed at the reference to Broadfoot. He did have a reputation for being more than a little self serving. The fact was that Hunter was right but he was disappointed that she had missed the obvious.

"Timothy Bermond's father is Sebastian Bermond."

The penny dropped and Hunter took a sharp intake of breath, "Oh, bloody hell."

Caslin nodded, "Now you see."

Further comment was halted as they approached Timothy. He clocked their arrival and broke away from his conversation, stepping forward to meet them. He thrust his hand into Caslin's.

"Glad you're here, Nate."

"It's been a while, Tim," Caslin said graciously, accepting the firm handshake. "I'm sorry it's under these circumstances."

"I know, me too. I saw that you were back in the area after that case you had last year. You were all over the papers." Caslin thought back, he didn't want to go there. "I considered calling you then but… well, it's been—"

"A long time. Don't worry about it, Tim. We're here to help," Caslin said and then introduced DS Hunter, who also took an offered hand.

"Thanks, Nate. Anything you can do will be very much appreciated."

Caslin could see the lines of concern etched into the face of his old friend. He barely recognised the boy that he used to know and absently wondered if the feeling was reciprocal. Tim was being polite but it was clear that he was deeply worried about his daughter.

"Forgive me for being blunt, Tim, but why do you think that something has happened to Natalie?"

Timothy lifted himself upright, almost as if reverting to a disciplined stance, reminiscent of a soldier on parade. Caslin considered it a byproduct of a public school education, one he was intimately associated with.

"This is so out of character for Natalie. She was thoroughly determined to partake in this research. She's talked about little else for months. I cannot fathom any reason why she would fail to attend, none at all."

"Even so, twenty-something girls can be spontaneous—"

"Not my Natalie. Believe me, there is something very wrong."

"Is there anything else?" Caslin asked, sensing reticence.

The man hesitated, meeting Caslin's eye. The passing moment was brief but telling.

"We've been getting calls, at the house."

"What type of calls, nuisance, malicious?"

Bermond shook his head, "No, they are always silent and then hang up."

"I get those all the time, they're usually automated."

"No, no, not those types of calls. They wouldn't concern me

at all. These are at all hours and someone is always on the end of the line. We can hear him."

"How do you know it's a man?" Hunter asked.

Bermond thought on it before shrugging the question off, "I don't know, we assumed so but... it's not just that, there are often sounds in the background. Like it's a public place, not an office or call centre but say a bar or a gathering, of some sort."

"Are they ever threatening?"

"They feel like it," he said, his tone fearful. "I know that probably sounds daft."

"Not at all, Tim," Caslin reassured him. "Why do you think these are threatening calls and do you have any idea who might be making them?"

Again, he shook his head in response, "This just feels wrong."

Caslin felt that they weren't going to get any further at the moment. There were occasions when he felt the need to push relatives to give up more information, believing that they had useful leads for him to follow but at the same time, he wasn't a monster. The man was extremely anxious and probably thrown by the whole situation. There were other things that Caslin could be doing in the meantime and pressing the parents could wait until later.

"Why don't you go home, Tim," he suggested. About to receive an objection to that idea, Caslin continued, "We can drop by later and have a more detailed conversation. I'll be in touch the minute I have any news. I give you my word. For now, you're not needed here but I dare say your wife needs you at home."

The last hit the right note and Bermond conceded the point. Once again, he shook hands with Caslin, thanking him for his involvement. Caslin called over a uniformed officer and requested that he arrange a ride home. The last thing he wanted was a preoccupied father causing a road accident on the way.

"The two of you go way back?" Hunter asked.

"School friends," Caslin said. "Until my parents divorced and my mother took me and my brother down south. I can't have seen Tim, for what... twenty-five, nearly thirty years, something like that."

"You didn't stay in touch?"

"I was twelve," Caslin said, as if that answered everything.

"What do you reckon, think there's anything to it?" Hunter asked as they watched the back of the retreating father.

Caslin blew out his cheeks. He recalled Timothy Bermond as a sensible, pragmatic boy, certainly not one to overreact to a given situation. Tim had always been a steady influence on the younger of the Caslin boys. As a result, he felt he should consider the possibility that there was more going on than it at first appeared. However, that friendship had been decades ago and people changed.

"Well, whatever's going on, we have to check it out. Once the press gets a hold of this, they're going to have a field day."

Hunter had to agree. A missing girl would most likely generate a few headlines in the absence of another major story. Throw in the fact that she was the granddaughter of the long serving MP for York Central, and you had a story with a massive public interest.

CHAPTER FOUR

THE DRIVE to the Bermond residence in Harrogate took less than twenty minutes. Hunter pulled the car up outside a large Edwardian townhouse, set back from the road with a well-manicured front garden acting as a buffer to the tree-lined street beyond. Caslin got out and glanced over to the house. Movement from within signalled their arrival had already registered. Caslin and Hunter had barely opened the gate when the front door opened. Both parents stood waiting for them, anxious expressions conveyed their expectation of the worst.

"Have you any news?" Timothy asked, as they mounted the double step to the porch.

Caslin shook his head, "Please could we go inside, so that we can talk."

"Of course."

They were beckoned in and shown directly into, what Caslin guessed to be, the sitting room. Little did he know it was the first of three reception rooms. The large bay window to the front enabled the passage of a great deal of natural light and Caslin was impressed with the surroundings. The house was opulent without drifting into decadence. The colour scheme was consistent with the furnishings and he figured the Bermonds had a sense of period style.

"Please take a seat," Catherine said, indicating the sofa to their left, one of a pair that faced each other, sprawling almost the width of the room. They did so and Caslin observed her while they all took their seats. Hunter sat next to him, whilst Tim stood to the left of his wife, who held tightly to his right hand. Caslin introduced them both, primarily for Catherine's sake, before moving to the subject of their daughter.

"Firstly, I must stress that at this time we have found no evidence that anything has happened to Natalie," Caslin said as gently as he could. Both parents seemed to relax but only slightly. "However, we are certainly taking your concerns seriously."

"It would help us if you could provide some information about her," Hunter said, taking out her notebook.

"What would you like to know?" Catherine asked.

"What type of person is she?" Caslin said.

"She's an amazing daughter, Nathaniel," Timothy replied. "She has never given us any cause for concern, such as this. She's a model student, straight As through college and has hit a distinction in each of her first two years at York."

"What is she reading?" Hunter said, despite already knowing the answer, attempting to ease them into the task at hand.

"Archaeology," he replied. "That was why she was due at Fountains Abbey today. They are carrying out a dig in partnership with the National Trust."

"Has anything like this ever happened before, anything peculiar? For example, last minute changes of plan that she failed to notify you of?" Caslin said. Both parents were taken aback.

"No, never," Timothy said. "We told you, she's a model student and daughter."

Hunter cast a glance sideways to Caslin but he didn't acknowledge it.

"What about boyfriends, anyone on the scene that you are aware of?" Hunter asked.

Again, Timothy shook his head, "She doesn't have time for any of that. What with her studies, the debating club, and all the sports that she's involved in, there wouldn't be enough hours in the day."

"Mrs Bermond?" Caslin turned the question on the mother, who had largely remained silent. She too, shook her head.

"No, not that I'm aware of."

"Does she live here, with the two of you?" Caslin asked.

"No, she's in halls at the university, Vanbrugh College. Fairfax House to be exact," Timothy said. "She obviously still has her room here, and she comes home sometimes, at the weekends."

"Not often, though. Not these days, anyway," Catherine added.

"We'd like to take a look at her room, a little later. If you don't mind?"

"Not at all," Tim said.

"What about friends, is there anyone specific that she is close to? Someone that she might go to, or confide in," Hunter asked, scribbling away in her pocketbook.

"She's a very popular girl," Timothy said, but Caslin could see the man's frustration building. "Look, I don't see how this is getting us anywhere. You should be out there looking for her."

"We are, Tim. I assure you, there're a lot of people doing just that," Caslin said, deliberately keeping his tone calm and controlled. "We just need a steer as to the best place to focus them, that's how this can help."

He appeared to settle down at that point, his shoulders sagging ever so slightly. His wife's hold of his hand grew tighter still.

"What is it you do with yourself these days, Tim?"

He glanced up at Caslin, "I work for a strategic marketing

consultancy, DYC, *Deep Yonder Consultants*. We have an office here, in Harrogate, and another in London."

"You're a little more than that, darling," Catherine rubbed the back of his hand with hers. Turning to Caslin she added, "He's a senior partner. He practically runs the place, by himself."

"That's an exaggeration," Timothy corrected his wife. "But I do put in the hours. That's true."

"Would there be anyone in your business dealings that could have a grudge against you?"

"Certainly not!"

"I have to ask, Tim. What about you, Mrs Bermond? Is there anyone that you've come across that might wish you or your family harm?"

She paused before answering, meeting Caslin's gaze head on with one of her own. He found her incredibly difficult to read. "No."

"It would help if we had an up to date photo of Natalie, do you have one that we could borrow? Also, could you provide us with her mobile phone number? I'm assuming that she has one," Hunter asked, flicking looks between the two parents.

"Who doesn't?" Timothy replied. "I can give it to you, but I've been calling it all morning and she hasn't answered once. It cuts straight to voicemail."

"That doesn't matter. We can try to get a hit from her signal, see where she's been, if not where she is," Caslin offered. "It may also be useful to see who she's been talking to in recent days. We'll get that from her provider."

"I'll see about getting you a photo," Catherine said, standing up and making to leave the room. At the threshold before passing into the hall, she stopped, appearing momentarily confused, "Forgive me, where are my manners? Would either of you like a cup of tea or coffee?"

"No, no, we will be fine. But thank you," Caslin said, without considering Hunter for a moment.

Timothy watched his wife leave and turned back to the

officers, a determined look on his face, "It's my father that you should be speaking to."

"Sebastian?" Caslin reiterated. Timothy nodded fervently.

"If someone has an axe to grind, no doubt it'll revolve around him."

Caslin sat back in his chair, casting a glance at Hunter who had, involuntarily, ceased writing at the mention of the MP. Sebastian Bermond had recently been appointed to the Common's Home Affairs Select Committee, one of the most high profile and influential, in the system. He had a fearsome reputation and was largely outspoken within his constituency, a trait that seemed to curry favour with the electorate.

"Why would you say that, Tim?" Caslin asked.

"I don't have any evidence, so don't ask me for it but I always knew that sooner or later, it would come back to bite us."

"If you have a specific—"

"Talk to him."

"Tim, I can't walk into his office and throw an accusation without any substance to back it up."

Tim glanced at Hunter, who in turn looked to Caslin. He nodded and Hunter got up and headed in the direction that Catherine had taken, leaving the two men alone.

"He's not clean, you know," Timothy offered in a conspiratorial tone.

"How so?" Caslin asked, before adding, "Off the record."

Tim took a deep breath, looking around before he spoke, as if to ensure they were alone, "My father and I are not close, Nathaniel. We've barely spoken in years."

Caslin could relate. "Then how can you think that he's involved?"

"Not involved, that's not what I said. Growing up, I used to hear things, come across people at the house from time to time. Things that I wasn't supposed to be aware of but I made it my business to know. I was curious."

"Go on."

"I didn't think much of it at the time, the late-night meetings, quiet chats with men who left via the rear access. As I grew older, I figured that these people weren't your average lobbyists or business associates."

"Who were they?" Caslin asked, intrigued.

"Well, I don't really know, not for sure."

Caslin noticed that his heart rate had increased with the anticipation but now he considered that this could be nothing but hearsay. Timothy sensed his waning interest and was keen to drive the point home.

"Listen, Nathaniel. Think about it for a second. Who is Natalie? She is my father's only grandchild. There would be no point in coming after me, for it's common knowledge that we can't stand each other." It may have been to some but certainly not to Caslin until now.

"Is he close to Natalie?"

"I've never sought to keep them apart. My issues with him are mine alone. There's no reason for Natalie to be a pawn in all of that."

"I don't know. There's a lot of supposition in there, Tim. Not much for me to work with, if I'm honest with you."

"Just talk to him, *please*," he implored him. "You'll recognise it the same as I did, I know you will. I remember you, Nathaniel. That's why I insisted you be on board."

Caslin rubbed at the back of his head, frowning at the same time. He had made a name for himself as one to ruffle feathers in the past. However, he had hoped that those days were behind him. Although, he always knew it to be a vain hope.

"Leave it with me," was the best response he could muster.

Catherine returned to the sitting room, Hunter trailing behind. The former clutched a photo of Natalie in her hand, apparently reluctant to pass it over. Almost as if to do so would be an admission that her daughter may not return. She tentatively passed it to Hunter, who smiled appreciatively.

"We'll get this back to you," Hunter said reassuringly.

"May we have a look at Natalie's bedroom now?" Caslin asked.

"Please, come with me," Timothy said, leading them out into the hall and on up the staircase. They passed a split level access to a family bathroom at the rear, before coming to an imposing landing. There were four doors off it, with another staircase further along, leading to the next floor. The presentation was once again without fault. "It's that one, the second left."

Timothy appeared as if he didn't want to enter the bedroom, perhaps not wanting to draw out more emotion than he could handle. Caslin thanked him and indicated that he could leave them to it. Gratefully, the father departed and went back downstairs, presumably to be with his wife.

Caslin and Hunter opened the door and went inside. The room was large, at least by the measures that Caslin placed on bedrooms. The window was cracked open and a cool breeze drifted over them. A single bed was set against one wall, a vanity unit to the side, beneath the sash window. On the adjacent wall was a desk, a laptop lay unopened upon it. Everything was well ordered, with no loose clutter. A few shelves were set out above, holding assorted knick knacks and an assortment of chick-lit paperbacks. A large, free standing wardrobe dominated the rear wall and a matching chest of drawers made up the remaining furnishings. All were high quality and crafted from an expensive hardwood, Caslin guessed, as he perused the room.

Hunter began to sift through the contents of the drawers, to the desk, while Caslin examined the wardrobe. The latter was stocked with a healthy amount of clothes, he figured they were fashionable without being certain, knowing so little about these things. The chest of drawers was also full and he felt slightly voyeuristic as he rummaged through her accumulated underwear. His searches yielded little. He glanced over to Hunter and flicked an eyebrow.

"There's nothing here that strikes me as particularly unusual. How about you?" she asked.

"Same," he replied. "It doesn't look like she was planning on going anywhere, not if this lots anything to go by."

"Most of her valuables will be at her digs, though, won't they?"

"The more intimate, personal things, laptop, diary… do people still keep those?"

"Some."

"Do you?" Caslin asked, playfully.

"That… is none of your business," Hunter replied in a reciprocal tone.

Caslin smiled, "I have a warrant card. Everything is my business."

There was something unusual here, Caslin figured, just not necessarily directly related to Natalie's disappearance. The overall impression of the room, and its occupant, was that she was tidy and respectful. There was no mess, no make-up or styling products left out, nor any jewellery to speak of. The trappings of modern media, fashion magazines, posters, the likes of which one would expect to be adorning the floor and walls of a girl's room were all absent. That surprised him. The colour scheme, wooden furnishings aside, was overwhelmingly pink. The thought occurred, eyeing the neatly stacked cuddly toys in one corner, that this was the room of a young child rather than that of a twenty-something. He wondered whether Natalie was immature for her age. That might explain the apparent disinterest in boys. Then again, perhaps her parents liked her that way.

Pulling the door to behind them, they crossed the landing and made their way back down. Timothy met them at the foot of the staircase.

"Did you find anything to help?" he asked optimistically.

"Nothing specific, no," Caslin replied. Sensing the deflation of his childhood friend, he offered a supportive hand to Timothy's shoulder. "Everything we see helps us to build a picture. Nothing is a waste of time."

Tim nodded and smiled, by way of gratitude at the sentiment. Caslin passed him one of his contact cards, insisting that he could be reached at any time of the day or night. He also promised to keep them in the loop and he bid them farewell.

Caslin heard the front door close before they made it down to the garden path. Hunter passed him the photograph and he scanned the young face before him. She was attractive with an infectious smile. A brunette, with long straight hair that carried to her shoulders, she was almost the spitting image of her mother. Reaching the pavement, he glanced back at the house whilst waiting for Hunter to locate the car keys. He saw Catherine standing in the bay, watching him intently. Her arms were crossed against her chest, her right hand absently playing with the gold necklace that she wore, her face, a picture of concentration.

"What do you make of what he was talking about?" Hunter asked, unlocking the car.

Caslin turned away from the house, opening the door to his side.

"What, the cloak and dagger stuff?"

"Yeah," Hunter said as they simultaneously got in. "Do you buy it?"

Caslin remained tight lipped as she started the car, mulling it over. They pulled out into traffic and he looked back at the house once more, but Catherine was gone.

"He wouldn't be the first MP to be up to something."

"Is that what he said?" Hunter asked.

"No, not in so many words," Caslin replied. That was part of the problem. Timothy Bermond hadn't really said anything useful at all.

"Do you think he's right? That Natalie's been abducted, I mean?"

"If you had asked me that a couple of hours ago, I would've said unlikely. But now... the water seems a little murkier, from where I'm standing."

"I know what you mean. They are pretty adamant."

"Begs the question, though, doesn't it?" Caslin said solemnly. "*How* they can be so sure?"

Caslin nodded but didn't comment further. It wasn't Timothy's conspiracy theory that had piqued his interest, more the couple's body language. He couldn't put his finger on what exactly, but something didn't add up. The challenge would be to figure it out and, with a bit of luck, pick up Natalie along the way. He was always one for a challenge. Looking over at the clock, set into the dashboard, he saw it had just turned three o'clock.

"Let's swing by the university and see if this image of perfection stacks up."

"Sir?" Hunter enquired, looking across at him.

"Come on, Sarah. I saw the look you gave me. You show me a twenty-year-old, university student, that's not interested in guys and I'll show you Terry Holt, picking a winner."

Hunter laughed. "Particularly if the said girl looks like that." She pointed to the photo in Caslin's hand. "Even if she wasn't interested in them, they would definitely be interested in her."

Caslin looked at the photo again. Hunter was right. The parents were always the last to know, the friends were the first.

CHAPTER FIVE

"WE'RE VERY proud of our Collegiate system, here in York," the young, postgraduate student said as they walked.

"How many colleges are there?" Hunter asked him.

One of the Resident College Tutors, Luke Wilcox, led them from the reception of Vanbrugh Nucleus and out onto the piazza. Caslin found the wraparound, shallow steps leading down to the paved area, sweeping out before them to the lake beyond, visually striking. The sixties prefab architecture lent itself to the set of a science fiction film rather than a traditional seat of learning. Students milled about, groups sitting on the edges of the quayside, awaiting boats that would never come. The weather had fared better in the afternoon, a bout of blue sky and sunshine, bringing the residents out to socialise on their wind down from the day.

"We have eight at the university, the latest formed within the last couple of years," Luke said with enthusiasm. Noting Caslin's appreciation of the scene, he went on, "You wouldn't think that Vanbrugh was opened during the second phase of the university's creation, would you?"

"When was that?" Hunter asked, appearing genuinely interested.

"1967, named after Sir John Vanbrugh. He designed Castle Howard, you know."

Caslin feigned interest. He had visited the castle as a child, located within ten miles of the city. He couldn't remember much about it.

"Is this one of the more popular colleges?" Caslin asked.

Luke shrugged, "They all are, in their own way. Because we're open access, they form their own communities that cross study boundaries."

"What does that mean, exactly?" Caslin asked, becoming irritated and struggling not to show it.

"You can apply to the college of your choice, irrespective of what subject you're reading. Each has its own distinct vibe if you will."

Hunter laughed, "Is Vanbrugh the party college, then?"

Luke met her laugh with one of his own, "No, you're thinking of Derwent. But let's keep that between us. Rivalry is still fierce, even amongst friends."

They skirted the piazza, hanging a left, and made their way to *The Warren*, the administrative centre of Vanbrugh. This building was far more in keeping with what Caslin had pictured when considering the University of York.

"This is the old Provost's House. We've been using it as the hub of the college since 2013. Upstairs we have the offices but there is a kitchen…"

The young man carried on with his diatribe, Caslin didn't care for it. He allowed Hunter to pay attention but personally, he doubted that anything useful would come out of him. Caslin was more interested in taking account of the surroundings in an attempt to better understand Natalie. If Vanbrugh wasn't the wild college, it was certainly a place for expression. The instrument library, which he saw in the Nucleus, as well as the many advertised events dotted around showed the emphasis placed on music. A variety of artworks were also commonplace wherever they went. Was Natalie a free thinker? Had she chosen this place for its independent spirit or was he reading too much into it? Perhaps she chose it from the prospectus and hoped for the best, like so many do with life changing decisions.

A brief visit to the office saw them learn where Natalie resided in Fairfax House, another period building, this one in Georgian style, a five-minute walk from the edge of campus. They approached via the well-tended gardens, again sporadically populated by students making the most of the clement afternoon. The building was made up of three wings, arranged in a U shape, with three floors per wing. Entering through a communal doorway, Caslin felt positively ancient as he viewed the fresh faces passing by him. He didn't usually consider himself to be old, not at thirty-nine, not unless his children were visiting anyway.

They mounted a flight of stairs to the second floor, turning right as they reached the landing. The rooms must have been uniform in size and shape as each door was equidistant from the next. Curious eyes scanned them as they walked.

"How many residents do you have, here in Fairfax House?" Caslin asked.

"We have capacity for ninety-one."

"And are you full?"

"Always." Luke sent him an easy smile.

"Fees haven't slowed the intake?"

"No, not at all. That's not something for the better universities to worry about."

Caslin wondered whether quality really had anything to do with it. The promise of a more successful future, via a university education, was a lure that never diminished.

"How well do you know Natalie?" Caslin asked. They had held back on explaining the background for their visit as much as possible, not wanting to set the rumour mill alight. That would happen soon enough.

"Not particularly well. I've come across her socially but never with my student welfare hat on."

"How much of that do you do?" Hunter asked.

"A fair bit," Luke replied. "If the students have concerns, they can come to me, in confidence. All the residential blocks have tutors and if not us, their college officers are usually available."

"Not so with Natalie?" Caslin reiterated for clarity.

"No, she is a very together person, as far as I know. This is hers."

They stopped before a door and Luke knocked, to which there was no answer. He withdrew a master key, unlocking the door and stepping aside.

"We'll take it from here," Hunter said, by way of thanks. "If you could hang around for a few minutes in case we have any further questions, it would be helpful."

"No problem. I'll wait in the common room," Luke said, indicating an area at the end of the corridor. They passed into the room, allowing the door to close behind them. Caslin was pleased to lose the narrator.

"Likes to talk, doesn't he?" he said dryly, keeping his voice low.

"He was being quite pleasant," she replied. Caslin frowned. "You're a miserable so and so, sometimes."

"*Sir*," he added. Hunter smiled.

They found themselves in comfortable surroundings for student life. The room was light, modern and well decorated. Caslin compared it to the damp, mouldy room that he remembered from his first year at university. A single bed, study workstation, wardrobe and minimal additional storage seemed more than adequate. Caslin was not shocked to find it in stark contrast to the room they explored at the Bermond's house. The order here was tempered with a mixture of chaos. Pictures, spread over the walls, of bands that Caslin had never heard of, tall ships sailing in foreign waters, and all peppered with snapshots of student life. The desk was strewn haphazardly with paper, random sheets and notebooks, left with no frame of context.

Opening the wardrobe, Caslin saw a noticeable change in style. Still of high quality but the clothes were less demure, arguably more contemporary.

"What do you make of this lot?" he asked Hunter, who stepped over and sifted through the rail.

"Definitely a step change from what she left at home."

"That's what I thought and none of her clothes seem particularly tired," Caslin replied, casting an eye over the desk. Everything on it appeared study related. Handwritten notes, from lectures, were dated at the top and text books were readily identifiable, amongst the clutter. He picked one up and read the cover, *Quantifying Diversity in Archaeology*. A light read if ever he saw one. Putting it down, his eye passed to a noticeboard, set above the desk. He took note of the calendar. Social engagements were well plotted. There was a gig planned for the forthcoming weekend, a group called *Iron light Stream*, a nonsensical name that was no doubt intended to mean something clever. Hunter was searching through the drawers at the base of the wardrobe.

"Anything?" he asked casually, opening the top drawer of the desk and looking at the contents. Beneath the first two folders lay a tablet, housed in a purple, suede case. Taking it out, he flipped it open. It was top end and even with his limited knowledge, he figured it to be expensive. Anyone with kids knew the cost of decent tech, these days.

"Slightly more risqué underwear than at home, plus a few extras," Hunter proffered.

"Extras?"

"A couple of aids, the likes of which we don't talk about in polite company," Hunter offered.

Caslin glanced over. He didn't need to look, it felt overly intrusive. He would take Hunter's word on it. "Not interested in boys, eh?"

Hunter smiled, "You never know, she could be interested in girls."

Caslin conceded the point. Further conversation was halted by the door opening, an individual launching herself into the room, at pace.

"Well it's about bloody time you got... oh," she said, pulling up, as she saw the police officers standing in Natalie's dorm. "Sorry, I... was looking for Natalie."

"And you are?" Caslin asked.

"Lottie, Charlotte Gibbs," she said, warily eyeing Caslin as she spoke. Her eyes flicked briefly to Hunter and back to Caslin. "I'm a friend of Natalie's. Who are you?"

"Police," Caslin said without breaking his gaze, taking out his warrant card. "Perhaps we could have a chat?"

Lottie appeared momentarily unsure before responding, "Sure. What's this about?"

"I CAN'T BELIEVE IT," Lottie said. She seemed genuinely upset that her friend had gone missing. "I've been texting her all day and not had a response."

Caslin made a mental note of that. They had found a quiet corner of the communal dining room, on the ground floor, to sit in. The areas upstairs were far too cramped to have a conversation without making it very public. The three of them nursed coffees, recently purchased by Hunter.

"Can you think of any reason that Natalie might have for taking a day to herself?"

Lottie emphatically shook her head, "No, not without telling me anyway."

"The two of you are close?" Caslin asked.

"Yes, we've been together at Fairfax since we were Freshers."

"You met here? I mean, you weren't friends before?"

"No, I'm from Gloucester. We hit it off and have been friends ever since. Do you think something's happened to her?"

"Do you?" Caslin replied.

Lottie sat back in her chair, her face a mask of the thoughts revolving in her head. "Why would anyone want to do something to her? She's so nice to everyone. She hasn't got an enemy in the world."

Caslin thought about that. Perhaps she didn't on campus but if she had been abducted, he would have to differ on the premise, for she would have at least one.

"Has Natalie done anything different to the norm, recently? Any behaviour that maybe didn't strike you as odd, at the time but does now?" Hunter asked, her pen hovering over her pocketbook.

Lottie met Hunter's eye and glanced to her coffee cup, on the table. Looking up again, she shrugged, "Can't say as I noticed anything, then or now."

"Does Natalie have a boyfriend?" Caslin enquired. Remembering Hunter's comment earlier, he added, "Or even a girlfriend... things being what they are, these days?"

Hunter's eyes crossed to meet his. Her face didn't break, but he knew she was smiling. Lottie took a sip of her coffee and shook her head, "No. She was seeing a guy last year, but it was only a couple of dates. She kicked him into touch pretty soon after."

Caslin loved the phraseology, probably an apt description for the majority of his own university love life. "Do you have this person's name?"

"I didn't really know him. He was from one of the other colleges. Sorry, I can't remember which one. Not sure that I ever knew," Lottie said with apparent regret. "Listen, I wish I could help more but I have a practice session to attend and I mustn't be late."

"Band?" Hunter asked.

Lottie smiled, "Hockey. May I go?"

Hunter looked to Caslin, who nodded.

"Thanks for your help, Lottie," Hunter said. "If we need to speak to you again, we'll find you. In the meantime, if anything comes to mind, give us a call?"

"Sure," Lottie replied with enthusiasm, taking the offered contact card. With that, she left in haste.

Caslin watched her go until she passed through the double exit doors, absently sipping at the coffee from his plastic cup. It was rancid.

"What do you make of that?" Hunter asked.

Caslin didn't have time to formulate a response as his phone rang. Taking it out from an inside pocket of his coat, he tapped the green answer tab.

"Caslin," he answered flatly. There was silence as he listened. Hunter cast a look around the dining room while she waited. "Two and a half... what... thousand? You must be bloody joking! I didn't even pay that for the sodding thing."

Hunter focussed her attention on the cup in her hand as Caslin hung up on the caller. He put thumb and forefinger to his eyes, exhaling a ragged gasp as he did so. "Problem?"

"Someone expects me to pay for their summer holiday," he replied, dryly. "Come on, let's get a shift on."

"Where are we going?"

"I need a lift," Caslin said. "I'm afraid you're going to be exposed to something no woman should ever have to be."

"Intriguing," Hunter said with a smile. "On the way, we can check in with DCI Inglis. Let him know what we've found out."

Caslin nodded, "Good idea. What have we found out?"

Hunter looked over, attempting to judge whether Caslin was testing her or merely kidding.

"She's one thing to her parents and another at university?"

"Agreed. Pretty sure it's commonplace with many students but I think this is different. The clothes are odd. Not in style but it's almost like there are two people."

"One reserved, with the other modern and expressive?" Hunter suggested. "Lottie's holding back."

"She's following the code," Caslin said.

"The code?"

"Under no circumstances do you speak to an adult and certainly not anyone official, about what is going on with your friend's personal life."

"Should we put her under a little pressure?"

"In due course," Caslin said before adding, "if necessary. Something's going on and I intend to find out what."

CHAPTER SIX

CASLIN LEFT Hunter in the car to call a report through to John Inglis. Walking up the path he saw that the lights were on indoors, a flicker of movement past the front window told him his father was home. Ignoring the front door, he trotted around the side and entered through a gate to the rear. As usual, the back door was unlocked and he couldn't help but think a retired copper ought to know better.

"Hi Dad, it's only me," he called as he walked into the kitchen, wiping his feet on the mat. There was no response but the sound of the television filtered through from the living room, football by the sound of it. Heading that way, he raised his voice even louder, "I've not heard from you in a while, so I thought I'd bet—"

His words stopped when he realised his father had company, someone that he recognised but hadn't seen for a while. He appeared gaunt in comparison to the last time they were together but even so, was still better than expected.

"Hello, little brother," Stefan said, with an easy smile.

Caslin was left open mouthed.

"What's the matter? Got nothing to say?" their father said, grinning from his armchair, nursing a can of beer in his lap.

"I'm... just—" Caslin stammered. "Hi, Stefan. Bit of a surprise."

His elder brother got up from the sofa, put his own beer on the coffee table and came over to greet him.

"That's okay, Nate," he said, fiercely embracing Caslin. "I should've told you I was staying. Dad and I had some catching up to do that's all. Let me take a look at you." Stefan stepped back, holding Caslin at arm's length. The latter suddenly feeling like a child again. His father and brother having a cosy chat and him feeling awkward, out of place, as if he was intruding. Their father returned his attention to the match, one from a European or lower league, somewhere nondescript, judging by the limited crowd and state of the pitch.

"How long have you been in town?" Caslin asked.

"Oh, a few days," Stefan replied. "Thought it about time I came up for a visit."

"Stopping long?"

"For Pete's sake, Nathaniel. Can't you drop the warrant card for five minutes and just be pleased to see your brother?"

"Dad," Caslin began but his rebuttal was interrupted.

"It's alright, Dad. That's Nate, always asking questions," Stefan said, grinning and, for a fleeting moment, resembling the boy of their youth, once more. "You're looking good, little brother. A bit of middle-age spread creeping up on you but apart from that, doing okay."

Caslin grunted, "I would say the same but you look like you need to eat something. Didn't they teach you how to feed yourself in the infantry?"

Stefan had served twelve years in the army, seeing tours of Iraq, Bosnia and Kosovo, in that time. The experiences left him struggling with the aftermath of military life and he had never fully adjusted. At least, not in Caslin's view.

"Below the belt, Nathaniel," his father said.

Caslin ignored him. "Where are you living these days? Still in Maidstone?"

Stefan shook his head, "It varies, you know. I've been working and it takes me all over."

Caslin was pleased that his elder brother had found employment. The last he'd heard, Stefan was still on benefits and looking likely to remain so.

"You going to grab a beer and sit down?" their father asked, not breaking his gaze from the television. It was a giant screen that dwarfed everything else in the room.

"No, can't. I'm still on the clock, so to speak," Caslin explained. "I've been meaning to stop by. I hadn't heard from you—"

"Well I am quite well, as you can see. So, there was no need."

All was said without looking up and Caslin knew he'd already outstayed his welcome. Regretting the decision to come, he said goodbye. A farewell not acknowledged by his father. Caslin figured he was already a little drunk, eyeing several empties on the sideboard. Stefan followed him out into the hallway. The strong odour of alcohol also lingered. Some things didn't change.

"Ignore him, Nate. You know what he's like."

"Only too well."

"Are you sure you can't stay for a drink?" Stefan asked.

Caslin shook his head, unlocking the front door.

"I really am still on shift," he said, stepping out onto the path and indicating Sarah Hunter, waiting in the car. She glanced over at the two men and then away.

"Oh, fair dos," Stefan said in understanding. "She your bit, is she?"

Caslin frowned, "Colleague. Listen, we should catch up, while you're around. We've not seen each other for ages."

"Three years, at least."

"Is it that long?" Caslin asked, shocked . Stefan nodded. "You got a car? Mine's a bit knackered."

"I'll borrow Dad's."

Of course, you will, Caslin thought but didn't say so. "He'll give you the address. I'll see you later."

Stefan watched as he walked to the car and got in. He had returned inside by the time Caslin looked back.

"Who was that?" Hunter asked, curious.

"Who, Golden Boy, back there?"

Hunter laughed, "He looked a lot like you. Your brother?"

"Aye, first born," Caslin said with candour. "What followed was merely disappointment."

"Well, at least you're not bitter," Hunter said, engaging first gear and moving off. "DCI Inglis wants us back at Fulford Road."

"What's he doing there?"

"Broadfoot wants Fulford as the base of operations."

"Because he can't be arsed to drive any further west, from his house."

"Probably," Hunter said, humouring him. "Makes it easier for us, too."

Caslin didn't comment. It would also make it harder for him to do *what he did best.* Watchful eyes were never too far from him, even having salvaged something of the downward spiral of his career, in recent times.

THE JOURNEY to Fulford Road only took fifteen minutes and then another ten to get through the press of waiting media, encamped at the entrance and setting up in the car park.

"Do you think the word's out?" Caslin asked sarcastically whilst Hunter negotiated the outside broadcast vehicles.

"We always knew there would be interest," she replied, picking one of the few available spaces, some distance from the station. It was raining again and Caslin cursed.

"They'll get in our way, always do."

"Are you going to do the press conferences then, same as usual?" Hunter mimicked his sarcasm.

Caslin didn't reply as both got out. Pulling his coat tightly about him, he braced himself against the rain and briskly walked to the station. Choosing to bypass the melee, they entered via the yard, passing through custody into the station proper. Making their way up towards CID, they bumped into Inglis on the stairs.

"Good follow-up on the girl," he offered as a compliment. Caslin thought it standard procedure but accepted it with good grace. Hunter was sent on her way but he asked Caslin to remain behind. "The media have cottoned on to who is missing. It'll be headlining the six o'clock news. Needless to say, people want answers."

"Don't we all, Guv," Caslin replied. He knew that Inglis was talking more about the senior ranks.

"Robertson and his team are working the car but it's not looking hopeful, from a forensic point of view. If anything happened, it most likely occurred outside of the vehicle."

"What about the surrounding area?"

"He's taken casts of those tyre impressions but other than that, we have little to go on."

"Little?" Caslin sensed there was more. "What *do* we have?"

"Some sketchy witness accounts of a vehicle in the area, at roughly the right time. The boards are being updated in the squad room, so you should familiarise yourself before the press conference."

"Sir?"

"Didn't I say? Sorry," Inglis looked at him for a moment, making Caslin feel self-conscious. "Are you okay, Nathaniel?"

Caslin was taken aback, "Yes, Guv. Why do you ask?"

"You're looking a bit peaky, if you don't mind me saying? Journalists are nothing to be intimidated by. Press conference at five-thirty. I want you alongside me."

Caslin was about to protest but Inglis left him without the opportunity. Instead, the DCI resumed his course downstairs to oversee the setting up of the room, for the press briefing. Caslin silently cursed. He reached for his phone, to check the time, but stopped when he realised his hand was shaking slightly. Not for the first time. Heading upstairs, he went to the gents, grateful to find it empty.

Taking in his appearance in the mirror, he realised Inglis was right. His eyes had a haunted look to them and his skin showed a tinge of grey, feeling clammy to the touch. Whilst considering that, he noticed his hands starting to sweat. Even though no-one had entered since he arrived, he glanced around anyway. Rifling through his pockets he located the blister strip. Running some water, he popped two pills through the foil and put them in his mouth. Washing them down with a mouthful of tap water, he rose up and took a deep breath.

Returning his gaze to the reflection, he filled the basin with cold water. Leaning over and splashing his face, he sought to revitalise his appearance, rubbing at his cheeks to regain some colour. Picking up the blister strip, he turned them over in his hand before secreting them away. Pausing only long enough to stare at himself for another moment, he turned and left, making his way to the squad room.

Most of those present were too busy to notice his arrival, phones pressed to ears and pens in hand. He slipped through the throng, acknowledging the odd greeting, making a beeline for the notice boards. The scene was documented with the key facts they had to hand, denoted on sticky notes. To one side a list of names had been compiled, known faces already familiar to the police. Caslin recognised two repeat sex offenders from the area. Officers had been allotted to some, no doubt tasked to ascertain their whereabouts. Lottie Gibbs had made another list, one of known associates. That list was frighteningly small. Alongside that were family members. Once again, names were allocated to investigate them. Caslin felt they were right to do so. Sadly, experience taught him that family members, or close associates, often perpetrated such crimes.

Finding the witness evidence, he was frustrated. The vehicle spotted in the area that morning, was anything from a red Range Rover to a white Jeep Cherokee and between two and ten years old. The information had been supplied by three eye witnesses and the only corroborative point that he could see, was that the vehicle had been parked on Fountains Lane. That was the location where Natalie's car had been found. The inconsistency was irritating but unsurprising. People would see something which was often apparently insignificant at the time. Therefore, when recollecting it, they would fail on the detail. The desire to help so strong, that their mind would fill in the gaps, hence the contradictions.

A whistle from the other end of the room caught his attention and he turned. DS Hunter beckoned him over. Approaching, he frowned at her.

"Not very ladylike, Sarah."

"I'm not much of a lady and besides," she said with a wry smile, "I've been working with you lot, too long."

"What's up?"

"Timothy and Catherine Bermond are downstairs. I thought you'd want to know."

"What are they doing here? The press frenzy will chew them up for the morning copy!"

"I think that's what the DCS is hoping for," Hunter said.

"Chum the waters, for the publicity?"

"Exactly."

"Christ," he exclaimed. "Putting them through it, when we don't know that she's in danger yet—"

"First twenty-four hours are the most important, you know that," Hunter countered. Caslin could only nod his understanding. "And the papers will go to town on it anyway, so we may as well use them."

"I'll go down, make sure they know what they'll be facing."

With that, Caslin hotfooted it downstairs. Reaching the ground floor, he saw Linda and asked her where the Bermonds were being kept. He was with them a few moments later. Timothy rose up from his seat, behind a table in the family room, a recently arranged place for people to wait, away from the prying eyes of police and public alike. He took Caslin's hand and thanked him for coming to see them. Catherine smiled momentarily but didn't stand. Caslin returned the smile.

"Have you spoken to my father?" Timothy asked.

Caslin shook his head, "Not yet, Tim. We're on the case, though. Has anyone spoken to you about the press conference? About what to expect?"

"Yes, we've got a prepared statement to read," he said, indicating a transcript on the table. "I'm told it's especially formulated to reach out to her, or to… someone who might…"

"I know," Caslin reassured him. The message would be a standard one, asking for Natalie to get in touch or for anyone with information to come forward. The next stage would only be enacted if they suspected, or knew for certain, that she was being held against her will. That message would speak directly to the abductor. For now, the plan would be to generate as many leads as possible. At this moment in time, they had little to go on but Caslin kept that to himself. Thus far, he had chosen not to make Timothy's accusation about Sebastian Bermond, a focal point of the investigation but if nothing turned up soon, he would have to pursue it. That would not go down well, not with anyone, except possibly with Natalie's father.

"Will you be there?" Catherine asked him.

"At the press conference?" he clarified, she nodded. "Yes, I'll be with you the whole time."

"Thank you," she said. Her expression was one of relief. His presence would be under protest but she didn't need to know that. Confident they were in good hands, Caslin excused himself, leaving the couple with a family liaison officer. Making his way back to CID, he bumped into Terry Holt on the stairs.

"Sir, I heard you were back. I've been looking for you."

"What's up, Terry?"

"I've been looking into this missing Tom—"

"Person," Caslin corrected.

"Yes, Sir... sorry," Holt bumbled. "Anyway, I went home with the mother, like you asked, and got some more details. She gave me a photo and stuff, pretty girl, and her mobile number."

"Turn something up?"

"I did, yeah," Holt went on, clearly gearing up to something. "I got her recent activity log from the supplier and she made a call around twelve-thirty a.m., the night she disappeared."

"Who to?"

"Us," Holt said, before quickly adding, "well, not us directly. She called 999."

"That's interesting. Have you got the transcript?"

"Better, I got the recording."

"And?"

Holt paused and their eyes met, "She claimed someone was trying to kill her."

CHAPTER SEVEN

"999 EMERGENCY, what service do you require?" the operator's voice was firm and efficient.

"Please help, they're trying to kill me!" an erratic, female voice pleaded.

"*Somebody is trying to kill you?*"

"Please help me."

"Where are you, madam?"

"I... I... don't know," the voice was fearful, lowering in tone and becoming an almost inaudible whisper. A loud bang could be heard, followed by two more, in quick succession. They were accompanied by a male voice in the background, muffled but apparently raised. The words spoken were indistinguishable due to the quality of the recording. "They're here... please," the voice tailed off before the call abruptly ended.

DC Holt clicked a button on the mouse and the playback ceased. Caslin indicated for him to replay it and Holt did so, from the beginning.

"That's it, that's all we have."

"Definitely from her mobile?"

"Confirmed," Holt replied. "The centre wasn't able to get a

location before she hung up. They logged the call for further investigation but it doesn't appear to have been followed up."

"Any reason?"

"Not officially but I reckon they chalked it off as a crank."

Caslin thought for a moment. "Can we get a ping from a tower, to give us a search area?"

"Way ahead of you, Sir," Holt answered with confidence. "The signal was picked up by two towers, which gave us a reference point. I plotted them on an Ordnance Survey map and I'm pretty sure I've narrowed it down."

Holt went over to his desk and picked up the map. Returning to the table he spread it out. Two blue circles were drawn, at their centres the transmitter relay towers, to mark the coverage of each.

"What do we have then?" Caslin asked as he eyed the area, south of York.

"Where the circles crossover is where we'll find the origin of the call."

"Good work, Terry," Caslin said genuinely. In a built up area or city, such a search zone might prove to be far too problematic to mount anything but a cursory examination. However, in this case, they had a shot. "I think it's safe to assume she was in a building, what with the banging and muffled shouting. Besides that, outside, even in the countryside you get a noticeable difference to the sound of a call."

"Agreed," Holt said. Looking at the map, he asked, "So how do you want to play it?"

Caslin pursed his lips. "Let's round up a few bodies and start knocking on doors."

Terry Holt left to seek out the duty inspector, to arrange some extra resource. In the meantime, Caslin turned his focus back to the map. The crossover of Holt's circles centred on a village that he knew well, being a little over four miles to the north east of his father's house. The village of Skipwith stood alone, surrounded by farmland. From memory, Caslin thought there were roughly a few hundred residents. The number of curtain twitchers that occupied those places was phenomenal. The likelihood that someone saw, or heard, something was a reasonable hypothesis at this stage. Tonight, was looking like a late one.

SKIPWITH WAS DRIPPING WITH MONEY. At least, that was how Caslin had always viewed the place. Well within the commuter belt but situated amongst beautiful countryside, the houses could sell for figures resembling telephone numbers. Scanning his pitiful entourage, he was thankful for the pleasant evening. The sun had set but heavy cloud cover kept the temperature up. Leaning his back against the car, he watched as the various officers went from door to door. Most of the properties here were detached, with many on large plots, and he considered that a lot could happen that people wouldn't see. He hoped that inherent nosiness would win out, over discrete liaisons. The last he expected was to find anyone openly admitting to entertaining prostitutes at the first time of asking.

Terry Holt came into view at the end of a gravelled driveway. Closing the gate, he cast a glance towards him and shook his head. Caslin hid the disappointment well as he marked off another address. They'd been at it for over an hour but thus far had drawn a blank. The majority of officers on shift were at the beck and call of the Bermond inquiry and he was spared only a half-dozen bodies. Hunter promised she would call if a significant lead came in following the press conference. So far, nothing had.

The radio crackled and he scooped it up off of the car's bonnet. There was someone he needed to speak to. The address was a two-minute walk away and he made it in quick time, bringing Holt with him. The house was a bungalow, set back from the main road, as most were. A tarmac drive curved around an immaculately manicured garden, giving the house two approaches from the highway. A uniformed constable met them at the entrance.

"Mrs Sheila Cosgrove, Sir," the constable said. "She was woken by a commotion on the night in question. I think you need to hear this."

Caslin nodded and allowed himself to be led up to the residence. She was elderly, well into her eighties, Caslin guessed, and as neatly turned out as her front lawn. Following introductions, she got to her story.

"I thought it was a dog shrieking during the night, not unheard of out here. Some people are so ignorant when it comes to their neighbours. They can make—"

"The noise, Mrs Cosgrove?" Caslin pushed, politely.

"Oh yes, well I thought it was a dog but then I heard a scream."

"A scream?"

She nodded enthusiastically. "I thought so, it was rather disturbing but then I heard nothing more, so I thought I'd go back to sleep."

"I see. What time was this?"

"I have no idea, it was very late, though," she said, thinking on it. "I retire around ten each night so it was later than that."

"Right," Caslin said, glancing towards the uniformed constable who appeared nervous at that point.

"Mrs Cosgrove, could you tell the inspector what you told me happened next?" the officer said swiftly.

"Oh, of course. I heard someone banging on my door."

"Who was that?" Caslin asked.

"I don't know," she replied. "By the time I got out of bed and went to the door, there was no-one there."

"Did you see anything when you looked out?"

"I'm afraid not," she said glumly. "I didn't open it, the door I mean. I just looked out of the window. You can't be too careful these days, can you?"

"Did you think to call anyone?" Caslin asked.

She shook her head. "No, I didn't really want to get involved. I thought I might have imagined it. Did I?"

"Okay, Mrs Cosgrove." Caslin ignored her question. "That's very useful information. Thank you very much. DC Holt will take a statement from you."

"That was at one o'clock."

"I beg your pardon," Caslin said. He had already turned to leave.

"It had just gone one o'clock in the morning, when I heard the banging."

"Are you certain?"

"Absolutely," she said defiantly. "I checked the time, when I went back to bed."

"Thanks again," Caslin said. Leaving her with Holt, he set off back down the driveway, considering what it all meant. Assuming the caller in the early hours was Melissa Brooke, she had somehow eluded her attackers but how far would she have run before seeking help? Not more than a few doors, he figured. Was she being chased when she ran to Mrs Cosgrove's and where would she have gone afterwards? The thought came to him, whilst assessing potential flight routes within the immediate vicinity, as to whether Melissa had made it as far as she was able.

Caslin walked back to his car and, using the radio, asked each officer to check in with any information. Nothing more had come to light. Barely a fifth of the village had been canvassed and it was already approaching nine o'clock. He needed to find that house. Terry Holt reappeared soon afterwards, striding purposefully towards him.

"Did she have anything else?"

"No," Terry replied. "I think she's a bit dotty but sound enough to trust on the basics. It's something else."

"Go on."

"Vale View," he indicated a house, four down from where

they stood. "I spoke to a lady there, a bit of a stroppy mare, if ever I met one, seemed really put out that I was delaying her evening. She had plans and *couldn't possibly be late.* She was away on business when we think Melissa went missing."

"And?"

"I didn't think about asking at the time, too busy checking out the Audi that she was getting into," he said. Caslin figured he was more likely to be checking her out but said nothing. "She was wearing a wedding ring."

"You didn't speak with the husband?"

"No, she was home alone but another car's just pulled up."

Caslin had missed that, so preoccupied was he with contemplating Melissa's escape. "Let's go and have a chat and see what he has to say for himself."

Vale View was an impressive detached house, stone built with an appealing frontage that stood out from others nearby. Caslin figured that his entire apartment in Kleiser's Court would fit into half of the ground floor. Their feet crunched on the pink marble chips as they passed the double garage and mounted the porch. Holt rang the bell and the wait lasted only seconds before a figure could be seen in the hall beyond.

A suited man, in his mid-forties answered the door, eyeing them both suspiciously. Caslin offered up his warrant card and decided to dispense with the preliminaries.

"We're here to discuss last Friday's visitor," he said sternly. Although the man's facial expression didn't change, Caslin noted that he glanced to either side of them, into the driveway beyond, before replying.

"I… I don't know—"

"Let's not waste any of your time, or mine," Caslin said. He knew that this was their target. His body language was screaming it.

"You had best come in."

Caslin looked to Holt, who was surprised at the exchange but followed. They stepped into a brightly lit, double height entrance hall. A contemporary, oak and glass staircase swept up from their right, two sets of double doors were to their front and left. The first was open and Caslin could see a living room beyond. The others were partly glazed and gave access to a spacious kitchen. Their host showed them into the living room, which was as impressive as the entrance hall.

"What is it that you do, Mister?" Caslin asked.

"Summerbee, Peter," the man offered, resignation in his tone. "I'm a partner in a share brokerage firm."

"Tell me about Friday, Mr Summerbee."

He sighed deeply and glanced at his watch, "I would like this to be concluded as soon as—"

"Before your wife gets home, I understand," Caslin offered. He had little time for people who used prostitution, whatever their reasoning. "Better to get it out quickly, then."

Summerbee looked at him nervously. The man seemed uncomfortable in his own skin. "My wife was away, I thought that some company would be… good. So… I booked someone."

"A prostitute?" Holt asked.

"An escort," he corrected. "I understood them to be discreet."

"What made you think that?" Caslin asked.

"I got the number from a friend. He said that they were always top."

"Top what?"

"Quality, obviously."

"It didn't go to plan, did it?" Caslin challenged him and Summerbee's reaction confirmed it. He sat down on the sofa, elbows to his knees and cradled his head in his hands.

"No, it was a bloody disaster."

"Tell us what happened."

Summerbee looked up at Caslin and took a deep breath. "She flipped out, that's what happened. I thought they were professionals but she completely lost it."

"What did you do to her?" Holt said, accusingly.

"Nothing, I swear!" he retorted. "I didn't have a chance to do something to her, not that I would you understand but she was barely through the door. I knew something was wrong, she was odd."

"Odd? In what way?" Caslin pressed.

"I don't know, she was high on something, I reckon," he said, eyes flicking between the officers standing in his living room. "They're supposed to be clean."

"Like you, you mean?" Caslin asked, sarcastically. Summerbee looked to the floor. "Were you alone?"

"Yes. Like I said, my wife was away."

"What happened next?"

"She went straight into the downstairs cloakroom and locked herself in."

"Just like that?" Holt said, his tone intimating that he found the narrative unconvincing.

"That's how it happened, I'm telling you. When she didn't come out after five minutes, I knocked on the door and there was no answer."

"And then?"

"I started banging on it and shouting at her. I didn't want some junkie overdosing on my toilet."

"Certainly not with your wife away," Holt said, scribbling down what was being said.

"Speaking of which, can we keep this between us—"

"We'll see what we can do," Caslin interjected. Their host smiled, looking relieved. "Keep talking."

"Right, yeah. Anyway, she burst out of the cloakroom and barged past me for the door."

"The front door?" Caslin asked.

"Exactly. It wasn't locked, so out she went. That's it."

"That was the last you saw of her?"

"Yes."

"What time was this?"

"Gone midnight for sure but I'd had a few. Look, whatever the bitch did, it's got nothing to do with me. Give me a ticket for soliciting, or whatever you call it and let's be done, yeah?"

Caslin looked to Holt, who shrugged almost imperceptibly but it was enough. So far, the account matched the timeline of the recording as well as the details offered in Mrs Cosgrove's description.

"Unfortunately, Mr Summerbee, it's just not that simple. You see, that *bitch*, as you so colourfully described her, has gone missing," Caslin paused for effect, "and you are the last person to be with her. She has a little girl at home, waiting to find out where her mum is."

Summerbee went a whiter shade of pale, his mouth trying to utter a response but no words came. Finally, he managed to regain some semblance of composure and string a coherent sentence together, blurting out, "No, no... I wasn't... you should ask the guy—"

"What guy?" Caslin asked.

"The one that was with her," Summerbee implored him, flailing hands driving home the point. "The... the driver."

"She came with a driver?"

"Yeah, he walked her to the door and spoke to me. I think he was checking me out. He was waiting in the car."

"And what did he do, when all of this went down?"

"I told you, she took off into the rain and he went after her."

"Chasing her?"

"That's what it looked like to me. She was screaming like a banshee!"

"Then what happened?"

"I don't know," he said, assessing the sceptical eyes viewing him. "Honestly. I shut the door. Bloody chuffed she was out of my house that's for certain. It was one time, a mistake... a big one. I looked out ten minutes later and the car was gone. You have to believe me."

"What car was it?" Caslin asked.

"I don't know. A silver saloon, maybe."

"Can you be more specific?"

"I'm not into cars, I'm sorry."

"What about the driver, tell us about him," Caslin said.

Summerbee thought about it for a moment, "Late thirties, perhaps early forties. Clean shaven. Sort of average looking."

That narrows it down, Caslin thought, "What about height, weight, hair colour?"

"Erm… average, I guess."

"Average hair colour?" Caslin persisted. He judged that this punter was trying to minimise his involvement in the investigation as much as possible. No doubt vainly hoping it would all go away.

"I didn't really pay him any attention. I was looking at the girl for pity's sake!"

"Right, I think we should get all this down, in a more formal manner," Caslin said, "back at the station."

Summerbee sat bolt upright as the realisation hit him, "I thought we were going to keep this… you know… on the quiet."

"Did you, Mr Summerbee?" Caslin said lightly.

"I haven't done anything." he said

"You can come of your own free will or you can be arrested."

"I haven't done anything.".

"Have it your own way. Perhaps your memory might improve with a change of surroundings. Do you want to call your wife first, or would you rather we let her know?"

CASLIN STOOD with Holt alongside him, watching the uniform vehicle reverse out of the driveway, Peter Summerbee sitting in the rear.

"Are you buying it?" Holt asked.

Caslin saw the car disappear from view and then he turned back towards the house. The story may well fit the facts as they understood them but those facts were scarce. With so many gaps in the events of the night, Caslin was damn sure that there was more to it.

"I'm not ready to buy anything, just yet. I want him put under some pressure. Start off with his clothes. Then move onto swabs and bodily scrapings, from every conceivable orifice. Afterwards, leave him in a cell for a few hours to think it all over. I want him believing we've got him nailed on," Caslin looked at Holt. "Only then, can we be sure he's given us everything. In the meantime, I'll wake up one of the almighty and get a search warrant, for this place. Iain Robertson and his team can tear it to pieces. If there's something to link him to Melissa, I want to find it."

"I'll do some digging and see if he's got a record, while I'm at it," Holt said. "I'll bet it wasn't his first time either, no matter what he says."

"I don't like this, Terry," Caslin said softly, biting his lower lip. "I don't like this one little bit."

CHAPTER EIGHT

"WHAT HAS ROBERTSON FOUND?" DCI Frank Stephens' tone had an unusual ring to it that he couldn't decode. Caslin bought a bit of time by sipping at his vending machine coffee, his third since three in the morning and it was now only six. It tasted awful.

"We have to give him more time."

"So that would be *nothing*, then?"

"Yes, Guv," Caslin accepted that the initial forensic search at Vale View had drawn nothing to link Summerbee with Melissa Brooke's disappearance. "He's only had eight—"

"Hours," Stephens finished. "Yes, and that's eight hours of overtime for a specialist team. That's costing me a fortune. And before you say it, I know, you can't put a price on a missing person."

"But you will," Caslin said.

"Too bloody right if it flushes my budget down the swanny."

Caslin sat back in his chair, the lack of sleep beginning to catch up with him but even so, he wondered what the DCI's problem was. He rubbed at tired eyes and almost lost the will to argue, almost. "It's worth it just to put the wind up that arse, Summerbee. He'll choke if he's done anything, you know the type."

"Well I hope you're right," Stephens said flatly. "Broadfoot already has his back up because you cleared off and missed the press conference."

That was a fair point. Caslin had ducked it but not without valid cause. "I'll apologise to him, Guv. It wasn't what I usually do." He then thought the same was necessary for the Bermonds.

"Usually you just bugger off."

"That's right," Caslin agreed.

"We're not going to be able to hold Summerbee beyond twenty-four hours, you know that?"

"Of course," Caslin said. Unless forensics found something at the house, Summerbee would walk. The chances of getting an extension to thirty-six hours were non-existent and a ninety-six, laughable. Their only suspect, if he could stretch to calling him that, was giving them very little. "May I go? I need to take a shower."

"Yes, you can and you do. I'd take care of that before you find Broadfoot, if I were you."

Caslin left the DCI's office. Entering the squad room, he found a bleary-eyed Terry Holt waiting for him.

"You're not going to believe what I have here, Sir," Holt said, a wry smile on his face. "Peter Summerbee is clean."

"Yes, I know. So, what have you got?" Caslin asked, eyeing the DC's computer screen.

"I have a Peter Dreyfuss here, who does have a record. It goes right up until he adopted his wife's maiden name."

"Interesting," Caslin said, keen to know more. "What for?"

"Two arrests for *Actual*, no convictions but he does have a fine for solicitation, from three years ago."

Caslin nodded as it came together in his head. Summerbee had more or less confirmed his knowledge of the system the night they brought him in. He pretty much requested a fine to get it over and done with. Caslin was irritated that he didn't pick up on it.

"Well, well, Peter," Caslin replied, pulling out a chair and sitting down. "It would seem our boy isn't as squeaky as he would have us believe. Slippery little shit, isn't he?"

"Sir?" Holt said.

"Never mind. Let's go and have another word, see if he feels more like opening up."

HALF AN HOUR LATER, the three of them were facing each other in an interview room. For the second time, Summerbee had waived his right to legal counsel. A career criminal would usually lodge that right immediately, thereby locking down the interview and stalling the investigation. An innocent person however, who felt they had nothing to hide, would often feel no need of counsel but then there were others who fell into a different category altogether. Those who enjoyed the game. The arrogant. The self important. These people thought they were smarter than everybody else, particularly the police. Caslin had figured this guy, up until now, to be firmly lodged in the second of those categories. He didn't appreciate being taken for a fool and therefore, chose not to beat about the bush.

"Tell me about your arrest for solicitation, three years ago, Mr Summerbee. Or would it be *Dreyfuss?*" The stress on the name, along with the intensity of Caslin's gaze, made a denial futile.

"Oh that," their suspect replied without skipping a beat. "A misunderstanding."

"The magistrate didn't agree."

"Opinions vary," Summerbee said, a half-smile crossing his face, "ancient history."

"And the two arrests for Actual Bodily Harm. Are they also ancient history?"

"Never passed to trial, those cases were dropped."

Caslin sat forward in his chair, locking eyes with the man across from him. "The victims were prostitutes, weren't they, Mr Summerbee?"

The smile widened into a broad grin. "I didn't know that and besides, how can they be victims of a crime, if one never took place?"

Caslin felt his anger building but maintained a professional level of calm. "Dropped because the victims withdrew their statements."

"And you and I both know that equates to the same thing. No evidence, no crime."

"Did you think you could throw us off with a simple name change, that it wouldn't show when we ran your prints?"

Summerbee shrugged, "You're the policeman."

"Anything to add to your earlier statement, bearing in mind our forensics team is currently cataloguing every detail of your house, as we speak?"

Summerbee leant back in his chair, stretching out his arms above him and yawning. "I do hope that they wiped their feet. Our carpets are *very* expensive. When my solicitor gets through with the wrongful arrest claim, I dare say she'll be expecting compensation to cover the clean-up and repair costs."

Caslin stared at him. He had misread this man. Expecting him to fold once put under pressure, he now realised that this was a player who not only knew the game but just as importantly, how the police played it.

"Is that right?" Caslin asked.

"Oh, didn't I mention it?" Summerbee said innocently. "I would like to see my solicitor now. Not your duty moron but my own. By my reckoning you have me for about another fourteen hours, so you best get a shifty on. Hadn't you?"

"Interview suspended," Holt said following a look from Caslin, "at 07:14."

Caslin watched as Summerbee was escorted back to his cell, before joining Holt on the walk back to CID. Mounting the stairs, Holt appeared visibly dejected.

"What was all that about?" Holt asked.

Caslin stopped and put his back against the wall. The

interview had been continuously revolving in his mind. "Wasting time."

"Whose? Ours?"

"Using up the allotted detention time," Caslin said. "He showed us the *buffoon card*, naïve, lonely husband, playing away. He bluffed and I bought it."

"What are we going to do now, Sir?" Holt asked.

"There's one thing from Melissa's call that's bothering me."

"Just the one?" Holt asked with no sarcastic intent.

"She said 'They'."

"Sir?"

"She said '*They* are trying to kill me'." Caslin looked to Holt. "Who are *they*?"

"The wife?" Holt asked.

Caslin considered that idea. Female murderers were far rarer than their male counterparts but it wasn't unheard of. "Should be easy enough to check if Mrs Summerbee was where she claims to be. Where was it again?"

"Away on business, Sir. I didn't ask where."

"Have a word with her and check it out. Then I want you to get into her husband's life, turn it upside down. I want details, his business dealings, employment history, where he's lived since he graduated from puberty, pant size, anything and everything, you can get. This bastard is hiding something and I want to know what."

"What about his solicitor?"

"Get custody to chase her up. Unless Iain Robertson finds something soon, I don't think we'll have cause to re-interview. I'm sure the call out charge for his counsel will be substantial. We'll hold him for the maximum. That'll give the boys and girls in paper suits a shot."

"Alright, I'll get on it," Holt said, his voice sounding fatigued.

"In the meantime, I'll have a word with Vice, this morning and see if I can find out who Melissa's been working for.

Someone other than her family will be missing the money if not her. Locating the driver—"

"If there is one," Holt said.

"You're right," Caslin said, although Melissa herself had always told her mother similar. "If there is one, he can verify or devastate our boy's version of events."

"Yes, Sir."

Caslin indicated for him to crack on but Holt looked momentarily lost and hesitated before moving off.

"Something wrong?" Holt turned back to face him.

"No, Sir, not really," Holt began. "I'm just a bit knackered."

"Half-hour for the Queen, Terry."

Holt frowned but nodded at the same time. The constable understood the reference to the unpaid daily overtime each officer was expected to give. He didn't argue about the eleven hours that followed. Caslin considered it karma for not having done his job properly in the first place. Only time would tell if the delay to the investigation would turn out to be pivotal in finding Melissa.

Now left alone, Caslin remained where he was. At this hour, hardly anyone was in. The station would soon be filling up and he knew it was going to be a busy day. Deciding that a shower and a set of clean clothes were in order, he set off to cadge a lift from uniform into the city. Heading back towards custody, his legs felt leaden, so he veered towards the elevators. That was a mistake. Calling the lift, he waited for only a few seconds before the ping sounded and the doors opened. He was faced with the towering figure of Kyle Broadfoot.

"I wondered when you would show up," the DCS said evenly. Immediately, Caslin knew the shower was going to have to wait.

"I owe you an apology, Sir. I was—"

"I know where you were," Broadfoot said, "and please don't insult my intelligence with a heartfelt apology. We both know you won't mean it."

"Sir," was all that Caslin could say.

"Next time, speaking to me directly would be advantageous. Understood?"

Caslin knew it was rhetorical, he nodded. "Of course, Sir."

"Walk with me, Inspector," Broadfoot instructed. Caslin fell into step, regretting not taking the stairs as the sound of the elevator doors closing, came to ear. "What was it about this other case that was so pressing?"

"A lead came through on a missing person, Sir. It needed to be followed up."

"Hmm," Broadfoot murmured as they walked. "Missing person? A minor?"

Caslin sensed that he knew more than he was letting on. "No, Sir. She's twenty-one."

"Any reason to think that something serious has occurred?"

"Possibly, we have someone in custody downstairs—"

"But you don't know for certain? I mean, she may well turn up in due course or have left of her own accord."

Caslin wondered what was going on. "You said to carry on with my caseload, Sir."

"Indeed, I did and I meant it." Broadfoot stopped and turned to him, looking around as he spoke. They were alone in the corridor. He lowered his voice, "However, low priority cases can afford to slip a little, can't they?"

"Melissa Brooke is a low priority, Sir?"

"That's for you to determine, Nathaniel," Broadfoot said, examining the lapel of his blazer, identifying and removing a bit of fluff with his thumb and forefinger. "I want to ensure that you have your priorities right, focus on what's important. Resources being what they are, you can always pick up the slack at a later date."

"I see, Sir," Caslin said, appearing thoughtful.

"Something on your mind, Nathaniel?"

"Seeing as you ask, Sir. I can see that Melissa Brooke isn't an ideal victim, unlike Natalie Bermond."

"Meaning?"

"Well, she's a prostitute, single parent from a council estate and has a documented drug habit. Let's face it, it's a bloody good job she isn't black—"

"I'll pretend I didn't hear that, Inspector," Broadfoot said with controlled authority. "I believe that I've been clear enough for you."

"Crystal clear, Sir."

"Good man," Broadfoot smiled. "Now, if you'll excuse me, I have an early meeting to attend. I trust you'll keep me advised of developments, following on from the press conference and morning papers?"

"Without doubt, Sir."

Once again, Caslin found himself on his own. Broadfoot's shoes echoing on the polished floor as he strode away. He swore under his breath. Rubbing at the back of his neck, he could feel a headache coming on. Reaching into his pocket he found his pills and popped one into his mouth, doing his best to swallow it without the aid of water. He needed some air and resumed his course. No longer were his legs bothering him, the conversation with Broadfoot keeping his mind occupied.

The refectory was clear of uniform and the custody suite was likewise, apart from those on shift. Abandoning the plan to arrange a lift, he went through the main reception and on out into the daylight. The brightness caused him to shield his eyes, having had no sleep and being under fluorescent neon for the previous eight hours. He retrieved his mobile and called for a taxi, only managing the briefest of conversations before the battery died. Confident that he had made the request in time, he walked up the path and sat down on the low wall to wait. The morning was crisp and the fresh air smelt good. He figured the painkiller was starting to take effect but, if truth be known, the sensations were no longer as stark as they used to be.

Glancing towards two large white vans, satellite dishes mounted on their roofs, he wondered how they had obtained permission to leave them there. Which hotel the press had taken over for the duration of their stakeout was another curiosity. No doubt they would descend on the station again shortly. Looking away, he hoped his cab would arrive before that happened. Having had more than his fair share of exposure in recent years, the thought of more was nauseating.

Hearing footsteps approaching he raised his gaze from the floor, wondering who would soon be greeting him. It was not the exchange he expected. A familiar face stood before him, red eyed and shaking with adrenalin. Whether it was a reaction borne of anger or frustration, he didn't know but here was Suzanne Brooke. Her arms were clamped to her sides, fists balled so tightly he could see the white of her knuckles. His expression changed from one of surprise to open bewilderment as she raised a hand and slapped him across the cheek. The blow stung but was hardly forceful.

"What the bloody—"

"You bastard!" she swore in his face, so close that he could see the spittle on her quivering lips, such was the ferocity of her speech.

"Mrs Brooke," he began, standing, but got no further.

"My daughter's not worth as much, is that it?" The question spat at him.

"It's not like—"

"You fucking coppers are all the same!" she shouted at him, tears falling. "You don't give a shit about my daughter... *and why*... because she had her problems and didn't go to the right school? Well she's worth ten of you..."

"Mrs Brooke," Caslin raised his voice just enough to get her attention, "we are working on your daughter's disappearance—"

"Where's my bloody press conference? My front page? Damn you." She moved to strike him again, only this time he caught her wrist as she lashed out.

"Mrs Brooke, this isn't going to help."

She collapsed into his arms, his grip all that kept her from sinking to the ground. As she sobbed, Caslin held her tightly as if cradling one of his children. She seemed so fragile to him at that moment, likely to shatter if he let her go. The anger, bravado and violence were all little more than an expression of grief and frustration. Were it his own daughter, Caslin knew he would tear the world apart to find her. He recognised the perception of inequality. To be fair to her, it wasn't merely perception. He felt the same.

"Find my daughter, Inspector," she almost whispered, pulling away from him. He saw in her face the impact that these past few days were having. The strain evident in her eyes, the stream of tears falling unchecked. He felt guilty.

"I am looking for her, believe me," he said reassuringly. A flashback to DCS Broadfoot came to mind and Caslin shoved it away. "I won't let her go, I promise."

She looked at him. That same look, the one she gave him the first day they met. She smiled weakly, wiping her face with the back of her hand. "I put my trust in you, Inspector."

Those words hurt more than the blow to the face. He hoped it was not misplaced but he didn't say so. "Can I buy you a cup of tea or coffee?"

She shook her head, "No, thank you. I must get back to my granddaughter. I don't want her to wake up and realise that I'm not there."

Caslin wondered who was watching her but chose not to ask. "If you need a ride, I have a—"

"No… but thanks," she said. Stepping away, she made to leave, before adding, "Just find Melissa, please."

Without another word, she walked away and didn't look back. Caslin felt the weight descend upon his shoulders. He took a deep breath as a taxi pulled into the car park. Acknowledging the driver with a wave, the car approached and he got in. They moved off. Caslin hadn't seen the photographer standing near to the junction with Fulford Road.

CHAPTER NINE

BITING INTO THE BACON ROLL, Caslin savoured the taste. It almost made up for going the entire night without sleep. A shower and change had worked wonders. The centre was busy but it always was, in the old town, a stone's throw from the Minster. He ate as he walked. His destination was less than a mile from the city limits and he needed the exercise. The sun shone in a cloudless sky, the warmth of summer finally arriving.

Wiping his hands with a paper napkin, he discarded it in a waste bin as he crossed the River Ouse, via Bridge Street, and on to Micklegate. The traffic buzzed around him but he took out his phone, anyway. Selecting the right contact, he dialled the number. The phone rang three times before he was connected to an automated service, lodged eighth in the queue. He had passed the Church of the Holy Trinity and gone beyond the city walls before he spoke to the receptionist. He asked if his repeat prescription was ready for collection.

"Dr Pradesh has requested you make an appointment, Mr Caslin."

"I beg your pardon?" he said, surprised. "Why?"

"I'm afraid I don't know but there's a note pinned to the repeat prescription. Would you like to make one now?"

Caslin dithered, quelling the fear threatening to rise from within. "Yes... please. When can you fit me in?"

"I'll just check," the receptionist said. "How is 9:45 on Tuesday?"

"That's nearly a week," Caslin said, frustration creeping into his voice. "Don't you have anything sooner?"

"I'm sorry, no, not unless it's an emergency. Should I book it?"

"Do that."

"That's confirmed, then. 9:45 on Tues—"

Caslin hung up. He was annoyed. Micklegate passed into the wealth of The Mount, with its tree-lined rows of Georgian townhouses. Eyeing the Elmbank Hotel up ahead, he took the next right and then Driffield Terrace was on his left. An imposing run of buildings, he sought one at the far end. Freshly painted white, it appeared to glow in the morning sunshine.

Realising he was sweating with the exertion of the walk, he wiped his face with the sleeve of his jacket. Approaching the front door, framed by ornate metal railings, he spied the security camera set high on the wall above. He rang the bell and didn't have long to wait. The door opened and he was met by a suited man, heavy set with a hawkish appearance.

"I'm here to meet with, Mr Durakovic," Caslin said, receiving no response. "He is expecting me." Caslin showed his warrant card and was bidden entry. Once inside, the noise from the traffic died instantly and he surveyed his surroundings. The interior was bathed in light, with white painted walls and the reflective aid of marble flooring, as far as the eye could see. A crystal chandelier illuminated the hall and stairwell, dividing the front and back of the house, and Caslin clocked another member of security on the half landing to the next floor. A suited body came up from a second stairwell to the rear, welcoming Caslin with a somewhat contrived smile.

"Inspector Caslin, I understand?"

Caslin brandished his warrant card again but it was waved away. "Please, no need for the formalities, Inspector. Do come with me."

The accent was former eastern bloc, Balkan he guessed, seeing as that was where his employer originated. Which of the former Yugoslav states in particular, he didn't know but nor did the Vice Squad, not for certain. Durakovic arrived in the UK on a Kosovan passport but beyond that, no-one had any details.

"Nice place," Caslin said, looking around as they walked.

"Indeed, it is. Grade II listed, architecturally designed and built in the mid-Nineteenth Century, and extensively refurbished since Mr Durakovic acquired the property, three years ago."

"Busy man," Caslin offered, as they bypassed an impressive contemporary kitchen, descending to lower ground level. The entirety of the basement area was given over to an office, bedecked in hardwood flooring with striking modernist fixtures and fittings. Evidently no expense had been spared. From here they walked out onto a rear terrace. Surprisingly secluded, bearing in mind their location, and set within a mature, landscaped garden of trees and raised terraces, sat Anton Durakovic. Another aid rose and stepped away. Caslin spotted at least three others, spaced periodically around the gardens. Stern faces, furtively glancing around the grounds as well as beyond the perimeter walls.

"Inspector, please join us. Would you like a coffee or perhaps something cooler?" Durakovic greeted him with an easy smile, noting Caslin's perspiration. The woman sitting to his right inclined her head in Caslin's direction. Caslin returned the greeting with one of his own but declined the drink, preferring to stand. "You English with your polite reservations," Durakovic said, the smile broadening. Caslin was unsure whether the comment was a compliment or a slight.

"Well, this isn't a social call," he said politely.

"Then what is it that I can do for you?"

"Melissa Brooke," Caslin said. The blank look on his host's face gave away little. "She works for you, Mr Durakovic."

"It is not a name that I recognise."

"Spare me the games. I'm really not in the mood. We both know you have your fingers in many grubby little pies, no need to dance around it."

"You are very... how should I put it... direct," Durakovic said, the smile fading.

"So, my DCI keeps telling me. Melissa Brooke," he repeated. "Please feel free to be just as... *direct.*"

"Then I shall, Inspector. My wife, Danika," he indicated the lady next to him, sipping at an espresso, "looks after our ladies."

"The call girls," Caslin offered.

"Escorts." Durakovic's smile returned.

"I believe that Melissa has resigned," Danika said. Caslin took the measure of her. She was dressed in a business suit, high quality too, judging by the cut. Her hair was cropped short, jet black and she had a Mediterranean skin tone to accompany her movie star looks. Glancing up at him, he couldn't read her through the classic sunglasses, obscuring her eyes.

"We both know that you don't get to resign from enterprises, such as yours."

"What exactly do you think that we run here, Inspector?"

Caslin ignored her question. "Why do you think that she has *resigned?*"

"She didn't turn up for work, at the weekend."

"She was working Friday."

"Was she?" Danika replied, returning to her coffee.

"What is this about, Inspector?" Durakovic asked. "I am a very busy man."

"Well you should be. Racketeering, fraud, drugs and prostitution are arduous pursuits at the best of times," Caslin said, eyes fixed on his host, a man clearly unused to being addressed in such a manner. Caslin didn't care. "Sorry, did I leave anything out? Money laundering, perhaps?"

"What is it that you want?" Durakovic said, all semblance of charm vanishing from his demeanour.

"She's missing and the last person seen with her was one of your drivers."

Danika flinched, almost imperceptibly but Caslin registered it. Durakovic sat back in his chair, appearing to relax and letting out a deep sigh.

"Now that is unfortunate, if it's the case?"

"It is," Caslin reiterated. "I want to speak with him."

Durakovic looked to his wife. Caslin couldn't see her response for she was sitting side on to him and facing her husband. Durakovic stood. With an open hand he indicated for Caslin to walk with him. He led him onto the gravel path that wound its way through the gardens. Caslin remained silent and nothing was said for a minute or two. Once out of earshot of his entourage, Durakovic spoke.

"I can see that you are a man of black and white, Inspector Caslin," he began. Caslin didn't comment. "For me, there are many grey areas. These are where I do my business. That is what I am, a businessman."

Caslin glanced across at him. "Your point?"

Durakovic smiled. "It is not good for my operation to have policemen sniffing around, visiting my home. It unsettles the true balance of things."

"Don't commit crime and you won't," Caslin replied flippantly.

"Business, Inspector. Now, regarding such," he continued, "should I have trouble with an employee, it is far more beneficial for all concerned, if I take care of it internally."

"Beneficial for whom?" Caslin asked.

"For all parties," Durakovic stated forcefully. "The employees, the management, the taxpayer."

"What are you saying?"

Anton Durakovic stopped and turned to face him, his expression conciliatory, "The man whom you seek is an employee. As such, he is part of our family, as are all my employees. When one of our family goes missing, we endeavour to find them. If another steps out of line, then it falls to me to punish him."

"You're also looking for Melissa?"

"And the driver."

Caslin was momentarily thrown, he hadn't expected that. That is, if it was true. "I want the driver's name."

"Inspector, I will be more than happy to provide it," Durakovic offered generously. "You should know however, that many of my employees originate from abroad, often living under the radar."

"Meaning?"

"Despite our best efforts, they can turn out to be illegally seeking employment. We try to vet them as best we can, but they have very sophisticated documentation these days."

"I wonder how they obtain that?" Caslin said lightly.

"You may find it is a fake name. That is all. I will provide it nevertheless. I wouldn't want you to think I was giving you… how should I say… the runaround."

"Perish the thought. What with you being a concerned citizen."

"Poor attitude can only be tolerated for so long, Inspector."

This time it was Caslin who stopped them walking. Turning to face Durakovic, he met his gaze. It was cold and unyielding. "Should I take that as a threat?"

"Helpful advice," he said with a straight face. "My associate, Karl, will provide you with the name that you seek. Please excuse me, for I have much to do today."

With one flick of his hand, a man appeared swiftly alongside them. The newcomer indicated for Caslin to go with him, which he did. They left Durakovic alone in his garden and returned to the house. A slip of paper was handed to him as he was shown to the door. Without ceremony, he was out on the street, the door closing behind him. Unfolding the paper, he read the name. Marco Handanovic.

Taking out his phone he opened up the contacts, trying to decide between Hunter and Holt, questions or misery? He opted for Hunter's incessant questioning and dialled her mobile. She answered quickly.

"Sarah, I need a lift."

"Where are you?"

"Just up the road, the Elmbank Hotel but I'm sweating."

"Give me five."

He hung up. Spotting a break in traffic he jogged across the road, heading for the hotel. Once there, he stopped in the shadow of the building, removing his jacket. Going over the meeting with Durakovic in his mind, he considered what he knew. The reality was that he couldn't be sure of the authenticity of anything spoken in that conversation. The man had a wealth of expertise in criminality behind him. Were they searching for the same people and if so, could Caslin get to them before he did? Moving in their own circles, it was conceivable that the web of contacts at Durakovic's disposal, plus his resources, would indicate Caslin may lose the race. The Balkan gangster had one thing going for him that no-one disputed, a fearsome reputation as someone not to cross.

Caslin figured that should Durakovic turn out to be on the level, even only slightly, he had a greater problem on his hands than that of a missing girl. How did the driver fit in to the equation, what were his motivations? Had he crossed the line and gotten too heavy handed with Melissa? One thing was certain; you didn't want Anton Durakovic hunting you down. The thought process halted as DS Hunter drew alongside. He got in and she pulled off before he managed to put on his seatbelt.

"Bloody hell, steady on." He struggled with the belt as she accelerated back into traffic.

"Sorry, Sir. But we've got to get over to Harrogate."

"Why, what's happened?"

Hunter took her eyes off the road for a second, glancing towards him, "Tim Bermond's received a text from Natalie's phone."

Caslin took that in, understanding the nuance in Hunter's choice of words as she negotiated the traffic joining the ring road, heading west. That wasn't a turn of events that he'd expected.

CHAPTER TEN

"HAVE YOU SPOKEN TO HIM, my father?"

"Tim, it's not as simple as—"

"It's my father, I'm telling you."

"Calm down," Caslin said, appealing for his childhood friend to cool off. Upon reaching the Bermond residence, he found half of CID already present. Broadfoot and Inglis were overseeing the setting up of communications whilst Caslin and Hunter attempted to offer reassurance to the parents.

"Well it's because of him, it *must* be. Why else would they come after my family? Timothy said Damn it, I'll never be free with him still around."

That struck Caslin as a somewhat strange comment to make but he said nothing. Tasked with being alongside Timothy, from the moment of arrival, Caslin hadn't yet viewed the text message and didn't know when he'd get the chance. Catherine sat on the sofa, her eyes red and the skin of her face appearing blotchy in patches, all evidence of her emotional fatigue. Timothy paced the drawing room, in a perpetual state of agitation.

"What did the text say?" Caslin asked.

Timothy stopped and looked at him whereas Catherine

stared straight ahead with no change in her expression. "It said they had her."

"What else?"

"To wait for instructions."

Caslin nodded and glanced towards Hunter. She stood off to the side of the room, notebook in hand, just in case. "Did they offer any detail, anything to indicate…" he let the question drop away, unsure of how to complete it.

"That she's still alive?" Timothy finished. Caslin met his eye.

"No, nothing."

Catherine's head sagged. Hunter moved to sit alongside her. Caslin found this a strange turn of events. If Natalie had been kidnapped for ransom, or another as yet undetermined motive, why wait until now to make their move? The story was all over the press and the police were heavily involved. Surely a kidnapper would want as little police presence as possible. He had never worked a kidnapping before but it seemed at odds. If, however, as Timothy declared, the idea was to pressurise or retaliate against his father, then standard rules may not apply.

"You seem pretty certain, Tim. Is there something that you're not telling me? If so, now would be a very good time," Caslin asked coolly.

"Just talk to my father."

Turning his back on Caslin, Timothy crossed to the bay window overlooking the garden. Caslin sighed quietly. Catching Hunter's eye, he let her know he'd be back and left the room. Finding DCI Inglis in the expansive kitchen, peering over the shoulder of a technician, he touched his arm to draw his attention and led him away.

"What is it, Nathaniel?"

"This isn't sitting right, Guv."

"How so?"

"The timeline doesn't make a lot of sense to me," Caslin said.

"I know, why the delay?" Inglis said. Caslin was pleased someone else was on his wavelength. "However, this is the only lead we have. Whoever sent the text certainly has Natalie's phone. They most likely know where she is."

"Unless of course, they found it," Caslin offered before adding, "or nicked it. With wall to wall coverage, it wouldn't take a genius to find out whom the phone belongs to. With that said, it's doubtful."

Inglis agreed but he was right, they had nothing else at that moment. They would wait for the next message and take it from there.

"We're hopeful we can get some idea of whereabouts by tracking where the message originated," Inglis said.

"Any details, yet?"

"York centre."

Caslin knew that was pretty useless information. The chances of pinpointing the sender's location, beyond a rough guess, were inconceivable. At least they knew their target was still in the area. They were joined by Kyle Broadfoot.

"We need to keep this as quiet as possible, away from the press," the DCS said.

"That won't be possible for long, Sir," Caslin said. "Not with the interest they've been showing."

"I agree with Nathaniel, Sir," Inglis added. "We'll need to move swiftly."

"Have we been through Natalie's computer yet?" Caslin asked.

John Inglis answered, "We carried out a cursory examination when IT arrived here today. She's a studious one, apparently not very interested in mundane web browsing or social media. The guys will take it away for a more detailed review but looks like a nonstarter."

"What about her grandfather? Has anyone looked into Sebastian Bermond?" Caslin asked. He considered now was as good a time as any to bring it up, seeing as the stakes had been raised.

"What of him?" Kyle Broadfoot replied.

"Tim alleges that this all leads back to him, or at least his past."

Broadfoot stared at Caslin. The man had a face for poker. "And what would you have me do with that information, Inspector?"

"Wouldn't hurt to ask, would it?" Caslin suggested. In his head he thought the reply would be *yes it would, very much.*

Broadfoot looked at John Inglis and then back to Caslin. Before any response could be uttered, the house phone rang. The hive of activity intensified for a few seconds before calm descended, leaving the house in eerie silence. An apprehensive Timothy was escorted into the room. He took a seat at the breakfast table and hesitantly answered the phone.

"Hello," he said softly, his voice almost cracking under the pressure.

"Listen carefully. Thirty thousand pounds is to be deposited into Natalie's current account," a heavily disguised but clearly male voice said. "This is to be done by close of business today."

"That's… not enough time," Timothy stammered.

"You'll manage," the voice said.

"I want to speak to my daughter," he asked forcefully. "I need to know she's okay."

The line went dead. All eyes turned to the officer hunched over a laptop, monitoring the call. He glanced up and shook his head, "Not a chance," he said, answering a silent question. They hadn't managed to trace the call. He shrugged, "We need more time, it was a mobile but at least we have the number." Excitement rose at that news but Caslin guessed it would be a prepaid burn phone. Criminals were often stupid but, in this case, he doubted so. Nonetheless, they would follow it up.

"Why thirty thousand?" Timothy asked. His expression was one of bewilderment. "Is that usual?"

"Certainly not a life changing sum, if you'll forgive me," Inglis said, the last towards Natalie's father.

"First instalment?" Broadfoot suggested.

Caslin shook his head, "I think he's clever."

"Go on," Broadfoot said as all eyes fell on Caslin.

Looking at the faces arranged about him, he continued, "It's not an insignificant amount but one that I expect Tim could get his hands on relatively quickly. Am I right?" Timothy nodded. "This guy doesn't want it dragging on, less chance of getting caught. The money moves in, I presume he has Natalie's bank card and pin to access it—"

"He must know we'll be watching," Broadfoot said.

"Watching where, every ATM in the United Kingdom? If he's savvy he can withdraw money at random, a bit at a time, and he knows we'll keep the account open as we try to catch him."

"Taking the cash in dribs and drabs will drag it out, surely?" Inglis said. "That's risky. On his part, I mean."

"True enough but," Caslin looked over at his school friend, considering whether to say what he was thinking or not.

Timothy stood firm, "I need to hear it, Nathaniel."

Caslin inclined his head, "I'm not convinced that money is the motive here. I reckon he could take it or leave it."

"Why do you say that?" Timothy asked, ahead of anyone else.

"The ransom call has come so long after Natalie's disappearance. If this was the plan, he would have got to you before you called us."

"Unless Mr Bermond moved faster than expected," Broadfoot countered. "Then he'd have to reconsider the plan."

Caslin accepted the logic was just as sound as his own. "Good point."

"The fact he has Natalie's pin and phone must be good news though, right?" Timothy said, grasping for a positive.

"It gives us something more to work with. In the meantime, I suggest you raise the money," Caslin said. The thought occurred that Natalie may have given over the pin code under duress. In that event, her presence would no longer be necessary. However, he chose not to voice that particular scenario.

"You think I should pay?" Timothy asked, his tone not confirming which way he thought he should go.

"It would keep the dialogue open, even if we're only playing along. We want to ensure every opportunity is maximised to bring your daughter home safely," Broadfoot explained. "Can you raise that much?"

"Easily. One call to the bank should do it but the money won't be accessible from Natalie's account, by the end of today."

"He'll know that," Caslin said. "He's just trying to impart a sense of urgency into proceedings. The money may show as uncleared funds as long as the bank plays ball."

"Should do, we all share the same bank. You keep saying 'he', do you think it's just the one?" Timothy said.

"That we don't know. Kidnappers often imply there's more than one, even when they act alone but at this stage it's only a turn of phrase."

Timothy accepted that, "I'll call the bank."

"Could you make the call from a mobile?" Inglis asked. "We need to keep the landline free."

"I will," Timothy said, leaving the room. Catherine stood in the doorway, her husband touching her forearm lightly as he passed. She fixed Caslin with a stare. When he returned it, she looked away, moving back in the direction of the drawing room.

After a few minutes, Caslin excused himself and went in search of her. He found her outside, having left the house via the utility room. She stood in the access passage, linking the front garden to the rear, beneath a canopy of foliage. Leaning with her back against the wall, she took a steep draw on a cigarette. He came alongside and leant against the wall as well.

"Do you have a spare?" he asked.

She looked at him with a sideways glance, "You have the look of a smoker."

He smiled, "I used to be but now, let's say, it's only on the odd occasion."

She took out a pack and offered it to him, he accepted. A

lighter was tucked inside and sparking up, the first drag tasted good, the second, not so much but he persisted. They stood in silence for a moment before Catherine spoke.

"You don't think this has anything to do with my father-in-law, do you?"

Caslin inclined his head slightly, "That remains to be seen but I keep an open mind. You, on the other hand, are absolutely certain it isn't, aren't you?"

She lowered her smoking hand and turned to face him, "Is it that obvious?"

Caslin breathed out, blowing smoke away from them, "Only to one who's looking. Why are you so sure it's nothing to do with Sebastian? Tim's positive."

"Everything is about his bloody father," she said, demonstrating a frustration at an apparent constant in her husband's life. "The man can do nothing right in his eyes."

"But you disagree?" Caslin asked. Catherine didn't answer but her body language suggested so. She took another drag, speaking as she exhaled.

"The man has his uses."

"Are you going to fill me in or do I have to guess?" Caslin had the sense that she was holding something back and it was apparently significant. From the first moment they had met, she had been less vocal than her husband. Now away from him, Caslin saw she was not as submissive as he had figured. There was a reserved strength within her. "Catherine, is it prescient to Natalie's disappearance?"

She threw her cigarette down to the ground, grinding it into the gravel with the ball of her foot, "Tim will be furious that I'm smoking again."

"You're hardly going out of your way to hide it."

"True enough," Catherine said, fixing him with a stare. "I'm usually far subtler but right now, I just don't care. Oh, what the hell, you'll probably find out at some point, regardless."

"Go on," Caslin encouraged.

"We all have a past, Inspector, and sometimes, no matter how hard you try to leave it behind... you just can't." Her eyes watered but tears didn't fall. Her expression was one of cold resignation, "Do you know what I mean by that?"

"I do," Caslin said solemnly. He wasn't humouring her.

"It seems a lifetime ago now but..." she swore under her breath, almost struggling to articulate her thoughts. "I'm not from a wealthy family, Inspector Caslin. We were young when my father left us, God knows where he is now, and my mother did her best. She rode us hard as kids. I think she wanted us to make something of ourselves so we wouldn't be reliant on others."

"Unlike her?" Caslin asked.

"Exactly," Catherine said. "He left her with nothing and it was a real struggle. Me, two sisters and no family to fall back on. When I look back at it now, she had it rough, working all hours. Often, we would look after each other because Mum was flitting between jobs. We did alright, though, somehow. Not saying that we've all made it but we turned out okay, as human beings, I mean. I was the only one to make it to university. One of my sisters got married, pretty much as soon as she left school and the other joined the navy."

"Does she still serve?"

"Yes, she's doing well. Not that we see much of one another. It's usually birthday cards and a phone call at Christmas."

Caslin's thoughts passed momentarily to Stefan. He could relate. "I have a brother like that."

She looked at him with searching eyes, assessing his integrity. She must have liked what she saw. "University was hard for me, Inspector. Not the studying, I enjoyed that. But I was a long way from home and even on a full grant, if you can remember those days, the money didn't go far? It was hard to make the numbers add up."

He sensed where this was going. "You had to work?"

"I did," she nodded. "For the first year or so, I had three jobs on the go but the hours were sporadic. In the second, I got into some difficulty with rent and… well, I was at the end of the line. I had repeated warnings from my landlord and my grades were slipping. For a time, I thought I was on my way out."

Caslin waited while she formed the words in her head, he guessed that speaking openly about this put her far from her comfort zone, "Take your time," he said reassuringly.

"It just came about, I hadn't planned it… but he said we could work it out."

"I see," Caslin said, trying to fill the awkward vacuum that followed the revelation. Catherine stayed silent for a further minute. She didn't come over as particularly distressed. Caslin perceived it more that she had come to terms with her past and now faced it with a steely resolve.

"I found it easier as time went on… and when the other work dried up…" she looked at him, her eyes being the window to her soul, "please don't judge me, Inspector. I'm not proud of what I used to be—"

"You should be," he interrupted her. "You made a success of your life, despite what you had to do. None of us can change who we were or what we did, no matter how much we may want to."

Catherine smiled weakly, apparently relieved at his response, "Thank you."

"Does Tim know?" he asked. She shook her head and looked downwards.

"No, but I guess he will, soon enough."

"How does this tie in with Natalie?" Caslin asked.

"It doesn't, at least not directly," Catherine said. "But a while back, a little over a year ago, I was contacted. Someone had found out… about my past, I've no idea how."

"Blackmail?"

"Yes, they were threatening to go to the papers with it, unless I gave them money."

"How much?"

"Twenty-five thousand."

Caslin mentally acknowledged that that was a similar figure to the ransom demand, "You paid?"

"I would've, believe me but I couldn't, not without Tim finding out. I don't have money of my own. Not that he controls the finances, you understand, it's just all in jointly held accounts. He would've noticed."

"So, what did you do?"

"I had two options, the way I saw it," she went on. "I either had to come clean with my husband, risking everything, or..."

"Or?"

"Or I find another way of raising the money."

"You chose the latter," Caslin said, rather than asked. Catherine nodded. "Let me guess, Sebastian?"

"I figured that he wouldn't want the scandal any more than I did and he had the means to pay. Twenty-five thousand is nothing to him."

"And did he stump up the money?"

"He did," she said, "and he handled the whole thing surprisingly well. He was far more dignified than I expected, or probably deserved. Not to say that he was happy but... he came through. Perhaps it was more for Natalie's sake, than mine."

"You think this is all related?"

Catherine shrugged with an accompanying shake of the head, "It could be a coincidence."

Caslin took a final draw on his cigarette before discarding it to the stones at his feet. There was a saying that he often adopted when coming across a coincidence. In his line of work, they usually took a great deal of planning.

CHAPTER ELEVEN

"WHERE IS IT WE'RE GOING?" Hunter asked.

"To see Sebastian Bermond," Caslin replied. Hunter glared at him. The sound of a car horn, accompanied by his shouting returned her attention to the road. "Jesus, Sarah! Watch the road, yeah."

"I thought Broadfoot didn't want us talking to him," Hunter replied, open mouthed.

Caslin kept quiet. She was almost correct, in that Broadfoot didn't sanction an approach to the serving MP but likewise, hadn't specifically dismissed the suggestion. Although Caslin knew that was only a technicality. He was on thin ice and would need to tread lightly.

"He'll be right," Caslin murmured.

"Do at least tell me you called ahead, please?" Caslin didn't respond. He was already formulating his strategy. Hunter swore.

"You'll not make DI if you keep up that language, young lady," Caslin said playfully. Sarah Hunter was only six years his junior.

"I'll not make DI if I spend much more time working with you, that's for bloody certain," she bit back. Caslin dropped the conversation, deciding to let her stew for a while.

The afternoon traffic grew heavier as they approached the outskirts of York, slowing their progress. Despite the surprising twist provided by Catherine, Caslin still felt uneasy about this entire affair. The kidnapping scenario wasn't sitting well with him. Besides that, there was definitely something strange going on within this family. Nothing and no-one was quite what they appeared to be. Taking out his phone, he called Terry Holt. The DC picked up within a few rings.

"Hello, Sir."

"Terry, I want you to run the name Marco Handanovic through the system, see what pops up. That's Marco with a 'c'."

"Yes, Sir. Who is he?" Holt asked.

"That's what I hope you'll find out."

"Okay, leave it with me. Bad news, Sir," Holt began.

"There usually is, Terry. What's up?"

"SOCO found nothing suspect at Summerbee's house and his lawyer was going bananas. DCI Stephens said we had to release him."

"Alright, Terry. Don't worry," Caslin said nonchalantly, inwardly seething. "What about his good lady wife?"

"She was in Bridport for two days, provided me with the name of the hotel and it checks out. I called them directly and they confirmed payment by card. It was definitely her. She stays there several times a year. They've offered us CCTV if we want it."

"Yes, I want it. Let's make sure. How did she take to her old man having a visitor?"

"Didn't bat an eye, Sir," Holt said. "I get the impression they have an arrangement. Either that or she's one cool customer. I wouldn't want to get on the wrong side of her, I tell you."

"Okay, keep digging," Caslin said.

"Will do."

Caslin returned the phone to his pocket and slipped into a train of thought. Peter Summerbee was still their best suspect. However, they needed to find the driver. Suzanne Brooke had insisted her daughter was always accompanied and the 999 call virtually confirmed that. Melissa didn't know where she was, someone else must have taken her out to Skipwith. Even so, Summerbee bugged him, the man had form and he set Caslin's radar off. Instinctively, he was disinclined to drop him so soon. It was altogether too convenient that another unidentified person was in place for him to point the finger at.

"Who's Marco Handanovic, Sir?" Hunter asked, the hissy fit apparently having subsided.

"Most likely a load of bollocks," Caslin replied. He indicated the forthcoming turning, "This is us, next left."

THE RECEPTION to Sebastian Bermond's constituency office was intimate. The front desk ran the full width of the room. Hunter and Caslin waited patiently on the padded benches, set in front of the expansive front window, overlooking the street. This wasn't an MP who spent a great deal on opulent surroundings. Caslin found the décor reminiscent of a taxi office or an Indian takeaway. Initially denied a time slot, due to lack of availability, Caslin had pointedly asked the receptionist to double check with the man himself. Two appointments were thereby pushed back to accommodate them.

Half an hour after arrival, they were shown through. The office was as drab and characterless as the waiting area. Sebastian Bermond MP seemed to notice Caslin giving the place a sneering once over and commented on it.

"Not exactly what the *Daily Mail* would have you believe are the trappings of power, are they?"

"Quite true, Sir," Caslin replied, taking the offered hand. He was a big man, far more fat than muscle and easily cleared six-three in height. That surprised Caslin. His son was nowhere near that tall and the MP never came across as such when appearing on the television news.

"Please, no need to stand on ceremony, call me Sebastian," the MP said as he shook Hunter's hand, in turn and offered them seats. Small plastic ones, similar to those Caslin remembered from school.

"Thank you for seeing us at such short notice, Sebastian," Caslin said politely.

"No problem at all," he replied. "I am being kept in the loop by your man... erm... what's his name, Broadfoot, Kyle Broadfoot. He didn't say anyone would be calling by today."

Hunter cast him a sideways look but Caslin ignored her and the comment. "It has been a little frenetic today but it's important for us to speak with you. It's a delicate subject, so I hope you can forgive the intrusion."

"Of course, Inspector. Anything that I can do, to help, I will. Whatever is it?"

"Catherine and her blackmailer," Caslin said calmly. He thought for a second that he heard Hunter's jaw hit the floor. Sebastian Bermond visibly flinched, then took a deep breath, looking first to the ceiling and then back to Caslin, exhaling slowly.

"Does Timothy know that you're here?"

"Not yet, Sir."

"I see," the MP rubbed at his chin, as if there was something there to irritate him. "I suppose it was churlish to expect that affair to remain a secret forever. What is it you would like to know?"

"Have you received any communication from them, since last year's event?" Caslin said. Hunter turned to him, all colour draining from her cheeks.

"I never had any then, or now. Do you think it's connected?"

Caslin shook his head, indicating that he didn't know, "We need to review all potential lines of investigation, under these circumstances, be them past or present. I hope you understand?"

"I thought that was all over with," he sighed. "I always

thought that strumpet wasn't good enough for Timothy and I told him so, the very day he married her."

Charming, Caslin thought, "And yet, you were okay with giving her twenty-five grand?" Again, Hunter glanced sideways, slapping her notebook down with force, a movement that Caslin judged as petulant rather than a sign of frustration.

"I'll do anything for my family, Inspector, within reason," Sebastian added in as cold a manner as Caslin had ever seen. "Besides, I acted more for my granddaughter than for her mother and my wayward son."

"She said similar."

"Good. I told her in no uncertain terms that I was not impressed. That sort of thing casts a long shadow over everyone around you. I didn't want Natalie to suffer such ignominy."

"You weren't bothered for yourself, then?" Caslin asked, not quite believing that to be the case.

"Tosh!" Sebastian said. "I'm too long in the tooth for something like that to damage me. My record speaks for itself."

"You referred to Timothy as wayward?"

"Perhaps... more flighty... than wayward. The boy could never stick at anything."

"He seems to be doing quite well, these days," Hunter said.

Sebastian snorted as he burst into a broad grin, "Gambling with other people's money? Yes, I don't doubt it. He was always quite adept with another's wallet. But I dare say his surname helps grease the wheels with certain people."

Caslin smiled, "Well thank you for clearing that up, Sir. Just to clarify, no-one has been in touch with you regarding Natalie?"

He shook his head emphatically, "No and if they do, I will be straight on to you."

"You wouldn't be tempted to go it alone, like last year?"

Sebastian fixed a stare on Caslin. Leaning forward he rested his elbows on the desk and formed a tent with his oversized fingers. "Inspector, my granddaughter means the world to me. I wouldn't take the chance, there is far too much at stake. Last year's escapade was entirely different. Reputations and not lives were at risk."

Shortly afterwards they were walking back to the car. No conversation had taken place since they left the office. Caslin could, however, feel Hunter's eyes burning a hole in the back of his skull. Reaching the car, she unlocked it and went to open the door.

"Okay, I'm sorry," Caslin offered, leaning on the roof.

"Sorry? Is that it?" Hunter said. Caslin regretted speaking; silence suddenly seemed much more appealing.

"What do you want me to say?"

"How about 'hey Sarah, there's this whole other blackmail thing going on' or 'you know, Sebastian paid a backhander to cover for a prossie, last year'. Anything along those lines would've been nice."

"I know," Caslin said with genuine contrition. "I am sorry, really. I hadn't got it all clear in my head that's all."

"And no-one else knows about this yet?"

"No, just us… and Catherine, obviously."

"Oh yes, her. Suddenly I don't feel a great deal of sympathy for her."

"Come on, Sarah," Caslin challenged. "You don't mean that."

Hunter got in the driver's side, slamming the door behind her. Caslin sighed and with a glance skyward, opened his door and also got in.

"What do we do now, then?" she asked him as he fastened his seatbelt.

"I want to go back and have another word with Natalie's friend, Lottie. It's about time she told us something useful."

"Okay, do you think she'll open up?"

"Well, things have changed," Caslin said, looking out of the window. "She's not just missing now. The game's changed, so must the rules."

"What did he mean when he talked about 'greasing the

wheels with *certain people'*?" Hunter asked, taking a left and heading out of the city.

"I don't know. The funny handshake brigade, perhaps."

"The masons?"

"Probably. It's as good as any other idea. After all, having the son of such a high profile person around couldn't hurt your business."

"Catherine says Timothy practically runs the place."

Caslin didn't reply. Perhaps Timothy was worth his weight, or perhaps everyone else had to shoulder it. People often had inflated opinions of their own capabilities or those of their partner. The father-to-son relationship, in this case, was evidently challenging from both sides. To Caslin, it was all beginning to feel like a busman's holiday.

THE DRIVE over to Fairfax House was short and yet, felt like it took an age. The summer warmth had arrived only to be accompanied by a frosty atmosphere inside the car. Pulling up outside the accommodation block, Caslin sought to make amends, if only slightly.

"The DCI said you acquitted yourself well, while I was off."

"Did he," Hunter replied with no break in her persistent scowl. She had stepped up to Acting DI whilst Caslin recuperated.

"He thinks you'll make a good inspector. That's high praise, particularly coming from him. You've passed all your exams as well, haven't you?"

"You don't have to suck up, Caslin," Hunter said, looking across at him. "Just don't keep me in the dark like that again… *ever.*"

He smiled and was pleased when she returned it. "I'm not lying though. I reckon the next position that comes up is most likely yours."

"I'd best stay clear of you then," she said.

His smile broadened, watching her get out of the car. He did likewise and they went in search of Lottie. They approached the main entrance and were buzzed in. Finding their way up to her dorm, they found no-one home. Asking a passing student of Lottie's possible whereabouts, they were directed to the gardens. Once outside they found her sitting on the lawn within a group of around a dozen. She saw them approach and the sweeping smile that had been on her face faded rapidly. She stood up and excused herself from the others, coming to meet them.

"I didn't expect to see you both so soon," she said with a contrived smile. "Have you found Natalie?"

Caslin eyed her with a stern expression, "No Lottie, we haven't and what's more, I think you *hoped* you wouldn't see us so soon."

She looked away then, appearing agitated, shifting her weight between her feet. "I don't know what you mean."

"Lottie, you must've seen the news," Hunter said . "If not, you will have heard. Natalie's in real trouble and you need to help us. Forget whatever it is you think you're doing for the best. You need to talk to us."

"I... I don't know what it is you want from me?"

Caslin said firmly, "I want you to tell us what it is we don't know. And you know what I mean by that, don't you?"

"I've not heard from her," Lottie said, "and I don't know her plans for that day."

"But?" Hunter added.

Lottie's expression changed and she exhaled heavily, "She had talked about skipping the dig and heading off with Stuart for the day but it was idle talk, you know. Her course *is* important to her."

"And who might Stuart be?" Caslin asked, irritated that this childish girl could keep this from them.

"He's her boyfriend, sort of," Lottie said.

"Sort of?" Caslin asked. "Well, is he, or isn't he?"

"He is."

"Does Stuart have a second name?"

"I don't know it," Lottie said, shaking her head. "Honestly, I swear."

"Where can we find him?" Hunter asked, equally annoyed.

"I don't know. He's not a student," she said, meeting Caslin's unforgiving stare. "I never see him on campus and he's hardly ever here, at the halls. You could check her laptop, they're always emailing and she has pictures of him on it, too."

"You mean her tablet?"

"No, she has a laptop," Lottie said, looking from one to the other.

Caslin and Hunter exchanged glances. "Her laptop is at her parents' house," Caslin said.

"Not that one. She has two. Didn't you search her room? She always leaves it in there and uses her mobile when she's out."

"Where?" Caslin asked.

"I'll show you," Lottie offered, leading them back inside.

ONCE THEY HAD access to Natalie's dorm room, Lottie swiftly retrieved the laptop from the top of the wardrobe, stashed beneath a board game and an old blanket. Bearing in mind the security doors and the locks to her private room, Caslin pondered the need for such concealment. As if reading his mind, Lottie responded.

"It's not only hidden from the other students, although they're well bad for stealing things from you. She didn't want her parents to see it, either."

"Why ever not?" Hunter asked.

Lottie shrugged, "She was always secretive about it, I don't know why."

"But you knew?" Caslin asked.

"There's not much I don't know."

"Then tell me about Stuart."

"Not my type," Lottie said, flashing him a smile. "Too old. Natalie was drawn to his sort, though. I think she likes the challenge."

"What is it about Stuart that's challenging?"

"There's an edge to him but I didn't like it. I'll bet he'll never amount to anything, all tattoos and partying. That's fun for a while but I want a bit more."

"Natalie?" Caslin pursued.

"Probably trying to piss her parents off, I expect." Lottie offered. "There's a lot of that about. I never saw him as being long term, for her."

Caslin thought about his own daughter and prayed that she wouldn't adopt a similar strategy in a few years' time. He opened the laptop and turned it on. Within moments the log in screen came up, he had been afraid of that.

"Do Natalie's parents know about Stuart?" Caslin asked, expecting her answer to confirm what he already knew.

"No way!" Lottie said, emphatically. Caslin was grateful that the Bermond's had been on the level about something, at least. "They would go mental, if they did. She would've told me."

"Better get this to the tech guys," Caslin said regrettably, looking at the password request.

Lottie laughed, "Why, because of her password?" She seemed incredulous.

"Well, do you know it?"

"They don't teach you much at police school, do they?" Lottie said, stepping in front of him and reaching for the keyboard. She used the glidepad to reboot the laptop. When the machine began its start-up sequence she held down the shift and a function key, halting the process and moving it into a different set up screen. Caslin was curious. Looking to Hunter, he silently mouthed the words *police school*. Hunter smiled before both refocussed their attention on Lottie. Caslin watched as she highlighted a command that said "Delete all users" and double tapped the glidepad. "It's so easy, I don't know why they bother with the security features," Lottie said aloud, almost to herself.

Within moments the laptop was up and running. The desktop background was a picture of Natalie, her arms draped around a tattooed male, appearing to be a number of years older than her. Caslin guessed him to be well into his thirties. He wore a vest and the body art that they could see decorated both arms, his upper chest and ran up the side of the neck, to his ear. He was muscular with a well lined face, sporting a closely-cropped beard and long black hair, tied into a pony tail. He bore a scar above the left eyebrow, running down and away from his eye, roughly two inches in length.

"This is Stuart?" Caslin asked Lottie. She nodded. "Looks like a catch."

"You can step aside now, Lottie," Hunter said. She did as requested and Hunter took over the search. There was a folder containing multiple pictures of the couple and several dozen media files that she chose not to open at that time. Caslin guided Lottie out into the corridor and checked they weren't within earshot of anyone nearby.

"Is there anything else that you're not telling us?" he asked. "This is serious and we can't afford to waste any more time."

"No, I can't think of anything. I promise," she emphasised the last, clearly intended to assure him that she was being truthful. "It's just that we agreed never to—"

"I get that but you've slowed us down. This might be significant and I hope for your sake it doesn't cost Natalie. It's about time you grew up a bit. You're not in the playground anymore."

Lottie's reaction demonstrated that she acknowledged her poor judgement. Caslin thought that, with hindsight, he was a little harsh on her but needed to convey the gravity of her choices. That way, next time she would be more forthcoming.

"I'm sorry," she mumbled.

Caslin pushed one of his contact cards into her hand, "If you think of anything else, I expect you to call me immediately. Do you understand?"

With that he excused her and she left. He returned to Natalie's room.

"You're not going to believe this," Hunter said as he entered.

"Why, what have you got? The identity of the secret boyfriend?"

"No, not yet but she's quite the little vlogger, our Natalie," Hunter said, glancing up at him. "Vlogging is when you—"

"I know what vlogging is," Caslin cut her off. "People videoing themselves, banging on about something or other. It's like writing shit about fuck all, isn't good enough anymore. What's her subject matter?"

"Well, her blogspot is subtitled 'Lies, deception and the secrets we keep'. I can't wait to explore what it is she has to say."

Caslin blew out his cheeks, "Strewth, what is it with this bloody family. Come on, let's take it back to Fulford and see what we can find."

CHAPTER TWELVE

THE SQUAD ROOM was relatively quiet. The lateness of the hour, coupled with the base of operations largely relocating to the Bermond's home in Harrogate were the contributing factors. Caslin passed through towards his office, spotting Terry Holt at his desk in the corner. The DC was hunched over and for a moment Caslin considered he had succumbed to fatigue. Crossing the room, he caught a glimpse of a photo on his desk.

"Keeping you up, Terry," he called out. Much to his surprise, Holt looked around, bright eyed and attentive.

"Not at all, Sir," Holt said. "I was just mulling things over."

"Have you been seconded to the Bermond investigation as well, then?"

"No, Sir," Holt said, visibly confused.

"What are you doing with a photo of Natalie, then?"

"What?" Holt replied, looking at his desk. "This is the one Suzanne Brooke gave me."

Caslin was surprised by his own error. Leaning forward he took another look, rightly enough it wasn't Natalie. At first glance it was an easy mistake to make.

"Frank Stephens about today?" Caslin asked after the DCI.

Holt shook his head, "Not this afternoon. He's in court on that Mitchell fraud case."

"Oh yes, I forgot," Caslin said. "How are you getting on with Summerbee and his business affairs?"

"Looks on the level, so far. He's filed everything on time, not missed any payments to Inland Revenue or the VAT man."

"Keep on it."

Caslin left Holt and went to his office. Sitting down he opened the folders on his desk and reviewed Iain Robertson's findings on Natalie's hatchback, found on Fountain's Lane. As expected they had no forensic evidence to indicate a struggle or anything to suggest that she had been taken ill in the vehicle. To all intents and purposes, the car had been parked in an orderly fashion. No personal belongings had been found inside. The fact it was left unlocked was all that stood out as unusual. The tyre patterns Robertson found at the scene were sufficiently detailed to enable identification of a brand and not only that, they were relatively new, judging by the tread depth. Bearing in mind the size, the initial hypothesis of them belonging to an SUV or similar was reasonable. Robertson said with high probability that a positive tyre match could be made, should a suspect be found.

"We need a suspect," he said quietly to himself.

"I might be able to help you with that," Hunter said from the doorway. So engrossed was he that he failed to notice her arrival. "I think I've identified Stuart."

"Good," Caslin said, sitting forward in his chair, excited at the prospect a tangible lead. "Who is he?"

"Stuart Nicol," Hunter said, walking in and passing an open file to Caslin. Immediately he recognised the face in the mugshot as that on Natalie's laptop. "He's a real charmer. Not a stranger to us, with three prior arrests for Grievous Bodily Harm but none of them stuck. He served two years for demanding money with menaces."

"Where was that?" Caslin asked absently, scanning the file before him.

"Up in Glasgow. He was released on licence four years ago. That was his last known address. Current whereabouts are unknown."

"I see he has a weapons conviction here," Caslin said.

"Yes, when he was sixteen he spent twelve months in young offenders, convicted of carrying a knife with intent to wound."

"Do we know what car he drives?" Caslin asked.

"Nothing registered to him with the DVLA."

Caslin was disappointed but figured that wasn't a surprise, "Must be every parent's dream to have him dating your daughter."

"Lottie was right though, the parents probably wouldn't be too keen, if they had known. Kidnapping would be one hell of a step up for him, though. I'm not convinced he has the intelligence to pull it off."

"Never underestimate someone's capacity to convince themselves of their own greatness."

"He's been seeing her for some time. Do you think he'd wait this long to pull a stunt like this?"

Caslin considered that point. Perhaps Nicol had been playing the long game, assessing what he would gain and waiting for the right time. "Maybe, I don't know. Hell, Natalie may have decided to kick him into touch and he thought, why not? It might explain the absence of a struggle. What have you got from the laptop?"

"I've left it with the tech guys, they're giving it the once over now," Hunter said. "I'll follow up as soon as we're done here."

"If we don't have intel on Nicol's whereabouts, I guess there's nothing in the system on his hangouts. What about known associates?"

Hunter shook her head, "Nothing local to tie him to. We don't even know why he's in our area." Caslin sat back in his chair, rubbing his eyes with thumb and forefinger. "You look like crap, Sir, if you don't mind me saying? When did you last sleep?"

Caslin shrugged off the question, "Can you get me a copy of the photo, Catherine gave you of Natalie, plus another of this little gem?" he indicated Stuart Nicol. "Lottie gave us a nightclub and a couple of pubs where they tend to hang out. I'll stop by tonight and see what I can get out of them."

Hunter nodded and left the office. Sitting in the silence that followed he considered closing his eyes but thought better of it. Thinking about his route for the evening, he would start with a visit to the Kings Arms, which he knew to be a decent pub. The clientele was predominantly from the university and it was a nice enough place, causing little trouble. The landlord was upstanding and would assist if he could. The club was Angels and Ice, somewhere to go when most elsewhere had shut their doors. The other pub, Lottie had described, was the Cloaked Beggar. That place was altogether another story and probably where Nicol would feel most at home.

Hunter returned with copies of the photographs, handing them over with a smile.

"Are you sure you don't want me to come with you?"

Caslin shook his head, "If you're that desperate for a date, Holt's looking a bit lonely these days." Hunter glanced through the window and saw Terry Holt, slyly leafing through his racing paper, attempting to look like he was hard at it.

"No, I'm not that desperate," she smiled, turning to leave. Reaching the doorway, she stopped and looked over her shoulder, "Oh and Sir," Caslin looked up, "don't flatter yourself."

Caslin laughed, "Let me know if you get anything useful from that laptop."

"I will."

Caslin looked at the clock on the wall of the squad room, it read 18:24. Deciding to head out, he told Terry Holt to go home and get some sleep, after first dropping him off in the city centre. A grateful DC didn't object and Caslin was within the city walls twenty minutes later. The Kings Arms pub was on the banks of the Ouse, well below street level. Caslin trotted down the flight of stone steps from the bridge above, negotiating a group of early revellers as they stumbled up. Being clement, the pub's vast numbers of patrons were enjoying the evening, sitting on the quayside. The days of canal boats shipping goods to the warehouses opposite were long gone and the buildings themselves were now flash apartments with a river view.

Passing through the entrance door into a traditional pub, the summer light was stripped away by dark wood and even darker carpets. The smell was typical for the pub and welcoming. With only those queuing for service present inside, Caslin made his way to the end of the bar and took a seat, eyeing the staff. One barman caught his eye and acknowledged him but there was no sign of the landlord.

Rather than leap in, Caslin waited and when his turn came, he ordered a pint of bitter. When the barmen returned he handed over a fiver and asked him to take a look at the photos. The young man was willing to help but barely recognised Natalie. He thought she probably did drink there but appeared much like any other student and they had hundreds of them. He was adamant however that Stuart Nicol didn't frequent the pub. Caslin thanked him and tried the other member of staff but she too, was of no help..

Finishing his drink, Caslin left. It had passed seven o'clock and, despite it being a week night, the pub was starting to fill. Taking a left turn, he walked along King's Staith before another left brought him to Clifford Street, a stone's throw from Angels and Ice. The club would be nigh on empty at this time. He guessed he would get more from the staff when quiet than later when the place was jumping. The doors were locked when he arrived, the club not opening until 8 p.m. but he hammered a fist on the door, anyway. It took several attempts before he got a response, a young woman unbolting the door and eyeing him warily. He didn't look like their usual customer.

"We're not open until—"

"Eight, I know. I can read," Caslin said, brandishing his warrant card. The door opened and he passed through. Not a place that he ever had cause to visit, the interior was new to him. Passing by the entrance foyer and cloak room, he went through a double door and up a flight of stairs before entering the club proper. A circular bar was centrally located, with a second tier that wrapped around the outside of the room, with viewing galleries to the dance floor and booths beneath. Everywhere he looked there was chrome and neon, contrasting with dark walls and floors. Grateful to not be present during opening hours, for this wasn't his kind of place, Caslin was directed to an office at the rear. Here he was introduced to Jacqui Morris, the manager of the club.

Smartly dressed in a sharp business suit, Caslin couldn't help but think she was more a banker than a club manager. Openly admitting that she spent little time on the floor of the club, Jacqui called for her door supervisor, Mike Berry. He looked more the part, tall with a shaved head, although slender and wiry and most certainly not the heavy-set individual one might expect. Speaking eloquently, Caslin knew the image was only part of his make-up. The man was likely to be ex-forces, he guessed, due to the way he carried himself and the order with which he went about his role.

"Yeah, I know these two," Berry said after Caslin passed him the photos. "She's often in here, sometimes twice in a week. Spends a fair bit of time chatting to the door staff. Not unusual that. Good fun as I recall."

"What about him?" Caslin asked.

Berry frowned, "Yes, not as often, mind you. I've seen him with her a handful of times but he's not a regular."

"Any trouble?"

"From her, no," he shook his head. "Him on the other hand, a different story. We had to throw him out once, a little while ago. Nothing too serious, an altercation at the bar. We already had an eye on him at the time so it didn't get the chance to escalate."

"What was it about, do you know?"

"The usual. Too much alcohol and someone chatting to his girl, I think. Not that we stopped to ask."

"Can you remember when you last saw him?"

"A week or two, maybe. Come to think of it, I reckon it was the weekend before last. They were both here, in a small group."

"With other students?"

"No, not this lot," Berry said. "That's why I remember it. I thought it an odd bunch for her to be running with. Not the usual crowd, aside from him obviously."

"Did he always arrive with her?"

Again, the doorman shook his head, "Can't say I remember them ever arriving together before. He's not really the student type, you know?"

Caslin thanked them for their help and left. The Cloaked Beggar, his last port of call, was located on Feasegate. The frontage suggested what lay beyond. Many of the bars and pubs around there were sleek and classy on the exterior, pushing for high end appearance. Not so the Cloaked Beggar. Peeling paintwork and signage, dating back decades.. Inside fared no better, threadbare carpets, whose original colouring was a forgotten memory and traditional décor, heavily stained by tar from days prior to the smoking ban.

When he entered, all eyes descended on him and the general hum of the half-filled pub dropped slightly as he approached the bar. Perhaps it was his imagination but conversation nearby appeared to cease when he came into earshot. The barman sidled up within a few moments, giving a brief nod in greeting.

"What can I get you?" he asked.

"Double Macallan, no ice," Caslin said. The barman got him his drink and took the ten-pound note on offer. As he handed him his change, Caslin asked casually, "You seen Stuart tonight?"

The barman eyed Caslin suspiciously, "Don't know any Stuart," he said flatly.

"Sure, you do, Stuart Nicol. He's in here all the time," Caslin replied, glancing around. "I owe him some money but can't get hold of him. Thought he might be about." The barman walked away without another word. Caslin heard a chuckle and turned to see from where it originated. The man sitting nearby, at the bar, smiled in his direction.

"I would've thought a man of your years would have more experience than that."

Caslin took in his measure, guessing he was in his fifties, rangy with blonde hair and beard, both shot through with grey. Casually dressed in jeans and a polo shirt, that had seen better days, he sported a stud earring in his right lobe and his face was well worn.

"Is that right?" Caslin asked, sipping at his drink.

"Yeah," the man said, "you should've just got your ID out and saved a few quid on the scotch."

Caslin smiled, "Is it that obvious?"

"You may have a shit suit on but people like you aren't friends with Nicol."

"Who said we were friends?" Caslin countered. "You know where I can find him?"

Again, the man laughed, "No. And if I did, I would hardly be likely to tell you."

"And here was me thinking we were getting on so well," Caslin replied. "I could always get some uniform down here to toss this place. Doubt they'll find anything but it'll piss you all off, no end."

The man thought about it for a second before looking around. "That would be a shame, what with the boys watching the football and all."

Caslin turned his attention to the big screen just as a shout went up, regarding some decision that went one way, rather than another. "We couldn't have that, could we,"

"He's not been in, not for days. Good enough?"

Caslin met his eye and deemed him to be on the level, as much as anyone in this place ever would be, "Who does he hang about with?"

"Go fuck yourself."

"Cheers," Caslin said, "but I prefer blondes." Swiftly finishing his drink and with a wink towards the unnamed man, he placed his glass on the bar. Leaving the pub, through a cloud of cigarette smoke from those congregating around the door, he found the mixture of fresh air and alcohol going to his head. He knew to avoid the booze with his medication but often chose to ignore the advice. Feeling slightly giddy, he set off towards Stonegate and his flat in Kleiser's Court.

The commercial heart of the city, near to the Minster, was quieter than usual. The shops were long closed and the bars and restaurants along the medieval streets, often tucked discreetly down alleys and in small courtyards, carried the noise away. Caslin became aware that he might not be alone. A few people were milling around, heading for drinks or a meal but he had the distinct feeling that he was being followed. Despite stopping a couple of times, feigning interest in shop windows, he couldn't catch sight of anyone. Ultimately dismissing it as paranoia, he resumed his course.

Taking a left onto Swinegate he spied someone he knew. Checking for traffic, he ducked between two oncoming cars and ran over the road to catch her up.

"Hey, Lisa," he said to the woman walking in the same direction.

"Hello, Mr Caslin," she replied, with a smile. "I've not seen you out here for a while."

"I've been keeping busy."

"Pleased to hear it," Lisa said. "Do you want to walk with me for a bit?"

He nodded, "It would be my pleasure. How's business?"

"Are you asking a professional question or just making small talk?"

He grinned, "The economy's picking up, so they tell us and I wondered if you'd seen an upturn?"

She laughed, "No matter what the state of the economy, people always make room to socialise. Some would rather go hungry. Were you looking for me or having an evening out?"

"A passing coincidence but seeing as you're here," Caslin went on. "What do you know about a guy called Durakovic?"

Lisa stopped walking, the smile fading from her face,

"Anton Durakovic? More than I'd like."

"You've come across him, then?"

"Not so much me," Lisa shook her head. "He's pretty new in things around here. I understand he's ruffled a few feathers amongst the established."

Caslin bobbed his head in understanding, "He's muscled his way in over the last couple of years."

"Doesn't play by the same rules. At least, that's what I'm led to believe. These former eastern bloc types rarely do. They operate like they did back home."

"Do you know where he's from?"

Lisa shook her head, "No idea and I hope not to get close enough to find out. Not that I have anything to worry about on that score."

"Why not?"

"So far he's not interested in my line of work. He goes for the more elite clients and people like me don't make enough, so it seems."

"Escorts only?"

"Yes. You know as well as I do, that with street girls you often get drug or alcohol dependency, or both. Durakovic likes his girls clean. They fetch more on the market."

They walked for a minute or so without conversation, Lisa's arm hooked through his. "Do you know Melissa

Brooke," Caslin asked casually. He felt her arm tense slightly against his.

"Mel? Yes," she replied. "Why do you ask?"

"Her mother has reported her missing."

Lisa took in a deep breath, "That's not good."

"She works for Durakovic," Caslin offered.

"I know," Lisa said, her tone implying she knew more.

"Should we be worried?"

Lisa stopped walking, turning to face him.

"I told her not to get involved with that lot. I said it was a bad move, particularly in her position."

"Her position?"

"Mel cleaned herself up a lot in the last year. Didn't want to be on the streets or even in the game, not that many of us do," the last words spoken were accompanied by a sad expression.

"Then why go to work for Durakovic?"

Lisa shrugged, "Money, why else? I saw her, must be what, a month ago? She was looking good, still sober and probably the best I've seen her in ages. She was raving about how things were going."

"With Durakovic?" Caslin inquired.

"Not so much, no. She said she was still definitely looking to get out and thought she'd figured a way to make it happen. Planning to get her daughter back too."

"I don't see Durakovic as the sort to let you walk away when you please."

"That's what I told her. Plus, if he found out about her former recreational habits… I doubted it would go down well. This business is unforgiving at the best of times and men like that… well, you know how it is."

"What did she say to that?"

"Wasn't bothered," Lisa replied forcefully. "Said she had it all planned out and that I wasn't to worry. It's almost like…"

"Like what?"

"I'm not sure… like she knew something that I didn't."

"Such as?"

"I took it that she had some kind of leverage, a way to get what she wanted. I thought she was playing with fire and told her so but... I'm not surprised she's gone missing, let's put it that way."

Caslin let the information sink in. It appeared as if Durakovic's reputation was not merely for show. He could be ruthless if necessary and Vice had told him that his girls didn't quit, at least not of their own accord. He wondered what Melissa thought she had that could facilitate her exit strategy. Would she have attempted to blackmail someone like Anton Durakovic? If so, she was a very brave young lady, or more likely, a foolish one.

"Word is that Durakovic's girls are accompanied. Is that right?"

"Oh yeah, always, Makes a big show of it, so you feel safe. Protecting his asset is arguably more like it."

That information tallied with the factual element of Summerbee's account. Caslin still wasn't prepared to give him the benefit of the doubt, not yet. "It was good to see you, Lisa," Caslin said, affectionately kissing her on the cheek. "Maybe you should think about a change?"

"We do what we have to," she replied.

"Take care of yourself out here, won't you?"

She smiled warmly, "I always do, Mr Caslin."

Resuming his course towards Stonegate, his thoughts oscillated between Natalie and Melissa Brooke. Two young girls who had grown up on separate sides of the track. One, who seemingly had everything going for her, whilst the other faced a struggle from the very moment she was born. Melissa, hell bent on bettering her life and in contrast, Natalie appeared to be flirting with a darker element in hers. The convergence of their lives to this eerily similar point, together with their distinct likeness, struck him as he slipped into the Coffee Yard, via one of the many medieval alleys linking the old streets of York. Stonegate was now only yards away.

Moving footfalls on the enclosed brick passage came to ear. Slow to react, he turned just in time to see the fist strike him on the left side of his face. Stunned, he staggered back, only managing to raise his arms in a defensive motion as more blows rained down. He fell against the wall, an involuntary shout emanating from somewhere within. Tucking his elbows in and protecting his head with his forearms, he sought to fend off the fists and feet that repeatedly thrashed at him.

Another shout could be heard in the melee and the blows suddenly lessened as another joined the fray. Caslin, momentarily winded, used the wall at his rear to brace against before launching himself at the nearest body. A whack to the head didn't slow him and he swung in retaliation, landing a glancing blow. A combination of flying fists later and it was all over. The attackers fled back down the passage from the direction they had come, a man giving chase. Caslin fell back against the wall, trying to catch his breath. The pursuing figure soon gave up and returned to Caslin's side. The enclosed Coffee Yard wasn't lit but Caslin recognised the voice as soon as he heard it.

"Life's certainly not dull around you is it, little brother?"

"Right enough," was all he could manage in reply, drawing deep breaths whilst probing his features, searching for damage before spitting blood to the floor.

"Good job I stopped by, by the look of it," Stefan said. Even in the gloom, Caslin could see the smile. "Come on, let's get to yours."

Two minutes later and the door to Caslin's apartment in Kleiser's Court closed behind them. Caslin pointed his brother in the direction of the living room and headed into the bathroom. Pulling on the light cord, he inspected his face in the mirror. Already one of his eyes was bloodshot and watering and there were several areas tender to the touch, which would no doubt look far worse in the morning. One of his teeth felt loose, wobbling when he ran his tongue against it.

"Bastards," he said to his own reflection. Rifling through his medicine cabinet, he located his painkillers. There were only four left in the strip and he knew there to be a further three in his jacket, nowhere near enough to see him through until Tuesday. Putting the box back, he closed the door and joined Stefan.

"What was all that about?" his brother asked.

"A couple of chancers, I expect," Caslin muttered. If truth be known, he had no idea but found it likely they had followed him from the Cloaked Beggar. Stefan appeared to accept the explanation and made no further comment. "Do you fancy a drink?" Caslin asked, crossing to the other side of the room and bringing down a bottle of Jura from a shelf. He went to pour out two glasses but found a shaking hand making it difficult. Holding the bottle with his left, he flexed the fingers in his right, to try and ease the movements. Moments later he passed one glass to his brother and sank into his armchair with the other. Stefan walked to the window and looked out onto Stonegate below.

"This place is a bit... old fashioned," Stefan said, glancing around at the exposed beams and dark panelling that lined the walls. "What would an agent call it, a fixer upper?"

Caslin snorted a laugh, "Either that or *in need of modernisation.*"

"They'd have a point," Stefan agreed. "When was this place last rewired?"

"If it looked like it belonged in the 21st Century, I couldn't afford the rent. The roof leaks, I've got mould, rot, both wet and dry and basically, I live here because no-one else wants to."

"I was sorry to hear about you and Karen," Stefan said, referencing Caslin's ex-wife.

"The old man fill you in, did he?"

Stefan nodded. Caslin frowned and then continued, "I'm sure it didn't go down quite the way he described."

"No matter, I'm sorry, all the same. How are the kids?"

"Doing okay," Caslin said, taking a sip of his drink. His nose stung and he could feel his bottom lip beginning to swell. "Staying long?"

From his position, facing the window, Stefan shrugged, "See how it goes. You know what Dad's like."

"Only too well."

Stefan turned around, sipping at his own scotch, "Don't be too hard on him, Nate. He doesn't mean to be difficult. He's actually alright—"

"Ha!" Caslin retorted. "Problem is, you and I have different fathers."

Stefan smiled, knowing better than to get involved in that debate. They didn't, but to Caslin it often felt that was the case. "I should apologise for not visiting sooner. You know, after what happened?"

Caslin fixed him with a stare, "I'm sure you had your reasons."

Stefan flicked an eyebrow, "Probably not very good ones, though," he said solemnly. "Don't take this the wrong way, Nate but are you okay?"

Caslin smiled, "I'll be fine, it's not the first kicking I've ever had."

"No, not that. I mean you've clearly got a problem."

Caslin's smile faded to a scowl, "What do you mean by that?"

Stefan put his glass down, taking a seat on the sofa opposite. "You can't kid a kidder, little brother. Your eyes are dilated, you're sweating and the shakes tell their own story."

"Piss off," Caslin bit back.

"I've been there. What are you taking? Whatever it is, I think you need to cut back—"

"You know nothing about it!" Caslin snapped, downing his drink and slamming the glass to the coffee table. "I've not seen nor heard from you in three years and you swan in, talking this shite. Who do you think you are?"

"Look," Stefan said in a conciliatory tone, "I know what it's like."

"I got bloody shot, Stefan."

"I *know* what it's like to be under fire," Stefan said. "At least I got to shoot back."

"Oh, we're not going to have this conversation again, are we? There are enough guns on the street without the police adding more."

"If you'd had a gun, maybe you would have got him first, that's all I'm saying."

"Or maybe he would have shot me in the *face* without a discussion," Caslin countered. Stefan dropped it, sitting back in his seat. Caslin stood up and went to pour another scotch, returning with the bottle. "Anyway, who are you to be lecturing me? How many jobs have you tried and failed at since you got out of the army? How many dives have you stayed in? You don't get to rock up and start calling the shots."

"You're right," Stefan said, offering up his hands in supplication. "You're right. It's not my place."

"What are you doing here?" Caslin asked. "With you, there's always a reason." Stefan nodded solemnly. If he was hurt by the slight he didn't let on.

"I wanted to speak to you—"

"Knew there would be something," Caslin replied, with more than a hint of malice. "About what?"

"It was about…" Stefan began, before looking away.

"About what?"

"I wanted to talk to you about Dad, that's all," Stefan said, shaking his head. "I'm a bit worried but… this probably isn't the time."

"Never a good time, Stefan. Never," Caslin said bitterly, nursing his scotch.

"Maybe I should just go."

"I think that'd be a good idea," Caslin replied, focussing on the drink in his hand.

"I'll find my own way out."

Caslin didn't look as Stefan passed out into the hallway. Instead he swallowed his drink in one fluid motion, immediately pouring another. He heard the door close and the latch click as it dropped into place. The noise of revellers in the street outside came to him, fading as they moved away. The darkness was descending and Caslin knew it. However, on this occasion, unlike many others in recent months, he chose not to fight it.

CHAPTER THIRTEEN

THE PERSISTENT RINGING of an alarm was irritating, no matter how much he tried to ignore it, it continued. Irritation turned to anger. The light from the window pierced his eyes as he awoke, shielding them with the back of his hand. The repeated pressing of his doorbell and muffled voices replaced the fading memories of Karen in the forefront of his mind.

"All right," he shouted, immediately regretting doing so. Standing up, his legs were stiff and his head pulsed with each movement. A glance at the bottle on the table, less than a finger remaining within, explained a great deal. "I'm coming!" he called out and the racket subsided. He unlocked the door and pulled it open, running a hand through his unkempt hair, still finding his bearings.

"About time, Sir," DS Hunter said, as he beckoned her in. She took stock of him. "What happened to you last night?"

Caslin exhaled heavily, "Make yourself useful and stick the kettle on, will you?"

Hunter was about to object but Caslin walked towards the bathroom, allowing the front door to swing closed on its own. Examining himself in the mirror, Caslin ignored the bruising that lined the left side of his face. Observing the dark rims beneath his eyes and stubble growth, he filled the basin with water. The shrieking floorboards of the hallway heralded Hunter's return from the kitchen, coming to stand the other side of the door.

"We'll have to make it coffee to go," she said aloud.

"Where are we going?" he asked, masking his face with foam, hissing as he touched a raw point of his face.

"We've found a body," Hunter said. Caslin stopped short of applying the razor. "We got a call around dawn, this morning."

"Where?"

"South of Thorganby, in the Derwent," Hunter said. "A local man was night fishing, didn't see her until daybreak."

Caslin paused, fearing the worst, "Anyone we know?"

Hunter didn't answer.

THE JOURNEY out to Thorganby took a half-hour and Caslin's head was still pounding when they pulled off Bonby Lane, parking on the verge. There were several uniform and CID cars already present. Greeted by John Inglis, he gave Caslin a withering look, inclining his head as he spoke.

"What on earth have you been up to?"

Caslin remained impassive, "Cut myself shaving."

Inglis glanced at Hunter who looked away. The DCI chose not to push the subject. They made the short walk across the wooded glade to the river's edge.

"It looks like she went in further up and got snagged in the bend, just over there." He indicated with a sweep of his arm. They both looked in that direction, towards a cluster of uniforms.

"Have you got her out yet?" Caslin asked.

Inglis shook his head, "We're letting the forensics team search the bank before we do that. There's no doubt that she's dead."

Caslin understood as soon as he reached the bank. The upper part of the body was clearly visible beneath the surface of the water. The current ebbed and flowed in such a way the extended hand appeared to be waving. The grey of the early morning sky, as well as a light breeze, added to the sense of foreboding. To the right, Caslin noted two special unit officers, donning their wetsuits to carry out the retrieval. From his vantage point, Caslin could make out that the body was evidently a female, Caucasian, with long dark hair.

As if reading his thoughts, Hunter said, "Do you think it's Natalie?"

He shrugged, "Well, if not then it's someone's daughter. I never hope to see anyone like this. Who found her, Guv?"

"Thomas Breckon," Inglis pointed out a man in the distance, dressed in waders and an all-weather coat, being spoken to by a colleague. "He was fishing at the turn. Apparently, it's a well-known spot for the local enthusiasts."

"Do we have any idea how she went in, witnesses or the like?"

"Not yet, no. Mr Breckon saw no-one else from the moment he arrived, last night around ten-thirty. We have teams scouring the riverbank, both upstream and down, looking for where she went in and any of her personal effects, handbag, clothing, that type of thing. She appears to be completely naked but we've found nothing, so far."

"Has Iain Robertson any idea how long she's been in the water?"

"Not without getting her out. That's going to be down to the pathologist to determine, I fear."

The divers entered the water. Caslin shuddered as he empathised with the thought of the cold water. In spite of their suits, the Derwent's temperature would still be a shock to the system. The speed of the flow and the depths at the nature reserve, a little further north, ensured the temperature remained fairly constant throughout the year. Caslin considered whether the girl died before she ended up in the water or whether hypothermia and drowning played a part.

Not able to take his eyes off the scene, he watched as she was released from the chains of nature that restricted her passage down river. Gently they brought her to the surface and back to the waiting team on the bank. Iain Robertson oversaw her removal from the water, his team clad in their forensic coveralls. Carried to the crest, they were able to get their first proper view of the victim. Her skin was pale with a tinge of blue, no doubt due to the cold, but a severe head injury was visible at the top of her right side. Her eyes were closed and she looked almost angelic, so serene was her expression. Once again, the likeness struck him and Caslin sighed in recognition. Inglis looked up from a kneeling position, at her side.

"Melissa Brooke," Caslin said evenly. "Been missing since Saturday morning."

"Well, she's not missing anymore," Inglis replied, standing up and coming alongside him. "She does look a lot like Natalie Bermond though, doesn't she?" Caslin nodded but made no comment.

"Can we link them?" Hunter asked, raising the prospect that was most likely on the mind of others present.

"Let's not get carried away," the DCI said. "After all, they may look similar and went missing within a few days of each other but that's all."

"Isn't that enough to consider it a possibility?" Hunter said.

Inglis met her eye, "Have you got anyone in the frame?"

Caslin spoke up, "We do, a local man. He's been in custody and we've searched his place but got nothing to link him directly to anything like this. He admits to being with her the night she disappeared but claims she left his place shortly after midnight."

"So, he was the last one to be seen with her?"

"Not what he says but we've been unable to corroborate his account, as yet."

"Dare I ask if there's a link to Natalie or the rest of the Bermonds?"

Caslin shrugged, "Nothing that we've come across. At the moment, I can barely even tie him to Melissa."

"Maybe you will now. Is it plausible? Tying him to two, I mean?"

Caslin shook his head, "He would have been a busy man if so."

"With an awful lot of front, too," Hunter added.

"I'll speak to Broadfoot but in the meantime, not a word, okay? The last thing we need is the press to tie the two together. We've got enough going on as it is."

They all accepted that on the face of it. However, since when did the press need encouragement? They were going to link the cases anyway, regardless of what they were told. He figured that was inevitable at this point.

"Whose case is Melissa Brooke?" Inglis asked.

"Mine," Caslin replied, "or it was. I have a DC still looking into it."

"Right, unless the DCS says otherwise, you can get on it," Inglis said, methodically working through his thought process. "Do what you have to, to rule him in or out. If you find anything to link them, fine, we'll bring the full resource to bear. Until then, the rest of the team stays focussed on the Bermond kidnapping. Fair enough?"

"Fair enough." Caslin looked down at Melissa. He noted numerous scratches across her arms, legs and upper body. They were deep, having brought blood to the surface of the affected area in several places. He watched her being zipped up in a bag for transport. His thoughts passed to Peter Summerbee. Skipwith was only a couple of miles south west of their location, as the crow flew, with not very much in between apart from farmland. Easily a journey that he could've made without being seen, in the dead of night. The forthcoming visit to see Suzanne Brooke reared up in his mind. The need to do so saddened him greatly. Despite her insistence that they find her daughter, Caslin thought that Suzanne already feared the worst. That came as no consolation to him nor would it to her. His headache was gone, along with all physical symptoms of the rigours of the previous night, to be replaced by a burning focus.

"We'll want answers on this one fast," Hunter said, joining him as they walked away from the others.

"Aye," Caslin agreed, scanning the immediate area. There was nothing to see. A small farm stood in the distance on the far side of the river and the odd sound further afield in Thorganby, carried on the breeze. "Call pathology and instil a sense of urgency in them. We need to know cause and time of death as soon as possible. Let's get some meat on the timeline following her 999 call on Friday night."

"Yes, Sir," Hunter replied, taking out her mobile. Caslin stopped and took in the scene once more. An early morning mist hung across the fields, soon to be stripped away by the sun, burning away the cloud cover. This was no place for a young woman to meet her end.

"And while I think about it," Caslin added, "speak to Terry Holt and find out if Anton Durakovic has any link to Peter Summerbee, business or otherwise."

"Sir?"

Caslin didn't respond but walked away from her to be alone with his thoughts. He replayed what Lisa had said to him only the day before. Melissa may well have thought her leverage enough to permanently get her off the game but instead, it could just have got her killed.

A whistle from behind him drew his attention. Turning, he saw DCI Inglis beckoning him over. Hunter fell into step and they reached him together.

"Come with me," Inglis said, his expression was stern.

"Where to, Guv?" Hunter asked.

"Upstream. The dog handler has something."

"Clothing?" Caslin asked but the DCI shook his head.

"Another body," Inglis paused, "or I should say, part of another body."

FOUR HUNDRED YARDS UPSTREAM, just inside the nature reserve of the Lower Derwent Valley, the dog handler made the discovery. What initially looked like a piece of dirty clothing turned out to be much more. Two forensics officers were laying out markers, preparing to catalogue the scene, while another set up her camera for the shots. Iain Robertson carefully lifted the edge of the material, a hessian sack dumped in a mass of brush in an open clearing. Caslin took in the remains. Impossible to tell which part of the body he was looking at, he figured it to be part of an upper torso. There was a tattoo visible in one patch of discoloured flesh. Perhaps a hand span in width, it was black, and depicted some kind of Gaelic symbol.

"How long do you think it's been here?" Caslin asked.

Robertson thought on it. A precise man, he was never keen to offer impromptu theories, "I would envisage six months but treat that with caution. These parts of the valley hold a lot of water, even in the summertime, and the type of soil might slow degeneration somewhat. I'll narrow it down once the pathologist has a look."

"Where's the rest of it?" Caslin asked. Unable to ascertain if this was a male or female, from what they had, he was generic in his description.

"We have another sack over there." Robertson pointed to a location twenty yards away, closer to the river where an officer was taping off an area. "Looks like parts of a leg."

"Parts?" Caslin voiced openly. He glanced up from the grisly contents of the sack and eyed the teams scouring their immediate location. At that point a shout went up nearby with yet another discovery. "Bloody hell," Caslin muttered under his breath. "What on earth have we stumbled onto?"

THE NATURE RESERVE was located east of York, within the triangle of Wheldrake, Storwood and East Cottingwith. Here the River Derwent flowed by on the west side, with the Pocklington Canal and The Beck joining from the east. Sandwiched between them was the reserve, made up of a mixture of scrubland and a large expanse of wetland. With the exception of a few working farms, to the east and the south, there was nothing else in the vicinity. Although Caslin could see that there were precious few vehicular access points, it was easy to envisage someone slipping in unobserved to deposit the remains.

"Widen the search area," Caslin said as Inglis came to stand with him. "We need it picked clean. If there's a crisp packet lying around, I want it examined."

"Agreed," Inglis said, turning to Robertson. "If you need more bodies, I'll make sure you get them. There are limited access points to this area and this guy didn't hike out with these sacks, so maybe we'll get lucky." Spotting the look on Caslin's face, Inglis raised his eyebrows in a questioning manner.

"Just thinking, Guv," Caslin said softly, "just thinking."

The opportunity for further conversation was broken by Caslin's phone ringing. Taking it from his pocket he saw the number was withheld. He walked away from the others and hit the answer tab.

"Caslin."

"Good morning, Inspector. It's Jimmy Sullivan."

Caslin's heart sank and he blew out his cheeks. The last thing he needed was to be fielding enquiries from one of the most annoying journalists in Yorkshire. "Morning, James. What can I do for you? Bearing in mind how busy I am, I'll warn you, it won't be much."

"I think you can drop whatever it is you've got on, for this."

Caslin was curious but sceptical. After all, it was Sullivan, "What do you want from me, Jimmy?"

"For once, perhaps it's what I can do for you. You'll not believe what landed on my desk this morning."

FORTY MINUTES LATER, Caslin and John Inglis had made their way into the city centre and were now standing beside Sullivan's desk. Once freelance, the journalist got a break in a major case involving Caslin, a break that cemented his return to contracted employment. A position at *The Post* was hardly the leading daily red top, where Sullivan had made his name but regardless, it was a decent role and a second chance.

"Who would have thought this for a turn of events, eh?" Sullivan said with a smile. Caslin knew the hack was loving this.

Caslin gently wiped the side of the desk with his shoe, smearing mud from the reserve on to it and wiping his foot on the carpet tiles to get rid of the remainder. He took a modicum of pleasure in the act. Sullivan noticed and shook his head. "Come on, Jimmy," Caslin said, "we've not got all day."

Sullivan reached into the top drawer of his pedestal and retrieved a brown envelope. Placing it on his desk, he indicated it with a nod. Caslin donned a pair of latex gloves and picked it up. The flap had not been sealed and he gently eased out the contents, a Polaroid snapshot of a young woman, easily identifiable as Natalie Bermond. The light where the picture was taken was evidently poor and the background was a plain blockwork wall, without detail. Natalie was visible, sitting with two hands holding up a copy of *The Post* to camera. Her expression was fearful, haunted even, with wide eyes that appeared to be pleading for help. Raising the picture closer, both Caslin and Inglis peered at the newspaper she held.

"Yesterday, September 16th," Sullivan offered in an attempt to spare their eyesight.

"You're sure?" Inglis asked.

"The lead story is our probe into dodgy spread betting at the racecourse," Sullivan offered. "Unmistakable. The runaway granddaughter of a local MP wasn't holding readers' attention."

"Well, that's proof of life," Inglis said, catching Caslin's reaction too late.

"Proof of life, eh?" Sullivan said aloud. "So, the missing has become the kidnapped, *getting juicy*. Have you spoken to him… or is it them?"

Caslin ignored the question, flipping the photo over and reading the handwriting on the reverse, whilst Inglis flapped at a response to Sullivan. The message simply read, *"30K be ready for the call"*. Inglis was still attempting to nullify the journalist when Caslin butted in.

"Who's had hold of this, Jimmy?"

Sullivan thought for a moment, "Me, my duty editor and… only those working in the mail room, this morning."

Caslin examined the envelope again. There was no postmark, "Hand delivered?"

Sullivan nodded, "I guess so, yeah. Are you going to tell me what's going on? I told my editor the other day, you lot were onto something big—"

"How would you know that?"

Sullivan shrugged, flashing him a half-smile. The DCI had never run across Sullivan before.

"Don't worry, Guv," Caslin said. "You have to spend at least fifteen minutes in Jimmy's company, in order to fully depreciate him."

Sullivan laughed, "That's harsh, Inspector. Very harsh indeed."

"Not a word of this leaves your building, Jimmy," Caslin said firmly.

"Now hold on a—"

"Not a word. Get your editor on the phone. We're going to need to have a little chat. While you're at it, you can chase up the mailroom staff and any CCTV footage of your post box."

Sullivan sat back in his chair, exhaling heavily and fixing Caslin with a stare. He knew not to mess about when Caslin used that tone. "You don't want much, do you?" he said, lifting the receiver.

CHAPTER FOURTEEN

"SHE WAS STILL alive when she went into the water."

"You're certain?"

"The volume of water in her lungs is categorical," Dr Taylor said. "Cause of death is drowning and definitely in the river, samples of which were taken and match up."

"What can you tell me about the head wound?" Caslin asked, moving to get a better view. Dr Alison Taylor had carried out the post mortem the same day she received the body, following Melissa's identification by her mother.

"That was a significant blow to the side of the head. It caused a massive depressed skull fracture and subsequent intraparenchymal haemorrhaging," she looked up, interpreting Caslin's expression. "A bleed on the brain that proves fatal in over forty percent of cases."

"Would she have been conscious?"

"After the blow?" Dr Taylor said.

Caslin nodded. "Highly unlikely. My guess would be she was struck down and either fell, or was thrown, into the river. Death followed soon after."

"How can you be sure?"

"Volume of blood in her system, the heart must have stopped pumping shortly after the injury."

"What caused it, in your opinion?"

"A large object of irregular shape and somewhat weighty. There were no splinters or elements of rust in the wound which could indicate if it was a timber or metal object. However, it is possible that the pressure of the river's current may have cleaned the wound, washing them away."

"What about these other injuries?" Caslin asked, pointing to the deep scratches he observed when Melissa was pulled from the water.

"They're fingernail abrasions. You can tell by the curved nature of the scratches, wide at the start and narrow at the end. Very unusual, I must say."

"How so?"

"Their locations," Dr Taylor said. Pointing at various parts of Melissa's body, she continued, "In sexual assault cases, we expect to find these wounds on areas where the assailant traditionally attacks. Notably these are the breasts, genitals, inside of the thighs and the anal region. Now we do have some signs of that in this instance but also to the shoulders, waistline, forearms and legs. I must admit I haven't seen the like of it before. Not in such volume, anyway. They were recent though. The blood and lymphs hadn't the time to dry, indicating they were very fresh indeed."

"How long ago?"

"These injuries form bright red scabs when they dry, which are slightly raised, within a twelve to twenty-four-hour period. The process hadn't occurred so they were definitely ante mortem and therefore very recent. All of which helps me to set a time of death, which I estimate to be five days ago."

"That puts her in the water sometime early Saturday, of this past weekend?"

"I agree," said Dr Taylor. "I'll be able to be more specific once my test results come back."

Caslin considered that for a moment, "Any other signs of sexual assault?"

Dr Taylor appeared thoughtful, retrieving her notes from a table, off to the side. "I'm not convinced that she was sexually assaulted, although some signs point in that direction. She'd recently had intercourse but there is none of the usual trauma one would expect in a violent assault. No tears or vaginal abrasions, for instance."

"Perhaps the violence came later?" Caslin suggested.

"Possibly," Dr Taylor conceded. "With that said, can you see these shallow bruises?" She leaned in and directed Caslin to two areas, one at the top of the inner left thigh and another, below the hip on the right. "They are caused by underwear being forcibly removed, usually torn off, rather than taken. Have you found her underwear?"

Caslin shook his head, "Not yet, still searching."

"Well, expect the fabric to show signs of damage," she frowned. "So, you see my dilemma. The bruising indicates force whereas the internals show nothing of the sort."

"Anything useful from underneath her fingernails, signs of defensive wounds or dare I ask, semen samples?"

Dr Taylor smiled at him, it was a knowing smile, "The water has cleaned away most forensic evidence, as I'm sure you well know but..."

"*But*," Caslin said, returning her smile.

"But I was able to retrieve some scrapings from under the nails. I've sent them to the lab already. You'll have to chase Leeds for the results. As for defensive wounds, no, I've not found any. All adds to the confused picture, doesn't it? I found this interesting," she said, indicating Melissa's feet, heavily ingrained with dirt on the sides and to the soles. These too, had many scratches but were clearly different to those on the rest of her body. "She was moving barefoot across rough, muddy ground. Evidently, she wasn't used to doing so, the skin has considerable damage. I doubt she was too careful about where she put her feet."

"Maybe she didn't have a choice," Caslin replied thoughtfully. "Have you got anywhere with the other body?"

Dr Taylor indicated for him to follow her. Together, they walked to the other end of her pathology lab.

"I've only managed the preliminaries, so far. Therefore, I can't give you very much, except that you have a further two victims."

"Two? Are you certain?"

Dr Taylor nodded enthusiastically, "Oh absolutely, yes. Unless you've come across a woman with two left legs before, I haven't. I would estimate that I have barely half the remains in their entirety. Your searches are still going on at the scene?"

"Yes, of course," Caslin replied. This case was turning more sinister by the hour. The forensic team at the scene had thus far produced four hessian sacks, the contents of each varying in size and degradation. "What else do you have? Anything we can use to identify them?"

"That will prove difficult. I don't have hands or feet and nor do I have a head, for either of them. I can tell you they are definitely female, that's clear from basic examination of the pelvic area, although the genitals have been removed—"

"Removed? What, surgically?"

"Nothing as precise, I'm afraid but bone structure doesn't lie. I would estimate their age range, with a reasonable degree of accuracy, between twenty-five and thirty-five."

"Too early for cause of death, I know but any idea how long they've been out there?"

"I'll need to run a battery of tests to be sure but my best guess would be around six to nine months. As for cause of death, with what we have, it would be pure conjecture at this point. You might get a DNA hit from the database but if not, without more to work with, I'll tell you now, it will be nigh on impossible to identify them."

"Are you able to determine whether they were killed at the reserve or merely dumped there?"

"I would say they were dumped. There's little or no mud or foliage present on the bodies which you would expect if they had been butchered at the scene. I choose that term particularly carefully. The mutilation is severe but has been done with reasonable precision, not in a frenzied manner. I think they died elsewhere and were then dumped."

Caslin's mind went into overdrive. Their initial search hadn't turned up any more remains. Presumably the rest would be held in other sacks but if they had been thrown into the river, or dumped in another location, finding them may prove difficult. Each of those already retrieved had been secured with cable ties, leaving the contents with no opportunity to spill. The missing heads, hands and feet were both intriguing and macabre, at the same time. Was it a case of concealing the identity of the victims or were they merely awaiting discovery? Another thought that came to him was the least palatable, that they were grisly souvenirs, trophies retained by the killer.

"I don't mean to be pushy, Alison," Caslin began, "but when do you think you'll be able to tell me more?"

Dr Taylor thought about it for a moment, "Tomorrow evening," she said confidently. "Perhaps over dinner?"

Caslin's eyes flicked up, meeting hers, unsure if he heard correctly. "Dinner?"

"Unless you already have plans, or can't spare the time," she said, flushing.

"No, no, not at all," Caslin stammered. "Everyone has to eat. Dinner sounds great."

"Good," Dr Taylor replied. "I'll get us a table. How about seven-thirty, at Domenicos?"

"Sounds great," Caslin said, immediately noting the repetition and clenching his eyes shut with that realisation.

"I'll book it."

CASLIN LEFT the mortuary with more than case facts spinning through his head. Despite the horrendous details he had just seen and heard, he was upbeat and he knew why. The previous year he had surreptitiously tried to engineer a date with Alison Taylor, almost succeeding, until a case got in the way. Believing the opportunity to be long since passed, he consigned her to the file of *might-have-beens*, perhaps doing so too early. The timing was little better on this occasion but he would find a way.

His phone rang as he made his way down the steps outside, it was Terry Holt.

"Sir, I've got nothing to link Summerbee with Durakovic and his business is clean. I thought I'd take a look at these previous cases he was involved with, maybe run down the witnesses and associates, see what turns up. Maybe somebody will remember something they didn't mention before?"

"Good idea, Terry," Caslin said. "This guy knows how to play and you only learn that through experience. If you haven't found a link, then it follows that he's hiding it pretty well. I also want you to check with Vice to see if there are any other prostitutes that have gone missing in the last six to nine months, particularly if they worked for, or were associated with, Anton Durakovic. How did you get on with Handanovic?"

"No hits, Sir," Holt replied. Caslin wasn't shocked by that. "He's not known to us. I can't find any record of him anywhere."

"Get back to me when you have something."

Caslin hung up. Finding no link between the two didn't mean there wasn't one. He realised he could be wrong about Summerbee but Caslin wasn't prepared to scrub him off the list just yet. There was no doubt in his mind that this man was concealing something and he planned to find out what. He went to put his phone away but changed his mind, calling DS Hunter instead. She answered quickly.

"What's going on with the Bermonds, any news?" he asked.

"Tim's arranged the money with the bank. They'll transfer it into Natalie's account via BACS, overnight. We're all set for a call, this end. Catherine and Tim are nervous but that's understandable. It's edged with some relief after seeing her photo."

"Any word from Tech on Natalie's laptop?"

"Sorry, Sir. What with everything, I haven't had time to check in with them. I'll get on to it."

Caslin asked to be kept informed and hung up, setting off into the city centre. The feeling returned – this kidnapping wasn't all that it was supposed to be. Everyone was hoping that the money transfer would signal a communication as to Natalie's whereabouts but Caslin's instincts told him that wouldn't happen. There was more to this than they were aware of. However, currently Caslin felt blindfolded, waiting on another to instigate the next phase of the operation. Stuart Nicol hadn't turned up yet and a man of his profile never stayed in the shadows for long. Caslin couldn't help but wonder why he had dropped off the radar. The CCTV footage obtained from outside the newspaper offices offered little. A figure, whose features were so obscured by dark clothing and a balaclava, that Caslin couldn't tell whether it was a man or a woman. The envelope and photo had been sent to forensics for processing, a lingering hope of DNA or a fingerprint, all that Caslin had to cling to.

Returning his thoughts to Melissa Brooke, he pondered the inconsistencies within the evidence. If Alison Taylor was right, in that the others were dumped there after being dismembered, then why would a killer change his modus operandi for Melissa? Killers were inherently ritualistic in how they went about things and rarely deviated from successful routines. Statistically that was the case anyway. However, there would always be exceptions and those were the hardest killers to track. Images of Melissa running through the brush, pursued by her assailant in the darkness, came to mind. He couldn't help but empathise with the fear she must have experienced. Had she fought for her life? Had she fled, only to be caught and killed?

Whether or not she had fallen into the water or been thrown, was another angle that he contemplated. Falling would have carried her away from the killer, thereby robbing him of the opportunity to dismember her in the same fashion as the others. Whereas, had she fled from him, or perhaps wounded him in some way, he may have been unable, or unwilling to carry out his usual procedure. An apparent knowledge of forensic practices of identification could have led him to throw her into the water, knowing that this would destroy the majority of evidence. If the latter was the case, then he was forensically aware. This would signify there was an intelligent killer out there, someone well versed in police procedure. One thing was certain, if he had killed several times, then he would almost certainly kill again. Caslin had to get to him before he sought to satisfy that hunger once more.

The hum of the traffic almost drowned out the sound of his ringing phone. Scrabbling around in his pocket, he managed to answer it before the voicemail kicked in.

"Hi Nate," an upbeat and familiar voice said. "I thought you could do with a pick me up."

Caslin smiled, "Hello Sara. How's London? Surviving without me?"

"Wouldn't have a clue," she replied. "I'm in York."

Caslin was momentarily thrown, "York... what are you doing in... here?"

"I'm on holiday. That is allowed, you know. You always told me how great it is up here so I thought I'd venture north."

"Really? I thought they never let you out of the cavern."

Sara laughed then, "True, they usually don't. Seeing the sun was a shock to the system, I can tell you."

Caslin took on a more settled tone, "How long are you here for?"

"A few days, a week, I'm not sure yet. See how it goes. Meet me for a drink?"

"Yes, of course. Things are a bit manic here—"

"I know. That's why I said *a drink*. This is your patch where shall we go?"

There was only one place where Caslin felt genuinely comfortable, "Lendal Cellars, around seven?"

"What's wrong with now?"

"I'm on duty."

"You sound like you're in town."

"I am."

"Well then?" Sara persisted. Caslin checked the time. It was pushing midday.

"I can be there in about fifteen minutes. We can call it an early lunch."

"Excellent," Sara replied. "And you're buying."

The call ended and Caslin realised he had stopped walking, much to the frustration of other pedestrians, now forced to negotiate the narrow space around him. He hadn't seen that call coming.

THE CELLARS WERE QUIET. No doubt trade would be picking up over the coming hour but for now, the vaulted, brick-lined lower seating area was theirs alone. The bright sunshine and warmth outside rapidly faded from memory as they read the menu. They were sitting well below ground level and the slight smell of damp appeared at odds with the social setting. Sara was seated opposite him, in a booth halfway along the length of the section. The recessed lighting illuminated them in a way that softened her angular features. He hadn't seen her in nearly two years and found her company strangely electrifying. Once before, that had been the case but now he figured it all over and done with.

"This place kind of suits you," Sara said, glancing around.

Caslin eyed her to see if she was mocking him somehow. She noticed. "It has a real character. It's charming in a way, stylish and yet dark and brooding."

Caslin laughed, "No-one has ever called me stylish."

"Well, I didn't say it was exact."

"Thank you very much," Caslin replied, smiling. Sara fixed him with a gaze, a stern expression appearing on her face. His smile dropped, "What is it, Sara?"

"You," she replied flatly. "You look like shit, Nate. In all seriousness, what's going on with you?"

Caslin sat back in his seat, exhaling heavily as he did so, "I could say the rigours of the job but you wouldn't buy that, would you?" She shook her head. In contrast to himself, Sara was looking radiant. Her hair was cut shorter than he remembered and probably a different colour, recollecting her more as a blonde but he chose not to mention it, just in case he was wrong. To be fair, she was ten years his junior, in that sweet spot of life where age enhances, rather than detracts from your appearance. Approaching forty, Caslin should still be able to say the same but he was the first to admit he wasn't taking care of himself. "Just going through a patch, you know how it is?"

"How long has it been?"

He laughed, nursing his pint, "Couple of years."

"How did it go with Karen?"

Caslin picked up a slight change in tone at the mention of the name. He shrugged.

"That's all done."

"I'm sorry," she said. He looked at her and could see she meant it. "I feel partly to blame for all that."

"You shouldn't," Caslin implored her, shaking his head. "You shouldn't. We were in trouble before you and I... long before our thing."

"Our *thing*?" Sara said with a crooked smile.

Caslin laughed, "Our whatever. It was hardly a relationship... fling... I don't know."

She reached across, placing a reassuring hand on his forearm, "I'm kidding. Karen blamed me though, didn't she?"

Caslin sipped from his glass, "Karen needed someone to blame. It wasn't enough just to blame me but..." he paused, arranging his thoughts, "you were a symptom, not the cause. I was the one looking outside the marriage, so ultimately it was my fault." He fell silent, finishing his drink.

"I'll order the food," Sara said, standing up. Moving off, she stopped and turned to him, "You could've called, you know."

He met her eye and nodded, "I know."

She resumed her course to the bar, Caslin watching her until she disappeared from view, mounting the steps to the next level. He hadn't told Sara that he and Karen had tried again the previous year after Caslin's shooting. Karen had halted the divorce proceedings. Was it through guilt that saw her do that or the very real thought of nearly losing him? He would never know the answer. Whatever the reasoning, it didn't matter. All was said and done. Shaking off the melancholy as Sara returned, he forced a big smile.

"So, what are your plans while you're in town?" he asked, sneering as a glass of coke was put down in front of him.

"You're still on duty, remember?" she said. "However, I did order you the Gourmet Burger. It comes with all the trimmings, including beer-battered bacon, if you can believe that? So, it's not a total washout."

"The heart stopper," Caslin said with a smile. "Nice. Plans?"

Sara retook her seat, shrugging off the question, "See how it goes. I was due the annual leave and couldn't think of anywhere I particularly fancied going. Then I thought of you and ended up here."

"I'm honoured."

"Don't be," Sara laughed. "I went out to Croatia, last year. This time I thought I would try the UK for a change. So, tell me about this case you're on?"

"Did you have one in mind?" Caslin countered.

"I saw you on the telly, when was it, Monday night? You were in the background when the news crew were interviewing your DCS about the Bermond girl."

"Eagle-eyed, Sara."

"Attention to detail is my business."

Now Caslin laughed, "Speaking of which, how is life at the Agency?"

"I would love to say it's all spooks, terror plots and non-stop action but in all honesty, it's mostly crunching data. Exciting stuff," Sara said with a flick of her eyebrows. "Unlike you and yours."

"What do you mean by that?" Caslin asked.

"You're like a magnet to big cases," she argued. "Or is that you can't leave anything alone and they grow arms and legs?"

Caslin smiled, "Aye, right enough there."

The conversation paused as the barman arrived with their food. They chatted as they ate and for the first time in months, he felt like life extended beyond the folders on his desk at Fulford Road. Time flew by and Caslin forced himself to head back to the station shortly before two o'clock, only after promising to meet Sara again later for a drink. He was already looking forward to it when they said their goodbyes.

CHAPTER FIFTEEN

"WHAT IS it you're getting at?" Caslin asked, throwing another couple of mints into his mouth. He was barely back at Fulford before Hunter accosted him en route to his office. Hunter, now standing in the doorway to his office, looked over her shoulder to check that no-one else was within earshot before she continued.

"This has been bothering me right from the start. Bearing in mind how we found the scene, not to mention her boyfriend's list of accolades, do you think we should consider a possible alternative to this being a kidnapping?"

"Such as?"

"Well, take a look at this," Hunter said, coming inside and passing him a clutch of papers. She closed the door to the office, raising an eyebrow from Caslin. He put the file down, a review of Robertson's initial findings from the nature reserve. Turning his attention to what Hunter gave him, they appeared to be a collection of essays. "They're printouts from Natalie's blog. I've not been through everything, yet but I've highlighted some interesting passages."

Caslin began flicking through, stopping at the specific sections she had indicated. The language struck him as intense. The first few highlighted words read "the truth never remains hidden" and "think on your sins". A little further, Natalie had written "retribution and vengeance are fair and just" and described how "the suffering will come from my hand". Under normal circumstances, Caslin would consider this the ramblings of an evangelical, taking the teachings of The Old Testament too literally.

"Is Natalie religious?" he asked.

"If she is, what the hell is she doing with Nicol?" Hunter said. "Her blog is obsessed with lies and deception. She's posted rants on subjects ranging from breach of trust, to lying and secrecy. It's always focussed on intimate relationships, not your conspiracy theorists and their *New World Order* nonsense. I would put money on it that she's talking about her mother. She writes under a pseudonym but it's definitely Natalie."

"I fear I know where you're going with this."

"What if it's not a kidnap? What if—"

"She's involved," Caslin finished. He sank back into his chair, allowing the thought to gestate. "Extortion rather than kidnap? You'll need more than—"

"How about the blackmail from last year?" Hunter offered, pointing back to the papers in Caslin's hand. He began wading through again, slowing as he neared the end. They were transcripts by the look of them. "MSN Messenger conversations," Hunter offered.

"What's that then?"

"It's software," Hunter explained. "Similar to text messaging but done over the computer. Copies of the dialogue are automatically saved in a folder, also logging date and time, unless you instruct the program otherwise."

"Discussing the blackmail?"

"Orchestrating it," Hunter confirmed. "We don't know who she was talking to. I've left it with Tech to find out. They said they'll prioritise it and get back to me."

"Cheeky little bitch," Caslin said under his breath. "Is there any venom directed at Tim?"

"Not so as I can see. Why do you ask?"

"It's one thing to put your mother through the mangle but another to do it to both parents. Unless of course, we're missing something."

"I know it's a bit of a leap but what if there's a different twist?"

Caslin looked up, "Go on."

"What if someone found out what she had done, within the family, I mean?"

Caslin didn't want to consider that. His head was already spinning. Remembering how fast Tim got to the scene the day Natalie disappeared, he shuddered. How well did he really know this man? A person could change a great deal over the course of three decades. He realised Hunter was waiting patiently for him to say something.

"Let's step up our search for Stuart Nicol. If Natalie carried out the blackmailing of her mother, he fits the bill as a likely accomplice. You said it yourself, kidnapping would be a massive step up for Nicol but extortion would come as second nature."

"What about Inglis and the DCS?" Hunter asked.

"You've not mentioned this to either of them?"

Hunter shook her head, "They're in a meeting with the chief constable."

Caslin thought about it, "Keep it between us for now. Put the word out that Nicol is a priority but nothing more. We don't want a suggestion like this to surface without a thorough check and we both know this station leaks like a sieve. We'll sit on it until I get a chance to speak with Inglis."

Hunter excused herself and Caslin was left alone with his thoughts. Tim's insistence on his father's complicity took on a new light as he mulled things over. Did he know that Sebastian was involved in dealings that could lead to his granddaughter's kidnapping? Or was this whole case merely a charade, masking

Tim's reaction to discovering the two women in his life were not what he believed them to be? The more he thought about it, the greater his desire to locate Stuart Nicol increased. The boyfriend could direct him away from those theories or, a growing fear, land him at the Bermond's door.

Thoughts turned to the unexpected arrival of Sara. He wasn't so naïve to believe she was in York on a sightseeing holiday. Their romance had been a whirlwind of a three-month affair, one that he regarded fondly, in his memory. Often, he felt their time together had been the right match at the wrong time. He found her company so easy. Never did he feel that he had to mind what he said or think about his actions. Caslin could be himself around her, for she liked him for who he genuinely was. Not even Karen, his wife of eleven years, could lay claim to that. With that said, could he envisage them together once again? The barrier to that scenario was always his wife and children but no longer. So why did he have reservations? Pushing the questions from his mind, he got up from his desk and went in search of a coffee.

Returning ten minutes later, steaming cup in hand, Caslin found DCS Broadfoot and John Inglis waiting in his office. Broadfoot was sitting in his chair flicking through the transcripts he'd left on his desk.

"I thought you were focussing on the prostitution murder?" Broadfoot said, with no hint of accusation.

"I am, Sir. This has just come to light after Tech processed Natalie Bermond's laptop," Caslin replied, directing a reassuring glance at Inglis. The latter appeared slightly put out to have not been made aware of this earlier. "A quarter of an hour ago, tops."

"This adds to our problems," Broadfoot said absently. Caslin detected something in his tone.

"Sir?" he enquired, reading an expression of frustration on Inglis' face at the same time.

"There's significant pressure being applied, Nathaniel."

"By whom, Sir? The chief constable?"

"We all have our masters, even the chief constable," Broadfoot replied noncommittally. "They're not pleased at the lack of progress in the Bermond kidnapping. They want us to consider handing it over to the National Crime Agency."

"No way!" Caslin was emphatic. Although he immediately recognised that was a call far beyond his pay grade. "They can't do any more than we already have."

"I know that," Broadfoot retorted, breaking his usual calmness with an uncharacteristic snarl. "But when it starts getting political, people move chairs around, regardless of whether you're sitting on them."

"Are we losing it?" Caslin asked, resigned to the answer.

"If we don't see movement within the next twenty-four to thirty-six hours, yes," Inglis said solemnly. "Until we saw this," he pointed at the papers on Caslin's desk, "we didn't have anything to go on, unless the kidnapper made a move for the money. You would agree that it might turn out to not even *be* a kidnapping?"

"That was our consideration also, Sir. Still no word at the Bermond's or movement at the bank?" Caslin asked for confirmation. Inglis shook his head. "Whether it's a kidnapping or not, they could be putting as much distance between them and us as possible before accessing the funds. We assume they'll draw small amounts at a time but maybe they want to hit the account with one large transfer."

"If that's the case, they'll be in for a shock," Inglis said. "The bank will delay any such attempt and we'll track them to source, even if they're abroad. We were prepared for that but thought it unlikely. However, this brings an altogether different perspective to the situation. The big question now is whether Natalie is in on it, or not?"

"We'll find out in due course," Caslin offered. He remained angry at top level interference in the case. Left alone to do their job, he was certain they'd get a result but tinkering from above only clouded the issue, diverting much needed focus away from the investigation. Broadfoot and Inglis left together, Caslin remaining behind. He saw Hunter wait until the senior officers had departed the squad room before getting up from her desk and coming towards his office. She lightly rapped her knuckles on the door frame, indicating over her shoulder with a nod of the head.

"That looked pretty heavy," she said inquisitively. "Anything I need to know about?"

Caslin fixed her with his gaze, "Put it this way, if you want to make DI anytime soon, we need some progress on the Bermond case?"

"Understood," Hunter replied. She lingered in the doorway, hesitant in her demeanour.

"Something else?" he asked.

"You probably don't want any more bad news but…"

"Okay, what is it?"

"Word is that there will be a march in the city centre tonight."

"A march?" Caslin frowned. "By whom?"

"Organised by an equality action group," Hunter said. "Protesting about our focus on the middle class white girl and calling for the same response for Melissa. I just heard Suzanne Brooke interviewed on the radio. She'll be at the forefront."

"Oh, for crying out…" he muttered, allowing the comment to tail off. "What's the good news?"

Hunter pursed her lips before answering, "Sorry."

"Great, there isn't any," Caslin said, putting his head in his hands and massaging his temples.

"Thought you should know," Hunter said, walking away.

***

THE FRUSTRATION of the afternoon was displaced momentarily by meeting up with Sara for dinner, at her hotel. Once again, she lifted him with a simple smile, although the double scotch may have assisted.

"Don't worry, I know full well what it's like when it rains down from above," Sara said after he had recounted an abridged version of the earlier conversation. "Not a great deal you can do about it, though."

Caslin hissed as he ordered them another drink from the bar, "It pisses me off. I hate being told what to do."

"Better get promoted then," Sara said playfully.

"Tried that," Caslin replied with a smile. "It didn't work out too well. And you always have a boss, no matter how high you go."

"Let's finish these and head into town," Sara said, draining her glass as soon as it was put before her. Caslin raised his eyebrows in surprise and glanced at the clock on the wall. It read 6:45.

"It'll be one hell of a night at that rate," he said sternly.

Sara shot him a devious smile, "Won't it just." She stood up and inclined her head, indicating for him to get a move on. With a shake of his own, he slid the scotch down his throat, replacing the glass on the bar. Sara hooked her arm through his and they made their way out through the lobby. "It's still warm, why not take me for a walk through the old town," she said. "Show me what York is all about."

Caslin frowned, "I think you've been reading too many of those tourist leaflets. You'll have us on a ghost tour next."

"There are ghost tours? Fantastic! That can go on the list."

"Behave yourself," Caslin said, smiling.

The hotel was right in the heart of the city and they were picking their way through the cobbled streets of The Shambles within minutes. Sara seemed genuinely interested in the collection of Tudor façades, often leaning at preposterous angles, as well as the mixture of artisan shop fronts, displaying their quirky merchandise. For his part, Caslin felt lightheaded. Despite his resilience to the effects of alcohol, built up through years of binging, he was struggling these days and he knew why. His doctor's appointment was still days away and he knew he would be in trouble before that. Perhaps his alcohol intake would soften the fall but he doubted it.

Reaching the end of the narrow street they were caught up in a press of people, far more than would usually be found on Low Petergate at this time of day. It took him a moment before Caslin realised this was the protest march. It wasn't the rabble-rousing scene he'd envisaged. Quite reserved. The group, consisted of both men and women. Even children were present, some walking alongside their parents with others in pushchairs. Caslin pulled Sara to the side and they watched as the marchers made their way towards the Minster. Many carried placards or unfurled banners, held by small groups but all bore the same message, that all women were equal, whatever their background. It appeared as if they had been requested to dress in white, for the vast majority had turned up sporting that colour. Caslin wondered if it was to signify the innocence of the victim, Melissa Brooke. A play on the prejudices often held against those in the sex trade. The thought crossed his mind how times had changed. Twenty years ago, public opinion would have viewed Melissa's death as largely of her own causing, stopping marginally short of outright blame.

"What are they protesting against exactly?" Sara asked in a hushed tone, fearful that she would be overheard.

"Me," Caslin replied softly. Sara glanced at him but he didn't elaborate. "Come on. Let's get another drink."

***

Whatever it was outside that woke Caslin, it had passed by the time he realised where he was. He could still feel the alcohol , despite a few hours' sleep. There was little cloud cover and he spied the moon illuminating the street outside. Unsure of the time, he looked for a clock at the bedside but there wasn't one.

Believing his phone to be in his jacket and not knowing where that was, he slipped from between the sheets. Sara didn't flinch as he tiptoed past her side of the bed, clearly grateful for the full moon, so he could avoid the pitfalls of an unfamiliar room in the dark. Gathering up his clothes, he slipped into the bathroom.

His phone had logged several missed calls, all from Hunter. Caslin silently cursed. Turning out the light, he crept back into the bedroom. Sara hadn't stirred and he paused, taking in her still form as she slept. An occasional flash of green light blinked in the corner of his eye. Glancing over, he saw it came from beneath some clothing on a chair. Moving over, Caslin eased the laptop out as quickly as he dared, casting his eye briefly in the direction of the bed as he did so. Lifting the screen, he saw it was in hibernation and swiped the glidepad, bringing it back into life. The hard drive firing up seemed excessively loud in the dead of night and he momentarily regretted the decision as movement under the sheets suggested he was about to be rumbled. The screen flickered, changing from matt black to a password request and Caslin exhaled heavily. Although not surprised, he was disappointed. Slowly, he eased the screen back down and replaced the machine where he had found it. Casting his mind back to Natalie's dorm, he wondered if he could recreate Lottie's trick with the password request but thought better of it.

With a final, fleeting look towards Sara, Caslin made his way over to the door and teased it open. Ensuring that the self close mechanism didn't slam it shut behind him, he found himself in the brightly lit corridor of the hotel. Wondering what on earth had made him think his actions that night were a good idea, he set off to find the lobby, looking up Hunter's number as he went.

CHAPTER SIXTEEN

"WHERE THE HELL ARE YOU?" Hunter asked, lowering her voice despite the background noise that threatened to drown her out.

"I lost signal," Caslin lied. "Why? What's going on?"

"We've had a hit from Natalie's bank account. The first withdrawal came just after midnight."

"Where?" Caslin asked, excitement creeping into his tone.

"Here in York," Hunter replied. "The person was gone by the time we got a car over there but we've pressed the bank for the ATM camera footage. It'll be here within the hour."

"I'm on my way," Caslin said, hanging up as he crossed the hotel lobby. With the briefest of acknowledgements to the night porter, he passed out into the street.

Being the early hours, no-one was about and that included taxi drivers. Caslin had to run to the nearest cab office to get a ride out to Fulford Road. Taking the stairs up to CID two at a time he made it into the squad room with only a light sheen of sweat on his forehead, having recovered from his run through the city centre. Inglis cast him a withering glance as Hunter crossed over to bring him up to date.

"Five hundred pounds was withdrawn at 00:18 from an ATM

in the city centre, we've just had the footage emailed to us from the bank's security office."

"That was quick."

"We put the bigger banks on notice this afternoon, most have stepped up for us," Hunter said. The two of them joined a cluster of officers waiting patiently around a computer screen as the file was first downloaded and then decrypted for viewing. The process seemed to be taking forever and the sense of anticipation in the air was palpable. At last the footage came up and within seconds, everyone let out a groan, almost in unison. Optimists had hoped for an identifiable face but the pessimists won out, as their suspect was clad in black, from a hooded coat to a full face balaclava, shrouding the features entirely. The video stream lasted for less than two minutes and nothing useful could be gleaned.

The air of expectation was replaced with one of deflation as they replayed the footage over and over. The grainy images masked the detail and illumination from the street lighting did little to help.

"I'll try and clean it up as best I can," the tech officer said solemnly, as the footage ceased playing.

"Do that," Inglis said. "I'll brief the DCS but in the meantime, Nathaniel," he indicated Caslin, "you and Hunter get down to that ATM and see if you can find anything that helps us. I'm not conceding defeat, just yet. If it's not too much trouble?"

"Will do, Sir," Caslin said.. No answer he could give would satisfactorily explain his absence so he needn't bother trying.

Caslin could feel Hunter's eyes burning a hole in the back of his head as they descended the stairs. Reaching the half landing he stopped, allowing her to come alongside.

"If you've got something to say, then say—"

"What are you playing at?" Hunter asked accusingly. "Look, you're my DI and if you really don't give a monkey's about your career, that's fine, but I bloody well care about mine!"

"You're not responsible for me—"

"Too right, I'm not but when you go AWOL it looks bad and I don't need to be associated with it, alright? Plus, I end up covering for you and that pisses me off."

"I'm not asking you to."

"No, you're not, are you," Hunter hissed, brushing past him and continuing on her course. Caslin cast his eyes skyward, took a deep breath and followed.

It was four-thirty when they reached the ATM on Clifford Street. There were a few early morning deliveries taking place but other than that, the area was deserted. Caslin had to admire the choice of location. They were central to the city but standing at an intersection where five routes converged, leaving plenty of options for a swift departure by vehicle or on foot.

"What do you think?" Hunter asked.

"He's certainly thought about it," Caslin replied. Hunter nodded as if she had come to the same conclusion.

"We could get some bodies down here, start knocking on some doors and see who was around at midnight?"

"Good idea, we might get lucky." Caslin didn't rate their chances. Looking around them, he could see a couple of restaurants who may still have had employees on site at that time but there was little else. The remainder of businesses in the area would have long since closed for the day. The precinct was only a stone's throw away but the bars and clubs were deeper into the centre and passing traffic, pedestrian or otherwise, would have been slight. Caslin spied something. "What does that look like to you?"

Hunter looked where he was pointing, across the street and down Castlegate. She saw what he had, a small camera mounted on the exterior of a three-storey, terraced building. It appeared to be pointing in their general direction. A board, sited above the entrance to the shop front, said the building was either for sale or available to let.

"I'll give the agents a call as soon as they open. I hope they kept it running," Hunter said although she seemed unconvinced.

"Oh, don't be disheartened," Caslin said with the hint of a smile, "we're due a break. While you're at it, let's get the footage of all the traffic cams in the area last night, maybe we can get a few vehicles to follow up on. This guy isn't a ghost. He'll show up somewhere."

"You couldn't get anything from it?" Caslin asked, evidently dismayed.

The tech officer shook his head and shrugged, "The quality isn't good enough to enhance any further. All I can give you is that it's a white male, probably about six feet in height, due to the position of his head in relation to the screen."

Despite spending much of the morning analysing the ATM footage, they still had little to go on. The image tantalised them with the perpetrator but the thickness of the clothing, available background lighting and poor picture quality, all transpired to make the recording almost useless. A full forensic examination of the cashpoint itself proved futile, leaving the team frustrated.

"This might cheer you up, Sir," Hunter said as she strode purposefully towards them, having returned from visiting the estate agents. "I got this from the surveillance camera on Castlegate," she said, brandishing a disc. "Now it doesn't cover the bank itself but does show Clifford Street, in the background."

They waited as Hunter put the disc in to the computer and brought up the recording. Once again, the quality was poor but as she fast forwarded through the footage to just after midnight, they saw what she was excited about. As the time index hit 00:15, a vehicle appeared in the bottom corner of the camera's view, although barely in shot. It was white, or grey, in colour and had stopped near to their bank on double yellow lines. Everyone waited in silence as the digital counter ticked along, past the time that the ATM was used to access Natalie's account.

"Come on, come on," Caslin mouthed quietly, hoping the vehicle would drive into shot, rather than reverse away.

"Here it comes," Hunter said as the vehicle moved off, passing directly through the camera's viewing angle. Several people gave a whoop of delight as the car crossed the screen and continued in the direction of Bridge Street and a route across the River Ouse.

"Does anyone recognise the make?" Caslin asked.

"Looks like a Japanese SUV to me," Holt offered.

"Let's see if Tech can do a better job cleaning this one up," Caslin said aloud.

"Right, new point of focus," Inglis said. "I want to know where this car went after this point. Utilise any resource we can find, traffic cameras, CCTV, petrol stations, find it, track it and see if we can get an index. There can't have been too many light coloured SUVs driving around town in the early hours. This is our guy, find him. Nathaniel, does Natalie's boyfriend have a vehicle registered to him."

Caslin shook his head, "No, nothing on file. Perhaps we should have a look at any other MisPers in the local area where witnesses mentioned a similar vehicle, there might be an index recorded. You never know."

"Agreed, get someone on it. Likewise, as soon as we can identify the model, I want DVLA records for all those registered in this area."

"That'll be hundreds, if not thousands, Guv," Hunter said, regretting mentioning it almost immediately.

"Better get to it then," Inglis replied. "Nathaniel, do you want to speak to the Bermonds or leave it to family liaison?"

"I'd rather speak to them later, Guv. Once we have something concrete," Caslin said, silently hoping that they would.

THE TEAM SET about their new tasks with a renewed vigour that had been sorely lacking in the previous few hours. Caslin walked into his office, a faraway look on his face. He failed to realise that Hunter had followed him in until he sat down. Her presence startled him.

"Something on your mind?"

"Just thinking, why that particular ATM?"

"Well you said it yourself, ease of access as well as multiple exit routes. Does it need to be any more complicated than that?"

"Perhaps," Caslin mused openly, "but everything he has done so far, has been meticulously planned. There is so little evidence left behind, it follows that this must have been as well."

"Unless she is in on it, then there wouldn't be a lot to leave behind."

"Even so, they would know we'll be watching the money. Why access it in York at all? Surely, this will be the hottest place to be, they would know that. This has been executed so well, they *would* know that."

"So, why then?" Hunter asked.

"I've no idea. It's a risky move, that's all. Arrogance, maybe?"

"Rubbing our face in it?"

Caslin chuckled, "There have been stranger things done, that's for sure. Hell, it's probably nothing. Maybe I'm reading too much into it."

"I thought you might want to read this," Hunter said, passing Caslin a copy of the local paper. The front page detailed the candlelit vigil, held outside the Minster on the previous night, the culmination of the protest march. Hunter left him to it and headed off to assist with obtaining, and then trawling through, all the digital data they could muster. For the first time, Caslin felt that they might actually be getting somewhere now that they had a tangible lead to follow. Scanning the headline and the image of a sombre Suzanne Brooke in the newspaper, Caslin couldn't help but think of Melissa. He said a silent prayer that they would have more success in finding Natalie, whichever direction the investigation took.

With that in mind, he called Iain Robertson to get an update on the search of the wildlife sanctuary. They hadn't located any more remains on the previous day and Caslin wanted to give Alison Taylor a decent chance of identifying those she had in her pathology lab.

"Anything for me, Iain?"

"I wish I could say yes, Nate," the Scot replied stoically. "We're going by fingertip, and we've widened the search area thirty percent, but we've turned up little else. We do have some clothing, a pair of knickers that may belong to one of the victims but besides that, nothing."

"Okay, any signs of damage that you can make out?" Caslin asked, thinking back on Dr Taylor's comments.

"None that I can see but I've bagged it and they're on their way to the lab. I'll let you know."

"Quick as you can, Iain. And the river?"

"Upstream and down, one mile with the former and so far, two with the latter but I have nothing for you. I'm sorry. It's very disappointing from my point of view."

"No need to apologise, Iain. Call me if you do find anything else, though," Caslin said before saying goodbye and hanging up. He hoped that Alison would have better news for him later that day. His mobile rang and taking it from his pocket he saw that it was Sara. Staring at the screen for a few moments, he watched as the call was passed to voicemail and he blew out his cheeks before tossing the phone onto the desk in front of him. Waiting for developments had never been one of his strong points, so Caslin decided to be proactive. Scooping up his phone once again, he called Alison Taylor. She answered within a few rings and appeared unsurprised at the caller.

"Intuitive, Inspector Caslin," she said playfully.

"How so?"

"You saved me a phone call."

"What do you have for me?"

"We have a DNA match on one of our bodies, the torso with the unusual tattoo. It comes back as an Irena Toskaya, a teenager reported missing last year."

"Good news, Alison, thanks. No joy with the other?"

"Sadly not, she's not known to us. Has the search turned up anything else for me?"

"No and it doesn't look promising, if I'm honest. Any word on the organic material found underneath Melissa Brooke's fingernails?"

"I'm expecting to get the results back tomorrow, at the latest, but I'll chase it up and see if I can get something for you by this evening. Still on for dinner?"

"Absolutely. Sounds—"

"Great?" she finished for him, stifling a laugh. Caslin felt his cheeks burn but took it in good humour.

"Indeed. Seven-thirty, do you want me to pick you up?" he asked before remembering that he didn't have a car.

"No, I'll meet you there, if that's okay?"

"Of course," he replied. They said their goodbyes and Caslin moved to the doorway of his office and shouted for Terry Holt. "*Irena Toskaya*, Terry. I want everything that you can get."

CHAPTER SEVENTEEN

"WELL, that puts yet another slant on things, doesn't it?"

"By all accounts it looks like she was raking it in," Hunter said absently.

"Quantify that for me, would you?" Caslin asked. The review of Natalie's hard drive, from the laptop secreted in her dorm room, had come back with startling information. Not only could they confirm Stuart Nicol's involvement in the blackmailing of Catherine Bermond, the previous year, but another income stream had come to light. The couple had been recording and uploading sex tapes of themselves, earning money for each view generated via the host website.

"There are dozens of videos, with over a hundred-thousand subscribers to her account. Millions of views, in total."

"English, please?"

"I've not got a figure yet, still waiting on the site's admin team. They promised to get back to me early this afternoon but we're talking tens of thousands of pounds worth of earnings, probably more."

"Over what period of time?"

"The past year and a bit. That was when she registered as a user on the site."

"Strewth. So, they don't necessarily need the money but then again, *need* is a relative term."

"What if," Hunter said thoughtfully, "Natalie was looking to break it off with Nicol? He would be losing out. Let's face it, he's the replaceable partner in that little enterprise."

"Good point," Caslin agreed. "I can throw another one into the mix. How identifiable is she? I don't mean visually on screen but have they been intelligent in the way they've gone about it?"

"Could someone have found out who, and where, she is and come looking?"

"Exactly, taken a keen interest in more than just her online presence?"

"Her profile is under a pseudonym, as is her blog but people can be pretty persistent when they want to get to you, via the internet. A loose comment here or there in a video, could've put her at risk. I'll have to go through each recording, plus all the comment threads to see what she put out there."

"Okay, do it," Caslin told her, "and light a fire under the site's owners while you're at it. Find out everything that they have. You may also need some help tracking the viewers. Look for anyone placing regular comments against the recordings. They may have looked to take it further."

"Yes, Sir," Hunter made to leave the office, pausing at the door. "Do you want to break it to Catherine and Tim?"

Caslin considered that for a moment. Perversely, that was a conversation that he was looking forward to. Should Tim or Catherine be holding out on him, this would bring about a reaction difficult to fake. Alternatively, thinking as a parent, he knew that this was unfolding into a nightmare scenario. "Leave it with me."

"Sir, have you got a sec?"

Caslin looked up to see DC Holt brush past the retreating form of Hunter. He appeared slightly edgy. "What is it, Terry?"

"After we saw that footage this morning, I had a thought. I

know I'm supposed to be working on the Melissa Brooke case but..."

"It's okay, Terry. What's on your mind?"

"Well, there was a report a while back about an encounter in Studley Park. I remember reading about it."

"What type of encounter?"

"A woman walking her dogs reported a weird exchange with a motorist, about six months ago. It spooked her to the point that she reported him to us."

"And?"

"And nothing, that's it. It's not our patch so I don't know what came of it."

"This interests us, why?"

"The driver was a male, in a white SUV."

Caslin sat back in his chair, pursing his lips. It might be nothing but then again, he figured they had nothing to lose. "Get on to the local boys and find out who she was. We'll go and have a chat. Well done, Terry."

———

BISHOPTON WAS SITUATED on the south western edge of Ripon, barely a mile from the entrance to Studley Park, where the ruins of Fountains Abbey could be found. Caslin was met at the front door by a lady in her forties, slight build with an expressive, welcoming face. She beckoned him in as he introduced himself, showing him through to the kitchen.

"I'm making tea, if you're interested."

"Yes, thank you very much, Mrs Jackson," Caslin said, taking a seat at the breakfast bar.

"Caitlyn, please," she replied as the kettle boiled.

"As I said on the phone, Caitlyn, we're investigating a case and your report from last year came to light. It may be significant, or it may not."

"Not to do with that young girl going missing, is it?"

"What makes you ask?"

"Well," she began, pouring the water into two mugs, "no reason, really. It's just that the man I came across was creepy and it's in the same area. That's all."

"I read your statement, from the time but could you go over it again for me?"

"Of course, if it will help. I got home from work around the usual time, half-past five, and set off to walk the dogs." Caslin glanced around. As if in response to that she added, "They are at my daughter's, we've just returned from a break and I've not picked them up. Anyway, I like to take them further afield and often drive over to Studley Park. I can let them off there and it won't bother anyone."

"Being the winter, it must have been dark, even at that time of the day."

"Oh yes, tipping it down as well, that evening. But that's what you do. The dogs have beacons on their collars and they don't go far, not these days, they're getting on. I hadn't even parked up when it happened. I knew a car was behind me, which in itself was unusual, on Studley Drive, at that time. Are you familiar with it?"

Caslin cast his mind back. Studley Drive was a direct route into the heart of the park, a tree-lined road with no infrastructure for as far as the eye could see. He nodded, "Yes, I am."

"At that time, in the winter you barely see anyone but this car was right up close and as I went along, he was flashing his lights at me. Accelerating up close and then dropping off. It was very odd. I slowed down and moved over, just enough to allow him to overtake, if that was his intention."

"And did he?"

Caitlyn shook her head, "No, he slowed even more and remained where he was. Then he flashed his lights again. I was beginning to think there was something wrong with my car. I wasn't sure what to do."

"What happened next?"

"I figured that he had decided to leave me to it after that because he sped up and overtook. A little way along was the car park I like to use and there he was, stopped in the middle of the road, still with his headlights on, just before the entrance. He was standing next to the car with his arm up, flagging me down."

"You didn't stop, did you?"

"Hell no," Caitlyn was emphatic. "By that point I was frightened. I didn't care what he wanted. My wheels could've been falling off and I wouldn't have stopped. I slowed down but passed by him, using the verge, and made my way home by the shortest route I could."

Caslin considered her story, thinking that she may have had a very lucky escape. "Did he follow?"

She shook her head, "No, I kept an eye out but never saw him again. I phoned my husband on the way, he was already home and met me on the driveway. I was shaking when I pulled up. It was all very strange."

"Can you describe the man to me? Any details that come to mind might prove significant."

"I'm not sure. Like I said to the policeman at the time, it was dark and the weather was terrible." She appeared thoughtful, choosing her words carefully. Caslin liked that. Too often witnesses talked and talked, almost for the sake of it. Many were attempting to be truly helpful, others to make the most of their moment in the spotlight. Caslin wanted detail and not conjecture. "He wore one of those all-weather walking coats but I know he was big. Tall and muscular, I mean, not fat."

"How can you be sure? I mean if he was wearing a coat?"

"It wasn't fully zipped up, and the wind was billowing out the body as well as the hood. He had on a white T-shirt underneath. I remember clearly because he was lit up in my headlights but was looking down, away from the beam, so I couldn't make out his face. His figure seemed to be well set, that's what I mean, full framed. He was definitely white, though, and had an angular face. Not old either."

"And the car?" Caslin took notes as he spoke. "Any idea of the make, model?"

"I'm sorry, Inspector," she said softly. "Cars really aren't my thing but it was white and large. More like a four-by-four than a van. I remember a lot of windows as well as lights. We have a great deal of farm traffic, off-road vehicles and the like, around these parts and you recognise the difference between domestic and working. His was certainly the former. I'm sorry if I'm not being useful."

"Not at all, Caitlyn. Tell me, what was it that made you so wary? He could have been a good Samaritan after all."

She paused before responding, "I can't really answer that. It all felt wrong, I know it'll sound clichéd but... the hairs on my neck were standing up and the longer it went on, the more I thought that I had to get home. I never saw his face clearly but everything about him seemed cold," she paused, as if remembering the sensation. "Like I said, I know it probably seems odd—"

"No," Caslin replied genuinely. "I think you made the right call that night."

"Is it connected, do you think, to that case with the girl?"

Caslin felt that there were similarities, too many to ignore. However, he knew better than to speak his mind at this point, "Probably not, Caitlyn, but I'll put the details into the system. You never know."

With that he stood up, thanked her for her time and she showed him to the door. Just as he was leaving, she called him back.

"It's probably nothing, Inspector but I remember a sticker in his rear window. I'm not sure if I mentioned it before."

"What was on it?" he asked, retrieving his pocketbook. "A car dealership?"

She shook her head, "I can't remember the words, sorry. But

it was white lettering on a green background. I'm certain about that."

"That's okay," Caslin replied, passing her one of his contact cards. "If you think of anything else, no matter how trivial you believe it to be, please call me."

She said that she would and returned inside. The front door was closed before Caslin got into the pool car, borrowed to make the visit. Taking out his mobile, he called Hunter. She answered within three rings.

"Sarah," Caslin said, "I know you're busy but we talked earlier about following up on missing persons. Have a look from December, no make it November, of last year. Start off with Yorkshire and then widen it. Specifically, any women who went missing after being last seen out and about."

"That'll be most, Sir," Hunter said honestly. "Why, have you found something?"

"Possibly the luckiest woman in North Yorkshire," Caslin said, staring back at the unassuming, suburban house he had just left. "I'm not sure if, or how, it will tie in but there's commonality to look into. How are you getting on with hunting down that car?"

"Slow progress. We have CCTV from three twenty-four-hour petrol stations and the footage from traffic cameras has just arrived, so we're on it."

"I'm heading back now. I should be there between six and half-past."

Caslin turned the key in the ignition and fired the engine into life. Setting off to Fulford Road, he couldn't help but feel that they were tantalisingly close to catching a break. His mind drifted as he drove and his brother slipped into his thoughts, primarily regarding their last conversation. Feeling guilty for the way he had spoken, Caslin decided he had to clear the air. Otherwise there was the distinct possibility that a few more years would pass before they spoke again. Now wasn't really the right time but he figured that he should spare an hour or so. If the team turned up anything, they knew where to reach him. In the meantime, he would call in at his father's.

The journey should have taken over an hour but Caslin shaved fifteen minutes off that. The rush hour traffic was steadily building and he was pleased to reach his father's, before the usual gridlock took hold. Approaching the front door, he knocked. After a few moments without reply he headed to the rear. Rapping his knuckles on the glass of the door to the kitchen, out of courtesy rather than with an expectation of an answer, he pushed it open and entered.

Calling out also brought no response and Caslin cast an eye about him. The oven was on and the door open, the internal fan going hell for leather. The intense heat emanating from within felt oppressive as he stepped over and turned the dial to off. Resting on the open door were four ready-made frozen pies, still in their foil trays and each blackened at the edges. The odour of burnt pastry filled the room. Moving into the living room, Caslin was disappointed to find his father and brother were both spark out, his father in his favourite chair and Stefan slumped across the sofa. Neither stirred as he addressed them. The cluster of crushed beer cans and a half empty bottle of scotch on the coffee table, indicated why. Both men were snoring and Caslin, having located the television remote, muted the commentary of the basketball match they were apparently watching.

Tossing the controller to the table, it bounced to the floor, taking several cans with it. Again, there was no movement from either of them. Cursing under his breath, Caslin thought about leaving but curiosity got the better of him. Crossing the room, he headed upstairs, the treads squeaking under his weight. He found where Stefan was sleeping. The room smelt like it was occupied by a teenager, stale sweat and a lack of fresh air. A canvas army bag was thrown off to the side of the bed alongside some scattered, dirty clothes. Casually, he flicked through them with the toe end of his shoe but there was little of interest.

Glancing around, he concluded that Stefan appeared to travel light.

Opening the drawers to the bedside table, he scanned the contents. The first held some underwear and he initially passed over the contents of the second, without sifting through them. However, as he pushed the drawer closed, his eye caught sight of a plastic bag tucked at the rear. Turning out the contents revealed several blister strips of tablets. The foil on the rear of the first was branded *Zyprexa*. The second was familiar to him, *Tramadol*, an opioid-based prescription painkiller. The temptation to pocket the Tramadol went through his mind, in a fleeting moment. Putting them back in the bag, he returned it to where he'd found it. Moving to open the next, he was startled by a voice from behind.

"Can I help you with something, little brother?"

Stefan's tone was edged with outright hostility. Caslin turned. He saw no point in a weak denial. "Sorry, Stefan. I... well... what can I say?"

"Dad's right. Always the copper, aren't you?"

"Always questioning, if that's what you mean, yes."

"Did you find what you were looking for?"

"The other day," Caslin said, without skipping a beat, "I got the impression that you had something on your mind."

"Is that right?"

"Do you want to talk about it?"

"How about we talk about your problem first." Caslin could smell the alcohol, seemingly oozing from every pore of his brother's skin.

"Maybe this isn't the best time," Caslin offered. "We could talk when—"

"When I've not caught you rifling through my stuff?" Stefan's tone was aggressive and the anger was visibly building. "I ought to punch you out."

"We're not kids anymore, Stef," Caslin said quietly, moving towards the door. Stefan stood rigidly, arms folded defiantly across his chest. Caslin had to turn sideways in order to slip out onto the landing. Without looking back, he walked downstairs feeling both embarrassed and awkward. His father was still sound asleep and so Caslin left via the front door. Stefan didn't materialise before his departure and as the latch clicked into place, Caslin exhaled deeply. His efforts at reconciliation had been dealt another substantial blow. On this occasion, it was undeniably his fault.

CHAPTER EIGHTEEN

"Irena Toskaya, Sir," Terry Holt began. "Reported missing eight months ago, in Leeds. She was twenty-one and a known tom... erm... sorry, sex worker. Originally from Latvia but relocated to the UK three years ago, along with her elder sister. It was the sister who reported her missing."

"Was she working when she went missing?" Caslin asked, glancing at the file.

"Not what her sister says, no. They had been on a night out but were separated in a club. Her sister left with someone else and figured Irena would make her own way home. She never showed."

"Do we know where she went after the club or have footage of her leaving?"

Holt shook his head, "The door camera has her leaving on her own, shortly after 2 a.m., heading in an easterly direction and there are no sightings after that. I've spoken with the investigating officer and they canvassed the area, sought out all available CCTV and got nothing. There was a street camera two hundred yards along the route she appeared to take but she never came into shot. Likelihood is she was grabbed, or offered a ride, somewhere in that space. No hits on her bank account, her passport or any use of her mobile phone. She vanished into thin air."

"Sounding familiar," Caslin mumbled. "Any leads at all?"

"Not a single one, until she turned up with us at the nature reserve. They're keen to know all that we've got. With no evidence to the contrary, their case is still open only as a MisPer. A DC Blake is heading over to review our findings. I thought that would be okay."

"Of course," Caslin said. He couldn't help but notice how attractive a young woman, Irena Toskaya was. The photos in her case file made her appear far older than her years but with her apparent lifestyle that wasn't a surprise. "I don't suppose that we know of any connection with Melissa Brooke, or more likely, Anton Durakovic?"

"It's something I'm already following up on," Holt proffered. "I spoke to Vice, over in Leeds, just before you got back. Durakovic has been expanding his operation in their direction but apparently only in the first few months of this year. There isn't a crossover in the timeline."

Caslin nodded thoughtfully. "Keep digging. Any connection, however tenuous is worth investigating. Speak to the sister again. See if she knew who the pimp was and if Irena was having trouble with him. Maybe she was also looking to get off the game or switch handlers. I don't want it to go another eight months before we make headway on this, Terry. You're doing a good job, keep at it."

Caslin's mobile rang and Terry Holt excused himself, returning to the squad room. Holding the file open with one hand, Caslin took his phone out with the other and answered it without looking at the screen.

"Caslin," he said flatly, scanning through Irena Toskaya's background as he spoke.

"Forgotten something," the softly spoken voice said, from the other end of the line. Caslin winced, looking up at the clock on the wall.

"I'm sorry, I'm on my way," he said, rising from behind his desk and grabbing his coat from the back of the chair. He half ran from the office, cursing himself all the way.

———

HIS DATE WAS FAR MORE forgiving than he expected. The time was pushing eight o'clock when he walked into Domenico's, on the edge of the city centre. Dr Taylor smiled warmly as he took a seat opposite her, passing his coat to the maître d' as he did so.

"Gentle jog, was it?" she asked, evidently noticing the sheen of perspiration.

"I did have to pick up the pace a little," he said apologetically. "I'm sorry, I got caught up—"

Holding up her hands to indicate there was no need for further apology, Alison sought to reassure him, "It's okay, Nathaniel. This is a sort of *working dinner* anyway, right?" Caslin nodded, although that acknowledgement saddened him slightly. He poured himself a glass from the bottle of water at the table.

"In which case, what do you have for me?"

"Well, for starters, I've ordered for you already," she pointedly looked into his eyes, a playful gleam in her own, "you were late, so I took the liberty. I hope that you like fish?"

"Love fish," Caslin said, returning her look with a smile.

"Secondly, I got the results back on the material beneath Melissa Brooke's fingernails as I left the office, this evening. But don't get too excited."

"Why not, is it unidentifiable?"

She shook her head, "Oh it's definitely identifiable. Unfortunately, it's hers."

"Her own DNA?"

Alison nodded solemnly, "Those scratches that seemed so odd across her body, well, it looks like the majority may have been self-inflicted. Apart from the injuries attributable to the vegetation, soles of her feet, ankles and so on."

"Are you sure?" Caslin sat back in his chair deflated.

"With the organic material, there is no doubt. The pattern was too strong. There are traces of another but not enough to form a working profile."

"Can you give me anything to work with?"

"We can try and separate the organic matter and attempt to elicit a stronger pattern but don't hold your breath. As for the self-harm, I'll have to do some more tests tomorrow but I should be able to confirm it. Melissa's fingernails were long and manicured so there will be a reasonable degree of correspondence between cause and injury."

"Why on earth would she do that?"

"Your guess is as good as mine, I'm afraid to say. Perhaps it was unintended, during a struggle but there is very little to suggest that to be the case and the number of apparently self-inflicted injuries is rather high."

Caslin nodded, "Do you have any good news for me?"

"Toxicology has confirmed that she had no illegal drugs in her system, so she wasn't high at the time of her death or in the weeks running up to it."

"Suzanne was right," he said softly.

"Who?"

"Oh, Melissa's mother. It was something she said. Sorry, I was just thinking out loud. Anything else?"

"Yes," Alison said, smiling, "the fish here is excellent. I also ordered a bottle of wine. I assumed that white would be okay, seeing as we're having fish."

Caslin smiled. If truth be known he always drank red, regardless of the meal but agreed that her choice was fine. A waiter appeared with their starting course of antipasti and a selection of breads. Caslin realised that he was starving. Work conversation was put aside as they began to eat. He found Alison very pleasant company. No, it was more than that. He hadn't felt so relaxed with another person in years. Even with Sara there was always an edge, no doubt related to the baggage of their relationship. However, this truly felt like a fresh beginning. He liked the feeling.

Caslin was impressed to learn that her expertise passed beyond her medical training, into sociology and psychology, having recently completed a master's degree in criminology, in her spare time.

"Do you have any thoughts on how, and why, we've come across our victims such as we have, in this case?" Caslin asked. The question was a logical route to follow and he wanted her take on it.

"Back to work, is it?" she asked, smiling.

"Genuinely interested in your opinion," he replied. "Even with my experience, this is an odd one."

"I can see why," she began. "That you have come across a killer's dumping ground is clear to me. The location lends itself to that conclusion with ease. The access, the remoteness of the surroundings, all fit nicely but then there is Melissa—"

"She doesn't fit the pattern, at all, does she?"

Alison shook her head.

"Exactly. The other victims were dismembered, crudely by all accounts, and almost certainly not at the reserve. In my opinion, they were killed elsewhere before being bagged and dumped. The lack of organic material found in and around the wounds of the body parts confirms that."

"So why would the killer change his MO for Melissa? Serial killers tend to be regimented in how they go about things, don't they? Significant deviations to their routines are not common once they have found their groove, so to speak."

"On the whole, I would tend to agree but that isn't always the case. The most successful are those that don't follow a pattern, or theirs is more random in nature. Thereby it becomes difficult to link the victims, helping to avoid detection and hampering you in tracking them down. I don't think that this is what you have here though."

"Why not?"

"The dismembered bodies are indicative of someone *with* a regimen. He is methodical, he knows what works for him. Therefore, I find it unlikely that he's an unpredictable killer, not that he wouldn't necessarily be open to changing his routine, mind you. I don't need to tell you that as serial killers become more successful, they can also become more confident, arrogant or even complacent. That could explain why Melissa's case is so different."

"It is still a massive detour from what he has done in the past."

"True enough. That could open up the suggestion that his blood lust is overpowering his judgement. Further actions could become ever more random or extreme."

"That notion fills me with joy," Caslin said sarcastically. Alison laughed.

"Of course, there may be another reason for dismembering his victims. He may well have known Irena and the other girl. Perhaps he had been seen with them or was a frequent client, assuming of course that the other girl was also a sex worker."

"I'm looking into whether it was a client or even a pimp who had access to them."

"The method of disposal could've been to hide the link to their killer, hence why we have incomplete remains. I don't see it as anyone sending a message to others as in a threat from a pimp."

"No?" Caslin asked, intrigued. "It would certainly convey intent."

"Those body parts could have lain out there for years. You only found them because Melissa ended up in the river. If your goal is to make a point by mutilating someone, then you ensure they're seen and usually, by those whom you intend to frighten."

"That's a good point. Unless the disappearance is enough by itself and, like you said, they could be traced back to the perpetrator."

"Indeed. but then that would lead you to ask once again,

why was Melissa taken out there to be killed? It doesn't make a lot of sense, particularly when you factor in the additional circumstances of her working nearby, along with the apparent self-harming."

As interesting and enlightening as Alison's insights were, they didn't help make sense of it . His thoughts drifted back to his conversation with Anton Durakovic. Perhaps the gangster had been on the level when suggesting Melissa's driver had crossed a line. Maybe he was the serial killer and their proximity to his dumping ground was too big a draw for him not to take the opportunity. At this point that conclusion fitted quite comfortably with the evidence they had. Furthermore, Marco Handanovic, if he truly existed, was proving elusive. Caslin had to admit that he hadn't given the lead too much credence and now that was bothering him. If it turned out to be the reality, then it was quite likely that Durakovic may have already dealt with it.

"Let me pick your brains regarding medicine, if you don't mind?" Caslin said, directing their conversation away from work, whilst the waiter cleared the plates of their main course.

"Another angle?" Alison said with a quick smile.

Caslin shook his head, "No, this isn't work related, I swear. It's more of a personal matter, nothing to do with the office. What can you tell me about a drug called *Zyprexa*? I could do an internet search but, seeing as you're here."

"That's okay," Alison replied, thinking on it for a moment. "From memory, I think it's a brand name for the generic drug, Olanzapine, one of the next generations of neuroleptics. It's an antipsychotic, used in the treatment of conditions like schizophrenia. Why do you ask?"

"Oh, I've just come across it and wondered what it was," Caslin said openly. "Tell me, is there anything I should know about it?"

"If you mean the potential for side effects, then they are always possible. Atypical antipsychotics, of which that is one, are powerful drugs," Alison said, nursing the half full glass of wine in her right hand. "This new wave is supposed to have fewer side effects than the older drugs but even so, they need to be taken correctly and with care."

"How do you mean, *correctly*?"

"Well, at the outset, it should be under strict guidance from a medical professional. That routine must then be adhered to. Any deviation from the treatment plan may result in a serious relapse of the patient's mental state and could potentially, be very dangerous."

"What might be the consequences," Caslin pressed, "of taking it, as well as not?" Alison inclined her head slightly, narrowing her gaze on him.

"Has this got you worried?"

Caslin smiled weakly, "No, not at all. I'm curious, that's all."

"Common side effects with antipsychotics are muscle rigidity, painful spasms, restlessness or in some cases, tremors. Irregularity in dosing could also bring about a recurrence of the underlying condition. How that might affect your... friend... is dependent on the seriousness of their illness. How bad is it, if you don't mind me asking?"

Caslin shook his head, "It's nothing like that, not really. Forget I mentioned it, it's probably nothing."

"Okay, I'm sorry. I didn't mean to pry," Alison said. Her intonation was that of a concerned friend, rather than a doctor or colleague.

"Thanks," Caslin said, feeling guilty for threatening to bring a downer to the evening. Trying to lighten the mood, he summoned the waiter for the dessert menu. "Let's push the boat out a bit, shall we?"

Alison smiled and he returned it. The waiter arrived as Caslin's phone rang in his pocket, bringing looks of consternation from the diners seated nearby. Indicating for her to order for him, he excused himself from the table and went over to the bar to take the call.

"We have a lead on Stuart Nicol, Sir," Hunter said gleefully. "One of my informants has been in touch."

"Where is he?"

"I'm on my way to find out. I'm meeting him on Skeldergate, in about fifteen minutes. Pick you up, on the way?" Caslin glanced back towards his table, Alison watching him intently.

"I'll make my own way, be there in ten." He hung up and crossed the room. His body language must have spoken volumes because he didn't get the opportunity to speak.

"You have to leave, don't you?" Alison said softly.

"I'm sorry, I do. I'll have to take a rain check on dessert."

The waiter stood nervously to one side. Alison smiled at him. "Perhaps, I will also give the dessert a miss and just have a coffee." The waiter nodded appreciatively and departed. Turning to Caslin, she raised an eyebrow, "Will dates with you always be so… unpredictable?"

Caslin's brow furrowed, "Quite possibly, yes."

"Interesting," she replied. He didn't know how to take that.

"I'm sorry. I've had a great evening."

"Me too," Alison said, the smile returning. "You have my number."

Caslin said goodbye and casually left. Slipping his coat on as made his way past the restaurant's frontage, looking through the windows in her direction, until she passed from view. Caslin immediately picked up the pace, shortly after, breaking into a sprint to the nearest taxi rank for the short journey across the city. It was only once in the back of a moving vehicle that he realised he hadn't thought about the evening's cost, let alone offered to pay for the meal. Evidently it had been a while since he was last on a date. Throwing the thought aside, he turned his focus towards Stuart Nicol.

CASLIN INDICATED for the driver to pull over, spotting Hunter at the side of the road. He passed forward a fiver and didn't wait for change. She acknowledged him as soon as he climbed out onto the pavement.

"This way," she instructed, heading for the steps down from the Skeldergate Bridge, to the banks of the Ouse below.

"Is this one of your more reliable ones?" Caslin asked.

Hunter nodded, "Seemingly he's into Nicol for a few quid, so wouldn't mind him dropping off for a bit." Once sheltered beneath the iron and stone structure, they didn't have long to wait before Hunter's informant arrived. He was shrouded in a green hoodie and approached with purpose but was evidently agitated as he came before them. He smiled in Hunter's direction and gave Caslin a cursory nod.

"Alright Mr Caslin, long time, no see."

"You keeping well, Tommy?"

"Always, Mr Caslin. Nose is clean," he said, sniffing loudly. Caslin took it as an unintentional action rather than a demonstration of the fact.

"What do you have for us, Tommy?" Hunter asked.

"You're after Nicol, aren't yer?" he said, Hunter nodded.

"Have you seen him?"

"He's about, Mrs Hunter. If you know where to look."

"That's why we come to people like you. Where is he?"

Tommy shifted nervously, glancing over his shoulder as if to make sure they weren't being observed. "I gather you want him pretty bad, seeing as everyone is asking. Maybe it's worth a little extra, if you know what I mean?"

"We see you alright, already," Hunter countered. Tommy was unimpressed.

"Big case on the go, though, isn't it? I reckon you could make some—" Caslin stepped forward, grabbing two fistfuls of Tommy's hoodie and pinning him against the wall behind him.

"Stop pissing around! Where is he, you useless little shit?"

Caslin had got his attention, "Steady on, Mr Caslin," Tommy

said softly as he was released. "You can't blame a guy for trying."

"Trying it on, you certainly are," Hunter added. "Where's Nicol?"

THE PUB WAS PACKED, with the evening's celebrations well under way. The target didn't pay any heed to the newcomer appearing alongside him, at the bar. Caslin nudged him in the ribs, with his elbow and only then did he look over.

"Watch it pal," he said in an aggressive tone.

"You're a hard one to find."

"Yeah, who's looking?" Nicol replied, turning to face him. Caslin brandished his warrant card and went to raise it just as Nicol headbutted him. Caslin fell back unceremoniously into a small group standing behind him, much to their collective anger. Scrabbling around for his identification, he got back to his feet in time to observe Nicol running out through the back of the pub. He set off along the same route, hastily cleared of other patrons by their suspect.

Bursting through the fire exit, next to the gents, Caslin found himself in an alley that ran the full width of the pub. To the left, the path led back to the main street, the right saw a kink in the alley leading deeper into the warren of the historic back streets. Caslin ran that way. Turning the corner, he caught sight of Nicol's retreating form and shouted after him but the fugitive didn't break stride. Beyond him, the open expanse of Silver Street beckoned and Caslin tried to close the distance as much as possible but knew he wouldn't make it up. Nicol was too quick for him and left the alley with at least a fifteen-metre advantage. Upon leaving the alley, Caslin saw him race across the road with a quick glance over his shoulder, in his direction. An oncoming car's tyres screeched as it swerved to avoid him, the driver's door opening as it passed, catching Nicol full frontal. He bounced off to his left, collapsing into a heap. The car stopped and its occupant clambered out, rolling Nicol onto his front before kneeling on his back and pinning his arms behind him.

Caslin pulled up and drew breath, it came in ragged gasps. He acknowledged the look from Hunter with a weary flick of his hand. She secured the handcuffs on Nicol, who lay groaning on the tarmac, apparently only dazed and not seriously hurt. A small crowd of revellers stopped to observe the entertainment, giving a Hunter a round of applause for her efforts which she reluctantly acknowledged to appease them. Caslin came over and helped her lift Nicol to his feet and deposit him in the back of the car.

"Took your time," he said as she closed the door.

"Funny," she replied, raising her eyebrows, "I was going to say the same to you."

"TELL me where I can find Natalie," Caslin asked for the third time. Stuart Nicol's demeanour didn't shift in the slightest. He remained slouching in his seat, staring straight ahead with an expression of bemused irritation. At least, that was how Caslin interpreted it. Nicol was no stranger to the interview room or the unwanted attention of law enforcement. It was clear that he was a fan of neither. Caslin sat back in his own chair. This was nothing new. People like Nicol wandered through almost each and every day of his professional career. Whether he cared for Natalie was irrelevant. As far as he was concerned, he had nothing to say. "Let's come at this from another direction," Caslin began, taking a more conciliatory stance, "Natalie is missing and her parents are being blackmailed for her return."

The last seemed to elicit a glimmer of interest from Nicol, who inclined his head slightly towards Caslin, gazing on him with his one good eye. The other was swollen shut, a byproduct of the earlier coming together with Hunter's car door. "So?"

Caslin was impressed. That was one word more than had been obtained from their suspect in the previous ten minutes. "You know, as well as we do, that you're no stranger to blackmail."

"Dunno what you're talking about."

Caslin opened his file and placed a sheet of paper on the table in front of him. Nicol ignored it.

"Email transcripts, between you and Natalie from last year. Do you want to read them?" Nicol didn't flinch but his eyelids flickered. It was an involuntary movement but Caslin noticed nonetheless.

"No comment."

"Okay, Stuart. Let me sum this up for you, as I see it. We've been looking for you over the past few days and, although it's not been easy, we found you here, in York. Now, when I find someone where I expect them to be, that gets a tick in my book. Well done. Secondly, you're sitting here, probably not fully appreciating the gravity of your current situation but nevertheless, you haven't asked for a solicitor. I've been around long enough to know that usually implies one of two things, arrogance or innocence. If I go for the latter, then that's another big tick in your favour. Looking good, so far. However, your girlfriend is missing and her parents are being put through it but you don't seem to give a damn, either way. Ask yourself, what should that mean to me as an investigating officer?"

Nicol took in a deep breath and visibly shuffled in his seat before meeting Caslin's eye. "What are you saying?"

"I'm saying that you can sit there being an arsehole, while we dance around the room," Caslin said forcefully, Hunter cast a sideways glance in his direction, "or you can start talking before I channel this entire investigation in your direction. Kidnapping, blackmail, who knows, even murder, all add up to the better years of your life, Stuart—"

"Now hold on a bloody minute, you can't—"

"Just watch me, boy," Caslin said, "just watch me."

"I've got nothing to do with any of that," Nicol said, lurching forward in his chair. "I've not seen Natalie for ages—"

"Last week," Hunter corrected him, "according to the CCTV from the club you were in."

"Yeah, okay. Last week. Doesn't mean I've got anything to do with her going missing. We knock around a bit but not recently. She's a head case."

"What do you mean by that?"

"She's a bloody lunatic is what I mean by that!"

"Your considered opinion?"

Nicol sank back, his shoulders sagging. "She's always got to be the centre of attention. I reckon she liked having me around for the bragging rights."

"Bragging rights?" Hunter said, taking notes.

"The bad boy at her side and all that," Nicol said. "She got off on it."

"The blackmail?" Caslin pressed.

"All her," Nicol said flatly.

"Well, there's a shock," Caslin answered.

"No, seriously. You got the emails, read 'em. I went along with it, yeah. It was easy money but it was on her, not me. Man, I thought it was cold to hit her own mother but I told you, *funny in the head.*" Nicol tapped the side of his temple as if to emphasise his point. "I ain't got nothing to do with what's going on. I'll hold my hands up to that shite in the past but all of this stuff, nah, no way. Do you *understand* what I'm saying?" Caslin thought about pointing out the rules of double negatives but realised he would be wasting his time.

"Well, let's see if we can make sure that you're telling us the truth. I want to know where you've been, who with and where you're tucking up safely at bedtime. Once we have that, I'm personally going to turn over every rock that you've kicked, sat or pissed on and more besides. When I've done all that, if you still look like you're on the level, I might consider letting you go.

Now do *you* understand what I am saying?" Nicol exhaled heavily, staring at the table in front of him.

"Whatever," was the barely audible response that he managed.

Terminating the interview, both Caslin and Hunter left the room, a uniformed officer escorting Nicol back to the cells.

"What do you make of him, Sir?" Hunter asked.

"He's not the sharpest, is he? I don't think society will be losing a cure for cancer if we put him away."

"You think this is above him?" she asked.

Caslin thought on it momentarily. "I'm not letting him off the hook, just yet. He seemed remarkably blasé about everything until he thought he might get fingered for it. You'd expect at least a modicum of concern for Natalie's wellbeing."

"Unless he thinks she's done it herself again."

"Or if he's involved, which brings us full circle," Caslin said aloud. "Put some smoke under his tree and let's see what makes takes flight."

"What about last year's blackmail? He basically confessed to it."

"I think the Bermonds have more going on at the moment. Once all this is done, we can see if they want to make a complaint but somehow I—"

"Doubt it," Hunter finished for him. Their conversation was halted as DCI Inglis appeared at the end of the corridor. He shouted to get their attention.

"You two, CID, now. We've got a lead on the SUV." Caslin and Hunter exchanged excited glances and set off for the squad room.

CHAPTER NINETEEN

"THE TRAFFIC WARDEN wrote out the ticket at half-past six on the evening of the first withdrawal. Now, granted that the SUV wasn't parked anywhere near to the centre, this guy is still worth a look," Inglis said with conviction.

Caslin cast his eye over the record of the vehicle's owner. Martin Soriza had a criminal record, not alarmingly lengthy but past misdemeanours included a caution for common assault against his partner, dated within the previous two years. "He lives over in Knottingley, West Yorkshire," Caslin said, reading from the page. "That's a good hour away. Do we know what business he has in York?"

Inglis shook his head, "As far as we can tell, he doesn't, which makes him interesting to me because he has no reason to be here."

"How do you want to play it, Guv?" Caslin asked.

"I don't want to spook him," Inglis said. "If he has Natalie, then I want to avoid a full on confrontation, if we go in mob handed that's what we could get. I want to minimise the threat to the hostage."

"On the other hand, Sir," Caslin said, "perhaps that's exactly what we need to do. Hit him so hard and fast that he has no time to harm her."

"Or do we follow him?" Hunter said. "If she's not at the address, then he might lead us to her."

Inglis considered his options, "All we have is a parking ticket, that he's reasonably local and his record to go on. It's pretty thin. Why do you think as you do?" Inglis asked Caslin.

"Using both speed and overwhelming force gives him less time to react or adapt but we need to avoid backing him in to a corner, as if he has no way out. If you want to take the softer approach, and we play it right, this could be over very quickly, without the need for kicking in doors. With the intelligence we have on him, we know he isn't married and apparently lives alone. This isn't a master criminal—"

"Perhaps he's making a step up," Inglis offered.

"Undoubtedly," Caslin agreed. "However, I see nothing here to indicate that he'll go down in a blaze of glory, quite the opposite. If he has an option to quit, I reckon he'll take it."

"Okay, let's do it Nathaniel's way and see where it gets us. Are you happy to take the lead?" Inglis asked Caslin.

"Absolutely," he replied. "Set ourselves for five in the morning, that's always been my preferred time. If you've been out partying, then you're most likely home and likewise, if you're working, then you probably haven't left yet. I recommend that we lock down the surrounding area and approach with caution but be ready to hit him hard and fast, should the need arise. If Natalie is inside, we don't want to risk a drawn-out hostage situation. Besides his record and what the housing association have told us, what else do we know about Soriza?"

"Not a lot," Inglis said. "The local tax office has no record of him working but we're still waiting for the DSS to come back to us with any welfare status they have on file. The locals tell me it's a rough area, in places but the estate has a real mix of the social strata."

"Those places have their jungle drums, even at that time.

We'll have a short window in which to deploy or we might as well announce it to the media right now that we're going in," Caslin said.

"Agreed, we want to be on scene and at it within a few minutes. Another factor to bear in mind, Soriza previously held a firearms license, although it expired three years ago."

"What did it cover?" Hunter asked.

"Two shotguns. A subsequent application for renewal was rejected, due to his assault conviction."

"So, he could be armed?" Caslin said thoughtfully.

"Perhaps the soft approach is the wrong one, after all?" Hunter said.

Caslin shook his head, looking at Soriza's file, "He doesn't strike me as particularly off the wall. The fact that he bothered to apply for a license demonstrates that. We'll have a firearms team in place when we go in, just in case."

ALONGSIDE OFFICERS from West Yorkshire Constabulary, the street within the local authority housing estate was cordoned off shortly before five the following morning. The early risers, heading out for work, found their passage from the estate blocked. Caslin stood fewer than fifty yards from number forty-two, Martin Soriza's house, and with one last glance over to DCI Inglis, he sought the go ahead. Inglis nodded and Caslin hit the dial tab on his phone. The phone rang a number of times before the call was picked up. All those gathered drew a sharp intake of breath upon hearing a woman's voice.

"Hello," she said, evidently having just woken up. Caslin's eyes flitted between the faces of his colleagues. Soriza was expected to be alone. They had wanted to avoid giving him the potential for gaining further hostages.

"Hi," Caslin said casually, "is Martin there?"

"Hang on," she said, clearly irritated. A muffled shout went up, calling someone to take the phone. No-one outside spoke. The sense of anticipation was palpable. A gruff voice came onto the line.

"Yeah, who is it?"

"Is that Martin, Martin Soriza?" Caslin asked.

"Yeah, who the hell is this?"

"Well, Martin, it's the police."

"*Police*? What do you want?"

"We need you to step outside, Martin," Caslin said, "and we need you to do it right now." There was silence but Caslin could hear breathing over the line, followed by a stressed voice in the background, haranguing Soriza about bringing the police to the door. "Martin?" Caslin persisted, "Did you hear what I said?"

"Erm… yeah, okay," he mumbled, "I'll be right there."

Caslin heard the line go dead and felt his chest tighten slightly. Had he made the right call? They'd know soon enough. He indicated for the firearms team to move in and watched as the officers, clad in black, took their positions within a few paces of either side of the front door. Those on point, to the left and right, had cover from two officers behind. Caslin knew a similar squad was at the rear. They waited, almost daring not to breathe. After a nerve racking few minutes, the front door cracked open and a female head poked out, glancing up and down the street. She was middle-aged and wrapped in a blue dressing gown, fear carved into her face. She was beckoned out and ushered off to one side before being instructed to lie face down on the pavement and taken into custody.

By now, curtains were twitching from the houses around them as the police activity became apparent. Seconds after the woman had left the house, their main suspect followed. He stepped out slowly, hands held aloft, dressed only in his pyjama bottoms, slippers and a white T-shirt. His face bore an expression akin to that of a rabbit caught in the headlights. Once he was also detained, Caslin and the team let out a collective sigh of relief.

"Let's get in there," he said aloud and what had been an exercise in subtlety, took a new turn. "Have them both transported back to Fulford Road in separate cars. We'll talk to them later."

Caslin allowed the firearms officers to carry out a sweep of the building before he entered. They found no initial sign that anyone else was present and the specialists withdrew. Caslin indicated for Hunter to lead the search downstairs, including the outbuildings to the rear, and he took a small contingent upstairs. Soriza was certainly not house proud, with an abundance of clutter everywhere. Picking their way through the mess, they systematically inspected the rooms. Every possible storage place was rammed with plastic bags, containing everything from sealed cartons of cigarettes to bottles of perfume and packaged lingerie. The cupboards held further boxes of branded shoes, clothing and DVDs. The latter appeared, in the main, to be crude counterfeits.

Caslin noted a hatch in the ceiling of the landing, giving access to the roof space. Seconds later a ladder was brought up and they entered the loft, scanning it by torchlight. The cramped area revealed yet more boxes and bags, all containing sportswear and other items but there was no sign of Natalie Bermond. Descending the ladder, Caslin found Hunter waiting for him.

"The garage is stuffed with gear, Sir," she proffered. "There are multiple recording units linked up. Soriza's got a heck of a sideline in pirate films going on, plus there's a mountain of other stuff. We've got everything from vodka to furry boots but there's something else you need to see."

"Something that points us towards Natalie?"

Hunter shrugged almost imperceptibly, "Come see."

They went downstairs through the kitchen and out into the rear garden. The area was paved over with concrete and they had to pick their way around rubbish bags and wheelie bins to get to the garage, a pebble-dashed, prefabricated structure, coming to the end of its useful life. Hunter led them inside and to the rear, past the racks of networked DVD recorders. Behind a pile of stacking crates, Caslin saw what Hunter was talking about. A small area had been given over to a single mattress, a bedside lamp positioned next to it. A heavy sleeping bag, clearly recently occupied, lay in the corner. Hunter pointed to some staining on the inside of the lining. Caslin knelt for a closer look.

"Could be blood," he said quietly.

"That's what I thought. Not a great deal though," Hunter replied, "probably from a small cut or a nosebleed."

"Nice place for camping, isn't it?" Caslin said with a degree of sarcasm, glancing at the damp patches on the floor, caused by the leaky, asbestos-sheeted roof. There were discarded food wrappers nearby, alongside a few empty soft drink cans and a half eaten sandwich. "Anything to indicate who's been sleeping here?"

"Not yet but my guess is it was recent. There are a couple of tablets and a laptop inside for Tech to get stuck into. They might shed some light on what Soriza's got going on."

"How about his car, the SUV? Any sign of it?"

"No but there's a transit parked on the hard standing to the front of the garage," Hunter said. "Forensics are already arranging transportation."

"Okay," Caslin said, pursing his lips. "Let's strip this place clean and see if we can get a link to Natalie. Perhaps Soriza has a plausible reason for all of this."

"I'm going to enjoy hearing that," Hunter replied dryly.

"MY CLIENT WISHES to make a statement before we go any further," Michael Jarvis, Soriza's solicitor, said evenly.

"We're looking forward to hearing his explanation," Caslin replied.

"Martin is prepared to hold his hands up to the possession and distribution of the counterfeit items found at his residence.

Furthermore, he is willing to cooperate fully with your investigation regarding the supply chain of the said items."

"That is big of him," Caslin replied. "Considering that he's bang to rights."

"Obviously there would be an expectation of a quid pro quo arrangement, regarding an appearance before the courts."

"I think that you are labouring under a misapprehension."

"How so?"

Caslin leant forward, "We're far less interested in knocking out dodgy imports than looking for a missing girl." Jarvis glanced across at his client who shifted nervously in his seat but said nothing.

"What girl?" the solicitor asked.

"Perhaps Mr Soriza would like to answer?" Caslin offered. "Bearing in mind that the sleeping bag, taken from his garage, is undergoing testing on the blood stains found on it."

Soriza folded his arms across his chest before meeting Caslin's gaze, "What of it?"

"An initial field test gave us the blood type O. Coincidentally, this is the same group as our missing girl. Can you offer an explanation for that?"

Soriza shrugged, "Could be anyone's. I understand that to be a common enough type. Hell, it might even have been there when I took on the house. That garage was full of stuff. It's probably not even mine. Do I look like the camping sort?"

"Should the DNA come back to the person we suspect," Caslin indicated to Jarvis, "then your client will be facing kidnapping, blackmail and potentially, a murder charge. My suggestion at this point would be to advise him that he should be a little more helpful." Caslin locked eyes with Soriza, who let a half-smile briefly cross his face. "Nothing to say, Mr Soriza?"

"No comment."

"Where is your car, Mr Soriza?"

"Don't have one," he replied dismissively.

"That's not what the DVLA are telling us," Caslin challenged.

"You've owned a white Toyota Land Cruiser for the last three years."

"Oh, *that* car," Soriza said with a sneer.

"Yes, that car. Where is it?"

"Sold it, months ago."

"Who to?"

"Don't remember."

"It's still registered to you."

"Not my fault, I gave him the V5 and sent off my part. Bloody Royal Mail. It's never been the same since they privatised it. You can't rely on anyone, these days."

"Where exactly are you going with this, Inspector?" Jarvis asked. "Do you have something specific in mind, with this line of questioning? My client is being cooperative but thus far, you are not getting to the point."

"The point, Mr Jarvis, is that the vehicle registered to your client," Caslin took out a copy of the parking ticket and a still from the CCTV near to the bank, laying them on the table, "is involved in the abduction of a young girl. The photograph is of the vehicle believed to be driven by the kidnapper, whilst obtaining access to some of the ransom money. We would like some answers."

Jarvis scooped up the photograph and compared it to the parking ticket before putting them both down, with a look of disdain. "Firstly, how does this prove the car in question has anything to do with the abduction? There is no shot of the license plate or the driver. Secondly, and most importantly, you have a parking ticket relating to my client's vehicle, which he denies being in possession of. I see nothing that proves these vehicles to be one and the same, let alone that Mr Soriza is involved in what you allege. Please tell me you have something more to go on than this?"

Caslin glanced at Hunter before seeing the return of Soriza's smile, except this time it broadened into a wide grin.

"I believe we should suspend the interview for a comfort

break," Caslin said. Jarvis was right. Until their forensic analysis of the house was complete and without the car, or self-incrimination, they had little to progress with. Both Soriza and his solicitor knew that.

Once clear of the interview room, Caslin let out a deep sigh of frustration. Hunter came alongside, leaning her back against the wall.

"He's a savvy one," she said.

"They both are," Caslin replied, "and Jarvis is also correct. At the moment, we're clutching at straws. Unless something comes back from Iain Robertson and his CSI team, we've got no leverage. Jarvis is representing Soriza's other half, too."

"So, there'll be no give with her, either."

"Exactly," Caslin replied, a wave of dejection washing over him. "Get on to Iain. Tell him we need something and we need it now."

"Will do, Sir," Hunter said, before heading back towards CID. Caslin felt his frustration mounting. Fatigue was setting in and rubbing at his face, he observed his left hand shaking. He made a fist and then relaxed the grip but it made little difference. His mind wandered to the forthcoming doctor's appointment and he was suddenly fearful. What if a prescription renewal wasn't forthcoming? There were other avenues, familiar to him, but it was nearly a year since he bought anything off the street and he had little appetite for it. For the moment at least, Caslin sought some fresh air. Making his way from the custody suite, he took a right and headed for the main entrance. He acknowledged a couple of officers passing in the opposite direction as he crossed the lobby and went outside.

The sun was high and with very little in the way of cloud cover, the early afternoon was pleasantly warm. Caslin had his hands in his pockets as he walked, his mind churning with their position in both of his primary cases. Each had leads to follow, some more promising than others but neither investigation had delivered the breakthrough he would've hoped for by now. His phone rang in his pocket and he answered it without checking the number.

"Hi Nate," Sara said. "If I didn't know better, I would say that you've been avoiding me."

Caslin snorted involuntarily, before smiling, "I'm sorry, Sara. I've just been—"

"Busy… ah," she replied. "The curse of a policeman."

"Alright," Caslin said with contrition, "I may have been avoiding you, ever so slightly. I have also, however, been busy."

"I don't doubt it. Listen, I'm still in York, is there any chance we can meet up?" Caslin didn't reply. "Nate… are you still there?"

Caslin stopped walking; he hadn't seen the approach of the Jaguar. Now it was stationary against the kerb, less than ten feet away from him. A suited man stood, casually leaning against the passenger side, beckoning Caslin to the open rear door. It was a face that he recognised.

"I'll have to call you back," he said to Sara flatly, before hanging up.

"Good afternoon, Inspector."

"Good afternoon, Karl," Caslin replied cautiously. "To what do I owe the pleasure?"

"Mr Durakovic would like a word with you. If you please," Karl said, indicating once again, for him to get in the car. "Mr Durakovic felt it polite to arrange transportation, seeing as your car is off the road." Caslin took a fleeting glance around before getting in, Karl closing the door behind him. The driver started the engine as Karl occupied the remaining front seat and they moved off, turning right onto Fulford Road and heading towards the city.

"What does your boss want to talk to me about?" Caslin asked. Neither man in the front responded. "Where is Durakovic?" Caslin asked, gazing out of the window as he spoke.

"You will see, soon enough," Karl replied. "Your phone, please."

"I beg your pardon?"

"Please give me your phone." Evidently the request was not optional in its take-up. Caslin took the handset from his pocket and pressed it into Karl's waiting hand, who promptly switched it off.

"Can I have a receipt for that?" Caslin asked quietly, Karl laughed. It was genuine.

"I will return it once you have spoken with Mr Durakovic."

The conversation ended there as Karl refused to interact further. Caslin paid attention to the route , circumventing the centre via the ring road and heading towards a large industrial complex, on the fringes of York. The site housed multiple warehouse units for all manner of companies. Caslin noted the premises of several large hauliers as well as units leased to smaller firms he hadn't heard of. They made their way through to the far end, entering a secure compound that bore no signage. Their approach must have been noted for as they slowed, a rolling shutter lifted and the driver eased into the warehouse beyond.

Caslin eyed another vehicle, a Range Rover, parked near the centre and they came to a stop. Two men were next to the vehicle and another, Anton Durakovic, stood a short distance away to the right. Karl left the vehicle, opened Caslin's door, and ushered him out. Approaching warily, Caslin took in his surroundings. The warehouse appeared to be little used. There were empty pallets stacked at one end and off to his left were packing crates, the contents of which he could only guess at. Beyond them were a flight of stairs leading to a mezzanine area, probably housing office facilities but that was in darkness.

"Nice place you have here," Caslin said, his voice carrying in the vast emptiness.

"One of my new premises," Durakovic replied, turning to

face the approaching Caslin. "Officially we are not operating here yet but will be, soon enough."

"As much as I appreciate the tour of your business interests," Caslin said, coming to stand before him, "why on earth am I here?"

"I felt that we should have a conversation."

"Is that so, regarding what?" said

"I am aware that you are taking an interest in what I do, Inspector Caslin. You know, as I well as I do, that I'm not overly pleased about this."

"You made that clear on our first meeting." said

"Indeed, I did, and seeing as you have been so active in my affairs, I felt it prudent to do likewise."

Caslin felt momentarily self-conscious, "What exactly do you mean by that?"

"Oh please, do not be alarmed, Inspector," Durakovic said with a smile. "When one is faced with an adversary, it would be negligent in the extreme to not consider him, would it not? A healthy level of arrogance is an asset for a man in my position but to dismiss your attention as insignificant would be considered foolish. Do you follow?"

"If you say so," Caslin said, trying to anticipate the course of this exchange.

"You and I are not so dissimilar, Inspector Caslin."

Caslin laughed, turning the heads of Durakovic's bodyguards, "I doubt that very much."

"Really, you do not see?" Durakovic shrugged. "We are both very focussed on our end goals. Perhaps in themselves, they are different but nonetheless, we are both prepared to make great sacrifices to achieve them. Look at me. I had to leave all that I knew, all that I had, to come to your great country. This was a lot, I can tell you."

"I'm pleased you like it here."

"And what about you? You chose your path and it cost you what... your marriage, your career?"

Caslin realised that Durakovic had been studying hard, "We make decisions throughout our lives before living with the consequences."

"No matter what the cost?"

Caslin nodded, "I'm able to sleep at night."

"If only that were true, Inspector. At least, not without a little help, anyway," Durakovic said, closing thumb and forefinger together, in front of an easy smile. Caslin felt a pang of anger in his chest, followed by one of fear as he considered just what Durakovic actually knew. Was he phishing?

"What's that supposed to mean?"

"It is far better for your blood pressure to remain calm," Durakovic said. "Like I said, we are similar, you and I. We do what we have to, in order to get by."

"We are nothing alike," Caslin said, a bitter edge to his tone. "People are afraid of you—"

"As they are of you," Durakovic countered. "People don't like the police, Inspector Caslin. They like firemen, love them... but the police... no. Why is that, do you think?"

Caslin shrugged, "You tell me."

"Because they are afraid of you... afraid of what you and your kind can do to them, if you so choose. In this, we are the same."

"Well, we're both busy men," Caslin said forcefully. "So, let's cut through the bollocks and get to the point."

"You appear a little stressed, Inspector. Perhaps you are due some of your medication? Or do you need a little something... off the books?" Caslin tensed, fearful that his reaction would be easily transmitted to all those present. "You should not be surprised. There is little that goes on in this city that passes me by, Inspector. I would offer you my assistance if I thought you would take it... with your little habit. I should say that quieter, shouldn't I, just in case someone overhears?" He leant in, adopting a mock conspiratorial tone. "That would be disastrous, wouldn't it? To think how you would explain yourself to your colleagues, what with your prior disciplinary issues and all. Besides that, how could you look Sean and little Elizabeth in the eye, with a clear conscience? Parents should set an example to their children. You carry a confused message."

Caslin quelled the rising panic within him at the mention of his children. It must have been visible as he spoke, "What do you want?"

"What do I *want*?" Durakovic said spread his hands wide. "Nothing."

Caslin couldn't help his scepticism, "Is that right?"

"Don't worry, I am a discreet man. I just felt it prudent to ensure we understood one another's position, nothing more than that." Caslin met Durakovic's gaze. There was a great deal unspoken in that one look.

"I see," he said slowly.

"Karl will drive you back to Fulford. As you say, we're busy men," Durakovic said, the smile fading, before turning his back. Their conversation was over. The sound of a car door opening nearby indicated that Karl was waiting.

CHAPTER TWENTY

THE RIDE back to Fulford Road was made in silence. Neither of Durakovic's associates offered conversation and nor did Caslin seek it. The Jaguar pulled up to the kerb and Karl turned to face him, handing his mobile back without saying a word. Stepping out, Caslin pushed the door closed and watched as the car accelerated away. The queasy feeling in the pit of his stomach had subsided but the sense of vulnerability that came along with it, remained firmly in place. Powering his phone back up, it beeped with several notifications. Two were missed calls and a third indicated voicemail. Checking the calls first, he saw one was from DS Hunter and the other, Catherine Bermond. Accessing his voicemail account, Caslin only listened to the beginning of the recording before hanging up. Quickly, he dialled Hunter's number, encouraging her to answer as the call connected.

"Sir, where are—"

"Out front," Caslin said, "swing round and pick me up on the way past. And get a move on."

"Okay," Hunter replied. "Where are we going?"

"I'll explain on the way but move… please… now."

Something in his tone must have resonated with Hunter

because she didn't say any more. Her car arrived from the rear of the station within a few minutes, Caslin clambering in before she even came to a halt.

"City centre," he instructed, clicking his seatbelt into place, in answer to Hunter's questioning look, "Sebastian Bermond's constituency office."

"Why are we going there?" Hunter asked, making the turn north, onto the Fulford Road.

"It's all going off."

The journey took less than ten minutes, with the benefit of the blue lights. A uniform car was already on the scene when they approached. Caslin ran inside, bypassing the unoccupied reception desk. Caslin needed only to follow the sounds coming to ear to know the whereabouts of those present. Entering Sebastian's office, Caslin found two uniformed officers in a standoff with Timothy Bermond. The latter stood over his father, laying prostate on the floor beneath him, blood pouring from several wounds to the face. For his part, Timothy's white shirt had blood spatter across the chest but Caslin assessed it to be his father's, rather than his own. More of a concern was the ornate letter opener that Tim was brandishing at the responding officers, coupled with a contorted facial expression of barely controlled rage.

Caslin identified himself to his colleagues, drawing Timothy's gaze in his direction. The two constables, one of whom had drawn his Taser, agreed to defer but held their stance.

"Tim, I need you to think about what you're doing here," Caslin said slowly, trying to defuse the situation.

"Do you know what this bastard has done to me?" Timothy Bermond spat the words, as he spoke. "Do you?"

Caslin knew. He had done ever since Catherine told him. Now she had made her husband aware and it would appear to have not gone down well. "This isn't going to help—"

"Help?" Tim said, "Not going to help whom?"

"Well for a start, it's not going to help Natalie," Caslin said softly. Momentarily he was concerned about adding emotional fuel to the fire but figured it to be a calculated risk.

Timothy appeared to flinch at the mention of his daughter before looking down at his father, "Let's see what he has to say about Natalie, then yeah? What else are you hiding from me?"

"No... nothing, Timothy," Sebastian mumbled, his speech twisted by a rapidly swelling face and the need to spit blood at regular intervals. Caslin figured Bermond senior had taken somewhat of a hammering before the first responders arrived. "I swear... I love that girl."

"What about my wife?" Timothy snapped. "Do you love her as well? Or was she just an extra, in lieu of payment?"

"Tim!" Caslin barked, drawing the focus back to him. "*You* called *me* in. You wanted my help." Timothy Bermond glanced away from his father, whose breathing was becoming more laboured and skin was turning pale. "You trusted me... you have to trust me again. Put down the blade, please. Whatever has happened, we can work through it, together but not if you don't listen to me. Natalie is going to need her father when I bring her back."

"You'll bring her back," Tim said, tears falling unbidden down his face.

"You know I will," Caslin said confidently.

"You don't understand what he's done to me."

"I do, Tim. Honestly, I do," Caslin said softly. "Please, give me the knife."

"They're all I have," Tim said, to no-one in particular. "He couldn't even let me have Catherine to myself... that only leaves Natalie." Caslin realised that despite Catherine's admission, he was still in the dark regarding the full story.

"She needs you to be strong, Tim," Caslin said, ducking his head to ensure they made eye contact. "She needs you." At the last, Timothy dropped the letter opener and released the grip on his father. Sebastian slumped to the floor while the uniformed officers took their opportunity and sprung to close the gap between them and subdue him. Hunter pushed past Caslin, kneeling at the side of the MP, shouting for the paramedics who entered immediately upon hearing the call. Caslin stepped back and looked on, whilst his school friend was led away, breathing a sigh of relief at the positive outcome. Hunter came to stand alongside.

"Well done, Sir."

"What for?" he asked. "Diffusing the moment or for lying to him."

"Sir?"

"Oh… forget it."

"Sometimes you have to do whatever it takes," Hunter said. Caslin was thrown back to his earlier conversation with Durakovic.

"What's that you said?"

Hunter shrugged, "Just that we do what we have to, to get by. Sometimes it isn't what we want but you still do it. Right?"

Caslin fixed her with a stare, "Yes, you're right."

Hunter cast her eye around the office. It looked like it had been ransacked. "To think, this is the last thing the Bermond's need at the moment. What do you reckon will happen to Tim?"

Caslin thought on it for a moment, "I think he gave the old man a bit of a pasting but that's about it. Knowing how their type close ranks when this stuff happens, I'll bet Sebastian won't want to press charges."

"One could argue that he deserved it," Hunter added solemnly.

Caslin shook his head, "Not for us to judge, Sarah. However, this incident might blow away some of the cobwebs in their family dynamic. I'm going to give Catherine a call and let her know what's going on." With that, he left the office and headed outside. Tim's wife had been frantic when leaving Caslin the voicemail. Having come clean to her husband about her chequered past, the blackmail and, seemingly, the extra demands that Timothy's father had made of her, sent him right off the deep end. Perhaps this altercation hadn't ended in the worst case scenario but had the police not intervened, the outcome could certainly have been different. Politicians seldom surprised Caslin with their antics but on this occasion, Sebastian had. He couldn't help but wonder what else Sebastian held in his closet of secrets.

A second patrol car was now parked outside, alongside the ambulance and Timothy was already in the process of being transported to the station. A small crowd had gathered to watch and Caslin was surprised not to see local media amongst them but figured it to be only a matter of time. Dialling Catherine's number, he moved out of earshot of those nearby. Waiting for the call to connect, he considered her actions in all this, both then and now. What a skeleton to keep hidden from those closest to you. Had unburdening herself been euphoric and would it be a short lived feeling?

"Catherine, it's Nathaniel Caslin—"

"Is Tim okay?"

"He's safe and well," Caslin assured her, "although we have had to take him into custody."

"My God! What has he done?"

"He'll be fine but Sebastian will need a short stint in hospital."

"He attacked him, didn't he? How serious is it?"

"Cuts and bruises. He's not a young man so it may take him some time to heal but like I said, he'll be fine."

"What about my husband?"

Caslin drew a deep breath, unsure of what he should say. He opted to be as open as possible, "That will depend on Sebastian, his recovery and what the CPS believe to be in the public interest."

Caslin could hear her choking back tears as she spoke, "This is all my fault…"

"Catherine, beating yourself up isn't going to make a whole lot of difference—"

"But if I hadn't told Tim—"

"He may well have found out another way," Caslin said as Hunter came to stand with him. "Look, you can always make a case for what you could, or should, have done in the past but that's what it is, the past. Focus on the present, focus on your family. Natalie is most important, right now. The rest can be ironed out in the coming days and weeks."

"Okay," Catherine said meekly, "thank you, Nathaniel."

"Call me if you need me," Caslin offered, "any time."

He hung up and turned to Hunter.

"That's us done here, Sir," Hunter said. "There was only one witness, Sebastian's secretary. It was her who called us when Tim burst in. I've taken her preliminary statement but she was keen to get over to the hospital. Uniform are tying everything off."

"Okay. Tell me, how is Iain Robertson and his team getting on with Martin Soriza's place?"

"Not good, from our point of view regarding Natalie, at least. We've got nothing to prove that she was in the house or his van but Iain reckons the latter has been scrubbed clean recently. For an old transit, it's just too clean."

"How recently?"

"Within the last week, Iain thinks."

"What about the DNA on the sleeping bag?"

"Fast tracking it but nothing yet," Hunter said apologetically. "Another thing, Sir?"

"What's that?"

"We're almost at the limit with Stuart Nicol."

"Bugger," Caslin muttered under his breath.

"We could always apply for an extension—"

"Except we have nothing substantive on him to do so." It went against his instincts to release Nicol. "He was the last person, on our radar, to have been seen with her. Plus, I don't like him."

"Do you think he's a better bet than Soriza?" Hunter asked, her tone indicating that she was unsure.

Caslin shrugged, "Right now it's coming down to probabilities, rather than evidence and I'd probably stick it on Nicol, if my hand was forced. You tossed his digs, didn't you?"

"I did," Hunter confirmed. "There was nothing there to tie him down. We can't hold him, can we?"

"No, we can't," Caslin said, regretting the inevitable outcome of their conversation. "Call the nick, get them to bail him but make sure he understands not to stray too far. If he pulls a disappearing act, I *will* find him and I'll drag him back to York, in chains."

"Will do, Sir," Hunter said, meeting Caslin's eye with an inquisitive look. "If we're not going back to Fulford Road, where are we going?"

"Soriza's car, the one he claims not to own."

"Yes, we haven't found it yet."

"No, but I'm interested in what he was doing here, in York. He denies making the trip but that car was certainly here. Let's take a ride out to where the parking ticket was issued. Rawcliffe wasn't it?"

"Yes, Shipton Road," Hunter confirmed. "What do you expect to find?"

"No idea but it was parked there for a reason. We'll just have to figure out what that was."

The journey to the north west of York took twenty minutes. A predominantly middle class residential area, with an array of large retail premises to be found on its northern edge, Rawcliffe seemed an odd place for their suspect to be spending his time. Shipton Road ran to the west, navigating the traffic away from the housing estates and separating them from an expanse of allotments and a sewage works. They parked the car alongside a small run of independent businesses and lock-up units, the only non-domestic buildings on the entire street. It was here that the white SUV had been ticketed on the evening in question.

The road was well travelled and Hunter had to raise her voice to be heard above the passing vehicles.

"Not a lot here, Sir."

Caslin had to agree. "Aye, let's ask around, see if the locals have come across anything odd in the past week or so." Hunter nodded and Caslin indicated for her to head off to one end of the run of buildings, whilst he went to the opposite. The first he entered was a kitchen showroom but found those inside to be of little use. The next was a secure lock-up but no-one answered his knocking. The roll shutters were down and the place appeared to be deserted. Intrigued by that, he entered the adjoining premises, an independent tile merchant. Little more than an open warehouse, packed with displays, the business was a father and son enterprise. The younger of the two men came across as more observant than his elderly father.

"Next door? Oh… that place must've been empty for nigh on two year."

"What's it used for these days?"

The man, identified as Terry Bartlett, thought on it for a moment, "It used to be a greengrocer. You know, supplying to the trade, restaurants and the like but they moved to a bigger site. Then it sat empty for ages."

"Thought it might be getting a new lease of life though," Donald, Terry's father chipped in.

"How so?" Caslin asked.

"Saw a bloke coming and going a little while back, figured he was moving in like."

"When was this?" Caslin asked, sensing a little excitement building.

"Few months since," Donald replied, glancing at his son, who nodded.

"Aye, that's about right," Terry said, "we spend a lot of time out the back, taking in deliveries of our customer orders and there was a guy coming and going. Just a handful of times though, never came too much. The place has never opened."

"Did you ever speak to him?" Caslin asked. Both Terry and his father shook their heads.

"It was a couple of evenings when I saw him," Terry added. "Usually I'm locking up around then and just want to get home."

"Can you describe him to me?"

"Erm… white, mid-to-late thirties, I would say. Big guy, too."

"Tall?"

"Yeah," Terry nodded, "but muscular, as well. I could tell he worked out or was well used to a physical job." The description piqued Caslin's interest, vague as it was. This man sounded remarkably similar to the one recollected by Caitlyn Jackson, following her encounter in Studley Park a few months back.

"Anything else come to mind, from either of you?"

Terry glanced at his father, who shrugged, "I've never seen him, only heard him."

"What did you hear him doing?" Caslin asked.

"Not him," Donald said, "just heard that car of his."

"What car?"

"That big white jeep thing that he was driving," Donald said scornfully, Caslin was now paying full attention. "He'd bring it right up to the rear and practically reverse it into the building. It makes a hell of a racket in an enclosed space."

"When was this?" Caslin asked quietly, almost frightened to ask the question.

"Well, as I say, I only hear him and it was maybe… a few days ago."

Caslin looked to Terry for confirmation, "A few days?"

Terry looked unsure but Donald spoke before his son could, "You were off on that delivery for the Johnsons, you weren't here."

"Thank you, gentlemen," Caslin said as he turned and

practically ran from the unit, almost colliding with Hunter at the door.

"Sorry, Sir. I've got noth—"

"Next door!" Caslin shouted over his shoulder as he passed her, heading for the adjacent building. Hunter caught up as Caslin once again, tried the front door. He grasped the handle but found no movement.

"What do we have?" Hunter asked as she pulled at the roller shutter, finding it secured in place.

"Lone man, matching our description and vehicle, has been visiting periodically. Keeps to himself, comes and goes with no apparent pattern and this place was always locked down. We've got to get inside."

Hunter stepped back and took out her mobile. She put a call into CID whilst scanning the unit for another entry point. There wasn't one. Her call was answered, "We need bodies out at Shipton Road, Rawcliffe. A building adjoining "Bartlett's Tile Emporium", we suspect that Natalie Bermond may be inside."

"I'm going around back," Caslin said, breaking into a run down the side access to the building. There was one window but it was obscured and covered with a metal grate, probably too small for Caslin to get through, anyway. The wall at the rear was barely five feet in height and Caslin managed to climb over with relative ease. At the rear he found another door and roller shutter. Both were locked but there was a larger window to the side, presumably to the office. This window was also grated and despite his best efforts, Caslin couldn't see through the grime to observe anything inside. There was a significant amount of decay in the fixings around the grate. Calling out, he caught the Bartlett's attention and they soon appeared from next door. "Do you have any bolt cutters?" he shouted to them.

"Yeah, in my van," Terry replied, running to the vehicle behind him. He returned minutes later, passing them to Caslin who now had Hunter alongside him.

"I've called it in. Support is on the way."

Caslin ran back to the office and set about trying to gain entry via the window. Despite the amount of rust, no matter how much he wrestled with it or tried to gain purchase, the grate refused to give.

"Damn it!" he cursed as frustration gave way to anger. Turning his attention to the access door, he found it was made of hardwood and sturdy, not one that he could put his foot through with any likelihood of success.

"Shall we get the fire brigade out?" Hunter asked.

Caslin shook his head, "No, I've got a better idea." Taking a step back, he told Hunter to do likewise before taking a swing and sending the bolt cutters through the pane of glass to the door. Following that with his boot, Caslin cleared away enough of the shattered safety glass to enable him to reach through, taking great care not to cut himself on the remnants. Lifting the latch, he opened the door and entered. Indicating for Hunter to explore the office, he edged forward. Peering into the gloom, he saw the unit was predominantly empty. Bringing his pocket Maglite to bear, he shone the beam around the interior. There were several plastic drums, stacked in the far corner, at one end. Other than that, there was little for him to see. An overwhelming smell of bleach or drain cleaner, accompanied by something far worse, carried in the air. The smell made him gag.

"Anything in there?" Hunter called out. Caslin covered his nose and mouth with his sleeve as he moved forward to inspect the drums. They had warning signs denoting hazardous waste was contained within and each had a metal seal to lock the contents inside. One seal was unclasped and Caslin guessed, judging that there was no other possibility that the smell was emanating from inside. With his elbow, he nudged the clasp out of place and with his free hand, lifted the lid, directing the torch downwards to reveal the contents.

Caslin's heart sank. The recognition was instant, despite the discolouration of the skin and the bloating. Not only had he found Natalie Bermond but she was staring up at him with the very same, haunted expression on her face, depicted in her proof of life photograph. Glancing at the wall behind the drum, Caslin concluded that the picture had most likely been taken here. The blockwork to the background was identical. The intense smell of decomposing flesh was becoming ever more apparent. Caslin knew that he would soon have to back out, not only to preserve the crime scene but also to avoid the stench. Before doing so, he leaned in closer. There was something about Natalie that struck him as odd, far odder than her being stuffed into a waste drum, the size of which was almost half his body mass. There was a reason that her expression remained unchanged. Her eyelids had been stitched open with thread.

"Sir!" Hunter called from behind him. "You really need to see this." Turning his light in the direction of her voice, he illuminated the office beyond. Crossing the unit, he walked in to see what she had found. Hunter was facing him, her torchlight illuminating the wall to his right.

"What is it?" he asked. She merely nodded in that direction. Caslin turned. Nothing could have surprised him more. Multiple images, all seemingly taken without the subject's knowledge, were pinned to a corkboard, on the wall. The stand out difference in this case was the subject in question.

"Looks like you have a fan, Sir."

"It does rather," Caslin replied dryly, his eyes scanning the photos of himself, many of which were staring back at him.

CHAPTER TWENTY-ONE

"Why you?" DCI Inglis asked. "There has to be a reason."

Caslin shrugged. "Agreed. Your guess is as good as mine. Maybe I've come across him before."

"How do you mean? Do you think you've nicked him once already?" Hunter suggested.

Again, Caslin was forced to admit he didn't know, "It's worth considering. I can't see any other motive."

"Any names spring to mind?" Inglis pressed.

"None that I can think of but," Caslin thought for a moment, racking his brain, as he had been for the past three hours since they'd discovered Natalie, "I've met some sick bastards in my time."

"Start formulating a list," Inglis said. "Then we can start running them down, find out where they are, whether they're local with the means to do something like this."

"What about Timothy Bermond?" Hunter offered, drawing a stern glance from the DCI. She voluntarily elaborated before anyone else had the opportunity to press her. "He asked for Caslin to be in on the case from the beginning, didn't he?"

"He did," Inglis replied.

"We all assumed it was because they were old school friends

but maybe he's been spinning this in his head for a while. We know he's volatile and Natalie was into some pretty messed up stuff that—"

"No father would be happy to find out about," Caslin finished for her. "He'd have to be incredibly calculating, bearing in mind how he reacted to the family secret and attacked his father, I'm not sure it fits. It's pretty thin as theories go."

"You'll need more than that," Inglis said flatly in Hunter's direction. "Check it out but for God's sake, do it discreetly." Their conversation was interrupted by DCS Kyle Broadfoot entering the office. Everyone greeted him as he sat down behind his desk. The landline rang and he answered, instructing the call to be put through. Once on speaker, Iain Robertson's booming Glaswegian voice came through clearly.

"Gentlemen, I have something for you from our initial assessment of the scene," Robertson began. "Natalie's body has been placed inside a hessian sack, similar to the other victims that we found at the nature reserve in the Derwent."

"Are they the same?" Caslin asked.

"Not one to speculate, as you know, until we get them back to the lab. It's one hell of a coincidence, though, and I know how you feel about those, Nathaniel."

Caslin sighed, "Do you have a time of death for us, Iain?"

"The clement weather and the method of storage, an airtight container, make it tricky to determine. However, I would expect last Monday night, perhaps into Tuesday but no later than that."

"That places it within twenty-four hours of her abduction," Caslin said aloud. "The ransom was just an afterthought. He stitched her eyes open for the camera shot, to make us believe she was alive."

"He had no intention of letting her go," Inglis said. "And you're right, he didn't plan the kidnapping for ransom, beforehand. Further to that; how she was found and the ransom demand indicates to me that it is unlikely to be Timothy Bermond."

"When did that suggestion surface?" Broadfoot interrupted.

"Sorry, Sir," Inglis replied. "It is potentially, a working theory."

"If you have the suspicion, then you must follow it up but tread carefully. I agree that the ransom appears too staged to have been planned. More likely this had a sexual motive but the pathologist can tell us."

"You suspected that from the beginning," Hunter said to Caslin, the accuracy of his prediction bringing him no satisfaction.

"Method of death?" Broadfoot queried.

"Most likely strangulation, Sir, due to the bruising around her throat," Robertson said. "But I'll also leave that to the pathologist to confirm."

"Anything that stands out to you, at the scene?" Caslin asked.

"Damnedest place I've ever investigated, Nathaniel. This is the cleanest crime scene I've visited. It's been scrubbed down so well that you could probably perform an operation here without fear of infection. Blood traces, hair samples, DNA of any note… utterly clean. We haven't even been able to lift a single print from the interior. We'll keep going but so far, we have nothing."

"Keep us apprised, Iain," Broadfoot said before hanging up. Turning to Caslin, he continued, "Now tell me about these photographs."

Caslin cleared his throat, indicating the folder on Broadfoot's desk. The DCS opened it, removing the contents and spreading them out before him. "They've been taken at various times and locations, in the past week, Sir. I have to admit to being completely unaware."

"I see," Broadfoot said quietly as he inspected the pictures. "Who is this?"

Caslin looked over, "Suzanne Brooke, Sir. Melissa's mother. We were talking outside, one morning last week."

"The missing prostitute, I remember," Broadfoot said,

without looking up. "And this one?" he raised a photo, contained within a see-through evidence bag.

"That's a friend of mine, Sir," Caslin said, recognising the image of Sara and himself.

"Could she be connected to this individual?"

Caslin shook his head, "I don't see how. She's only in the city on holiday. I wasn't aware in advance that she was coming up."

"Is she still here?"

In all honesty, Caslin didn't know but figured he could find out. "I'll give her a call."

"Do that," Broadfoot said, meeting his eye. "There may be a connection, however unlikely, and we need to know. Beyond that, make sure she's safe."

Caslin hadn't considered Sara's safety in all this, something he immediately felt guilty about. So far, he had only viewed himself as the focus. "I'll call her as soon as we are through."

"And whose car is this?" Broadfoot asked. Caslin knew it was Durakovic's Jaguar, picking him up from outside the station but he didn't voice the fact.

"Just an acquaintance, offering me a lift," Caslin replied. "My car was in the garage."

Broadfoot sensed his reticence, "I understand that this is interfering in your personal life, Inspector. However, we may need to look at all of these people in some detail, to rule them in or out, depending on what we find. Vague answers only muddy the waters further and could be interpreted as a deflection."

Caslin took in a deep breath, "That's not my intention, Sir. It's only that... I see myself as the constant in these pictures, not those I'm with."

"Indeed," Broadfoot said. "Well, this person is taking a keen interest in you, Nathaniel. I suggest we all figure out why. It might just be the break we need. Tell me," he looked to Inglis, "any CCTV from the unit where we found Natalie Bermond?"

Inglis shook his head, "No, the internal cameras were disconnected. All we have is the footage from the warehouse next door but theirs are trained on their own premises and not this one."

"Can they give us help with identification?"

Caslin responded, "They are working with a sketch artist at the moment. We'll have something this evening. Have the Bermond's been advised, Sir?"

"Family liaison are with them as we speak."

"And is Timothy to be charged following this morning's... altercation?"

"Yet to be determined but as of now, no charges are being levied at the request of the victim," Broadfoot replied curtly. "Who owns the unit in question?"

"Leased out on a short term tenancy, Sir," Hunter offered. "We have the name of a Duncan Shiach to follow up on, he is listed as the tenant. Paid all six months up front, in cash."

"And what do we know about Mr Shiach?"

"British national, resident in Scotland. He served in the army and has a long history of medical issues," Caslin said.

"Excellent," Broadfoot said enthusiastically. "He sounds promising."

"Except that he's ninety-four years old and resides in a nursing home in Inverness," DCI Inglis said, almost apologetically.

Broadfoot frowned, "Not as promising as I first thought, then. Look in and around him anyway, see what turns up. I think that's all, gentlemen. You have enough to be getting on with. Shall we have an update meeting at... say, eight o'clock?" There was a murmur of agreement and the office began to empty. "Stay a moment, would you, Nathaniel?"

The others filtered out and Caslin pushed the door closed after Hunter left, silently wondering if she was bothered by the DCS referring only to the "gentlemen".

"Sir?" Caslin said.

"First off," Broadfoot began, appearing to be searching for the right words, "Sebastian Bermond..."

"Sir?"

"He wants to speak with you… and only you… about the events of yesterday. I don't mind telling you that that makes me nervous."

"Why, Sir, if you don't mind my asking?"

Broadfoot shook his head, "We are under scrutiny, Nathaniel. I fear that this latest… well, let us say, the complexities of this case are sending ripples out around it."

"Sebastian is an influential man—"

"With a great deal of friends," Broadfoot said, locking eyes with his junior, "and I am not sure where this particular branch is reaching out to."

"I understand, Sir," Caslin said but he didn't, really. Whether the DCS was looking after his own reputation, that of his team or hoping to avoid the approach of a career-damaging situation, Caslin didn't know? There was always the possibility that he was concerned with justice but Caslin dismissed the thought, almost as soon as it came to mind.

"Tread carefully, Nathaniel. You may find the ground beneath your feet to be porous. Secondly, I've had a conversation with the chief constable," Broadfoot said, his tone taking a different tack. Caslin felt his heart rate increase but with no understanding as to why.

"About what, Sir?" he asked.

"During the eighties, we uncovered a list of serving officers' names, from forces across the country. It was suspected to be an IRA hit list, or at least, suggestive of one."

"I heard about it, Sir."

"The Home Office provided special dispensation to allow any officer, named on that list, to withdraw a firearm from the armoury. The chief constable is extending that courtesy to you, Nathaniel. Should you wish to take advantage of it."

"I'm not entirely sure that's necessary, Sir."

"It's your decision but I would strongly advise you to think on it," Broadfoot said solemnly. "This is a sick mind at work and apparently, for some reason, you are well in his sights."

"All the same, Sir. I'm not a fan of guns," Caslin replied honestly. With his personal experience, he had a deep seated displeasure of them.

"Indeed, I understand. Your choice," Broadfoot said. "The offer will remain open."

"Thank you, Sir. For the consideration," Caslin said before excusing himself and heading back down to CID. Stopping on the stairwell, he glanced around to see if he was alone. Taking out his mobile, he dialled Sara's number. She answered within a few moments.

"Is the length of this call going to be longer than the previous one?" Sara asked sarcastically.

Caslin flinched, "I'm sorry I didn't get back to you, something came—"

"Up? I got that loud and clear."

"I'm sorry, Sara. Listen, can we meet?"

There was a brief silence while all Caslin could hear was his own breathing. "Of course. When were you thinking?"

"Now," Caslin said.

"Okay, you know where I'm staying... and my room number."

"Maybe we could meet in the lobby?"

"Really?" Sara's tone changed. "Do you need a chaperone?"

"No, no, nothing like that."

"Then I'll be in the bar. The least you can do is buy me a drink."

"I can do that," Caslin said with a smile. "I'll be there in twenty."

THE BAR WAS DOING a brisk trade. The mix of tourists and business people enjoying their early drinks before heading out into the city for a meal, lent the lounge a pleasant atmosphere. Caslin located Sara in a booth overlooking the River Ouse, flowing by, reflecting the evening sunshine.

"So, what was with the *creeping out in the dead of night* routine?" she asked accusingly as he took his seat. A waiter approached and Caslin ordered a scotch and another glass of white wine for Sara.

"I had work to do and didn't want to wake you," Caslin said. It wasn't entirely a lie.

"And the subsequent radio silence?"

"Oh, for crying out loud," Caslin said, irritated. "It's not like you've never met me before, you know what I'm—"

"Relax, Nate," Sara said, breaking into laughter. "We're not married or anything. Perhaps I was just hoping for more this time."

"Perhaps I'm not capable of more," he replied.

"Definitely capable of self-pity, though," she said cuttingly. Caslin was taken aback. "I know, a bit harsh."

"Too bloody right it is." Sara smiled, "You deserved it."

Caslin returned the smile, "Aye, probably."

"So, if you're not looking for anything… romantic—"

"*Romantic*, is it?"

"Or whatever *it* is," Sara went on, "what are we doing here?"

Caslin cleared his throat, rubbing at his face, "Someone has been following me. Taking snaps here and there, activities of very little interest."

"Does this include me?"

"Yes, it does."

"Pleased to hear that I am an *activity of very little interest*," she said playfully.

"I didn't mean… anyway, my bosses want to know who you are and whether you could be connected."

"To what, the photographer?" she asked, Caslin nodded. "Pretty certain I won't be but who is he and why's he following you?"

"That's just it," Caslin paused for breath as he sought the right words. There weren't any. "He's a killer, and a particularly ruthless one, by all accounts."

Sara sat back in her seat, finishing the glass of wine just as the waiter arrived with the next. She picked up the fresh glass before the dead ones were cleared. "And why is he following you?"

"I don't know."

"Do you fit his MO," she asked, "middle-aged men in a mid-life crisis, suffering from low self-esteem?"

"Oh, thank you very much, for that," Caslin grinned, Sara matched it. "No, I don't. He appears to go for younger women, often sex workers but apparently not exclusively so. His latest doesn't quite fit with street walkers or call girls."

"But she is involved in the sex trade?"

Caslin nodded , "Sort of… amateur internet stuff."

"Growing trade."

"Is it?" Caslin asked, trying to read her expression. Was she knowledgeable or merely making conversation?

"Yes, criminal gangs have cottoned on to the internet as a method of exploiting women. It's big business on the continent so I'm not surprised that it's making its way over here."

"You don't… you know?" Caslin asked.

"No, I bloody don't. You, cheeky sod!" Sara flicked the back of her hand in his general direction. "I'm good at my job, that's all."

"I had to ask, seeing as you're in the know," Caslin laughed. He took a sip of his scotch and a thought came to him. "Speaking of your job," he leaned in towards her in a conspiratorial way, she mirrored the motion. "How does a gangster from a non-EU country obtain leave to remain in the UK, when we seem to know virtually nothing about him?"

Sara sat back in her seat, nursing the glass in her hand. She was thoughtful for a moment, "I would expect it revolves around several factors but…"

Caslin waited expectantly, "But…"

"Why are we talking hypotheticals, when we could head up to my room and maybe, see the night through this time?" she said with a gleam in her eye. Caslin recognised it as much as he did the growing desire to do just that. He broke her gaze.

"I have to get back to Fulford," he said reluctantly, rising from his seat.

"That's a shame," Sara said, sipping her wine and looking around the bar. "I'll have to find some other way of entertaining myself, won't I?"

Caslin felt a pang of jealousy although he knew her to be winding him up. "Whatever you do, take care. This guy is dangerous and until we know what he's about, anyone around me should—"

"Well that's the point, Nate, isn't it. I'm not around you, am I?"

"I'll be in touch," Caslin replied, ignoring the barb and draining the remainder of his drink. He moved for his wallet but Sara raised a hand.

"Don't worry, I'll put it on my room."

"Thanks," he said before smiling at her, unsure of what else he should say.

"I'll be seeing you, Nathaniel Caslin," Sara said. He left without another word, pondering what she meant with her choice of phrase and tone. Realising that he would never figure women out, especially this particular one, he pushed the thoughts from his mind.

The evening was warm with clear skies. On a normal day this would give him pleasure but Caslin found himself analysing anyone that came into view holding a camera or a mobile phone. Why was he so fascinating to this individual? There were multiple detectives working the case but it was him who had garnered the attention. More names from his past cascaded through his head but each time, he found reasons to discard them. Caslin's frustration was building. Taking out his phone, he called Hunter. "Tell me about Duncan Shiach."

"Following on from the initial search, I've spoken to the locals in Police Scotland."

"What have they said?"

"He has no priors. A law-abiding citizen by all accounts," Hunter said. "They even went to his care home to ensure our information was correct."

"Is it?"

"Absolutely," Hunter confirmed. "Shiach has advanced dementia and has been bedridden for the last four years. We'll get nothing from him as he's rarely lucid, according to the staff. He's definitely not our man. The residential address that the imposter used to rent the unit does however, check out as Shiach's former home."

"Our guy could be a relative or associate of his?"

"Or obtained the information off of the web. It's not difficult to find this stuff."

"Nevertheless," Caslin went on, "run a background on his relatives, children, nephews, whomever you can find. We might catch a break."

"Will do, Sir," Hunter said. "Are you coming back in?"

"On my way," Caslin replied and hung up. The distance between York and Inverness could easily be crossed with the internet but he had a sense that there was something more to this, something obvious that he hadn't considered. So far, this killer had been calculating, never making a mistake, as far as they could tell. Sooner or later, Caslin suspected he would, for they always did. He had to be switched on enough to notice.

CHAPTER TWENTY-TWO

"SECOND FLOOR, ROOM 216," the receptionist said. "Please make yourself known to the Ward Sister and she will take you through."

The atmosphere was convivial and lifted his mood if only slightly. The stark contrast between here and the NHS hospital were undeniable. Caslin thanked her and looked for the lifts. He was directed to his right. Pressing the call button, he looked around while he waited. A young woman passed him, surgical tape crisscrossed her face and she was supported by a nurse who failed to stop smiling as they went by. Whether anyone liked it or not, much of the private healthcare seemed to be aimed at cosmetic surgeries these days, both lucrative and apparently, very much in demand.

The doors opened. Caslin allowed the occupants to leave and stepped in, shaking his head. The question of why he was here, played over and over in his mind, much as it had done since learning of Sebastian's desire to see him. The notification chime sounded and the doors parted. He located the reception desk and from there, was escorted to Sebastian's room. The armed police officer, standing guard outside, highlighted his destination. Having identified himself, brandishing his warrant card, he was bidden entry.

Sebastian Bermond glanced in his direction, as Caslin entered, turning his gaze away from the outside view. He was seated by the window, a cane resting between his knees. Dressed in flannel pyjamas and a woollen dressing gown, the MP appeared slightly crestfallen as Caslin approached.

"Good morning, Detective Inspector," he said warmly, any sign of a beaten man, clear only in the bruising to his face. "Thank you for coming to visit me."

"Good morning, Sir," Caslin replied politely, resisting the urge to correct him on the motivation for his presence. He didn't know it was optional.

"Please, take a seat," Sebastian said, indicating the chair in front of him. Caslin did so, clearing his throat as he got comfortable.

"Forgive me for being blunt, Mr Bermond, but why did you want to see me in particular?"

"To thank you, in the first instance," the MP said, his expression taking on a faraway look. "This is very difficult for me... for all of us, I should imagine. I have never known Timothy react in such a way before. It was an eye opener. I wasn't aware that he had it in him," he said with a dry chuckle but Caslin sensed it was one with very little, genuine humour.

"Indeed, Sir," Caslin said, silently contemplating how fortunate Sebastian Bermond had been. Hypothetically inserting himself into the situation, Caslin wondered how he would've reacted. "It is certainly difficult to air one's linen in such a public manner, anyway."

Sebastian inclined his head slightly, "It is my fear for my son, your friend, that has drawn you to me here. You see, we have many... private matters that we would rather remain, within the family."

"Unfortunately, that would appear to no longer be the case," Caslin said without any intent to offend.

"Perhaps," Sebastian said, absently lifting an index finger to gently probe his swollen eye, "however, none of the tawdrier allegations shall ever see the light of day."

"Is that so?"

"Quite so, Nathaniel," Sebastian said with a half-smile. "Do you mind, if I call you, Nathaniel?"

Caslin shrugged, assessing the attempted familiarity to be contrived. "If you wish. You seem confident."

Bermond's expression broke into a grin, "Oh, I am. You see, such pernicious allegations aimed at me could be rather damaging—"

"I would've thought shagging your son's wife, would fit that description, yes."

Bermond faltered at the interruption but the break was only temporary, "My team are seeking assurances as we speak, that such spurious claims are not aired in the public domain."

"Through the courts?" Caslin asked.

Sebastian nodded, "Should that prove fruitless, I fear the worst for my son."

"Not for yourself?"

"Of course not," Sebastian said, sitting back in his chair. "It is Catherine who will come out of it with her reputation in tatters. Some of it may come my way, for a time but it will pass. I always told Timothy that she wasn't good enough for him. I found there to be something… below stairs, about her. If you understand what I mean?"

"Not really, Sir, no."

"Her history, her activities, they will all impact on public perception. These things are always about credibility. How many cases have you had, Inspector, where a rapist walked free because the victim had… how should we say… a promiscuous nature, or the mugger who never faced trial because the key witness was a homeless alcoholic? Credibility. That is where the narrative is won or lost." Caslin knew that he had a point but he was damned if he would voice it.

"What of Timothy?"

"My son would fare little better, what with his past. As I said before, I fear for him. The pressure that he is under may well bring on one of his episodes."

"Episodes?"

"Another of those private matters, Nathaniel," Bermond said, with a knowing look. "Timothy has struggled over the years, with the stresses of life. This has left him prone to seeking solace in a different world, one of fantasy, one where he feels secure. Bringing all of this into the public domain, no doubt unavoidable under the circumstances, would be catastrophic for Timothy's mental health. Not least, it may encourage some to point a finger in his direction, regarding Natalie's disappearance."

Caslin felt a shot of anger pulse through him, "Your reputation would be tarnished as well. Mud sticks—"

"With a lifetime of unblemished, public service behind me? The embarrassment would dissipate soon enough. I should imagine that I would be cast as the victim in all of this, managing to drag my son through life, with all the trials that came along with him."

"Natalie is the victim in all of this," Caslin said coldly.

Sebastian nodded his agreement, "Unarguably. However, Nathaniel, you should be aware that I am not a man to suffer fools. Nor do I allow myself to be a spectator regarding events that swirl about me. With any given situation, there is always someone who has failed and it is that person who will often pay the highest price."

Caslin felt there to be an implied threat, somewhere within that statement, "What does that mean, Sir?"

Bermond fixed him with a stare, "You do not reach my position in government, without learning to sidestep one or two... inconveniences. Put it this way, if the music stops playing, you'll not find me left standing, without a chair."

"What is it you're looking for, from me?"

"You're an old friend of Timothy's. He trusts you, for some reason," Bermond said, his tone becoming more congenial. "Perhaps you could speak with him? Help him to understand what is at stake in all of this?"

"What exactly, is at stake, Sir?"

"The family's reputation, his marriage... the future," Bermond said, evenly. "Take your pick. You're a smart man, Nathaniel. I will be making no further comment on my son's actions today. There will be no formal complaint."

"It may not be as simple as that. You didn't make the call to us."

"No charges will be brought, Inspector. You and I are well aware of that fact. It just hasn't been made public."

"And, provided Timothy keeps his silence—"

"Which he will. Once you've spoken with him, in any light. Then we can all focus on what is the most important task at hand. That being, finding my granddaughter, Natalie."

"You have faith in my influence, clearly."

"As I said, you are an intelligent man. I'm certain you will be able to see what is for the best, for all parties."

"Is there anything else?"

"No, I believe that covers everything," Bermond said. Caslin stood, making to leave. The MP called after him before he reached the door, "I love my son, Inspector. Irrespective of what you may think, never doubt that. When all else is said and done, it's your blood ties that carry you through life. Regardless of what crosses between you, those bonds are unbreakable."

"Good day, Mr Bermond," Caslin said over his shoulder.

"Good day, Inspector," Sebastian said quietly.

Caslin contemplated the situation as he made his way out of the hospital. There were far too many people who knew what had happened to keep it quiet, not without a court injunction, anyway. He was left to consider what he would say to Timothy, currently resident in the cells at Fulford Road.

"No, I'm sorry. I can't be sure."

"Take as much time as you need," Caslin said calmly.

Terry Bartlett shook his head, "I just don't know. It could be but I remember him being younger than this bloke. I'm really sorry."

"Okay, thanks, Mr Bartlett," Caslin said, trying to hide his disappointment. Having found a potential eye witness, Caslin had been hopeful of more. He buzzed the intercom, drawing the attention of the uniform on the other side of the mirror. "You can send them out, thanks." He watched in silence as Martin Soriza strode purposefully from the room, alongside the assortment of others participating in the line-up. Thanking their witness once more, Caslin excused himself. Stepping out into the corridor he was confronted by Jarvis, Soriza's solicitor.

"I trust that this will put paid to your little witch hunt, against my client?"

"Our investigations are ongoing. There is still the matter of the dried blood, found on the sleeping bag in your client's garage that he's offered no explanation for."

"Having a blood stain on an old sleeping bag is not a chargeable offence, is it?"

"Your client is free to leave, provided he complies with the agreed bail arrangements. For now, at least," Caslin replied over his shoulder, moving past and beginning to walk away.

"You're wasting your time," the solicitor called after him. "How do you think the court of public opinion, let alone your hierarchy, would judge you wasting time and effort on a slum landlord, while a girl's life hangs in the balance?" Caslin stopped, his interest piqued. Turning, he walked back to stand before Jarvis.

"Go on, then. You've got my attention."

"Martin knows you have nothing on him because, for once, he's not guilty of what you're levelling at him. Check his assets.

I'm sure you will. He owns several properties in Pontefract and another in Castleford. He lets out rooms or more accurately, beds."

"Relevance?" Caslin pressed.

Jarvis glanced around, ensuring no-one else would overhear, "Not everyone in these places are registered tenants. Several are probably not registered in this country—"

"Illegals?"

"Probably," Jarvis said, "but I'm not a party to that. The point is, the straw you're grasping has Martin renting out a mattress in his garage, to a migrant worker. That's it."

"Then why won't he tell us this?"

"Because he's not daft, Inspector. You have him on counterfeiting. He's hardly going to throw himself under a bus, voluntarily. Ask him in the interview room and he'll most likely deny it but let's face it, you'll still be wasting time and resources better spent finding the victim and not sparring with scum like Soriza."

"High opinion of your client, Mr Jarvis?"

"I have bills to pay, the same as everyone else."

"And he pays well, doesn't he?" Caslin said dryly.

The solicitor pulled himself upright, "You're wasting your time, Inspector."

"For large parts of every day," Caslin replied under his breath, walking away. Hunter appeared before him and fell into step.

"No joy with Soriza?" she asked. Caslin shook his head. "That's nought for two, then with Stuart Nicol also being a bust. Where do we go from here?"

Caslin stopped, exhaling heavily as he turned to face her. "What do we have on Duncan Shiach's relatives and associates?"

"A couple of promising candidates," Hunter began. "He had two children, a boy and a girl. Now, the girl died in a car accident, some fifteen years ago but her son provides a lead that piques my interest. He's done time in Glasgow."

"What for?"

"Two cases of ABH and affray, served six months," Hunter said. "He was far from the model prisoner, by all accounts. This was a few years ago, mind you. Add that to a stalking investigation and he makes for interesting reading."

"That he does. Where is he now?"

"Working on it, Sir," Hunter replied. "Police Scotland are trying to track him down. They believe it's possible that he moved south when local work dried up, during the financial crisis. When he was working, it was on construction sites, mostly labouring. It'd be fair to imagine that he's in the same ball park, physically, as who we're looking for."

"Labouring though," Caslin thought aloud, "often that's infrequent and cash-in-hand. I wouldn't expect to find him on any lists, particularly if he doesn't want to be found. How about in England or Wales? Any priors?"

"He was arrested on Teeside previously, for common assault," Hunter said, reading from her pocketbook. "That ended in a caution, about three years ago."

"Get his name and picture circulated and check the database for any intelligence. Contact the NCA if you have the urge. It's a little low brow for them but you never know, they might be useful for a change."

"Will do, Sir. What are you going to do next?"

Caslin thought on it, "I'm considering getting Caitlyn Jackson in."

"The woman from Studley Park?"

Caslin nodded, "Yes, her encounter might be unrelated but somehow I doubt it."

"Do you think she'll be able to pick one of them out? It was some time ago."

"To be honest, I don't but it could be worth a shot. Having anything to try and put the squeeze on Nicol or Soriza would be good right about now."

"Any word from the lab on that blood stain we found at Soriza's?"

Caslin shook his head, "Nothing positive. They've confirmed the blood type is a match to Natalie but are struggling with obtaining a workable DNA profile. It's some problem with exposure to chemicals causing degradation to the pattern. They're trying."

"Have you considered putting Timothy Bermond, in a line-up?" Hunter asked, her tone such that she appeared fearful to utter the words.

Caslin shot her a dark look, "There isn't a great deal of enthusiasm for that line of inquiry. Without more to go on, the fallout would be immense. Plus, we already have two suspects that we're parading around. To add a third would look like we're clueless."

"Wouldn't be far off."

"Speak for yourself," Caslin smiled as he spoke. "See if you can find any crossover between Tim's movements and any of our crime scenes, or victims, for that matter. If anything turns up, then we can go further. At the moment, you just have an instinctive notion. Am I right?" Hunter nodded but appeared reticent to leave it there. "If you've something to add, Sarah, spit it out."

"Don't take this the wrong way, Sir…"

"But you're about to say something offensive."

Hunter shook her head, "Is your friendship with Timothy getting in the way?"

"Clouding my judgement, you mean?"

"Not clouding, as such but—"

"We were friends in a different age," Caslin said. "If there's something to look at, I'll look. In the meantime, take any concerns to Inglis or Broadfoot, by all means. If you feel the need?" The last was said pointedly.

"Yes, Sir. That's not necessary. I'm sorry that I mentioned it."

Hunter left Caslin with his thoughts. Caitlyn was a very long shot and hinted at desperation on his part. Another failed line-up would do little else than give weight to the respective solicitors to have the investigation into their clients dropped. He decided against bringing her in unless there was a substantial change in their position. Caslin's phone rang. Taking it out he didn't recognise the number but it was local.

"Caslin," he answered.

"Hello. Is that Nathaniel?" a tentative male voice said.

"Yes, it is. Who is this?"

"Vincent Meechan. I'm a neighbour of your father's."

"I see. What is it I can do for you, Mr Meechan?" Caslin asked absently, heading in Hunter's direction with his mind pondering his next move.

"I'm so sorry to trouble you but your father gave me your number to call, if necessary. I think he was worried after that fall he had."

"Fall?" Caslin asked, stopping in his tracks.

"You remember; the one he had last year," Meechan said, matter-of-factly, "when he sprained his wrist. It scared him, I think."

"Oh that," Caslin lied, whilst contemplating why his father hadn't spoken of it to him.

"As I say, I'm terribly sorry to bother you, I know—"

"What's wrong, Mr Meechan?"

"Well, I heard some commotion from his place, earlier today. I wasn't listening in, you understand but voices rose and it seemed to be getting heated."

Caslin sighed, wondering which of the two, his father or brother, had overdone it by mid-afternoon, "My brother is stopping at the moment. Sometimes our family can be a little... exuberant."

Meechan laughed nervously, "Happens to the best of them. It did appear as if it was more than that though. I didn't pop round, I'm not one to pry but for a moment I considered phoning the..." he hesitated.

"Police?"

"Well, yes," Meechan replied. The anxiety in his voice was evident. "I don't want to cause any trouble but your father is an elderly man, as am I—"

"It's okay, Mr Meechan," Caslin reassured him, disguising his irritation. The last thing he needed was uniform attending a domestic at his father's house. "You did the right thing. Tell me, has it settled down or is it still going on?"

"Oh, it went quiet an hour or two ago but like I said, there was one heck of a rumpus. I wasn't sure if I should call you but—"

"Leave it with me," Caslin said in as upbeat a manner as he could manage. "I'll stop by and make sure everything's okay. I appreciate the call." Hanging up, Caslin knew he would have to go out to his father's, in Selby. A phone call would be quicker but most likely the skills of diplomacy, well honed in his youth, would be required. That necessitated face to face conversation. Heading downstairs he considered why his father would communicate his worries and frailties to a neighbour rather than his son? Turning his thoughts to Stefan's impromptu visit, he had been expecting something like this to happen sooner or later. It was only ever a matter of time where his brother was concerned; trouble followed him like stink on shit. Upon reaching the yard he was disappointed to find there wasn't a pool car going spare and he silently cursed. He gave Hunter a call.

"Sarah, I need a lift somewhere," he said after she had picked up.

"Right now, Sir?" she asked. "I'm pretty busy up here."

"In that case, can I borrow your car? I wouldn't ask if it wasn't important."

Hunter thought on it for a moment. Caslin knew how much she hated his driving and the response was predictable. "No, I'll come down and drive you. Where are we going?"

"Tell you once we're on the way," Caslin said, hanging up.

He didn't have to wait long before she joined him. They made their way to her car. She unlocked it just as he revealed where they were heading.

"Are you bloody kidding me, Sir?" she protested. "I've just had to blag my way out of CID and you want a lift to your father's?"

"I know what it looks like but it's important, trust me," Caslin said, brushing aside her indignation. He could feel the piercing stare burning into him. Glancing towards her, his expression conveyed the fact that he wasn't lying, "Please, Sarah. I need—"

"I don't want to hear any more about it," she said, opening her door and getting in. He too, climbed into the car, closing his door softly. Glancing over, once again drew a repetition of her statement. "Not one word," she said, firing the engine into life.

The journey to Selby didn't take long at that time of night. The house was in darkness but that meant nothing. Caslin knew they'd be home. His father's car was in the driveway and seeing as it was nearing ten-thirty, he expected to find both men passed out in front of the television. Caslin got out of the car. Leaning in, one hand on the roof and the other, the door, he spoke to Hunter.

"I shouldn't be long. Hang on here for a bit, would you?"

"Sure," she replied curtly. "I've not got anything better to do."

Caslin ignored the sarcasm and turned his back on the car. Trotting up the path to the front door, he rapped his knuckles on the glass. After a few moments with no response, he knocked again, rattling the letter box with his other hand just for good measure. With still no answer, he went down the side passage and entered the rear garden, as he had done many times before. He was surprised to see the door to the kitchen slightly ajar. Giving it a nudge inward he called out into the darkness, only to receive no reply. Realising that there was no sound emanating from inside, Caslin felt the hairs on his neck standing up. He took two steps into the kitchen and stopped. Nothing.

Reaching out towards the light switch, he waited a few moments for the neon tube to stutter into life. The kitchen table appeared to be set for lunch with plates, cups, bread and cheese, lying untouched. Tentatively, he walked towards the living room. In the gloom of the interior, he saw a figure lying on the floor. Unmistakably, it was his father. Rushing forward, Caslin turned on the nearest light, only to reveal a scene of carnage. The living room had been overturned in somewhat of a violent fashion, furniture and debris were scattered everywhere. His father lay amongst broken glass, blood seeping from a head wound that made Caslin fear the worst.

Kneeling down, he inspected the injury, searching for a pulse whilst reaching for his mobile. The handset was caught in his jacket pocket and Caslin cursed openly, whilst wrestling to free it. He called for an ambulance. His father was breathing but it was shallow and after initially struggling to find a pulse, he now found it to be scarily faint. He made a second call to Hunter, telling her to get inside. Meanwhile, supporting his father's head, he sought to stem the blood flow as best he could. Calling out to Stefan, he listened intently but again there was no answer.

"Damn it!" he said harshly. Hunter burst through the kitchen door moments later.

"Jesus!"

"Grab a clean towel from the kitchen. They should be in the second drawer down," Caslin nodded roughly in the right direction. She returned swiftly. "Take over from me, would you? I need to check the rest of the house. Ambulance is on its way."

"What's happened here?" she asked but Caslin didn't reply as he set off. Unsure of whether they were alone, he took his time. Rapidly ascertaining that the downstairs was clear, he reached the stairs. Further progress was taken with caution. Peering up with each step, he tried to preempt what might come from above. Every sense was heightened as he listened for the telltale signs that someone was waiting for him. Finding his brother unconscious would be the lesser of the two scenarios that currently occupied his thoughts. On the landing, he moved with more confidence. Going room by room, he found each untouched in comparison to the havoc wrought below, his mind went into overdrive with the possibilities of what had occurred. Satisfied that they were alone, Caslin called down to Hunter.

"It's clear," he shouted. "There's no-one else here." He didn't hear her response but he was pleased to recognise the approaching sirens . For once the response times were decent. Before heading downstairs, he ducked back into Stefan's room, making a beeline for the drawers that his brother had caught him sifting through previously. Fearful of what he'd find, he wanted the opportunity before others began looking for answers. All of Stefan's gear was still present and a quick check saw that included the drugs. For a moment Caslin lingered on the blister strip of Zyprexa, playing thoughts over and over, before tossing them onto the bed. Opening the last drawer, he rummaged through the contents. His fingers brushed against something cold and smooth. Without looking, he knew what it was. Removing the semiautomatic pistol, Caslin's heart skipped a beat.

Examining it, he found it was a Makarov and evidently quite old. There were dings and scratches from grip to barrel. It was a cold war relic but Caslin found the slide in perfect working order, a round already chambered. Removing the clip, he found it full. Hefting the weapon, he smelt the breach in an attempt to determine whether it had been recently fired. Thankfully, it didn't appear so.

"Shit, Stefan," he muttered to himself. "What the bloody hell are you into?"

A call came to his ear from downstairs. The paramedics had entered the house. Caslin had to think fast. Slipping the Makarov into the rear waistband of his trousers, he hurried downstairs just as the first of the paramedics knelt alongside his stricken father. Caslin was pleased to hear the old man groan. Despite everything, that was promising. Hunter came to stand next to him.

"He's taken a beating, Sir," she said, apologetically. "Any sign of your brother?" Caslin shook his head. "What do you think happened?"

"I can't see any sign of forced entry but the back door was open when we got here."

"Anything upstairs?" Hunter asked.

Caslin looked her square in the eye, his internal battle buried deep beneath the surface. "No, nothing," he said as convincingly as he could. He felt her gaze linger on him for a moment before she too, looked down at his father, lying between the medics.

"I phoned DCI Inglis, Sir," Hunter said. "I had to, under the circumstances."

Caslin glanced in her direction and nodded, "Yes, that was the right thing to do. Don't worry. What did he say?"

"Not a lot. He's coming out but said he'd see you at the hospital, later."

"I'll be here when he arrives—"

"Nathaniel," Hunter interrupted him, she seldom used his first name. "You need to be with your father."

"I *need* to work out what's gone on here," Caslin countered.

"Inglis runs things by the book. You know that as well as I do. There's no way he'll let you be in the middle of this."

Caslin momentarily let his frustration show, "Whether it's official, or not, do you think I'll let it go?" he hissed at her.

Hunter took a deep breath, "No. I don't doubt that but at the moment you should be with him. What if he wakes up and wants to tell you what happened and you're not there, or what if…?" she left the last unspoken.

Caslin hated to admit it but she was bang on. One of the paramedics advised them that they were going to make the move in a couple of minutes, seeking help with the lift. Caslin acknowledged that before addressing Hunter. "You're right. Tell Inglis I'll see him at the hospital."

"Do you think… look, we know you're in this guy's sights. Do you think this is him, trying to hurt you?"

Caslin shook his head in a manner more aligned with uncertainty than a rejection of the notion, "Why would he target my family like this, specifically?"

"To make you suffer, maybe. He doesn't appear to be playing by the book. Perhaps you have come across him after all?" Hunter appeared thoughtful. "Your brother isn't here."

Caslin met her eye, desperately trying to read her thoughts and not betray his own, "No, he's not. What's your point?"

"Just that we should consider the possibility… that he's…"

"What?"

"Been abducted… it's got to be a consideration."

"It has," Caslin said solemnly, looking towards the paramedics, one of whom signalled for assistance. The thought hadn't occurred to him. Even now, he figured that to be the least likely of the scenarios currently running through his head. However, he chose to keep his thoughts to himself and remained silent.

CHAPTER TWENTY-THREE

"TELL ME ABOUT YOUR BROTHER."

Caslin stood at the window, staring at any number of nondescript points of the city, visible from their elevation. The third floor waiting area within York Hospital was scant of detail, tired and sterile. The warm, orange glow emanating from the city centre, in contrast, appeared attractive in the small hours. "What is it that you want to know?" Caslin replied.

John Inglis was seated behind him, where he had been for the past half-hour, waiting. His patience must have worn thin. "You don't appear particularly worried about Stefan."

"Should I be?"

"Hunter is of the opinion that your father's attack is linked to our case."

"That's possible."

"But you don't think so, do you?" Inglis pressed.

Caslin turned away from the window, taking a seat opposite the DCI, "Stefan can take care of himself. He always has done."

"With respect, Nathaniel. You're not answering my question. I need to know if I should be reallocating resources in this direction, or not?"

Caslin shook his head. How was he supposed to walk the

line between familial loyalty and professionalism? His father had been admitted, assessed and moved directly into theatre for surgery. Little beyond seeking permission for the operation had been offered by the medical team and now he waited. Time to think, to ponder. Time to realise what had, in all likelihood, occurred. "If I were you, I would leave everyone where they are."

Inglis appeared taken aback. "What is it that you're not telling me?"

"What do you mean by that?"

"If there is the possibility that your brother has been abducted—"

"Doubtful," Caslin interrupted. "Although preferable, under the circumstances."

"Please explain," Inglis asked, sitting back in his chair.

"A friend of my father's called me this evening. He overheard an argument earlier in the day. It wasn't entirely a surprise, for me, to find things as they were. I didn't expect my father to be... well... as he was. My brother has had his problems, over the years." said Inglis was unimpressed with the ambiguity and showed it. Caslin offered up the detail, "He saw active service in the army and, let's just say, has failed to reintegrate into civvy street. He's always been something of a misfit and, after leaving the military, struggled with... illegal drugs... authority... stuff like that."

"Is he prone to violent behaviour?" Inglis asked softly.

Caslin met his eye, "No, never. At least, not until now but..."

"But what?"

"I'm loathe to link the two but he has a... at least, I understand that he has a disorder of some kind. The fact of the matter is that his medication could and I stress, *could*, give leave to outbursts, if he's not been taking them consistently."

"I see," Inglis said, processing the information. "You said *understand*. Does that mean you don't know?"

"Correct. We haven't discussed it."

"And yet, you believe this is most likely to be the cause of your father's attack?" Caslin nodded in response. The DCI exhaled slowly, "So we had better put his description out there and get him picked up. Is there a chance that he might harm someone else?"

Caslin looked to the ceiling, his expression one of genuine anguish, "I have no idea, I'm sorry. We're not particularly close."

Conversation broke off when a doctor appeared at the nurses' station and was redirected towards them. Caslin felt apprehensive as she approached, trying to infer his father's condition from her body language. He failed miserably.

"Mr Caslin?" she asked, he nodded. "I'm Doctor Ramirez, consultant neurosurgeon, here at the hospital."

"How is my father?" Caslin asked. Her flat expression and matching tone indicated to him that the news was not positive.

"Your father is in a critical condition," she began. Caslin felt his heart sink. "I'm sure I don't need to tell you that he is an elderly man and his injuries are worse than we originally thought. He came through the procedure without developing any further complications and is therefore stable, which we must take as a positive, at this point."

"What's... wrong...?" Caslin asked, struggling to find the right words.

"He suffered a severe trauma to the brain and it has begun to swell. When it does this, it pushes against his skull."

"What can you do?"

"Until the swelling subsides, not a great deal. We have removed a section of your father's skull to enable us to drain away the leaking blood, from the haemorrhage. This in turn, will alleviate the pressure caused by the swelling. For now, we must wait and see how he responds in the next twenty-four to thirty-six hours."

Caslin rubbed at his face gently with both palms, "Did he regain consciousness?"

Dr Ramirez shook her head, "No, he didn't come around at

all. We have placed him in a medically induced coma for the time being and will keep him that way until he stabilises. I'm sorry. I wish I could give you better news."

"Thank you, Doctor," Caslin said almost inaudibly.

"I don't wish to appear negative regarding his prognosis… there are no guarantees in these cases. Your father is in recovery where he will be monitored throughout the night. The nurses can arrange for you to spend some time with him. Please excuse me." Caslin thanked her once again. Returning to his seat, he found the weight of the world descend upon his shoulders.

"Perhaps you should take some time to be with your father?" Inglis offered. "We can crack on without you. Once his condition… you know." Caslin raised his head and looked across. He didn't speak but merely nodded. "Is there anyone I can call for you?"

Caslin shook his head, "No, thank you. I'll take care of it."

"Have you tried to contact your brother?"

Caslin nodded, "The call went straight to voicemail. I couldn't find his mobile at the house, so I'm assuming that he still has it."

"Give me the details and I'll see if we can track it to a location."

Caslin agreed and read out Stefan's number, Inglis took note.

"Any idea where he may have gone?"

Caslin blew out his cheeks, "Not really, no. You might find him propping up a bar somewhere. As far as I know, he hasn't anywhere in particular to go."

"Is there anything else that you think we should know?" Inglis asked. Caslin shook his head. The DCI said goodbye and Caslin found himself alone with his thoughts.

Apart from Stefan, there was their mother but his parents divorced decades ago and he couldn't see her dropping everything to attend. Once there was more definitive information he would let her know but saw no need to burden her with bad news at this time of night. Reaching into his pocket, he took out his dwindling supply of painkillers. Crossing over to the water fountain, he popped one from the strip and swallowed it before heading to the nurses' station. From there he was shown to his father.

Caslin took a deep breath and gathered himself before easing the door open. Over the years, he'd been exposed to people in all manner of shocking conditions, however, on this occasion, there carried with it a terrifying feeling of helplessness. His father lay in a bed, connected to a drip and several pieces of automated medical equipment. A monitor whirred away, depicting the old man's heartbeat with an occasional beep to remind him that it was still there. An artificial ventilator assisted with his breathing. Caslin caught sight of his own reflection in the solitary window to the outside as he approached, appearing ashen faced. Fighting tears, he came to stand next to the bedside. Before him, his father looked every bit as frail as his seventy-four years denoted.

Tentatively, he placed his palm on the back of his father's hand. The skin felt cool and was grey in colour. Caslin found the contrast between the man lying before him and the one he was used to, quite striking. Gently squeezing his hand, there was no reaction. Trying to think of something prophetic to say, and being unable to do so, Caslin stood in momentary silence.

"I'm sorry I wasn't there for you, Dad," he said softly. The words sounded hollow. His father had reiterated time after time that he wouldn't ever go into hospital. His choice would be to remain at home, under any circumstances, rather than face the indignity of fulltime care. Caslin remembered those conversations now. It seemed an odd stance to take, bearing in mind what can befall you in life. His father appeared, at least on the surface, to be resigned to passing when it was his time and wanted to face it on his own terms when the moment came. "You don't always get to choose," he said quietly, reflecting on those memories.

At that point his mobile rang which surprised him, what with it having passed three in the morning. Taking it out, he saw it was Terry Holt. Not considering ignoring it for a second, he clicked the answer tab.

"Sir, I'm sorry to call so late... early... whatever. Did I wake you?"

Caslin realised Holt was somehow unaware of the evening's events and didn't bother to enlighten him. "No, what's up, Terry?"

"Hunter gave me some follow up to do on this old boy, up in Inverness."

"Duncan Shiach?"

"That's the chap. I was looking at staff members who might be interesting and I turned something up so I ran with it."

"Go on."

"Most of them were locals and they tend not to move around much but I came across this one guy, Mark Rabiot. He was an agency worker, there on and off over a period of nine months."

"Does he have a record?"

"No, not that I'm aware of. He's an Australian national, here on permanent leave to remain since he married one of ours."

"Why is he so interesting?"

"He stood out from the list as one likely to move about, bearing in mind he's travelled halfway around the world to be here. Anyway, he's a specialist in caring for dementia patients, cognitive therapy and the like. I did some digging—"

"It's late, Terry."

"He's working *here*, in York."

A flicker of anticipation coursed through him, "I like that."

"Thought you might. Secondly, looks like he could've been working in Leeds when Irena Toskaya went missing."

"A lot of people work in Leeds—"

"How many worked in Inverness with access to Shiach's personal information, then Leeds around the time of Irena's disappearance and now here in York?"

"Well, you have a way with words, Terry. Do you have an

address?" Caslin left the recovery room and stepped into the corridor.

"Yes, it's in New Earswick."

"Pick me up from the hospital on your way, would you?"

"Hospit... what are you doing there?"

"Later, Terry," Caslin replied. "Have you been onto Inglis with this?"

"Can't get an answer from him, nor Hunter for that matter. Shouldn't we sit on it until the morning?"

Caslin's gaze drifted back to his father. A pang of guilt knotted in his chest. His place was here and he knew it. His father would make it or he wouldn't. That was the reality and Caslin also knew he could do nothing to influence the outcome. "My call, Terry. Let's check him out before we get everyone all excited—"

Caslin almost collided with a doctor as he resumed his course to the stairwell, so preoccupied was he with the conversation. "Sorry," he muttered under his breath, making his way through the door. Looking back over his shoulder, he saw the man cast him a sideways glance before continuing on. Caslin stopped. Terry Holt was still talking but he had ceased listening. Taking a couple of steps backwards, he eased open the door. At the far end of the corridor, the same doctor reached a turn. Once again, he glanced towards Caslin before disappearing from view. There was something about the expression on his face, the eye contact, the body language, that piqued his interest.

"Sir?" Holt said. "Are you still there?"

"I'm here, Terry," Caslin said absently, although his focus had moved to the ward reception desk. He moved in that direction, drawing the attention of the nurse. "Excuse me," he asked, "which doctors are on shift tonight?"

The nurse appeared a little surprised at the question but answered, "Doctors Shaw and Ramirez, although the latter is on call and present only for your father's case."

"And Dr Shaw," Caslin continued, "is he on his rounds?"

"*She* is on her rest break. Is there anything I can help you with?"

Caslin stood still, fighting the instinct that was gnawing away at him, "Is there anyone else on shift tonight?"

"On this floor?" she clarified. He nodded. "No, not directly but others do have access. This is the twenty-four-hour, trauma ward. Besides ICU, there are those requiring close monitoring before they can be moved to a general ward."

"Right," Caslin said, as if he understood. He remained there, his mind ticking over with the phone still pressed to his ear.

"Mr Caslin," the nurse persisted, "is there something that you need?"

"No. No, there isn't, thank you," he said, walking away. His attention returned to Terry Holt. "I'll wait for you outside, Terry."

"I'll be there in about twenty minutes," Holt replied in far too upbeat a manner for that time of night, before hanging up.

Caslin headed for the stairs. Upon reaching them, he put his hand upon the door before the unnamed doctor appeared at the end of the corridor again. Seeing Caslin looking in his direction, he stopped, turned slowly on his heel and headed back in the direction from where he'd come.

"Doctor," Caslin called out. The man didn't stop and if anything, sped up. "Doctor!" Caslin raised his voice but to no avail. Glancing at the nurses' station, he saw it was no longer manned. Letting go of the door, he set off down the corridor at a trot, his footfalls echoing on the polished floor. Reaching the T junction, he glanced to the left but there was no-one in sight. Slowing his pace, Caslin continued on, giving each room, he passed, a cursory inspection. Most were in darkness, some were locked, all were apparently unoccupied. His head told him that he was wasting his time but the feeling that something wasn't right had returned.

A ping came to his ear and he knew it was the sound of an elevator notification. Breaking into a run, Caslin made it to the lifts as the doors closed. He frantically pressed the *call* button but the machinery had already engaged. Stepping back, he looked at the digital counter, registering that it was heading down. Turning, Caslin ran to the nearest stairwell and descended as fast as he dared, bracing against the wall several times, on the way. Reaching the second floor, he heard the clatter of metal hit the ground. Realising that Stefan's gun had slipped from his waistband. Caslin retrieved it before looking at the elevator again. It hadn't stopped and he resumed his descent. By the time he made it to the ground floor, he was sweating and breathing heavily in equal measure. The display indicated that it was now stationary at the Lower Ground. Caslin headed that way.

Coming to what was the basement level, he slowed. Edging through the double doors and out of the stairwell, he walked into semi-darkness. Only the occasional lighting illuminated the corridor. Listening intently, he sought an indication of which direction to take but nothing came to his ear. It was a toss of the coin and he chose left for no other reason than that direction was well lit. With each step he doubted his decision, contemplating whether or not paranoia had got the better of him?

He heard something faint and froze. Listening intently, he waited, his own increased heartbeat was all that registered. Dismissing it as a trick of the mind, he set off, only to hear the same sound repeated. This time he was sure and moved with caution, almost hugging the wall. Approaching another stairwell, Caslin glanced along the corridor for some indication of what to expect, his eyes straining in the gloom. No more sound came his way and just as an acceptance that he was alone began to dawn on him, a body moved from the shadows. An involuntary yelp came from somewhere inside him, akin to the sound of a startled cat.

"What are you doing down here?" a male voice barked at him, before training the beam of a torch into his face. Caslin blinked, holding a hand up to shield his eyes. He could make out the lapels of a uniform on the figure's shoulder, beyond the intense light.

"Police," he uttered in response, as if that answered everything.

"Show me your ID," the man commanded. Caslin reluctantly took out his wallet, brandishing his warrant card. The security guard appeared satisfied and redirected the beam of his torch away from Caslin, who in turn was grateful. Caslin got a grip of himself.

"Have you come across anyone else down here?"

"No, there's no-one here but you."

"What about staff members?" Caslin pressed, glancing beyond the stocky man's frame. "Anyone at all?"

The man shook his head, "No, just you. What are you doing down here, this is off limits to the public."

"I saw…" he began, "I thought I saw someone suspicious and followed him."

"Suspicious how?"

Caslin shrugged, "A doctor. At least, he was dressed like one."

"A doctor, here in the hospital? That's strange."

Caslin ignored the sarcasm, believing he had fortuitously encountered the one guard who runs the NHS. "Anything out of the ordinary?"

"No-one dodgy… apart from you. Should I be arranging a search?"

Caslin concluded that wouldn't be necessary, "No, it's probably my imagination. Forget it."

"I'll escort you back upstairs."

"Okay," Caslin replied flatly, still looking along the corridor in expectation of seeing something. He didn't.

CHAPTER TWENTY-FOUR

"ENLIGHTEN ME, ON RABIOT," Caslin asked as soon as he got into Terry Holt's car, outside the hospital.

"Are you okay, Sir?"

Caslin cast him a look, "Yes, I'm fine. Rabiot?"

Holt didn't question further, although Caslin knew the DC was itching to know what he was doing at the hospital in the middle of the night. "Like I said on the phone, he's an Aussie national, been living here for years. Married to Samantha, a British national, and they have an eight-year-old daughter. No priors on any of them."

Caslin digested the information, "So this is a bit of a leap to link him to all this?"

"Absolutely," Holt agreed. "Everything is circumstantial. I wouldn't be looking at him if he hadn't been present at locations relevant to our timeframe."

"What about at home?"

"In Oz?" Holt clarified, taking his eyes off the road momentarily, Caslin nodded. "That's where it gets interesting. A man of the same name was detained under their Crimes Act, in Victoria. That covers domestic violence but also incidences of stalking."

"Any conviction?" Holt took a left turn. New Earswick was to be found to the north east of the city centre, barely five minutes' drive from the hospital.

"No, he was said and released without charge. I'm still waiting to find out if this is the same guy. The local police are trying to help us with that but if it is him, then—"

"We have somebody with form," Caslin finished. "Where's he working now?"

Holt shrugged, taking the first left as they entered their destination neighbourhood, "No idea, as yet. I know he's not on the current NHS register but I'll have to wait until the morning for the private centres."

They pulled up at the kerbside and looked around. New Earswick was an established estate of terraced and semidetached, brick houses, set in leafy surroundings. At this time of night all was still, with almost every house in darkness. Holt indicated which one was Rabiot's registered address. It was a nondescript, mid-terraced dwelling, set within a low hedgerow boundary. The garden appeared to be well maintained as did the house.

"Do we go in?" Holt asked.

"I didn't come out here to sit and watch," Caslin said, getting out of the car. Holt followed, although unsure whether it was the right move. "Problem, Terry?"

"It's just… with Soriza, we went in with all the bells and whistles."

"And this time it's just us?"

"Exactly," Holt said. "What if—"

"Oh, shut up, Terry. Come on."

Without another word, Caslin was off up the path, a reluctant DC in tow. Reaching the front door, Caslin rang the bell before hammering on the pane with a closed fist for good measure. After no response, he did so again. Stepping back, he looked up as a light came on upstairs.

"Wakey, wakey," Caslin said under his breath. Moments later

the hallway beyond the door was illuminated as a figure descended the stairs.

"Who is it?" a female voice called.

"Police," Caslin said. The door cracked open, security chain in place, and a pair of brown eyes peaked through. Caslin brandished his warrant card. "Forgive the time. Please may we come in?" The door was closed and they heard the sound of the chain being unhooked. Then they found themselves looking at a young woman, slight in stature, drawing a dressing gown tightly about her, a look of fear in her eyes.

"Is it Mark? What's happened?" she asked, the fear transmitting in her tone.

"Mark is your husband?" Caslin responded and she nodded. "May we come in?" She nodded again, stepping back and giving them room to enter. The hall was narrow and she ushered them into the living room.

"Is Mark okay?" she asked again.

"As far as we know," Caslin said, glancing around. "You are Samantha Rabiot?" he asked and she confirmed it. "Do you know of Mark's whereabouts?"

"Of course, he's at work."

"And where is that?" Holt asked.

"He's rostered on emergency call-outs, has been for months but I don't know where he is right now. Why do you ask?" her tone had changed to one of confusion.

"What kind of emergency?" Caslin asked, slowly pacing the room, his eyes scanning the scene as he went.

"Mental health issues and stuff," she indicated to him, "like when your lot have a problem with someone and he comes out to assess their mental state."

"To determine if they're a danger to themselves or others?" Caslin asked.

"Yes," Samantha replied. Wide awake now, it was beginning to dawn on her that this wasn't a welfare visit. "Why are you here?"

Caslin stopped before the fire, taking in the pictures on the mantel before him in a casual manner. "When will Mark be home? We need to have a word with him."

"About what?"

"A patient of his, one whose care he was involved with, up in Scotland," Caslin answered without breaking step.

"At nearly four in the morning?"

"It's very important that we speak to him, Mrs Rabiot," Caslin said. "Do you mind if my colleague has a look around?"

"He's not here," she replied flatly.

"Would you mind?" Caslin asked again.

"Help yourself but don't wake up my daughter," she said with a dismissive gesture, "I don't want her being scared to death by finding a strange man in her bedroom." Holt left the room, heading for the stairs. It was clear that they were the only ones present on the ground floor, what with it being largely open plan.

"When did you last see your husband, Mrs Rabiot?" Her eyes followed the back of Terry Holt as he disappeared upstairs.

"This afternoon, before he was called out."

"What time was that?"

"A little after four, I think."

"And he received a call? You heard it?"

Samantha shook her head, "Come to think of it, no. I went to the bathroom and when I came back, he said he had to go."

"Where was he for the rest of the day?"

"Here, with me."

"All day?"

"Yes. Why do you ask?"

Caslin ignored her question, "Did Mark say where he was going?"

Again, she shook her head, "No, he didn't say but he never does. It's all personal. You know, what with data protection and all that."

Caslin smiled and dipped his head, "Yes, of course." Holt

reappeared from upstairs, shaking his head as he descended the stairs.

"No sign," he offered in confirmation.

"Do you work, Mrs Rabiot?" Caslin asked.

"No, not since we had Jenna. Luckily with Mark's pay, I don't have to."

"Tell me, do you have your husband's mobile number to hand?"

"Only his personal phone. Not his work one."

"How comes?" Holt asked.

"He says he's not allowed to take personal calls on it, so I have to ring his own one."

"Can we have it?" Caslin asked. She nodded and went to retrieve her own. Returning from the kitchen, she was scrolling through the contacts as she spoke.

"You won't reach him, though. He never takes his personal phone with him to work. It's not insured by the NHS so if it were broken, he'd not be able to claim. That's why he leaves it here. It's there, on the table."

Caslin glanced at the dining table. A smart phone. Inclining his head, he asked, "May I?"

Samantha shrugged, "I guess so."

Crossing over, Caslin lifted it up and turned it on. The pass code screen came up and he looked to her again, "Do you know it?"

"Sorry, I don't. Look, what's this all about and don't tell me it's routine because it bloody well isn't."

Caslin put the phone down. Reaching into his pocket, he took out one of his contact cards and passed it to her. "When Mark comes home, please call me or have him do so."

Samantha took the card and cast her eyes over it with a wary glance, "Are you going to tell me what this is about, or not?"

Caslin eyed the montage of photos on the mantel. They depicted family days out, not dissimilar to those he and Karen used to display at their home. "Good looking girl," he said, pointing to one of which, he presumed, was their daughter. A sure fire way to get onside with a parent was always to praise their offspring.

Samantha smiled, "Thank you. We think so. She'll be nine next month. Can't believe it."

Caslin smiled, "I feel that way about mine. There don't appear to be many here of her father."

"Mark hates being in pictures. He always insists on holding the camera. Taking photos is one of his things, you know but I still get him occasionally," Samantha replied, crossing the room to stand before a bookcase, nestled into the alcove alongside the chimney breast. Reaching up to a high shelf, she took down a frame and passed it to him. It was a shot of Mark, his arms draped over their daughter's shoulders, both smiling at the camera on a sunny day. Caslin's blood ran cold. Momentarily stunned, he didn't react as fear and then panic surged within him. The frame slipped from his fingers, clattering to the wooden floor at his feet.

"Hey!" Samantha said but Caslin pushed past her.

"Terry, the car, now!" he barked, hurrying to the door. Caslin didn't register Holt's surprise, for he was already passing through the front door and out into the predawn light.

"Sir?" Holt replied, pulling the door closed behind him and running to catch up, which he only managed when they reached the vehicle.

"He's there, Terry," Caslin said as Holt unlocked the doors. Both men got in. Caslin met the questioning gaze as the key turned in the ignition. "He's at the bloody hospital. I saw him there before you picked me up."

"Do you think he's work—"

"No," Caslin cut him off, reaching for Holt's radio on the dashboard, "my father's there. Come on, Terry, punch it!" he ordered. Holt didn't comprehend what was going on but accepted the conveyed urgency and accelerated away with a wail from the tyres, the engine straining its way up through the lower gears. Putting the radio to his lips, Caslin rattled off his identification, "This is DI Caslin, Fulford Road. I need urgent assistance at York Hospital ICU. I'm requesting an armed response vehicle. Suspect on scene, approach with caution. Individual is potentially armed and should be considered extremely dangerous. Suspect is a white IC1 male, dark hair, approximately six-two and may well be posing as a member of medical staff."

The voice from control crackled an immediate response, "Received, all available units are being redirected. Please be advised that ETA on armed response will be fifteen minutes."

"Bugger," Caslin said aloud, he knew they would be on the scene a full ten minutes before them. Pressing the transmit button, he acknowledged the information, "Understood. Please advise that two plain clothes officers will be on the scene."

"Received," crackled the reply. Caslin dropped the radio into his lap, cursing himself as he did so.

"I bloody knew there was something wrong with that guy," he said. Holt glanced over but the comment was lost on him.

"Maybe she's right and I'm wrong and he is working at the hospital."

"He has no place on the trauma ward, Terry, no place at all."

"Why do you think he would be on the ward?" Holt asked, obviously confused by proceedings.

"My father was attacked in his home, this afternoon."

Holt returned his attention to the drive, focussing on getting there as soon as possible. Taking out his phone, Caslin looked up the hospital's number and once again, cursed himself for not making a note of the extension to the ICU. Telephoning the switchboard, his frustration grew as the automated service kicked in, offering him numbered options. Selecting the security office, he waited for the call to connect, murmuring his encouragement for them to answer. Choosing not to underplay his hand, he rapidly filled them in, "This is Detective Inspector Caslin from Fulford Road. You have a suspect on site, wanted for murder. He has been seen in and around the ICU and could potentially be targeting a patient in your care. You need to take all appropriate measures to secure the ICU. Police units are on their way. Do not approach and exercise extreme caution."

"We'll be ready," a startled voice replied. Caslin hung up.

"Come on, Terry," Caslin implored him. "Get us there."

"We're not far off," Holt reassured him, as they flew through a junction on the wrong side of the road, Caslin bracing himself against the dashboard. "We don't know that it's him—"

"It's him, Terry. I'm telling you. It's the way he looked at me. He recognised me but I didn't bloody see it." Holt took the turn into the hospital and they screeched to a halt outside Accident and Emergency. Caslin was out of the car in a flash, Holt not far behind. There was no sign of a uniformed response and Caslin put a hand on the DC's shoulder. "Wait for the others."

"No way," Holt protested. "I'm coming."

"*Wait*, Terry. That's an order. When they arrive, find the security office and bring up the CCTV. You might find him before I do." The constable was about to protest further but Caslin cut him off, "He's my father and I won't put you at risk," Caslin said, walking backwards before turning and taking off into the building, leaving Holt no option but to follow the instruction.

"Damn you."

Caslin heard Terry curse him under his breath.

Caslin's footfalls sounded heavily as he ran along the corridors, scanning the signage for directions to the Intensive Care Unit. Considering the stairs to be a less conspicuous approach, he took them two at a time. His progress slowed as he hit the third floor and the entrance to the ICU. The security door had been wedged open with a waste bin, negating the need for him to use the intercom to the nurses' station. Peering through the window, he could see nothing of note. His heart was beating rapidly and he was breathing heavily from the exertion of the run. Taking a moment to collect himself, Caslin removed the concealed Makarov. Easing the slide across, he ensured that a round was chambered and the safety was off.

Taking a deep breath, he gently pushed the door open. The hinges squeaked. It sounded impossibly loud, in the silence of the corridor, and Caslin waited before passing through. There was no movement in response and a quick glance towards the nursing station, saw it unmanned. With both hands gripping the pistol, almost for comfort, he made his way over to the desk. His palms were sweating and he had to work hard to control his breathing. Not wishing to call out, he leaned over the desk, to see into the office beyond. On the floor lay a body, it was a woman and even from the rear, Caslin knew it was the nurse he had spoken to earlier. A flash of panic shot through him as he took in the pool of crimson liquid, spreading out from under her. Looking to left and right for a signal of the attacker, he saw none.

Every fibre in his being urged him to run to his father but his moral code forced him to hold back. Slipping behind the desk, Caslin got as close to the nurse as he dared, not wishing to step in her blood and knelt. Reaching for a pulse proved futile, she had been dead for a while. A wide-eyed stare, one that he had seen far too often, conveyed the fact that life had passed from her and not painlessly. Caslin stood, returning his focus to the surroundings. He listened intently but nothing untoward came to him. Fear gnawed away at his confidence and he moved slowly but with purpose, towards the recovery room.

Approaching, Caslin could see the blinds were down, shrouding the interior. Coming to stand before the closed door, he paused. Crouching in order to give him an edge, he shifted his weight onto the balls of his feet. Reaffirming his grip on the pistol, in his right hand, he reached forward with his left and braced himself. Closing his eyes, he mouthed a silent prayer and shoved the door inwards. Hurling himself forward, firearm extended, he dived in. The dramatic entrance was met with silence. The room was empty. Everything was in order, with no evidence of a struggle.

Stepping back out into the corridor, Caslin returned to the desk. A quick search located the ward list and he found his father's name handwritten against Room Three. Resuming the search, he hugged the walls as he went. His progress was slow as he repeatedly checked around him, peering through each and every doorway that he came to. Reaching the room, he heard a sound from behind. Caslin froze. Taking a deep breath, he resolved to spin on his heel and bring the Makarov to bear, only catching himself at the last moment.

"Armed police!" a booming voice shouted, "remain as you are. Do not move or I will shoot you." Caslin followed the command. There was a moment of silence where the air seemed to crackle with tension. "Extend your right hand and release the weapon, or I will shoot you." Caslin was in no doubt as to whether it was an idle threat and did as instructed.

"I'm DI Caslin," he offered, noting that his voice broke slightly when he spoke.

"Turn around when I say... and do so... slowly," was the next instruction. He complied, finding two Maglite beams, mounted on submachine guns, trained on him. Beyond the glare, he could make out the uniforms of the armed response officers. From behind them came Terry Holt. Caslin was grateful to see him.

"That's Inspector Caslin, alright," Holt said and with that, the officers made to continue with their sweep.

"This is the target room," Caslin said, stepping aside. Retrieving the Makarov, as the men, dressed in black combat fatigues, took their positions either side of the doorway, Caslin breathed a sigh of relief. They entered with him only a step behind. He was relieved to see his father lying somewhat peacefully in bed, monitors attached, and he clearly breathing.

"Sir," Holt said softly. Caslin glanced up from his father and looked to where the DC was indicating. The relief, that had been palpable, evaporated in an instant. On the far side of the room, sitting in the visitor's chair was a security guard, the very same man whom Caslin had encountered in the basement, earlier that night. Only now, he was sitting bolt upright, eyes open, with the handle of a hunting knife protruding from his chest. The blade had pierced his lungs and the victim had coughed up a great deal of blood that had subsequently cascaded down to his chest.

Caslin approached warily, spying a sheet of paper resting against the blade, on the dead man's chest. Reaching out, he gently straightened it, to read it. There were two words, apparently written in the victim's blood. They simply read "back soon".

"Fuck me," Caslin said quietly, before casting a glance towards his father.

CHAPTER TWENTY-FIVE

"And where the hell did you get the gun from?"

Caslin hung his head, looking to the floor with thumbs pressed to his temples, hiding the grimace from the senior officers, standing before him. The headache was intense, with sharp pains pulsing through him every few seconds.

"DC Holt brings you a fresh suspect and the two of you dive in, without adequate consideration of the consequences—"

"What happened here tonight has nothing to do with us going to Rabiot's house," Caslin snapped.

"Is that right?" DCS Broadfoot asked, his usually calm manner taking on an aggressive edge that Caslin was unfamiliar with. "And you know that, how? He may have seen you at his house and reacted."

"There's no evidence for that, Sir. He was already at the hospital."

"Which is where you were supposed to be," DCI Inglis said. "You should have called me immediately, when Holt brought you the information. Your judgement is clearly impaired and you're not in a fit state of mind to be—"

"I'm beginning to question if you're fit to be on duty, at all," Broadfoot blasted him, ensuring everyone fell silent. There was unarguable logic behind that point but Caslin chose not to offer his agreement. "We can discuss that later and perhaps then, you'll have a decent explanation for carrying an illegal firearm. You were given dispensation to draw a weapon from the armoury and you knocked it back."

"I know," Caslin replied wearily, rubbing at his face. A glance towards the clock on the wall saw the hands tick past 7 a.m. and he stifled a yawn. "I'm sorry. I guess I wasn't thinking straight."

Further conversation was halted by a knock at the door. Hunter entered, casting a concerned look towards Caslin, before addressing the DCS.

"We've carried out the second sweep of the building but there's no sign. We have all the major intersections covered, in a three-mile radius, carrying out stop and search."

"Widen it," Caslin offered. John Inglis shot him a dark look.

"Do as he says. Increase the area to six miles," Broadfoot said, "and get his name, description and any other known information to the surrounding forces. I want a net thrown far and wide."

"He's not running," Caslin said, as a matter of fact.

"And how have you come to that?" Broadfoot asked with a sneer, losing patience. "He's managed to stay in the shadows so far."

"He's already changed his MO," Caslin replied, with little attempt to hide his own frustration, "and that implies he's developing, moving on."

"Moving on?" Inglis asked, seating himself on the Registrar's desk, whose office they had procured.

"We're assuming that he's our killer and if so, he went for women, young women, usually prostitutes but not necessarily so. Whatever made him move for Natalie, I don't know but maybe... that was a moment when this all changed for him. Somehow he's taking an interest in me and..."

"Your family?" Inglis said.

"Yes," Caslin replied flatly.

"He's upping the ante?" Broadfoot suggested.

"Perhaps?" said Caslin. "Some of these head cases are itching to get caught, after a while. They want their footnote in history. Is this Rabiot? Or is he just bored and trying to increase the thrill. Either way, how far he's planning to take it is another matter. He'll have to assume that we know who he is, by now. If he runs, he won't get far. This guy strikes me as a planner, meticulous in detailing what he wants and how to go about getting it. He's not about to walk away, let alone run. There's an end goal and he'll already have it in mind. We're a step behind, at least one anyway. We need to think ahead and get there before him."

"Any suggestions on how we do that?" Broadfoot asked.

Caslin appeared visually deflated, "No, I hadn't got that far. Damn my head hurts," he muttered, massaging his temples.

"Your brother?" Inglis asked. Caslin opened his eyes, flicking them in the DCI's direction.

"I don't know. Last night, I was so sure but now... the argument that was overheard..."

"It could've been Rabiot?"

"Yes, but if he'd managed to overpower Stefan, which wouldn't have been easy unless he didn't see him coming, where is he now?"

"There was no evidence of another person's blood at your father's place, which would indicate that Stefan was not badly injured. Would he have gone willingly?"

Caslin shook his head, "I doubt it but maybe, if he felt there was no other option? He must have been conscious."

"How can you be so sure?" Inglis asked.

"An unconscious man may as well be twice as heavy, when you try to lift them. It's not as easy as people think. Even a guy of Rabiot's physique would have struggled to shift Stefan more than a few feet. Let alone into a car outside. Particularly without the nosey neighbour catching on. What's bugging me is that if it wasn't Rabiot who attacked my father at his home, then how did he know we would be here, at the hospital? It's just not adding up."

"He's been following you, we know that already. We'll have to keep an open mind," Inglis offered. "Iain Robertson can go back over your father's place and see if we can shed some light on what happened. In the meantime, let's see if our search offers anything up. Your brother's description is out there so maybe we'll get a break."

"What about Stefan's phone?"

"No joy," Inglis said. "It's not been used, nor is it transmitting a location but the phone company will notify us of any change."

"I'm posting an armed guard on your father's room for the foreseeable future, until we can figure this out," Broadfoot said. "You should spend some time with him because I want you back at Fulford for a debriefing, this afternoon."

"Yes, Sir. Thank you."

"I can arrange for—"

"No thank you, Sir. I know what you're going to offer and I appreciate the thought but I don't want, or need, a bodyguard."

"That's your decision," Broadfoot said, glancing at John Inglis. "Until this afternoon then." Caslin nodded his understanding. "And Nathaniel," Caslin looked up, meeting Broadfoot's gaze, "it had better be good."

"Yes, Sir. I know."

Broadfoot left the room. Inglis let out a deep sigh, releasing some of the pent up tension.

"It's a good job you let your friend know about Rabiot," Inglis mused openly. Caslin glanced over to him.

"How do you mean?"

"Your friend… in the pictures, Rabiot took. Until we get him, we can't be sure but it looks like he's your stalker and therefore, Natalie Bermond's killer. You let your friend know, didn't you?"

"Yes, of course. In any event, she can look after herself," Caslin replied. "Why did you mention it?"

Inglis shrugged, "Just toying with possibilities. Where will he go, what will he do next? If, and I accept it's a big *if*, he came for your family, then maybe the end game you're talking about is targeting those closest to you. Seems plausible, doesn't it? Anyone close to you could be the next—"

"Bloody hell!"

"What is it?"

Caslin locked eyes with him, "Alison."

"Alison?"

"Taylor."

"The pathologist?"

Caslin was already making for the door. Inglis moved after him, "What about her?"

Caslin quickened his pace, "We had dinner last week. I should've warned her but... she wasn't in any of the photos."

"My car's outside," Inglis said, concern edging into his tone. "We can get some uniform over there as well, just in case." Within minutes they'd set off to make the short trip across the city to Dr Taylor's office.

Caslin put a call into the control room, requesting assistance. They had no definitive evidence that Rabiot was heading that way but nevertheless, he felt uneasy as they flew through red lights with their sirens blaring. He looked up Alison's number and rang it, remaining tight lipped as the call connected, before passing almost immediately to her voicemail. Cursing, he hung up. Switching to her office entry in his contacts, he tried again, only for the call to ring out. Replacing the phone in his pocket, he cursed once more.

"Maybe she's in the lab?" Inglis said aloud.

"Maybe," Caslin replied quietly. Pulling up outside, Caslin noted Alison's car was in her allotted space, one of the few present. A marked patrol car arrived as they clambered out. Inglis addressed the two uniformed officers inside.

"One of you with me," he instructed, pointing to the second constable, "Markson, you're with Caslin. Weapons drawn, take no risks. Understood?" he said the last while looking directly at Caslin, who nodded.

"You head for her office and we'll take the lab," Caslin said.

They entered the building and Inglis took off up the stairs, taking the steps two at a time. Caslin went to the left, in the direction of pathology, located on the ground floor, with PC Markson in tow. The latter drew his Taser and they progressed purposefully. A movement ahead caused them to pull up as a door opened. A woman, wearing a white laboratory coat, stepped out in front of them and gasped as they startled her. It wasn't Dr Taylor.

"Have you seen Alison, this morning?" Caslin asked.

"Yes… a little while ago," she stammered.

"Where was she?".

"In her office—"

"Thanks," he said, making to turn back the way they had come.

"But she was on her way to pathology, when I left," the woman said. "I'm sure she'll still be there. Is something wrong?"

"We hope not," Caslin replied, "but you should be somewhere public, until we make sure."

"Where?" she asked, appearing confused.

"More officers will be arriving soon. The car park is probably best," he said, resuming his course. Approaching the entrance to the labs cautiously, Caslin indicated they should continue in silence. Easing the outer door open, they listened intently but no sounds came to them. Caslin took the lead and they passed through. The corridor was wide with several doors leading off it, on either side. Caslin knew where Dr Taylor worked but they couldn't disregard the other rooms. A cursory inspection found several were locked and the others were empty. Coming to the pathology lab, Caslin paused and took a deep breath. An image of what they found at the hospital came to mind and he swallowed hard, finding his mouth dry. A shaft of light crept out from under the door, broken momentarily by movement from within.

With a glance towards Markson to check he was ready, Caslin silently mouthed a three count whilst gripping the handle. Easing the door open, he allowed the armed officer to go first, with himself only a half-step behind. The refrigerated storage units ensured a blast of cold air met them as they entered. The room was partially lit with every third neon tube engaged, lending the room an ethereal appearance and leaving much in shadow. Ahead of them, to the right, the adjoining office glowed brightly. A solitary cadaver lay on an autopsy table, shrouded entirely by a green cover and the remainder of the tables and equipment appeared clean and unused.

Caslin indicated the office with a flick of his hand and the constable nodded in agreement. Both men edged forward, putting a few paces between them. Resisting the urge to call out, Caslin wanted to find Dr Taylor hunched over her laptop, deep in thought. Coming to the office door, he once again executed a slow count and pushed it open. Stepping through he found the small room was also empty. Perhaps her colleague had been wrong and Alison was in her office after all? Feeling a gentle tap on his shoulder, he turned to see Markson indicating they should return to the lab. An enquiring look saw the constable remove his left hand from the Taser and indicate the autopsy table. It took a moment to register what he was intimating. The movement was almost imperceptible but was still movement, nonetheless. The sheet covering the cadaver was elevating and falling with regularity. Either the corpse had reanimated or the person beneath it was most certainly alive.

They slipped back in and Caslin took up a position to the left, Markson the right, bringing his Taser to bear. Caslin slowly took a hold of the cloth, at the top corner, taking care not to be too deliberate. In one motion he whipped the cover back and both officers involuntarily stepped back. Dr Taylor lay on the autopsy table, fully clothed, pale and unconscious but clearly breathing, albeit in a shallow manner. There were no visible indications of injury and Caslin apprehensively edged closer, the faint whiff of chloroform coming to him, as he leaned in to her.

"He's probably still here—"

"I am," said a voice from behind. Both men turned, only for two gunshots to reverberate around the laboratory in quick succession. Caslin saw Markson go down, discharging the Taser as he fell. The darts shot forward, taking Rabiot square in the chest but despite a grunt of pain, the weapon failed to bring him down. The constable hit the tiled floor hard, his Taser clattering down alongside him. Caslin's ears were ringing but he launched himself forward, trying to press home an advantage whilst Rabiot was disorientated. Pushing the gun away with his left hand, Caslin struck out at Rabiot's face, with his right. The Australian staggered backwards and Caslin followed through with his full weight, throwing himself head first into his opponent's abdomen in an attempt to knock him off balance and into the wall behind. Both men stumbled but Rabiot was first to regain the upper hand. Driving an elbow down onto the back of Caslin's head, he followed that move with a knee to the chest and levered Caslin to one side, before shoving him away. He attempted to bring the pistol to bear but Caslin grasped his forearm at the wrist, ensuring the gun was directed away and pushed back with all his strength.

The men grappled for supremacy, Rabiot's superior size and strength forcing Caslin backwards. They cannoned repeatedly off of the walls and equipment in their apparent life or death struggle. Caslin let out a frustrated scream, putting every ounce of energy into repelling the attacks but with little success. He was losing with every second that passed and he knew it. The barrel of the gun was edging closer towards him and panic set in. Rabiot must've sensed Caslin's strength dissipating, redoubling his efforts and straining every sinew to overpower him. Caslin launched a headbutt but it failed to land and he found himself off balance with his opponent pressing for an advantage. Falling backwards and gathering pace, Caslin sought to right himself. He struck something solid at waist height and before he could react, Rabiot had him pinned down across an autopsy table, one hand locked around his throat with the other trying to level the gun at his face. Caslin scrabbled at Rabiot's grip, struggling to breathe while his weaker left hand was losing the battle over the weapon. His thoughts momentarily became confused and his vision blurred before settling into a tunnel effect. Rabiot's demonic, focussed expression, now all that he could see.

Suddenly the grip loosened fractionally and Caslin found a second wind. Managing to shift his opponent's weight from atop him to the side, he had just enough freedom to plant his feet and pull himself upright. Drawing breath sharply, Caslin was surprised not to feel the impact of the expected bullet. Instead Rabiot turned away from him, lashing out with his weapon. Alison fell as she was pistol whipped across the side of the head, collapsing to the floor along with the desk lamp she had struck her assailant with. Rabiot spun back around but by now, had lost the momentum and Caslin leapt forward and on this occasion, landing a headbutt on to the bridge of Rabiot's nose. The larger man faltered and Caslin kicked out, sending the gun from Rabiot's grasp and spinning across the floor. Launching a blistering combination of punches, Caslin felt a surge of anticipation at taking the lead for the first time but still, the other kept coming back at him.

Drawing on his own reserves, Rabiot launched a counter attack that pushed Caslin onto the back foot, once again. Stepping away, to give himself some space, Caslin was dismayed to see his opponent draw a knife, concealed down by his ankle. Tearing off his jacket, he wrapped it around one hand and forearm, to vainly offer some form of protection. Rabiot flew at him like a man possessed, slashing wildly to the left and right. Caslin deflected the blows away from him as best he could. They circled each other and Caslin cast a brief eye over Alison, trying to ascertain her injury. It was impossible to tell but for now, she remained motionless. The thought occurred that there was no margin for error. He knew if he lost this fight, both of them were as good as dead.

"I'm disappointed in you," Rabiot said, in between ragged draws of breath.

"Is that right?" Caslin replied, not taking his eye off of him.

"This isn't how we were supposed to meet." Caslin saw an opportunity to buy time.

"How about we call it a day now? What do you think?" Rabiot shook his head, an action accompanied by a half-smile.

"If this is where it has to be, then so be it." He jumped forward, swinging the knife in a wide arc. Caslin leapt backwards, the blade missing him by inches. Taking refuge behind an autopsy table, Caslin used it as a barrier to allow some breathing space. Assistance would arrive soon enough and the longer he kept Rabiot at bay, the greater his chances of a positive ending.

"Why focus on me, Mark? Bit of a change, isn't it?" Caslin asked, gently bracing himself against the table.

"It's like anything else, after a while," Rabiot replied, edging to his left. Caslin mirrored the movement in the opposite direction, maintaining the defensive advantage.

"Life in general?"

"Things become too easy… too dull…" Rabiot said coldly. "A little freshening up, from time to time is required."

"You're another attention seeker, desperate for his mother's affection? Looking to get caught, to have your moment in the sun, like so many others?" Caslin glanced at PC Markson, on the floor. He knew he was dead.

"My family are close. My mother loves me very much. They are good people," Rabiot said with a grin.

"Many psychos convince themselves of that."

"You must have chased some idiots in the past, if that's what you think this is."

"I've brought down all kinds," Caslin countered. "Why me, Mark?"

Rabiot shrugged, "Why not?"

"I thought we were done with the bullshit. Why me?" Rabiot appeared thoughtful but that gave no indication that Caslin could relax.

"You're a challenge, a worthy adversary. I saw you on the TV. You didn't want to be there. You're not playing at being a policeman, you wear it on your sleeve. There are very few that you meet with genuine passion, these days."

"Usually I would take that as a compliment."

"You should/said Being passionate is something we share."

"For different things though, I dare say."

"What I do is too easy. No-one has ever got close to me—"

"How long have you been doing this?" Caslin asked, drawing a laugh from Rabiot. It was a sound so nonchalant that it chilled Caslin to his core.

"You know, there was this campaign once, up in Sunderland, to find a couple of missing pensioners. No-one even realises that they're dead, three years on. Imagine that. How many people go missing every year? Two… three thousand… more?"

"At least," Caslin conceded.

"All it takes is preparation. The army taught me that."

"Where did you serve?" Caslin asked, his eyes flitting towards the door. Rabiot noticed.

"Expecting someone?"

"Hoping, more like, seeing as we're being honest."

"Let them come."

"Until then," Caslin said, "tell me where you get your love of… this…"

"Craft?" Rabiot finished, Caslin inclined his head. "Advanced recon. Seven years."

"My brother was infantry," Caslin offered. "Where is he?"

Rabiot's expression split a broad grin, "Oh… wouldn't you just like me to give you all the answers? Despite so many positive attributes, this is why you still disappoint me, Inspector Caslin."

"How's that?"

"You bear such an emotional strain, day to day, and on the whole, you manage it quite well. And yet, you don't see what's happening right under your nose, even with those closest to you."

Now Caslin forced a smile, "You sound like a shrink, I once knew."

"That's my job. It requires an innate ability to focus, to bring order to the chaos."

"Why Natalie Bermond?"

"I didn't know who she was," Rabiot said flippantly. "You see, that's where things changed… my routines… my plans."

"You watch your targets, don't you? Like you did me?"

"You wouldn't believe the lengths that I have gone to," Rabiot boasted.

"Try me."

Rabiot smiled, appearing to mull it over, "I guess it can't hurt. I move around a lot, for my work. Even when I'm settled, the opportunity to travel is a constant. The possibilities are almost endless. To be a stranger in a town, or city, is a liberating experience. A place unconnected to me makes it simple. I take a train, a flight, whichever suits, then hire a car and drive to another city, at the reaches of the mileage allowance. From there, a target usually flags itself up in a short time."

"How do you choose?"

"If you sit in a park on a summer's day, outside a coffee shop or hell, even take a walk around a supermarket," he chuckled, "one or two people will catch the eye. Have you ever done that, watched someone without them knowing? I'll bet you have. Probably a woman, right?"

"You follow them?"

"Of course. They lead me home and that's where the

excitement ramps up. I weigh up the risks versus the opportunities."

"Such as?"

"Is there an integral garage? It's easier to break into the house proper without being seen or heard. Do they have kids or a dog? How close are their neighbours? Should I take them in their home or transport them elsewhere and what do I do with them once I'm through?"

"You're a twisted bastard," Caslin said.

"That couple I mentioned, in Sunderland, were a test," Rabiot spoke excitedly, recounting the event. "He was a big guy, so I took them while they slept. A gun, a couple of cable ties and a promise that I was only there to rob, kept any resistance to a minimum and made them compliant."

"But you didn't stick to that, did you?"

Rabiot shook his head, "No. I took them out to a derelict farmhouse that I'd come across on another trip. The project went like clockwork, as they do, until the husband got loose, anyway. I had him tied to a chair in the basement but I guess he couldn't handle listening to her screaming. He managed to get upstairs and rush me, like some kind of hero—"

"What happened?"

"I beat him to death, in front of his wife," Rabiot said with a frown. "Man, that guy really pissed me off. I had plans for him and he damn well ruined them. It just meant that I spent longer on her that's all." Caslin felt rage building from the pit of his stomach but he maintained his composure although his voice took on a tone of controlled anger.

"Who were they?"

Rabiot shrugged, "I remember her screaming for Jeff but seriously, how would I know? I left them there, in the farmhouse, covered up with an old length of carpet that I found lying about. They're probably still there, stinking the place out, by now."

"You speak about this stuff like you saw it in a film."

"I tell you, when I was a kid, not more than seven or eight, I was mucking about in the bush with some friends. I'd lifted a gun from my old man's cabinet. We came across a cat and I figured it'd be fun if I shot it. It screeched like nothing I'd heard before, ran around in circles for at least ten minutes, before it died. Funniest thing I'd ever seen but when I looked at my friends, they were horrified. One of the girls threw up, right there."

"Is there a moral to that story?"

"I learned something, that day, and it's seen me right ever since."

"Which was?"

"Never let people know who you are or what you're thinking. I'm different to people like them, people like you."

"No argument from me," Caslin said. "What about Natalie? You said things changed."

"Yeah. With hindsight, she was probably a mistake. Too close to home."

"Complacent? You broke your own rules?"

Rabiot nodded, "I should've known better. I never act on impulse. I've spent years planning, scouting locations, planting my kill boxes—"

"Kill boxes?" Caslin asked.

"Old recon trick. I stash equipment around the country, buried in fields, others off of laybys, remote but reachable. I can prep a weapon, place it in an airtight container and it'll still be ready to fire when I come back to it, even years off. Anything else I need, cable ties, rope, bleach, are all there."

"Bleach?"

"Or drain cleaner, whatever was easy to hand. Wipes out the DNA. The less I travel with, the more likely I am to pass unnoticed. Turn the mobile off, use only cash. I may as well be a ghost, in and out before anyone realises someone was ever there."

"This time, with Natalie?"

"Too impulsive. I saw her. I wanted her, so I took her. Nice girl. I enjoyed her company, albeit briefly." The callous tone left Caslin certain that he was facing a sociopath.

"The ransom?"

"Spur of the moment. Too good an opportunity to miss—"

"You're out of work… and you have a family to feed." The last comment seemed to strike a chord as the mask of determination faded if only slightly. Caslin couldn't drop his guard. Rabiot was talkative but both men knew this was merely a pause. "You broke your own rule. That was risky."

"Yeah, you're right. Finding out who she was and the next day, going back and rigging that photograph took a bit of doing but it worked."

"You have a family of your own, you have a daughter. Did you think of her when you set out on all of this?"

"Leave them out of it."

Caslin sensed he had found the chink in the armour.

"Can't though, can we? How do you think all this is going to affect her when it comes out, her school friends… your wife?"

"I told you to leave them out of it!" He lunged forward, scrambling unceremoniously over the table between them, startling Caslin with a vicious attack that he only just managed to fend off.

The fight was joined once more, Caslin endeavouring to hold his ground. Such was the sustained nature of the assault that he found the respite had been of little benefit. Deflecting blow after blow, he found himself back pedalling faster than he had space to manoeuvre into. In the corner of his eye, he saw Alison crawling towards the entrance. Backing away, deeper into the room, he took a calculated gamble and put their attacker between them, enabling her to reach the door unobserved.

Caslin was momentarily relieved to see her reach safety but that proved short lived, for Rabiot was upon him, in a heartbeat. Once at the rear wall, there was nowhere else to go and he found himself pinned against it, a blade at his throat. Checkmate.

"I thought that this might end with the two of us, together," Rabiot whispered to Caslin, "but it wasn't supposed to happen yet. I underestimated you."

"Sorry to disappoint," Caslin replied genuinely, trying not to convey the terror that he now felt.

"We're leaving, you and me."

Caslin blinked, "You think I'm going to walk out with you?" Rabiot stepped back but held the blade before him, well within striking distance of Caslin's face.

"Yes, I do," he said calmly.

The entrance doors were thrown open, DCI Inglis in the lead. Rabiot grasped Caslin by the shoulder and spun him around, using him as a shield, brandishing the knife close to his throat.

"Mark Rabiot!" Inglis barked. "This is over."

"That's my decision, not yours. Back off."

"You're not leaving here," Inglis said flatly as Rabiot inched forward, pushing Caslin before him.

"Easy for you to say, Guv," Caslin muttered quietly, the distance between them closing. Rabiot nudged Caslin forward almost to arm's length but kept the blade touching the base of his skull. With his free hand, Rabiot reached into his coat pocket and withdrew an object. Caslin saw Inglis' resolve falter and the accompanying officer looked across for guidance, his Taser trained on the advancing pair. Rabiot held the grenade aloft for all, except Caslin, to see before using his teeth to remove the pin. He spat it to the floor. Caslin noted it and raised his eyes heavenward.

"What do I do, Sir?" the constable asked.

"Put the knife down," Inglis instructed Rabiot. "Give it up. There's no need for anyone else to die here, today."

"Move aside or I promise you, we will *all die*," Rabiot said, stepping forward and wrapping an arm around Caslin, returning the point of the knife to his throat. No-one present was in any doubt that he meant what he said.

"We can't do that," Inglis said but his tone implied a lack of faith in that pronouncement.

"Where's my brother?" Caslin asked quietly, turning his head sideways to look at his abductor.

"Shut up," Rabiot replied. "I said back off!" he shouted at Inglis, who stood his ground, barring the exit.

"What do we tell your daughter?" Caslin asked.

"*I told you to shut up,*" Rabiot hissed.

"Simple question, Mark. You may never see her again. What should we tell her?"

Rabiot hesitated for a fraction of a second but it was enough. Caslin brought his forearm up, under Rabiot's, brushing the blade away. Twisting his body, he levered himself away from the Australian's flailing grasp. The moment was seized and the constable discharged his Taser. Caslin shrieked as the two were momentarily still in contact when the darts struck home. On this occasion, the weapon delivered more of a blow, bringing Rabiot to his knees. He screamed in pain but was far from incapacitated. Caslin lurched away, trying to run but found his legs unsupportive and he faltered. Inglis looped one arm under his and practically hurled both men towards the door. Firm hands seized him from the other side, as the constable also took hold, dragging him forward. The three officers clattered through the double doors and into the corridor beyond. Such was their pace, off balance, they stumbled over each other, colliding and crashing to the floor. Inglis landed atop Caslin, who exhaled heavily as he impacted the ground. An attempt to draw breath proved futile as a sensational force struck him, forcing him down. Fighting for air, he found none to be had, as a wave of heat washed over him and he clamped his eyes shut, silently screaming until it passed.

As quickly as it began, it was over. Caslin gasped for breath. The relief of the oxygen was surpassed by the acrid smell, taste and subsequent coughing that came with it. To his left, Inglis was up on his haunches, coughing in spasm, a swirl of dark smoke passing about him. Caslin tried not to but his body forced him to draw breath, this time in a smaller volume, only to reject it once more. Feeling something trickling down the side of his face, he tentatively inspected it. Despite finding it wet and sticky he was unable to process what had happened. Looking to his right he saw the uniformed officer, on one knee, bracing himself against the wall. He was mouthing something to him but Caslin couldn't make it out. There was blood running from his ear. His own were ringing, impossibly loud, and he reached up with one hand to find his head too sensitive to touch.

Rolling onto his side, Caslin levered himself up onto one elbow, amongst the debris and looked back towards the pathology lab. The smoke was still thick but beginning to dissipate as a draught pulled it through the building. The doors were missing, the frames warped and twisted at a peculiar angle. He could make out no detail beyond them for everything was shrouded in a veil of darkness.

"Now it's over," he said aloud but no-one heard the words.

CHAPTER TWENTY-SIX

"You have a mild concussion, nothing to be too concerned about," the doctor told him. Caslin gingerly probed the left side of his body with his fingers.

"Forgive me if I disagree," he replied, wincing as he pressed too hard.

The doctor smiled, "The x-rays show three fractures to your ribs. Your bruising will develop further over the next couple of days and they'll be sensitive for a time but other than that, there'll be no lasting damage. You were lucky." Caslin nodded his agreement but, sitting in a triage cubicle at York Hospital, he felt far from it. The last he remembered was his attempt to stand, following the explosion in Dr Taylor's pathology lab. The next he knew he was waking in an ambulance heading for the hospital. "I see no need for you to stay in overnight, unless you feel any significant change in your pain levels, nausea or vomiting. Come back to us if you do. In the meantime, I'll prescribe you some pain relief to tide you over."

"Thank you, Doctor," Caslin replied, annoyed with himself for the flash of anticipation within him upon hearing the last. DCS Broadfoot, concern etched onto his face, arrived as the curtain to the cubicle was drawn back. Despite the apparent conclusion to the case, he still carried an air of apprehension about him, as if the weight was yet to lift. That struck Caslin as odd, for Broadfoot was the archetypal man manager and consummate politician, always seemingly at ease with himself, no matter what pressure was put upon him.

"Good to see you, Nathaniel," he said, extending his hand. Caslin took it. "You're in better shape than I was expecting."

"The others?" Caslin asked.

"Well enough." Caslin observed his grave expression. "I'm afraid that PC Markson didn't pull through." That news wasn't a surprise to him.

"I didn't know him particularly well."

"Married, two young children," Broadfoot said solemnly, answering the perceived question.

"Is Alison okay?" Broadfoot's demeanour shifted, taking on a more upbeat tone.

"Yes, Dr Taylor needed treatment for a head injury but I've been reassured that she'll make a full recovery. Lucky woman. What with you and John turning up when you did." *There was that word again*, Caslin thought. "What drew you to her, this morning?"

Caslin shook his head and shrugged, "I hadn't warned her. We knew that he was following me, possibly targeting those near to me and it didn't cross my mind until today, that he may have seen us together."

"You're close, the two of you?" Caslin took the measure of the question. The last he wanted was to become the focus of station gossip, at least no more than he already was.

"No, not really. We had a meal whilst going over her findings on Melissa Brooke that's all. Probably why—"

"It slipped your mind to warn her," Broadfoot finished.

"Exactly," Caslin agreed. "Stupid oversight, really."

"It's probably a reasonable one. Don't beat yourself up too much, Nathaniel. Plenty of time to analyse all of this, in the coming days," Broadfoot said. He looked away from him at that point and Caslin was momentarily fearful of what was coming next. "We haven't had any joy in the search for your brother, yet. That's not to say that we won't, mind you. I have Hunter leading a team over at Rabiot's house, as we speak. They'll take it apart looking for any indication of where Stefan might be." Caslin appreciated the focus shifting to the search for his brother.

"Thank you, Sir. If there's anything, I'm sure she'll find it."

"I've every confidence in her and the team. We're treating Stefan as if he were one of our own. Have you spoken with your father?"

Caslin shook his head, "No, he'll likely be out for a while yet but I'll call in on him when we're through here, make sure there hasn't been a change in his condition."

"Don't let me hold you up," Broadfoot said, making to leave. "I'll touch base with you later, to arrange a debrief."

Caslin picked his jacket up from the end of the bed, dusting it off with the palm of his hand. The mixed aroma of smoke along with the grenade's cordite, was strong upon it. He threw it across his arm rather than put it on. Leaving the cubicle, his thoughts turned to his brother and what had become of him. Choosing to think positively, going against all empirical experience, he racked his brains to figure out where Rabiot could have taken him. With a twisted sociopath, he was in no doubt that Rabiot was such a person, there were no end to the possibilities nor the motives for abducting his brother. Tears welled in his eyes and he fought to suppress the avalanche of emotion, threatening to overwhelm him. They hadn't been close for many years but family duty and blood ties, were forged in steel. The sense of guilt, of being the one among them who should've been in a position to protect his family, weighed heavily upon him.

Leaving A and E, he walked to the lifts. His side was sore and he felt lightheaded so ignoring the stairs were justified, on this occasion. Pressing the button to call the lift, he played over their confrontation, in his mind. There must have been something that was said, at the very least a hint, of what he had done with

Stefan. Mulling over the timeline, as the doors opened with a chime, he realised that Rabiot had a narrow window in which to leave with Stefan and take him somewhere else, let alone dispose of his body. There were only a few hours between the abduction and Rabiot's sighting, by Caslin, at the hospital. Where could he have been and how far could he have gone, in the intervening time? The abduction implied that Rabiot wanted him alive, for whatever purpose. Therefore, the logic would follow that his brother was still alive. Dr Taylor had been knocked out with chloroform, perhaps Stefan was given the same treatment or was restrained in some other way. Why though, with the perfect opportunity to do so, hadn't Rabiot inflicted an emotional blow by revealing or implying, the nature of his brother's fate?

Once the lift ascended to the third floor, the doors parted and Caslin stepped out. He was buzzed through the security entrance to his father's ward, one he had not visited previously. The events of the night before had seen the closure of much of the ICU, for it was still a crime scene. In the meantime, those patients who could be moved had been transferred to nearby facilities. There was still an armed policeman standing outside his father's room and Caslin brandished his warrant card, despite being recognised on sight, and was bidden entry.

He felt a crushing blow, observing his father lying in the bed, pale and gaunt. His shallow breathing pattern, along with the regular accompaniment of a beep from a monitor, all there was to indicate he was still with them. His face was badly swollen with areas of deep blue and black, symptomatic of the beating that he had taken at the hands of Rabiot. Even were his father not in a medically induced coma, it was doubtful he'd be able to open his eyes, such was his physical condition. Pulling the visitor's chair as close as he dared without fear of interfering with the equipment, Caslin sat down. Leaning forward, elbows to his knees, he put his head in his hands and closed his eyes, looking to the floor. The only time in memory that he'd felt this helpless had been the day Karen asked him to leave, his marriage and career in tatters. Reaching out, he placed a hand on his father's forearm. There was no response but he hadn't expected one.

Turning his thoughts back to Rabiot, Caslin tried once more to make sense of what motivated the abduction. He had goaded Caslin, pointing out his lack of knowledge about those people closest to him. It was true that he'd underestimated the dangers they were exposed to. Having discovered the wall of pictures detailing his own prominence in the case, he should have reacted differently. There had been a collective failure in understanding the threat. Looking at his father, the guilt washed over him in a tsunami effect.

"I'm sorry, Dad," he said quietly. "I should have known better." There was a knock on the door and he glanced sideways. The officer outside held the door open, indicating another visitor. It was Alison Taylor. She inclined her head slightly to check it was okay to enter. He beckoned her in with a weak smile.

"Kyle told me you'd be here," she said coming to stand alongside him. "I hope I'm not intruding."

Caslin shook his head, noting she was on first name terms with the Chief Super, "Of course not. It's good to see you." She reached out, placing a reassuring hand on his shoulder. Instinctively, he moved his hand to meet hers. "I'm sorry that I brought you into all this."

"Nonsense," she replied. "*He* brought me into it. If you hadn't come when you did—"

"We should've known... I... should've known, you were at risk."

"How could you possibly? Men like him are few and far between, thankfully," she said. He rose from the chair, offering her his seat. She made to decline but he insisted.

"I was coming to see you, once I had visited my father. How are you?"

"I've one hell of a headache but I'll be okay, Nate."

He observed the dressing on the side of her head.

"How is it?" he asked, eyeing the area.

"Fourteen stitches," she replied with only the hint of a smile, before continuing, "but I'm alive. Largely, thanks to you."

Caslin chuckled, "I could say the same."

"Call it even?"

"You can buy me dinner," he said with a grin, before the feeling of guilt returned at his shockingly inappropriate sense of timing. The grin faded rapidly.

"Name it," Alison replied. "I think once this is settled, we could all do with some time off. Kyle tells me that they're looking for your brother?" Caslin looked away, rubbing at his eyes. "I hope they find him." He nodded but couldn't think of any words to convey his feelings about the situation.

"Me too," he said meekly, which he realised was a wholly inadequate response, under the circumstances.

"I have a lift home waiting for me, downstairs," she said, standing up. "I could stay, if you would prefer?"

Caslin shook his head, "I think you should go home, get some rest. Try to put today behind you."

"It's no trouble, I'd be happy to."

"Thanks," Caslin said, genuinely, "but I'm not great company and don't see that changing anytime soon. Besides, Broadfoot... Kyle... will want me back at Fulford Road soon enough, to explain myself."

"Okay," Alison replied, squeezing his arm affectionately. "You know where I am, if you want to talk." She backed away, offering him a warm smile as she turned away. He occupied the vacated chair. Returning his attention to his father, he didn't notice at first that she was still at the door. Almost as an afterthought, she looked over her shoulder. "I know this isn't really the time but I meant to ask you, how did you know about Melissa Brooke's condition?" Caslin looked at her, confused.

"Condition?"

"Yes, her medical condition. You got me thinking, after we had dinner and I reran her bloodwork."

"Looking for what?"

"Prescription drugs as opposed to the illegals."

"What did you find?"

"The Zyprexa, the antipsychotic that you asked me about."

"What about it?"

"Melissa had it in her system," she said. "I chased up her medical records and she had a long history of treatment for paranoid schizophrenia. Zyprexa was one of several medications that she had been taking for quite some time." Caslin sat in silence, processing the information.

"I knew she'd had a drug problem, in her past. Her mother and a… colleague, told me that."

"You didn't know about her mental state?"

Caslin shook his head, "Not to that extent, no. Thinking about it, not at all, really."

"Oh… I'm sorry," Alison said, flushing with embarrassment. "I figured you were just a great detective."

Caslin smiled at the last, "I am an exceptional detective. I just choose to hide it well." Alison excused herself and left, the door swinging closed behind her. Taking out his mobile phone, he stared at the blank screen. Tossing it gently within his palm, he toyed with the details over and over, in his mind. That information had tweaked something in his subconscious and he sought to pull it together. The door opened and a nurse entered. Seeing the phone, she tutted.

"Please could you step out, if you're planning to use that? The signal can interfere with the machines," she said, indicating his father.

"Really? I thought that was a myth."

"Well, whatever it is, it's policy," she replied, politely and Caslin didn't take offence. He got up and left the room. Stepping out into the corridor, he acknowledged the protection officer and walked towards the ward exit, scrolling through his contacts as he went. Coming to stand before the lifts, he found the number he was searching for and hit dial whilst summoning the lift. The phone call took a moment to connect and he was forced to wait a number of rings before the recipient answered.

"Well, it's about time. I was expecting your call," a familiar voice said without even the most basic of greetings.

"I know where you'll be," Caslin replied, returning the lack of courtesy. "I'll be there within an hour."

"I think you should be able to make it in less than thirty minutes. It would be prudent to do so."

"One hour," he replied curtly. The call ended as the doors opened. Caslin put his phone back in his pocket and stepped in, pressing the ground floor button. He now knew what he had to do. The guilt, the self-doubt, any feeling of blame had gone, to be replaced by a focussed rage. Only one course of action remained open to him and with it came a feeling of dread, gathering in the pit of his stomach.

CHAPTER TWENTY-SEVEN

CASLIN PASSED the cabbie a ten-pound note and got out, not waiting for his change. Mounting the steps into the station, he passed Linda on the desk but gave her only a cursory greeting as he went through the security door to the station proper. Barely acknowledging anyone who crossed his path, he took a left and headed downstairs, to the basement level. The archives and the evidence rooms were of no interest to him and when he reached his destination, he stood outside, taking a deep breath before turning the handle and walking through.

"Hello, Maurice," Caslin greeted the desk sergeant, a fixture of Fulford Road, not far off retirement. He looked up from his paperwork, smiled and crossed to the counter.

"It's good to see you're okay, Nate. You look a little banged up if you don't mind me saying? Nasty business. Any word on your brother?"

Caslin shook his head, "Not yet. Listen, I'm a bit pushed for time but that executive order that came down from upstairs, regarding—"

"You drawing a firearm?" Maurice finished for him, Caslin nodded.

"I'd like to take the Chief up on it." The desk sergeant

appeared taken aback. Caslin recognised his reticence and continued, "It's not been countermanded, has it?"

"No, no, of course not," Maurice shook his head. "I thought that—"

"So, can I draw a weapon, or not?"

"I... I... don't see why not but why—"

"Until this investigation is complete, I want... I need to be able to protect my family. You can understand that, can't you?"

Maurice visibly relaxed, "Of course, bear with me." He retreated from the counter and punched his security code into a door behind him before disappearing into the armoury. Caslin glanced around him, his eyes flitting nervously towards the security camera, mounted in the ceiling. Maurice reappeared within a couple of minutes, two boxes held out before him. He placed them down on the counter and reached for a clipboard. Scribbling details down onto a form he told Caslin what he was issuing him.

"This is a Glock 17. It's the standard model, 9mm and carries a seventeen round capacity, in each magazine. It weighs a little over nine-hundred grams, fully loaded, and has a 'safe action' trigger. You'll be far less likely to accidentally shoot yourself or anyone else, for that matter."

"Things have moved on from the old six shooter, then," Caslin replied, appearing nonchalant.

Maurice glanced up from his clipboard with a serious expression, "I know you've had your training on semiautomatic firearms. Can you handle this weapon confidently? If not—"

"I can," Caslin assured him. "I can. Sorry, I didn't mean to be flippant."

"Okay then," Maurice said, returning to his paperwork. "I'm also issuing you a box of ammunition. I'll expect everything documented here to be returned, assuming that you have no need to discharge the weapon, once you no longer have need of it."

"Understood," Caslin replied. Maurice passed him the clipboard.

"Please double check what I've put down, read the declaration at the bottom and sign." Caslin did so and passed it back. The armoury sergeant pushed the boxes towards him and Caslin scooped them up. "It's a reliable bit of kit. It won't let you down."

"Thanks," Caslin said. Once back out in the corridor, he made his way to the archive room. No-one was present inside and he quickly opened the boxes. The pistol was well maintained and having fed two magazines, he lodged the first back into the pistol, chambering a round and placed the second in his jacket pocket. Concealing the weapon in the rear waistband of his trousers, he stashed the now empty boxes on a shelf, behind some archived files. Forcing himself to calm his nerves, he returned to the corridor and made his way back upstairs. Feeling on edge, making his way through the station, he left without speaking to anyone. Once clear of Fulford Road he stopped and called a taxi, arranging to be picked up from the nearby Holly Lodge Hotel.

The taxi arrived within five minutes and the ride out took just shy of twenty, for the rush hour traffic had long since subsided. Indicating for them to pull in at the side of the road, the driver protested as they were still on the highway but Caslin dismissed his concerns. Again, he didn't wait for his change and got out. The car accelerated away and Caslin took in his surroundings. Many of the warehouse units in view, were deserted and locked up for the night. Only those loading delivery vans or with nightshift processes had anything but security lights on.

He waited for a break in the traffic and then trotted across the carriageway to enter the industrial estate. Realising that the allotted hour had passed some time ago, he broke into a run. The pace caused him no end of discomfort and having covered barely half of the distance, he found himself grimacing with every step.

Slowing as he approached the far end of the through road, he dropped to his haunches, not only to get his breath back but also to give him a chance to survey the ground. With no intention of walking up to the main gate, he decided the adjacent facility to the left, was his best bet. The entrance gate was relatively easy to overcome and he landed deftly on the other side. There were several gate cameras trained on him at that point but they weren't his immediate concern. Quickly covering the ground between the gate and the building proper, he used it to mask his advance.

There was no visible activity within the compound next door but he figured that belied what was inside. Moving around the compound, he looked for any weakness which he could exploit, in order to scale the perimeter fence separating the two units, unseen. He found such a point at the south eastern corner, where he judged there to be a gap in the continuance of the security cameras. If he was wrong, he would be in big trouble and very quickly. The fence was roughly eight feet in height with three lengths of razor wire, set at forty-five degrees, along the length of the crest. Taking off his jacket, he wrapped it around one arm and, with one last check that he wouldn't be seen, he ran to the fence. The chain links rattled as he clambered up, throwing his jacket across the razor wire to give him some protection as he negotiated the final ascent. With some difficulty, far slower than he would've liked, he managed to haul himself over the top and dropped to the other side. He landed unceremoniously on concrete and collapsed into a heap, knocking the wind from his lungs.

Leaving his jacket atop the fence, he drew his weapon and cautiously moved towards the warehouse. It was of steel-framed construction with corrugated infill panels. The windows were largely confined to the mezzanine area, where the offices were housed and alongside the access points to the building, at the front and rear. Apart from the emergency exits, there were no internal viewpoints in his direction, allowing Caslin to approach unobserved. From memory, he tried to recall the interior layout of the building. It had been largely empty, the one and only time that he had been here previously and he considered how that may have changed. If so, there was a good chance of concealing himself within, provided he could gain entry. Any further planning, beyond his end goal, would have to wait. Whatever he encountered inside would impact the strategy and he wouldn't know that until he was there. Hugging the side of the building, he made his way to the rear.

Reaching the corner, he pressed himself against the wall before risking a glance. Four cars were parked alongside each other, two of which he recognised. Again, there was no movement and he ducked down, making his way under the windows at the rear, so as not to be seen. They were expecting him; of that he was certain. Standing next to an entrance door, he chanced a look through the nearest window. Inside were rows of storage racks, running into the distance. All were arranged symmetrically with regular spacing between them. Many were filled to capacity with shrink wrapped items, stored on pallets, at various levels. Caslin could only guess at what was contained within them. Probably legitimate wares being used as a front for laundering, smuggling or a combination of the two and more besides.

With his confidence boosted by the potential for him to slip in unnoticed, he tried the handle of the door and was relieved to find it unlocked. The hinges were well oiled and the door gave way with little effort and more importantly, little noise. Passing through, he eased it closed behind him and scampered towards the racking, seeking shelter while he got his bearings. There were muffled voices coming from further in, the sound echoing in the cavernous roof space. Caslin couldn't distinguish them and therefore had no idea how many people were talking, let alone present, but evidently, he was at a distinct disadvantage on the numbers front. Moving with purpose, as quickly as he dared for fear of discovery, he progressed between the racks, making his way towards the voices.

Knowing he was closing in on their position but still unable to see them, Caslin paused to assess his options. The prospect of coming to a negotiated settlement was rapidly dismissed. If he had believed in that solution, he wouldn't have adopted this clandestine approach. Seizing the initiative would most likely yield the best outcome. All of them would have to be neutralised in one motion. Feeling the trigger, Caslin shifted his grip, fearful of accidently discharging the weapon with its safety lever being built into the trigger mechanism. Too much pressure and he might accidentally shoot himself, whilst seeking to control the adrenalin pulsing through him. His heart was hammering and his hands trembling at the prospect of the forthcoming confrontation. Inaction was giving fear a chance to assert itself. He knew it was now or never. Stooping low, he passed through the next run of racking, figuring it to be the penultimate row before he would clap eyes upon his quarry. The assessment was accurate, for once in the next aisle he could see figures moving beyond the pallets, in fleeting glimpses. He counted six that he could see, too many to overpower in a straight fight but if he held his nerve and got the jump on them, he had a chance.

The familiar trilling of his ringtone, bursting into life, sent him into a panic. Silently cursing whilst scrabbling through his pockets to silence it, proved ultimately futile, as bodies honed into view before him. Caslin leapt forward, weapon raised, bellowing commands.

"Police, stand down your weapons!" he screamed. He wasn't the only one shouting for each of them were equally vocal although in another language. With their weapons drawn, levelled at him, the standoff continued with neither side backing down. Everyone was apparently unwilling to open fire. "Stand down!" Caslin reiterated, fear edging his tone. Something in the corner of his eye made him look up, just in time to see a figure drop from above. The blow to his head was sudden and everything immediately went dark. The sensation of falling was strangely comforting and Caslin instinctively tried to keep hold of his gun but all feeling left him.

THE FLOOR WAS cold and hard, the back of his head grating against it as he moved. Images of people and colour passed in and out of his vision. For a moment he thought he was upside down only to feel his feet hit the concrete as he came to a sudden stop. Those foreign voices carried in the air about him, only this time without the menace. Darkness followed. He heard muffled voices, along with a stinging feeling on his face, not once but again and again, in a regular pattern. Opening his eyes, he saw a familiar face standing over him. He received another slap, seemingly for good measure. Caslin had no idea how long he had been out.

"He's awake," Karl said, this time in English.

"Good," Caslin heard another say, from a short distance away, knowing it was Durakovic himself. "Why not bring the family back together." At that point, two men roughly manhandled Caslin upright before aggressively dragging him forward and dropping him back to the ground. His head swam and his vision blurred momentarily before righting itself. Looking in the direction that he was facing, he observed someone sitting in a chair, less than two metres away. Caslin realised that he knew him but even so, he was barely recognisable. The face was so pulped and bloodied that he hardly resembled him at all. Neither of his eyes could open and his lips were swollen and split in several places. Blood streamed in equal measure from numerous other injuries. Even so, Caslin knew that this was his brother, Stefan.

"Hey, big brother. Some kind of mess you're in," he said, only half joking. Stefan didn't acknowledge him, he couldn't. His head did shift from lolling to the right, over to the left. Whether that was intentional or not, Caslin couldn't tell. Stefan had both arms tied behind him and his legs were tethered to the chair, at his ankles, with cable ties. Anton Durakovic ambled into view, coming to stand between the brothers. Looking at Caslin, lying at his feet, he inclined his head. Extending his arm, Karl stepped forward, passing him a gun. Durakovic inspected the weapon. Caslin recognised his Glock.

"What was your plan?" the gangster asked him. "Were you going to sneak in here, kill me and rescue your brother? Was that it?" Caslin didn't reply verbally. He leaned to his right and spat on the floor. Durakovic smiled, "Still the defiance. A sign of spirit. I like that," he said, grinning. "It won't do you any good, though."

"Is that so?" Caslin said, levering himself into a sitting position. Two men made to intercept him as he tried to stand, only for their boss to wave them away. "I figure that you have about ten minutes to end this peacefully, before everything hits the fan."

Durakovic laughed, "You would make a lousy poker player, Inspector. A very lousy player indeed. There is no-one outside, we have checked. There are no helicopters, no police cars and most certainly, no cavalry riding to your rescue."

"That's one massive gamble for you to take," Caslin said as convincingly as he could manage.

"Perhaps so," Durakovic replied. "But unlike you, I am an exceptional poker player. I don't like to lose. If you come off worse in my world, more often than not, you end up dead."

"A bit dramatic, if you don't mind me saying?" Caslin said, glancing around. There were eight men present, not including the boss, Stefan and himself.

"Seeing as we have a little time, let me tell you a story," Durakovic said as Karl came alongside him, putting a chair down for him to sit on. Caslin inclined his head. Something told him that he wasn't going to enjoy Jackanory today. "Imagine the most scenic picture you can, rolling fields, a river valley framed on all sides by rugged and yet, beautiful mountains. All of which crafted by God to inspire poets the world over."

"Wonderful," Caslin muttered but his sarcasm was ignored.

"That was where I grew up, a small town called Žepa. Do you know it?"

"Should I?"

Durakovic shrugged, "No, probably not. It's in Bosnia now, although for my early life it was in the Federal Republic of Yugoslavia. A beautiful place... tainted by such pain."

"Pain?"

"I left in '95, when the Serbs took the town. I had stayed longer than I probably should have, to be with my mother and sister. Our father was away, serving in the army but I ran when the shelling started. We knew what happened to Bosniak men at the hands of our enemies. Žepa is not far from Srebineca and Goražde if that helps you at all?"

"It does," Caslin nodded.

"Think of me, eighteen years old with nothing but... how do you English say... the shirt on my back, fleeing into the mountains? Those few of us spent the rest of the summer and all of the following winter, in that terrain. A life harsher than I could ever have imagined possible. At least, not one that I could foresee surviving. I learnt a lot about myself and the world around me, in those days."

"Please enlighten me," Caslin said. Stefan groaned and he glanced at his brother but besides the sounds, he didn't move.

"I learned first that I could survive, even when the odds appear virtually impossible and always stacked against me. Second, that I should never take for granted what life has to offer, for it can vanish in an instant. You know my father disappeared during the Homeland War. We have no idea what became of him. My mother? She was forced to watch as my sister was raped by the VRS—"

"The VRS?"

"The Serbs," Durakovic said flatly. "Then they raped her. My sister, Irena, could never come to terms with it. She fell pregnant by one of them and took her own life, along with that of her unborn child, rather than live with her shame."

"For them, I am sorry," Caslin said with sincerity. Durakovic looked to him, reading his response as genuine.

"As for my mother, she died of a broken heart. Her husband missing, presumably dead. The loss of her daughter and, as far as she knew anyway, her son, who perished in the mountains. You see, life depletes your resolve, unless you can find a way to strengthen it and push back. Valuable lessons. Harsh but valuable, all the same. Whatever life throws in your direction you must turn it to your advantage."

Caslin sniffed loudly, "Great story. Why tell me this?"

Durakovic shrugged, "I felt you should at least have an understanding of who it is you have come up against. Perhaps you can then understand why I utilise the methods that I do." Caslin looked past him, at his brother.

"Your methods are brutal."

"Do you think?" Durakovic said, also looking at the beaten figure that vaguely resembled Stefan. "This… this is nothing. In my country and that of my former adopted home in Kosovo, I have seen… and done, far worse."

"Is there a point to it?"

"There's always a point," Durakovic said. "Even if only to send a message."

"To whom?"

The gangster took on an intense expression, his tone menacing, "*Anyone* who even dares to think they can take what is mine."

"Melissa Brooke?" Caslin asked.

"Melissa Brooke," Durakovic confirmed. "Employees can look but they never get to touch my girls and most certainly, *never* get to keep them!"

"Their mistake was to fall in love—"

"You're quite right. Love clouds the mind and alters perception. Your brother made an error and now he is paying the price."

"He didn't kill her," Caslin said, shaking his head.

"Something that he was emphatic about," Durakovic nodded his agreement. Turning to Stefan, he smiled and then shot him, high in the leg. Stefan arched in his chair, the accompanying scream was chilling.

"He didn't fucking do it!" Caslin shouted.

"To be fair to your brother, he has been consistent as well as quite convincing. But if not him, then who—"

"No-one," Caslin interrupted, eyeing his brother with concern. Stefan whimpered, tears falling unbidden from swollen eyes and mixing with the sheen of perspiration and wet blood, on his skin.

"What do you mean?" Durakovic asked, a look of surprise crossing in his face as he casually aimed his gun towards Stefan, in a circular motion.

"No-one killed Melissa," Caslin said calmly, locking eyes with his captor who appeared about to protest. "She's a... was... a paranoid schizophrenic, prone to bouts of delusion. That night, she thought people were trying to kill her and she took off."

"If what you're saying is true, then how did she come to die?"

"She bore no signs of having been attacked, no signs of sexual assault but many of self-harming. Clawing at her own skin indicates that she thought... we'll never know for sure... but during bouts of psychosis, like this, people can see things that aren't there, insects, snakes, and they think they're being smothered. She was trying to get away from whatever she was seeing. The tearing off of her clothes, the self-inflicted wounds all over her body... it's the only logical conclusion."

"The murderer you've been seeking... it's not your brother?"

"No, we caught the killer, or at least... he's dead. Melissa wasn't one of his victims, she just stumbled into one of his dumping grounds... probably tripped in the dark, hit her head on the way down and tumbled into the river."

"She drowned? What... *by accident*?" Durakovic sounded incredulous.

"Like I said, it's the *only* logical conclusion." Durakovic pulled himself upright in his chair, casting a glance towards Karl, who shrugged almost imperceptibly.

"This is a very interesting theory that you have," he said to Caslin. "Completely unprovable."

"Nor can it be proven that she was murdered."

"Neither of which changes the fact that your brother, here," he said, indicating Stefan with the barrel of the Glock, "planned to rob me of my merchandise. This makes me look bad, weak and I cannot allow that to pass."

"So, what are you going to do?" Caslin asked, holding his arms out from his sides, palms upwards. "If you kill my brother, I won't stop until I've brought you down."

Durakovic laughed then, it was a deep sound of genuine humour, "You British and your sense of honour and fair play. I thought you would've left that in your Imperial past. I'll tell you this. After my world was destroyed, survival became my only focus. To do so, I had to make myself indispensable to some of the most unpleasant people imaginable. You see, when you have nothing left to lose, things become far simpler."

"How so?"

"It is good that you ask. My fledgling country, emerging from the shadows of her Soviet past, required people of talent to ensure we could stand on our own. Our government was overseen by the UN, for many years, whilst we constructed the apparatus of statehood. If anything positive came from decades of Communism and the Homeland War, it was the acceptance of a need for security. I provided that. Many years on from the events of Žepa, I used my position to track down the man who ordered the attack on my family. I have found there to be few in this world who will not... accommodate... your wishes, when money is the temptation."

"Isn't that the truth?"

"He had no recollection of my sister, my mother, or the actions of his men in Žepa. Whether that was true or not, is largely irrelevant. They were nothing to him. That day, he learned the third lesson that has carried me through the rest of my life."

"Oh please, do tell," Caslin said.

"When you become a monster, you must ensure there are no blood ties to come after you." Caslin's heart froze when those words were uttered.

"Do you think you can kill a British policeman and get away with it?" Caslin said, trying hard to disguise the terror.

"I told you, Inspector Caslin. I have made myself indispensable."

"What does that actually mean?"

"It means that he has friends," a recognisable voice said, from above. Caslin turned to look up towards the mezzanine. Descending the stairs was the last person he expected to see, Sara. She stopped halfway, leaning on the steel balustrade, sighing deeply. "Nate, you always manage to put yourself right in the heart of it, don't you?"

Caslin was dumbstruck, "Sara, what the fuck is going on?"

She shook her head, glancing away, "Like Anton said, he has made himself extremely useful over the years."

Durakovic's face split a broad grin, "Ask yourself, how I got into your country? How is it that I am able to do what I do whilst keeping your kind at arm's length?"

"Exactly what I'd like to bloody well know," Caslin practically shouted, glaring up at Sara.

"When you live in our world, Nate, sometimes you have to play by different rules—"

"Bullshit!" Caslin threw back at her. "Are you going to stand there and let him kill Stefan... *me*?"

Sara took on a pained expression, "It's not my call, Nate. I'm sorry." With that she turned around and walked back up the stairs.

"Sara!" Caslin shouted after her, fighting the rising panic. Upon reaching the landing she stopped but didn't look back.

"Do what you're going to do, Anton but make it quick and make it clean."

"Sara," Caslin called after her again, only with less conviction. She passed from view, without acknowledging his calls. "Fuck!"

"Now you're learning the ways of my world, Inspector Caslin. For what it is worth to you, I am sorry that it has come to this."

"Really?" Caslin said sarcastically, looking around, desperately seeking a solution.

"No," Durakovic said, grinning once again. "You are a hypocritical man, with your flexible morals and illiterate notions of right and wrong. The world is not fair and you should've accepted that a long time ago. Had you done so, you might have lived longer."

Durakovic raised the Glock, pointing it directly at Caslin who gritted his teeth. The first shot sounded and Caslin flinched, Durakovic took a round high in the chest. A second followed, striking him slightly to the right of the first. All present turned to where the shots had come from as more rained down upon them, the sound reverberating around the warehouse with earsplitting clarity. Two of the bodyguards fell in quick succession before they could draw their weapons. The remainder broke for cover. Caslin ran forward and threw himself against his brother, knocking the chair over and sending them both crashing to the floor. Stefan grunted as they hit the ground, Caslin shielding him with his own body. Looking up, he saw Sara on the gantry above, unleashing another volley of fire from an assault rifle, onto those below. Despite being outnumbered, she had them pinned down from an elevated position and they were, for the time being at least, outgunned by her superior firepower.

Caslin struggled at the restraints, binding Stefan to the chair. Durakovic's men were returning fire but only in Sara's direction. So far, they were ignoring him. Realising there was no way he could release his brother without a knife, he resorted to dragging him, chair and all, towards a pallet stack in order to use it as cover. As he struggled past, he stooped to retrieve the Glock from the floor alongside Durakovic, the gangster's lifeless eyes staring directly at him. The action didn't go unnoticed. Almost immediately, concentrated fire centred on his position. Wood splintered all around him as he threw them both behind their makeshift sanctuary. Something grazed the side of Caslin's face and he let out a scream of pain and frustration, sinking to his knees. Seeing his dilemma, Sara turned her fire on Caslin's attackers. Another body fell backwards with part of his head missing.

Taking advantage of the respite Sara was granting him, Caslin checked Stefan for further injury. Relieved to find nothing new, he inspected the leg wound. A rudimentary check, all that he could manage, revealed what looked like a clean through-and-through, having missed any major artery. Stefan grunted as he applied pressure to try and stem the bleeding as best he could. Touching his forearm to his own face, he judged it most likely superficial, probably caused by a shard of wood or a deflected bullet fragment. Movement in the corner of his eye indicated someone was attempting to try and outflank his position. Caslin let off a couple of rounds but failed to halt the advance. To his relief, Sara managed what he couldn't and drove the assailant back into cover under a hail of gunfire.

Caslin was unsure how tenable his position was but he was unable to move Stefan. His brother was in no fit state to stand, let alone run and any attempt to carry him out would be an act of suicide. A flash of colour to his left sent Caslin diving to the floor, bringing his gun to bear as a second muzzle flash erupted in front of him. Squeezing the trigger, he put two rounds into a faceless body. By his reckoning that reduced the enemy's combatants by half.

The realisation that remaining where they were would get them both killed sooner rather than later, struck him. Caslin inspected Stefan's restraints, once again. Pulling at the ties did nothing to loosen them but it did make his brother moan, almost inaudible against the backdrop of gunfire. Following the initial bedlam of Sara's assault, the confrontation had degenerated into a random pattern of sporadic bursts, as those taken by surprise tried to improve their standing. They realised that Sara held the advantage and they'd need to avoid going toe to toe with her or they'd likely lose out. Durakovic himself, along with several others were a testament to that.

The lessening of the exchanges did little to allay Caslin's fears. His eyes scanned the surrounding area for a blade, of any description, that he could use to free his brother. There were none. He swore under his breath. Examining the chair, he found it to be old and not in the greatest condition. One of the rear legs had snapped off, most likely when Caslin bundled him over. The entrance door, to the side of the frontal shutters, was tantalisingly close. With Sara providing elevated cover, they had a chance. He figured they were safe for the time being as all of Durakovic's men had gone to ground. A single shot rang out, ricocheting off the gantry above. Sara returned the compliment with a burst from her rifle and all fell silent again. The sound of movement above saw Caslin lose sight of Sara as she shifted location.

Caslin applied some pressure to the first of the chair legs to which his brother was tied. There was a bit of give and Caslin levered Stefan onto his side, set himself and drove his foot down as hard as he could. The leg split off at the joint. With great effort, he shifted Stefan's weight in order to give him purchase on the remaining leg, keeping Stefan bound to the chair. The ungracious movement appeared to rouse him from his barely conscious state and he growled, clearly in pain.

"Fucking hell, Nate!" he swore in almost incoherent speech, such was the swelling to his face.

"Nice to see you too," Caslin replied as he delivered another stamp to the chair. This time the leg failed to break. Another blow brought yet more cussing at him. A figure stepped into view and Caslin raised the Glock only to see his would-be attacker pitch sideways, at pace, with two rounds lodged in his back and side. A glance up saw Sara looking down the barrel at him.

"Get a move on," she shouted, turning her attention elsewhere. Caslin nodded and redoubled his efforts. With three more kicks, his brother was free. Caslin dragged him to his feet, putting one arm over his shoulder and supporting him at the waist. One last glance around to check if they should go was greeted by another shout. "Move. Now." Caslin didn't wait to be told a second time and without looking, he set off for the door. Stefan groaned. Evidently his body had also taken something of a hammering since his capture. Gunfire exploded into life behind them but Caslin continued on, the Glock, now held in his left hand, would be pretty useless as he couldn't turn and fire with any degree of speed or accuracy. The sound of Sara's weapon resounded in the confines of the warehouse. He had no doubt she had their back. The thought of how she would escape briefly came to mind but there was nothing he could do about that; she would find a way. At least, that's what he told himself as they reached the exit.

Once outside, Caslin realised he had no plan for how to make their escape. They were shuffling forward but Stefan was struggling and Caslin bore the load, practically dragging him onwards. His ears were ringing so loudly that the traffic noise from the nearby main road, was lost to him. Glancing over his shoulder for signs of pursuit, he was pleased to see none. They pressed on towards the main gate, some sixty yards, distant. This was another major obstacle. Caslin knew it to be mechanically operated and easily nine feet, in height. He had little chance of getting over it and Stefan had none, in his condition. Thirty feet away, a buzzer sounded along with the reassuring clank of the mechanism, kicking into life. The metal barrier began to open in, towards them. Caslin grinned.

"Sara, I fucking love you," he said with excitement.

"What's that, little brother?" Stefan mumbled.

"Just our guardian angel, nothing to worry about." His response was followed by the sound of another exchange of fire from within the building. It sounded to Caslin that it was two pistols trading blows with Sara's rifle, as the shots came on top of each other. Then there was silence. Caslin stood at the gate, supporting Stefan, looking back at the warehouse. His common sense told him to run but his attachment to Sara threatened to draw him back into the fray. As if reading his mind, Stefan caught his attention.

"I think she can take care of herself, a lot better than we can," he said with a grimace, one borne of agony. Caslin glanced at him and nodded. They continued through the gate, heading for the main road. "When are your mates going to turn up?" Stefan mumbled.

Caslin, breathing heavily at the exertion of aiding his brother, said, through deep draws of breath, "If someone's reported the shots, then any minute but this one's off the books."

"Terrific. You can never find a policeman when you need one, eh?"

Caslin laughed, giving a short respite from the tension, "Too true."

In the corner of his eye, he saw a lone figure vacate the building behind them, before breaking into a run. He knew immediately that it was Sara. From the rear, a car made the turn and accelerated along the length of the building towards the main gate. Sara, by now running at full pelt across the open compound, glanced over her shoulder upon hearing the engine pick up. She turned and dropped to one knee, levelling the rifle in the direction of the vehicle. As it rapidly closed the distance between them, she let off two short, controlled bursts. The first struck the windscreen and the second, the engine housing. The car veered to the left and then the right, before spinning out of control, colliding with the perimeter fence and eventually coming to a stop.

Sara approached the vehicle cautiously, whose engine was still running despite giving off substantial amounts of smoke and steam. The passenger door creaked open and she raised her rifle, depressing the trigger. A loud clicking sounded but the weapon failed to fire. Karl stepped from the vehicle, blood visibly streaming from a wound at the side of his head, to the left of his temple. He raised his pistol and fired. Sara's empty rifle dropped to the tarmac alongside her as she fell. Karl came to stand over her, stamping on the shoulder that he'd just put a bullet into. Sara screamed in agony. Leaning forward, he pressed the barrel of his weapon against her forehead.

"I'm going to fucking kill you, you bitch," he spat at her. Sara stared up at him with uncompromising defiance.

"I don't think you're going to do that," Caslin said evenly. He stood less than three metres away, his gun trained on Karl.

CHAPTER TWENTY-EIGHT

"Well, this is interesting," Karl said with a smile reminiscent of his employer, who lay dead in the building behind them.

"Are you in a hurry to join Anton?" Caslin asked.

"Feel free to shoot him, any time you like," Sara said in an icy tone. From the look in her eyes, Caslin knew she meant it.

"We find ourselves in quite a dilemma, Inspector," Karl said, before returning his attention to Sara, lying prostrate at his feet. "Do not come any closer or your friend will die." He reapplied pressure to her shoulder with the ball of his foot as if to emphasise the point. Sara grimaced.

"She dies, you die," Caslin said flatly, a nervous adjustment of the weapon in his hands, giving away a lack of confidence in handling the situation.

"I might live long enough to see your head come off, you piece of shit," Sara said, locking eyes with Karl. His smile broadened into a wide grin.

"I always told Anton that you couldn't be trusted—"

"And he believed you," Sara confirmed, wincing as she spoke. "Collectively, we needed each other."

"Indeed," Karl agreed, "until such time as the costs became

too great. However, Anton is dead. Do you believe that the time has passed?"

"What are you talking about?" Caslin said.

"Has it?" Karl repeated, ignoring the question entirely.

Sara narrowed her gaze, turning the scenario over, in her mind, "Durakovic went too far, even by his standards."

"He underestimated you and played this whole situation badly," Karl said.

"Very," Sara replied.

"So, in the scheme of things, nothing has really changed, has it?" Karl asked with a flick of his eyebrows.

She shook her head, "I see no reason."

"Sara?" Caslin persisted. "What's going on?" Karl looked at him and then back to her.

"Nate, please be quiet and let the grown-ups talk for a bit, would you?"

"What the fuck?" Caslin muttered to himself.

"I fear that we do not have a great deal of time," Karl said, still with his gun lodged against her forehead. He indicated Caslin, "His colleagues will be here, at any moment."

Sara nodded, "We will all have a great deal of explaining to do, unless—"

"We can conclude this negotiation quickly?" Karl finished. Caslin's senses were heightened, shifting his weight between his feet, nervously. He felt well out of this loop.

"Lower your weapon," Caslin said.

"Perhaps you could do the same?" Karl replied, irritated. Caslin was about to protest but Sara spoke first.

"You can lower your gun, Nate."

"Excuse me?" Caslin said with more than a hint of surprise in his tone.

"Do as I say, Nathaniel, please." He looked to her, inquisitively. "No-one else needs to die here, today."

"You're going to let him go, aren't you?"

"Yes," she said emphatically.

"You've got to be fucking kidding me—"

"You're both going to lower your weapons and we are all leaving," Sara said with authority. "This is going to take some clearing up and it'll be far easier if none of us are here when your lot arrive."

"Business as usual?" Caslin asked, barely controlling his anger. "You know who this is, the things he's done?"

"More so, than anyone," Sara replied. "Don't be so naïve. It's the way of things."

"Bollocks."

"Clock's ticking," Karl said softly. "We all walk or some of us die. I have nothing more to offer."

Sara looked at Caslin, "It's on you, Nate. I know what I'm doing, trust me." Caslin let out an involuntary laugh. The sound of sirens in the distance could now be heard and he looked in that direction. Blue light was flickering in the skyline, to the south.

"The ticking's getting louder," Karl said, now looking directly at Caslin. With one last fleeting glance at Sara, Caslin lowered the Glock. Karl immediately did likewise but neither man took their finger off the trigger nor their eyes off each other as Sara struggled to her feet. Karl backed away, picking up speed as the volume of the sirens got ever louder. Holstering his weapon when he reached the car, he dragged the lifeless body of his associate out through the passenger door, depositing him onto the tarmac. Clambering across and into the driver's seat, he revved the engine excessively, before accelerating off the grass verge, around the two of them and out of the compound.

"We need to move," Sara said whilst Caslin watched the car depart. A surge of rage threatened to rise from within him. "Where's Stefan?"

"Out there," Caslin nodded towards the road beyond. "When did you realise that they had my brother?"

"Not now, Nate, for Christ's sake," she said, moving off. He gripped her forearm and stepped across, blocking her passage.

The rough handling sent a shockwave of pain through her shoulder and she glared at him. Caslin didn't care. "Seriously, are we going to do this now?"

"When?" Caslin snarled. "Would you have done anything if I hadn't turned up, when I did? Or would you have let them kill him?"

"Nate, you're hurting me," she said, indicating his hand with her eyes. He released his hold. Her expression softened and their eyes met. "I didn't know he was your brother, believe me," she implored him. "He was working for Durakovic under a different name, probably in case it came up that he was related to a copper. I found out today and... for the record... I didn't have a bloody clue what I was going to do about it before you showed up, doing your feeble John Wayne impression."

"John Way— what?"

"I left the back door open for you and you *still* managed to get yourself caught. What with that and squaring up to Anton like you're in the *Magnificent Seven* or something—"

"You're talking old westerns—"

"We have to move, now," Sara hissed. "I have a car at the rear of that warehouse," she indicated a grey building several hundred yards further along the road, "they have their own access road from the bypass, for bringing up heavy plant. If we're quick, we can get clear. Now please, can we go?" Caslin nodded and Sara recovered her rifle, grunting as she stooped to pick it up. She swore whilst attempting to collapse the stock, something she couldn't do with only one good arm. Caslin took it and did it for her. She slipped the strap over her other shoulder and they set off for the gate.

"Are you going to be alright?" Caslin asked, looking at the blood creeping out from beneath the cover of her jacket.

"I'll be fine," she replied but he remained less than convinced.

Stefan was where Caslin had left him, lying just beyond the crest of the grass verge surrounding the compound. Caslin hoisted him up and they managed to cover the ground fast enough to conceal themselves from view before the first response vehicles arrived. Propping Stefan upright, against the wall of the building, he found his brother more coherent than when he had left him.

"You need to put pressure on, front and back—"

"I know," Stefan replied, doing as instructed. From their position of relative obscurity, Caslin watched as three patrol cars came to a stop near to the entrance of the compound. The second was an armed response vehicle and the officers moved to the rear, popping the boot and assembling their equipment. Other colleagues observed the warehouse, sheltering behind their cars. Caslin had no idea if an active threat remained on the premises or not. Looking back to Sara, she beckoned him forward. Kneeling, Caslin looped Stefan's arm around his shoulder, lifted him and made his way towards her.

With all the police attention behind them, they made their way towards Sara's car without further delay. It was a mid-size saloon and Caslin lay Stefan down on the rear seat.

"Here, use this," Sara said, tossing him a T-shirt from within a bag on the passenger seat. Caslin thanked her and knelt alongside his brother. Using the material, he fashioned a tourniquet for Stefan's leg. His brother groaned as he applied it but didn't complain. Concerned about how much blood he had lost, Caslin got into the car alongside his brother. He saw Sara stuff a clutch of wadding underneath her blouse and into her own wound.

"You okay?" he asked.

"Yeah, don't worry."

"Do you want me to drive?"

"No, it's fine. We don't have far to go."

"Where are we going?"

Sara didn't reply as she put the car into gear and they moved off, without lights, towards the exit. Pulling up, Caslin noticed the eight-foot high gate was secured with a combination lock.

Sara trotted over to it and within seconds was sliding the chain link barrier away to their left. He decided not to bother asking her how she knew the code. Once back in the car, they passed through quietly and Caslin got out to close the gate behind them, casting a wary glance at the emerging police presence in the distance. Returning to the car he got in and, once more without the aid of headlights, they picked their way up the bumpy, gravel track until they reached the slip road onto the bypass. Another gate barred their way but this was no hindrance to Sara and within minutes, they were well away from the scene. Caslin cast an eye skyward, Sara watching him.

"Looks like the air cover is needed elsewhere, tonight," she said. Caslin glanced at her, wondering if she knew something that he didn't. Dismissing the thought as paranoia, he turned his attention to Stefan. He had either fallen asleep or passed out, Caslin couldn't determine which but his breathing appeared to be regular and unobstructed. Furtively looking in her mirrors, Sara watched to ensure they had escaped unobserved and seemed comfortable that was the case.

"Stefan needs a doctor," he said.

"Don't worry, I know someone," she replied, not taking her eyes off the road.

"We have to get to a hospital." Sara shot him a dark and slightly patronising look in the rearview mirror.

"Too many questions. You know as well as I do that gunshot wounds have to be reported to the police. It'll be fine, trust me."

"There's that phrase again," he said without attempting to mask the sarcasm. "How am I supposed to be able to do that?" Sara smiled although she must've known there was no intended humour.

"Under your seat, there's a bag. In it, you'll find a mobile. Can you pass it to me?" Caslin did so. Tapping a number in from memory, she waited patiently for the call to be answered. It was, within a few rings. "I need a reservation," she said. There was a man's voice at the other end but the sound was muffled and

Caslin couldn't make out the reply. "Yeah, dinner for two," she said nonchalantly. Seconds later, Sara hung up the call and tossed the phone onto the passenger seat, the action causing her some discomfort in the shoulder. "Fifteen minutes," was all she said, wincing as she spoke. Caslin could see her skin was growing pale and a sheen of perspiration had formed on her brow. She was in trouble, regardless of her protestations.

The remainder of the journey was done in silence, apart from the occasional groan from Stefan, in the rear. Caslin had lost track of their direction and he was confused when they pulled into a multi-unit retail park. Bringing them to a stop, Sara looked at Stefan and then Caslin.

"Can you manage to get your brother to the rear of this building?" she indicated to their left. He looked, taking in the U-shaped complex they were parked in and nodded. "Good, you'll find double, fire exit doors around back. I'll meet you there in two minutes. I need to see a man about a dog."

"Where…?" Caslin was about to ask but she got out without another word, briskly walking over to an Audi, parked sixty yards away, on the other side of the car park. She got into the passenger seat and Caslin tried in vain, to make out the driver. With some difficulty, he hauled Stefan from the rear seat and half carried, half dragged his brother to the rear, as instructed. Having found the doors, he waited, supporting Stefan, who was slipping in and out of consciousness. Suddenly struck by the surreal nature of the evening, Caslin wondered how on earth they would make it back to normality.

The unlocking of bolts on the other side of the door, brought back his focus. Unsure of what to expect when they opened, he braced himself as the leftmost door was pushed out. The face of a young man, in his late thirties, appeared, looking them up and down. Caslin didn't speak.

"It'd be better if I checked your friend out inside," the man said. He stepped aside, allowing them enough room for Caslin to ease Stefan through the opening. Once past, the door was closed behind them and the bolts secured. There were cages arranged along the wall for three metres, at floor level and another row above, at waist height. Their presence was noted by several of the occupants. A dog came to the front near them, its nose sniffing the air around them. "This way," their host offered, walking past and beckoning them to follow. "Do you need any help?"

"No, I've got him," Caslin replied. They made their way through another door, across a corridor and into an ancillary room. Sara was already present, stripped to the waist, a trauma pad pressed to her shoulder. "How are you?" Caslin asked, "And please don't say *okay*."

Sara smiled weakly, "I've had better days."

"Put him down here," the man said, pointing to a bench off to Caslin's right. He did so, lying Stefan down as gently as he could.

"What's your name?" Caslin asked.

"Call me whatever you want, I don't care," the man offered without looking up. He took a pair of surgical scissors, cutting through the base of Stefan's trouser leg and slicing them all the way to his hip. Caslin took that to mean introductions wouldn't be forthcoming.

"In that case, *Dave*," Caslin said dryly, "can you patch up my brother?" The man glanced up and smiled.

"It looks clean enough."

"Do you know what you're doing... with people, I mean?"

"He's a former combat medic," Sara said. "He'll do just fine."

Caslin was comforted by that and stepped away in order to give him room to work. Crossing over to stand with Sara, he offered to assist, for which she was grateful. Taking a clean pad, he swapped the dressing and pressed down. Sara flinched but said nothing.

"So, is this guy one of yours?" he asked, his trembling hands causing discomfort where they were supposed to be soothing.

"Steady on, Nate," Sara said, perhaps more confrontationally than intended.

"Sorry," he replied, "I can't stop them shaking."

"It's the adrenalin. Now we've stopped, it's catching up on you."

"I… I've never shot anything… anyone… before, let alone killed—"

"Them or us, Nate," Sara cut him off, coldly. "That's what you have to tell yourself, them or us." Caslin looked into her eyes, seeing a steel in her that he'd never noticed previously and moved the conversation backwards.

"Is he one of yours, then?"

"Better if you don't know, really," she replied. Caslin dropped it.

"What was all that with Karl, back there?" he asked, lowering his voice. *Dave* didn't seem to be paying them any attention but even so, Caslin didn't want to risk being overheard.

"He'll have his uses," Sara said in an equally conspiratorial tone, "if he survives the next couple of days, anyway."

"Survives?"

"Danika," Sara replied coldly.

"Anton's wife?"

"Yep," Sara said, fixing him with a stare. "If Karl thinks he can just slide into Anton's place without breaking step, he'll be in for a shock."

"She'll try to take it on herself?"

"Absolutely," she said, adopting a faraway look. "Although I expect Karl knows that too and will try and get the drop on her. If they both establish their positions, you shouldn't need to worry about them for a while. They'll tear the organisation apart vying for control."

"And if one succeeds?" Caslin asked.

"Then have no doubt, you'll find the other floating down the Ouse, in a couple of days… or not at all. Either way, with their connections, there will still be business to be done."

"Business?" Caslin asked with no attempt to shield his contempt.

"Yes, business," Sara replied.

"You think Danika will work with you, after what you did to her husband?"

Sara grinned, "Who says it was me? She'll think it was Karl. His word will count for nothing once he makes his play."

Caslin shook his head, "How the hell do you get any sleep at night?"

"It's my job, Nate."

"Speaking of which, since when have you been a field agent? I thought you were just a data monkey?"

"None of us are ever *just* anything," Sara said. "My doctorate gave me a detailed knowledge of the Balkans. That's what brought Anton and I together."

"That holiday you mentioned, in Croatia, last year, was to do with him?" Caslin asked, Sara nodded. "I should have guessed. It was far too convenient for you to drop by unannounced—"

Sara reached out and gently touched his cheek, "I had to protect my asset but you should know, it's not all smoke and mirrors, Nate. Not with you."

"How can I know that?" he replied, leaving their contact for only a fraction longer before inclining his face away from her touch.

"I guess you can't," she replied, looking down. "Whether you choose to believe me or not, it's the truth. I suppose it's a question of faith." Caslin was about to respond but they were interrupted.

"Your turn," the vet said, coming to stand before Sara. Caslin removed the gauze from her wound and made way, returning to Stefan. His leg was heavily bandaged and Caslin was pleased to see he was awake.

"How are you feeling?"

"Like I've been shot," he replied with a half-smile.

"Funny that," Caslin said.

"The doc gave me something, I can already feel it kicking in."
Caslin glanced at *Dave*, cleaning Sara's bullet wound.

"Hopefully you'll not start licking your balls."

"Eh?"

"Forget it," Caslin said under his breath.

"What's the plan, little brother?" Stefan asked.

Caslin shrugged, "Working on it but... if I'm honest, I'm a bit out of my depth, here."

"Stefan and I need to go silent for a while," Sara said, speaking over the vet's shoulder.

"By silent, you mean..."

"I mean vanish," Sara confirmed.

"How do you suggest we arrange that?" Caslin asked.

"Stefan can come with me. In the meantime, you get back to work and do what you do... this evening however, stays between us."

"Easy as that, huh?" Caslin said.

"Easy as," Sara confirmed. "When can we move?" she asked the man working on getting the bullet out of her shoulder tissue before hissing at the pain he was causing.

"How long before you have to?" he asked.

"Two, maybe three hours."

The vet sucked air through his teeth, "I can patch you up but you've lost a fair bit of blood. Sooner rather than later, you're going to have to stop for longer."

"We only need to wait long enough to arrange an out, then we're gone."

"You'll be okay here, for a while. That should give you some time. I'll get you some food and water, while you wait."

"Thanks," Sara said. Turning her gaze to Caslin, she said, "You should get going before you're missed. Probably, they'll expect you to be with your father." Caslin looked at her before glancing at Stefan.

"I can't leave—"

"Yes, you can and you must. We'll be all right. I'll take care of

Stefan. You have my word but you being here will only make it harder for us to slip out of York, unnoticed."

"Where will you go?"

"I have resources behind me, remember?"

"And Stefan? Everyone's looking for him."

"He can call you in a couple of days, to tell you about his impromptu holiday. I'm sure he'll be surprised when hearing about your father's attack."

"Seriously?" Caslin asked.

"It'll fit, don't worry." Caslin had to admit that it was a plausible option, taking care of a number of the issues they faced. He looked at Stefan who met his gaze.

"Sounds good to me, little brother. I can't see any other way out of this, not for me anyway."

Caslin nodded his agreement, "Okay, I'll go back to the hospital and be with Dad."

"How is he?" Stefan asked. With all that had occurred, Caslin hadn't realised that his brother wouldn't know about their father's welfare.

"Banged up," Caslin said. "He's in a bad way. They put him into a medically induced coma. It's a waiting game now."

Stefan bobbed his head solemnly, "They came at us from the front and the back. Dad answered the door. I didn't see it coming. I never thought they'd figure I'd be there. I—"

"What happened, happened. It's too late to play the blame game. No-one wins at that."

"Is it true… what you said about Mel?"

"Yes, I believe so."

A tear ran down Stefan's cheek, he tried to catch it with the back of his hand but missed, "I was trying to get her out, you know? We both wanted that. I thought we could do it. We were going to build something proper, for us and her kid."

"You should've come to me—"

"I did but…"

"I wasn't ready to listen, was I?" Caslin said softly, a familiar wave of guilt washing over him. "I'm sorry, Stef. Really, I am." Conversation stopped for a time, while Stefan reflected on his loss and Sara was stitched up. She was also given a shot of something, Caslin didn't know what but he guessed it was for the pain.

"Dave here, could fix you up with some Oxycodone, if you need it?" Sara said to Caslin.

"Are you in pain?" the vet asked him.

Caslin shook his head, "No, I'll be fine." Although, if the truth were known, the voice in his head was screaming out to accept the offer.

"Pleased to hear it, Nate," Sara said with a knowing look. "You should get going. The longer you're off the grid, the less likely we are to pull this off."

Caslin said goodbye to his brother, not knowing when they would next speak, let alone see each other again. He thanked the unnamed man for aiding them and lastly came to Sara. The other two distracted themselves, in order to give them some space but Caslin led her out into the corridor, ensuring their privacy.

"Promise me that you'll take care of my brother."

"I will," she said. "Everything will show that he was out of the country when all this went down. He'll be in the clear."

"And you? Will I... will I see you again?"

"Do you want to?"

"I... I... think so."

"Thanks Nate, that really pulls on a girl's heartstrings."

"I'm sorry, it's just that... it's like you see the world through a blacklight."

"I know. It's a lot to take in," she said, looking to the floor, as if not wanting to say the words.

"I should go," Caslin said quietly. Sara nodded but wouldn't verbally agree. Her eyes welled up, but she tried her hardest to hide the fact. Unlocking the bolts, he reached for the bar and pushed the door open. Stepping out into the night, he paused.

Holding the door open with one hand, he looked back. "Yul Brynner."

"What?" Sara said, touching the palm of her hand to her eye before looking across at him.

"*The Magnificent Seven*. It was Yul Brynner, not John Wayne," Caslin said, forcing a smile.

"Are you sure?"

"Positive."

"You'll have to prove that to me, one day."

"It's a date," he said over his shoulder, turning and walking away as the door swung closed behind him.

CHAPTER TWENTY-NINE

"Are you sure she didn't suffer?"

"I don't believe so," Caslin said with sincerity. "What happened to Melissa was terrible but, in my opinion… a tragic accident. There was no-one to blame." Suzanne Brooke glanced first to Hunter, before turning to meet his eye, seeking to judge whether he was being truthful or merely attempting to spare her more anguish.

"I would disagree with you there," she said, her voice threatening to break. "I'm her mother. I should've done more."

Caslin broke the eye contact, "As parents, we always think we can do more. I've lost count of the number of people who have said exactly that to me, over the years. To be honest, I've even said it myself." Suzanne reached across and affectionately patted his knee.

"You're a good man, Mr Caslin. One day it'll probably come as a relief that I didn't lose my Melissa to someone like… well, you know? Right now, though, it doesn't help at all. Can you promise me?" Caslin cast an eye over the toddler, playing near to them, with the toys they had brought for her.

"To be honest, it can't be proven either way. That said, all my years on the force… my experience, tells me that's exactly what happened. I can only go where the evidence leads me. You might like to know that Melissa was looking to get out of the business and change her life, for the better."

"Really?" Suzanne replied. "I've heard that many times before."

"I spoke to people in and around her and I know it's true. You were right, she *was* clean and often talked about her dreams for the future, one together with her daughter." Caslin had decided not to bring up Stefan's relationship with Melissa, for fear of over complicating the narrative. To do so would no doubt lead to more questions and could, possibly, in Suzanne's mind at least, affect his impartiality in the case.

"I'm pleased she was thinking of Isabel. Whatever was happening in her life, she always made time for her." She nearly broke, then, her voice cracking but she held it together, if only just. It was evident, to Caslin, that the grandmother was doing all she could to maintain her composure for the toddler's sake.

"It will get easier," Caslin offered, the words sounded hollow and felt meaningless, as he uttered them.

"I'm sure," she replied. Looking to her granddaughter and lowering her voice, her next question was but a whisper, "She keeps asking when her mummy's coming home? I don't know what to say, I really don't." Caslin said nothing. He didn't have the words either. What do you tell a two-year-old who is missing their mother, a mother who will never return?

After a moment, he said, "Show her as much love as possible."

"No shortage of that, I can assure you," Suzanne replied with a smile, one instantly matched by the little girl. At that point, Caslin saw Melissa in the child's expression.

"I don't wish to tell you what to—"

"No please," she interrupted him, "do so. I'll take anything that you have, right now."

Caslin nodded, "When you feel able, do your best to talk about her mother as much as you can and encourage her to do likewise. That way, with a bit of luck, she'll still feel her mother is a part of her life… and of yours."

———

A FINAL WAVE saw Suzanne Brooke close the door as Caslin reached the end of the driveway. He unlocked the car, glancing at Hunter as she opened the passenger side door.

"It never gets easier, does it, Sir?" she said across the roof of the car, her eyes transfixed on the little girl, waving to them from the living room window. She waved back, smiling.

"Not ones like this, no," he replied, also acknowledging Isabel before getting in. The visit was one he'd been dreading but the weight was lifting, at least in part. He could have left it to family liaison but not only was he adamant that he should take the time, it was also the perfect reason to vacate Fulford Road. Casting his mind back to the morning meeting, Caslin let out a deep sigh.

"That's your take on it, is it?"

"It's all in my report, Sir."

"Hmmm," DCS Broadfoot mused, almost inaudibly. Seconds later, he closed the file on his desk, drumming his fingers lightly, on the cover whilst he took in Caslin's measure.

"It's good to hear that your father will be making a full recovery."

"Thank you, Sir. Physically, anyway," Caslin replied. "It'll take some time but, regarding his mental state… well, that's a different matter altogether. The entire episode has been a lot for him to take in. I'm sure we'll get there, though."

"That generation were built of sterner stuff."

"Yes, Sir. So, they often tell me."

"No leads on the attacker?"

"Hunter's working on it but there's little to go on."

"Any more word from your brother…," he paused, searching for the name, "Stefan, isn't it?"

"Yes. Not since the phone call, the day before yesterday, Sir, no," Caslin offered, straight faced.

"Spain, wasn't it?"

"Majorca, Sir."

"Hmmm," Broadfoot murmured again, absently eyeing something invisible on his desk. "Rather fortuitous that he missed the attack at your father's house."

"Not for my father," Caslin replied.

"Quite so," Broadfoot said, locking eyes with his inspector. "Upped and left without a word, then?"

"To me, Sir, that's right but we're not really close. About par for the course, really."

"And your father?"

"He has no recollection of the two days prior to the attack, Sir. The doctors have said it may come back to him but... he's not a young man." Broadfoot's gaze lingered on Caslin and he was unsure whether his credibility was about to be called into question. Then again, as both men knew, the reality wasn't what had happened but what could be proven and on that, Caslin still held the majority of the cards.

"In any event, it would appear that Mark Rabiot is rapidly becoming yesterday's news. Our media-driven society moves at breakneck speed. Today, everyone's focussed on an outbreak of internecine fighting."

"Sir?"

"Amongst the rich and shameless of our local underworld," Broadfoot explained. "Apparently, there's a power grab under way and I'm minded to not let it get out of hand. It would be better if more of it didn't spill over, onto the streets. Random beatings of known gang affiliates and an arson tells me it's threatening to get out of hand. Any further escalation could bring unwanted attention to our city. Not wishing to rush you, Nathaniel, but it would be good to have you back in the office. All hands on deck and all that."

"Never a dull day, in York, Sir."

"Well, I guess that just about clears it up," Broadfoot said in an upbeat manner. Caslin almost made it to the door before the DCS called after him. "There is still the matter of the firearms."

"Sir?" Caslin had asked innocently.

"I'm still waiting for an explanation as to how you ended up with an unregistered, eastern bloc Makarov in your possession."

"My father's attacker must have dropped it during their struggle. He's a tough old bastard when he wants to be."

Broadfoot frowned, "And you didn't mention this before because... why, exactly?"

Caslin shrugged, "There was a lot going on, Sir. Emotional trauma and so forth, I guess. I secured the weapon and took charge of it. At that point, I was still unsure whether a suspect was on the premises. It would have been negligent of me to leave it in situ."

"Under the circumstances, that seems... plausible. Drawing the weapon inside a public hospital, however, is not an insignificant matter, regardless of the circumstances. I'll probably recommend nothing more than a reprimand be placed on your file but the final judgement will be out of my hands, you understand?"

"Absolutely, Sir."

"What about your police-issued firearm?"

"What of it, Sir?"

"The weapon was returned to the armoury with far fewer rounds than you signed it out with." Caslin drew a deep breath and pulled himself upright.

"It's been a long time since I'd had a gun. I needed to get my eye in, for safety reasons if nothing else."

"I considered that also," Broadfoot replied. Caslin then made to leave but, once again, was stopped from doing so. "The thing is, I checked with the range and you aren't logged in as attending at any time since drawing the weapon. Care to explain?" Caslin flicked his eyes towards Broadfoot and away again, shaking his head slightly.

"Administrative oversight?" he said softly. Broadfoot stood, resting balled fists on the desk in front of him. He stared hard at Caslin, almost forcing him to meet the gaze. It felt uncomfortable.

"My thoughts exactly," Broadfoot said, before reseating himself. "Carry on."

CASLIN TURNED the key in the ignition and the engine fired into life. A now familiar grinding sound came to his ear whilst trying to select first. Casting one last glance towards the house, a curtain twitched, if only slightly, despite the windows being closed. There was no sign of Isabel. Suzanne Brooke had a difficult journey ahead of her. Hunter frowned as he fought with the gearbox. Giving up on first gear he selected third, second having become a distant memory. Repeatedly depressing the accelerator to generate enough revs, enabled him to move off without stalling but with a deafening roar of the engine. Thinking about it as they crawled away, the presence of Isabel should provide a measure of comfort to Suzanne, whilst coming to terms with the loss of her own daughter. Even bearing that in mind, he knew her personal trials were only just beginning.

The gearbox was disintegrating with each passing mile and at every roundabout, intersection or congested stretch of road, progress proved ever trickier to navigate. Worried he would stall the car approaching a line of stationary cars, he took a left turn into a quieter side street. The change in pace caused the car to lurch forward as he endeavoured to generate the revs needed to keep going. Another vehicle making the turn behind him, apparently frustrated at his lack of progress, pulled out to overtake. Accelerating past on his right, Caslin raised an apologetic hand towards the driver. Realising he was never going to make it back to Fulford Road, he slipped the car into neutral and coasted to a standstill. The car that had overtaken pulled into the kerbside, a little way further down the road. Caslin looked to Hunter.

"I'm sorry. It looks like we're walking from here."

Hunter grinned back at him, "At least if we walk, we'll make it."

Caslin grinned, "Aye. Fair poin—" The force of the impact, to the rear snapped his head backwards. The seatbelt tensioners locked in and the wind rushed from his lungs. Time passed slowly. The shot of pain racing up his neck, coupled with the confusion sent his mind blank. Attempting to get his bearings, he could tell the car had lurched forwards, partially mounting the kerb but was once again, stationary. Turning to Hunter, who appeared visibly dazed, he asked, "You okay?"

Her head lolled slightly. Raising it, she was about to respond but instead pointed forwards with a weak gesture, unable to get enough words out.

"There…"

Caslin looked forward just in time to see the car that had overtaken them, coming back, at speed. Transfixed on the white glow emitted from the reversing lights, all he managed was to shout, "Brace—" as the car slammed into the front of his. The airbags deployed, the sensation of hitting them over in an instant. Blinking to clear his vision, he struggled, what with a mist of white powder and the assault on his senses. There was a dull noise, a constant, in the background. In reality, it was the horn, sounding as a result of the collision and apparently set to continue doing so. Movement outside drew his attention. Still in shock, it was a moment before he realised the men, clambering out of the car in front, were wearing ski masks. Hunter responded first, scrabbling for the radio that had bounced into the well, at her feet. Bringing it up, she depressed the call button.

"Control—" her call for help was cut short as the passenger window shattered in upon her. Assailants from the car behind had reached them first, setting about the windows with baseball bats. Hunter shrieked and involuntarily crouched, towards the centre of the car. Caslin did likewise as his window exploded inwards, cradling his head with his arms in an effort to protect it from the glass raining down. The others joined in and the windscreen was swiftly battered into submission. The corresponding sounds from the attack sent waves of terror through the occupants, who felt utterly powerless. Hunter dropped the radio in favour of self-protection but as quickly as it had begun, the attack was over.

Tentatively, Caslin lowered his forearm and took a look out of the smashed window, to his right. Their assailants were already some distance away and covering the ground with speed. Taking a deep breath, he looked through the smashed rear window, at which point believed they were now safe. Glancing over, he put a comforting hand onto Hunter's forearm, although he noted his was shaking almost uncontrollably.

"It's alright, they're gone," he said, his voice wavering. She dropped her arms from their defensive stance and looked around, peering through the strands of hair that covered her face. Chunks of glass dropped from her hair as she sat upright.

"For fuck's sake," she whispered under her breath. Caslin pulled the handle and pushed the door open, remnants of the window fell about his hand and he recoiled. Pushing aside the deflated airbag, he got out onto unsteady feet. The car horn sounded louder now as if the volume was increasing along with the realisation of what had occurred. Stepping away, he looked back at the car. It was a mess. The vehicle that had shunted them from the rear, an SUV, was wedged into the crumple zone. At the front, the car that'd slammed into them had embedded itself into the bonnet. It was no wonder the horn had a mind of its own, sounding the death throes of his car. Hunter also got out, assessing the scene from the other side of the car. Raising her voice to be heard above the din and glancing around, she called out.

"What the bloody hell was all that about?"

Caslin took a deep breath, before turning to face her, "Someone was sending me a message."

"Who?" Hunter said. "And why?"

Caslin looked away, mulling it over. Karl or Danika? He didn't know which. Both would have due cause to take issue with him. Whatever deal either may have made with the intelligence services, he clearly wasn't part of the package. Apparently, nothing was off limits to these people. The message was straightforward as would be his response. If he were to interfere with them further, they'd left him in no doubt they'd be willing to put him down. Caslin recognised there and then, at some point in the future, their paths were going to cross. On that day, he would have a choice to make and it would be a simple one. Whether it would be a lawful one, remained to be seen. In the meantime, a momentary wave of gratitude washed over him, bringing out a smile.

"What exactly about this, do you find so funny?" said

Caslin looked back towards her, indicating the car with a casual flick of his hand, "In a strange sort of way, they've done me a favour."

"How do you figure that?"

"My insurance. I'm fully comprehensive."

Order the next book in the series from Amazon or click here;
The Dogs in the Street - Dark Yorkshire Book 3

FREE BOOK GIVEAWAY

Visit the author's website at **www.jmdalgliesh.com** and sign up to the VIP Club and be first to receive news and previews of forthcoming works.

Here you can download a FREE eBook novella exclusive to club members;

Life & Death - A Hidden Norfolk novella

Never miss a new release.

No spam, ever, guaranteed. You can unsubscribe at any time.

ARE YOU ABLE TO HELP?

Enjoy this book? You could make a real difference.

Because reviews are critical to the success of an author's career, if you have enjoyed this novel, please do me a massive favour by entering one onto Amazon.

Type the following link into your internet search bar to go to the Amazon page and leave a review;

http://mybook.to/Blacklight

If you prefer not to follow the link please visit the Amazon sales page where you purchased the title in order to leave a review.

THE DOGS IN THE STREET - PREVIEW

DARK YORKSHIRE - BOOK 3

THE THUNDERING SOUND of the water filling the bathtub was barely audible over the shrieks of excitement emanating from the children. Nicola smiled at the irony. It would take nigh on thirty minutes to coax them away from the TV or their tablets and get them upstairs but once there, less than three before impatience set in at the wait to get in the water. A frustrated voice cut through as the children's mother filled their cups with squash. Chris was suffering. She felt his pain.

Leaving the kitchen, fingers looped through the handles of both cups, allowing her a free hand she flicked off the light and nudged the dog out from under her feet. Passing through the dining room, scooping up Ethan's reading book on the way she made it to the bottom of the stairs before the chime of the doorbell brought her to a halt with one foot on the first tread. The sound of splashing and laughter came from upstairs and the initial intent to ignore the caller was cast aside. Gently placing the cups on the adjacent window sill, alongside *The Lion's Paw*, Nicola stepped over to the front door.

It was still light, mid-evening and a caller wasn't unheard of although unannounced was somewhat unusual. The suited figure, viewed through the obscured glass, waited patiently hands clasped before him. Nicola unlatched the door and swung it open. Greeted with a smile the caller addressed her.

"Mrs Fairchild?" he asked, she nodded. "Please accept my apologies for calling at this time but I have a letter for your husband. Is he home?" He indicated a manila envelope clutched in his left hand.

"Yes, he is," she glanced over her shoulder up the stairs, considering whether to call out. Realising the kids would be unattended she thought better of it. "Bear with me a moment, I'll just have to swap with him. He's upstairs bathing the children."

"Certainly. I don't mind waiting."

Pushing the door to but not closed, Nicola retreated. Leaving the bedtime offerings on the window sill she trotted upstairs and eased the bathroom door open. Met with a barrage of joy from within she broke into a smile as first Ethan and then Molly flicked bubbles at their unsuspecting father who chided them with fake fury. Leaning on the door and raising her voice to be heard she got her husband's attention.

"Chris, there's someone to see you." He looked up at her, from his kneeling position.

"Who is it?"

"I don't know. Someone from work I think."

"Okay. Take over here would you?" Turning sideways, allowing him to pass, Nicola knelt alongside the bathtub as the door closed behind him. Molly threw her mother a cheeky glance before ducking her hands beneath the waves created by a plunging Ethan at the other end.

"Don't even think about it young lady," she said firmly, albeit with a smile. Muffled voices came to ear from downstairs but try as she might the subject matter was unintelligible. Not that she was bothered. Ethan yelled as Molly launched a boat full of water in his direction catching him off guard. "Behave, both of you," she stated calmly, hoping to draw a line under the impending retaliation from the eldest.

"I didn't do anything!" Ethan protested.

"You did!" Molly screamed back.

"Both of you, enough, please," their mother stated evenly. The conversation downstairs had ceased. Chris would be coming back up and she could take him up on that offering of twenty minutes of peace, a well-earned break on a day like today. He had promised her at least that after arriving home later than expected, from the office. Time passed but the door remained closed and with each minute, Nicola felt her patience ebb away. Whatever it was could wait until later, if not tomorrow, surely? Throughout the course of their nine-years of marriage, she had been conditioned to understand how the markets worked. Chris could, and notoriously did, work on well into the night but not today. He'd promised.

"I want daddy to wash my hair," Molly whined. "You get water in my eyes."

"Yeah, me too," Ethan stated.

"Me three," she replied. "I'll duck out and see where your Father's got to. Play nicely for a second."

Leaving the bathroom door open, Nicola stepped out. Not wanting to interrupt his conversation if the visitor was still present she listened. Not hearing anything but feeling a breeze blow across her from the open front door, she moved across the landing to the top of the stairs.

"Chris," she called out. No reply. "For Pete's sake," she muttered under her breath. Calling out over her shoulder as she descended addressing the children, "Popping downstairs, kids. Look after each other for a minute."

"Okay!" came a double shout from the bathroom. Reaching the first turn on the staircase she stopped. The front door rocked back and forth ever so gently. Chris sat on the floor, back against the wall open mouthed, staring straight ahead. He looked serene. All that was out of place were the two black marks on the front of his white shirt and another on his forehead above the bridge of his nose. The sound of increasing rainfall striking the mosaic tiles of the porch outside was accompanied by a drop in temperature, carried indoors on the breeze.

"Chris?" Nicola asked quietly, in a questioning tone. One of hope rather than expectation. The sounds of squabbling came from above and behind her, the children battling over something or other but the argument was lost to her. The spray of crimson on the wall above her husband now beginning to run as the force of gravity exerted itself had her transfixed. "Chris," she said once more. This time to herself.

Order the next book in the series from Amazon or click here;
The Dogs in the Street - Dark Yorkshire Book 3

ALSO BY J M DALGLIESH

The Dark Yorkshire Series

Divided House

Blacklight

The Dogs in the Street

Blood Money

Fear the Past

The Sixth Precept

Box Sets

Dark Yorkshire Books 1-3

Dark Yorkshire Books 4-6

The Hidden Norfolk Series

One Lost Soul

Bury Your Past

Kill Our Sins

Tell No Tales

Hear No Evil*

*Pre-order

Life and Death**

**FREE eBook - A Hidden Norfolk novella - visit jmdalgliesh.com

Audiobooks

The entire Dark Yorkshire series is available in audio format, read by the award-winning Greg Patmore.

Divided House

Blacklight

The Dogs in the street

Blood Money

Fear the Past

The Sixth Precept

Audiobook Box Sets

Dark Yorkshire Books 1-3

Dark Yorkshire Books 4-6

*Hidden Norfolk audiobooks arriving 2020

Printed in Great Britain
by Amazon